Once Chosen

Ben Aldred

Dedicated to Amelia, my dearest muse

Special Thanks to Clayton, Esa, Fin, k8, Marcus, Mark, and Sarah

Contents

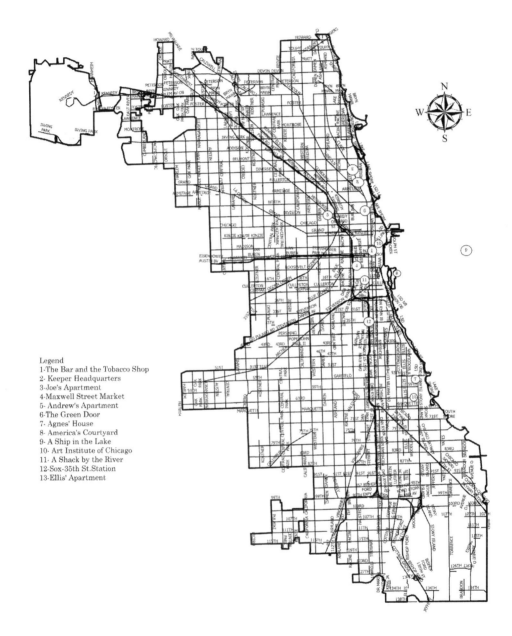

Legend
1-The Bar and the Tobacco Shop
2- Keeper Headquarters
3-Joe's Apartment
4-Maxwell Street Market
5- Andrew's Apartment
6-The Green Door
7- Agnes' House
8- America's Courtyard
9- A Ship in the Lake
10- Art Institute of Chicago
11- A Shack by the River
12-Sox-35th St.Station
13-Ellis' Apartment

Prelude

Where do you even start with something like this? It's not every day that your entire world falls apart. Everything that happens has so many things leading up to it, so many causes and effects that it's impossible to say where one story ends, and another begins. Every choice you make is just a product of a lifetime of experience and you could spend an eternity trying to track the things that led into the simplest event. And when your whole life falls apart and takes one of the fundamental truths of magical society with it? Where could I even start?

Besides, I don't even really know what kind of story it is. Do I start with the attack on my birthday? Do I start when I first learned the identity of the traitor to the Conclave? Do I start when I realized I was falling in love at the worst possible moment? Maybe I could start when I learned the horrible truth or when my life fell apart around me? Hell, I could start back when I first learned I was the Chosen One? Alright, no, I'll spare you that. 25 years of waiting around for destiny is too much to subject anyone to. Trust me, I speak from experience.

No, I just have to pick a starting point and fill in when things stop making sense. And as cliche as it sounds, I might as well start with the day she walked into my bar.

Chapter 1

Tuesday, June 9th, 2015

"Are you the Chosen One?"

I was putting a pour spout in a fresh bottle of gin, so my back was to the bar. I turned around slowly, bottle in hand, ready for anything, that wasn't always a friendly question. "I'm sorry?"

"We were wondering if you were the Chosen One." There were two women standing at the bar, still mostly empty a little before 4pm on a Tuesday. The one on the left, the shorter of the two with a deep tan was smiling at me. The one on the right had an enigmatic half-smile. Both were watching me closely.

I gave them a smile, "That depends...are you selling something?"

"What? No. Not at all!" The smiling one lost her smile and waved her hands in front of her.

I kept my smile, gauging the reaction, it seemed genuine enough, "Then are you here to start trouble?" I gave a playful wag of my head, could be a joke, could be a pre-fight taunt, though the odds were tilting towards the former pretty quickly.

"NoNoNo, we're just..." The smiling woman began to look worried and looked to her silent friend.

"I don't know, I could start some trouble." The woman on the right gave a subtle twitch of the eyebrow and her friend gave a little 'oh', realizing the joke.

"I'll keep that in mind. But yes, I'm the Chosen One." I set down the bottle below the bar and extended my hand. "Joe Palevsky, at your service...literally."

The smiling one took my hand and shook it vigorously with both of hers. "I'm Miriam and this is Jennifer. It's an honor to meet you." I blanched a little at that, though I didn't let it show. It was always weird to be honored for something you haven't done yet, even if it was a prophesied inevitability.

I set the bottle back on the bar shelf. "Right, yeah. Well, welcome to Brando's. You here to gawk, or here to drink? Gawking at the Chosen One is normally 20 an hour, but it might be less if you have a coupon."

Jennifer looked briefly in her purse. "Well, I forgot my coupon book back home, so I guess we'll have to drink."

"That's a pretty popular choice." I nodded to a businessman coming in from the back entrance and leaned in a bit. "Though, just to be clear, this isn't an exclusive place, so don't go too overboard on the magic talk. I know it's pretty empty now, but..."

"Oh, of course, no problem." Miriam nodded.

"Sure." Jennifer shrugged, unbothered.

"Also, do you ladies have some ID? Standard procedure." I took their IDs and took some quick mental notes, just in case there was actual trouble, before handing them back. "So, What's your pleasure?" I instantly regretted the phrasing, but it was out before I could get it back.

Miriam looked at the shelves before picking up the drink menu. "I'll have…. come back to me."

Jennifer pointed to the top shelf. "Is that Angel's Envy?"

"Good choice, how do you take it?" I pulled down the bottle.

"One ice cube." She held up a finger and smiled. I pulled out a single cube and dropped it gently into a rocks glass, pouring in a few fingers.

"I will haaaaaave a Margarita?" Miriam tilted her head as she decided, and it came out uncertain.

"True."

"What?" Miriam looked confused, though Jennifer breathed out the hint of a laugh from her nose.

"Thought you were testing my skills in prophecy. I'm generally rubbish without my tools, and I think the owner would get upset if I started consulting pigeon entrails before every order, but I think I got that one right." I began to make the margarita as I talked, and they laughed.

"Start a tab." Jennifer handed me a heavy black credit card as I put the drinks on the bar.

"Thanks!" Miriam looked over to Jennifer, who waved to indicate it was no problem.

"So, you local or visiting?" I poured out the shaker from the margarita and began to tidy things away.

"I'm local." Miriam was a little hesitant, probably not originally from Chicago, less than 5 years here I guessed, enough to claim it, not enough to be confident.

"I'm…newly local? In the process of moving here. A few things to still settle." Jennifer extended a hand and waggled it a bit to emphasize the uncertainty.

"We're celebrating." Miriam put her arm around Jennifer's shoulder, it only emphasized the height difference between them.

"Well, welcome to Chicago. Don't ask for ketchup on a hot dog unless you like being teased, definitely check-out the Neo-Futurists and memorize the Cubs home schedule if you ever plan on taking the red line." That was a practiced line. I had welcomed enough folks to the city between official Conclave contacts and general visitors that I had it down to a science. Something they probably already knew, something they probably didn't and an actual piece of advice. I change up the local food recommendation or theater company for the older or terminally dignified, but I knew my business and a first impression couldn't hurt.

Jennifer moved to sit at the bar. "Mind if we sit a while?"

"As long as you're drinking and don't mind me chopping garnishes. The bar back called in sick and backup won't be here until 6ish."

Miriam waved a hand. "Oh, that's fine! We're also here for the karaoke later, so we can get out of the way when things get busy."

"You've got a while to wait on that." I pulled out a lemon and a knife and began to peel off some strips of zest.

"It takes a few drinks to get Jenny in a singing mood." She nodded over to Jennifer who rolled her eyes but nodded.

"So, you two in the craft or just family?"

Miriam piped up. "We're Kappa Tau Omegas."

"Ah, I should have guessed."

Jennifer turned her head, giving me a sidelong look. "Should you have? Based on what?"

"Right, yes. Well, look at that! A dragon!" I jokingly pointed towards the back of the bar, though neither of them actually looked. "No, a pair of well-dressed women walk into the bar, looking for the Chosen One, not looking to start trouble. It's a reasonable guess. Unless there's a new neutral coven of witches run by Kate Spade." That got a chuckle. "I'll be back in a second, we're low on olives."

I went back to the storage closet and shook my head for a moment, taking a deep breath before grabbing the jar of olives and heading back out. As I did, I heard Miriam talking.

"I guess when you said we could find the Chosen One at a bar I thought he'd be sitting in a dark corner dispensing wisdom and justice."

"Maybe he does that on weekends? Anyway, he's a little older than I expected, but easy enough on the eyes. Especially around the rear. Tell you what, next round, order something top shelf, I want to see him reach." Jennifer's comment was flattering, though I felt a little self-conscious about some of the bottles I'd have to restock.

"Jennifer Davis! You are incorrigible!"

"Miriam Ashley, you sound like someone's maiden aunt." The two of them laughed, though they quieted as I heard the door open.

As I came around the corner with the jar of olives, I saw Andrew pulling up a seat around the corner of the bar from Miriam and Jennifer. I dropped a napkin in front of him and returned his nod of greeting. "Hey Andrew, the usual? This is Miriam and Jennifer, they're in the trade, Kappas. This is Andrew, he owns the tobacco shop across the street, supplies a lot of folks."

Andrew nodded to each of the women as I poured some ginger beer into a rocks glass behind the counter. "Nice to meet you."

Miriam spoke first, but stumbled slightly, looking at Jennifer. "Charmed...I mean, nice to meet you."

"Hi." Jennifer gave a short nod of greeting.

Andrew looked back to me, "You all alone back there? I have a few from Sunday if you have the time." He pulled a clipped crossword from out of the book he was carrying.

I shook my head, "Maybe later on, it's just me here for now. Sorry I had to cancel Sunday, Mrs. Mulaney thought she had a poltergeist and wouldn't let me go until I searched the entire attic."

Jennifer said, "What did it end up being?"

"Her asshole of a cat familiar. Actually, Andrew could you watch things here for a minute while I go downstairs to switch out a keg?"

"Sure thing."

"Talk amongst yourselves." I gestured between them as I went downstairs. Give Andrew a chance to size them up and let me flip the Goose Island 312. It only took a few minutes and when I came back, Miriam was in the middle of talking.

"I mostly just help with event planning and site arrangement, making sure we aren't on an Old Indian Burial Ground or something." As she said it, I saw Andrew flinch very slightly, not enough that someone who didn't know him would see, but enough for me to read the microaggression's effect. "It's nice and I like my coworkers, which is what really matters, right?"

Andrew nodded as she said it. "If that's what matters to you, then yes."

Jennifer raised her glass. "Could I get another?" As I was making it, the door opened again, and some business folks walked in. Jennifer pointed over to a corner table as I delivered the drink. "And we'll take that for the table over there." The two of them decamped to the corner and Andrew settled into his book as I served the suits.

The rest of the evening was hectic and mostly irrelevant, honestly. My substitute bar back finally arrived, and I was able to get ahead of things, but Andrew spent most of his time in his book and I didn't really see Jennifer and Miriam until the end of the night except to pour drinks, though I did note Jennifer's continued preference for high shelf bottles. Finally, the two of them approached the bar, bags in hand.

"I'll go grab a cab." Miriam waved to me as she headed out. "Nice to meet you."

Jennifer turned to me as Miriam left. "Time to settle the score."

I turned back to the register, watching her in the mirror. "Sure thing. Nice work on Lady Marmalade, you two rehearse?"

Jennifer blushed slightly; its effect enhanced by the bourbon. "Sorority talent show. Sticks with you even...a few years later."

I waved the implication away. "A gentleman never asks. Here's your card and receipt."

Jennifer signed and looked me up and down. "You're not quite what I was expecting."

"You were expecting me?"

"You know what I mean, you grow up with stories of the Chosen Ones over the years, I thought you'd be..." She trailed off, pensive.

I waited for a moment before filling in. "Taller? Younger? Sporting an impressive facial scar?"

She smiled at the joke, not quite laughing. "Different. But like...not in a bad way."

"Well, that's a relief."

She reached into her purse and pulled out a matchbook, opening it and writing a number on it. "Here. If you get a few moments between pouring drinks and saving the world." She handed it to me, winked and headed out of the bar.

Chapter 2

There are days I love living in Chicago. I may not be able to travel, but the world comes to visit me often enough. "I'll take the pad kra prao and the pla rad prik. Am I saying those right?" I was nearly yelling to be heard by the vendor, one of the hazards of getting lunch at a street festival. She nodded with a little head turn to indicate close enough. "And are these actually ant eggs or is that just a poetic name?"

"They are real, would you like a sample?"

"No need, I'll take an order. Oh, and do you have any...." I trailed off as I pulled out my money clip and Jennifer's matchbook came out with it. This was the third time today that it had hitched a ride with something from my pocket. It had come out with my mailbox key and with my Ventra card and each time, it had the same effect, distracting me from the task at hand. I looked back at the waiting vendor as she smiled expectantly. "Drinks! Do you have drinks?"

A few minutes later, I backed into Andrew's shop, holding my bags of food. "Andrew my man, I got some surprises today, you up for some authentic Thai street food?"

Andrew greeted me with a smile as I turned around. "That what I'm hearing from the post office?"

"Yeah, you should take fifteen and check out the dancers. But not til we've eaten."

Andrew cleared off the side of the counter, tucking a few glass pipes back into the case and putting a box of cigars back on the shelf. We spread out the food containers and spent a few minutes trying out the different options, interrupted by a few futures traders buying lotto tickets, a cigar connoisseur in a rush and a kid who had lost his license, but was absolutely 18, and surely Andrew could just believe him and sell him cigarettes. After the kid left in a huff, Andrew pulled the paper out of his satchel and popped it on the counter.

"So, what's giving you trouble today?" I popped an ant egg in my mouth as I leaned back against the window.

Andrew looked at the puzzle, "Roman Senate House?"

"Roman Senate House. Any Letters?"

"5. Blank, u, Blank, Blank, a." Andrew's face was serious.

"Curia." I said with confidence. "I could bore you to death with Ancient Rome trivia. It's actually part of my combat training, the 'Great March of Civilization' lecture attack, a guaranteed knock-out within earshot."

"I parry with post-colonial theory. "Andrew filled in the blanks with a smile, not looking up.

"Well played, well played."

Andrew scanned the puzzle for other problems. "Here's one. Skis with high-speed turns. Six letters."

I counted in my head. "Wedels, w.e.d.e.l.s" Andrew looked surprised as I spelled it out. "My parents were really into skiing before I was taken away for training. We'd do Switzerland, Colorado, Quebec. I mean, they still are as far as I know."

Andrew wrote in the answer, "Not a lot of skiing at Pine Ridge. Plenty of snow, not many hills."

I shook my head noncommittally, leaving some silence. Andrew didn't talk much about his childhood on the reservation. If he felt like talking about it, he would, but I knew from experience pushing wouldn't help. He returned my noncommittal shake with one of his own and returned to the crossword. "Here's another. View from Sandusky?" He pronounced the word putting emphasis on the first syllable.

"San-DUS-kee," I corrected. "small city in Northern Ohio in between Toledo and Cleveland. Home of Cedar Point amusement park, former stop on the underground railroad, overlooks Lake Erie."

Andrew looked quizzically at me, so I continued. "Look, I know ridiculous trivia about every metropolitan statistical area that borders the Great Lakes. There was a period where Casimir was worried my prophecy might refer to somewhere other than Chicago, so I had to learn about everything that is technically a city bordering the Great Lakes, US and Canada." I shrugged, "Perks of being the Chosen One."

"Erie fits." Andrew said, scribbling on the newspaper with his pen.

"Sandusky means 'water in pools' in Wyandot." I popped another ant egg in my mouth.

"That knowledge will surely prove useful." Andrew rolled his eyes and began filling in a few more clues around the new answers. "Nine letters, cheap. Second letter i, ends with ly. Miserly doesn't fit."

I counted letters with my fingers "Niggardly. Though...is that one of those words that comes from some really racist origin and now everyone uses like it's no big deal?"

Andrew shrugged and turned to the cash register computer to look it up. "I think you're overstating how much 'everyone' uses the term. It looks like it's from Old English, same as the term niggling, no relation to the slur."

I gave it some thought. "Still, way too easy to be misheard. I'll chalk that one up there with pusillanimous as words not to use any more."

Andrew filled in the spaces on the crossword. "Sorry for your loss." He smiled.

I pulled the drinks out of the bag. "You want the mango soda or the milk drink?"

Andrew pointed to the can and cracked it open. I checked the bottle top and pulled out my keys. The matchbook was stuck in the bottle opener. "Weird. What do you think?" I handed the matchbook to Andrew.

Andrew looked at it and up at me. "Whiskey or Margarita?"

"Whiskey."

Andrew nodded and looked it over. "Congratulations, you got a number. I imagine that's not too hard for the Chosen One." Andrew gave a sly smile.

"Hey, I haven't played that angle since I was a teenager, alright a young twentysomething. Okay, it was an eclipse conference, and I was going through a dry spell. I can't help it if she came looking for me."

"That much is true." Andrew turned it over in his hands, but before he could continue the shop door opened. I looked over to see a tall young Black man with short, neat hair standing in the doorway. He was wearing jeans and a t-shirt depicting a man in silhouette over the word Disip. He glanced at me and then at Andrew, an uneasy look on his face.

Andrew nodded hello, "Rock, this is Joe, he's in the trade." Andrew didn't out me as a Keeper usually. His customers weren't nihilists, but he didn't want the attention. The man visibly relaxed as he stepped in. "Joe, this is Rock, a customer of mine from Haiti."

I stood as Andrew made his introductions and shook Rock's hand. "Nice to meet you."

Rock looked over to Andrew, "You got them?"

Andrew reached below the counter and pulled out a plastic grocery bag. He put it on the counter and reached inside, pulling out a white and red pack of cigarettes labeled 'comme il faut'. "Ten packs, as requested."

Rock smiled at the bag, looking highly satisfied. He reached into his pocket and pulled out a handful of twenties. "Thank you. Nothing like the stuff from home." He looked over at me as he paid. "Loa just don't like Marlboros."

Andrew and I nodded in agreement as he put the cash in the register. Rock shook both of our hands again before he left, smiling and humming to himself. As he left, Andrew picked up the matchbook and looked it over. Opening and closing it, he turned it over in his hands.

I waited a moment before I asked him. "So, what do you think? You have a better instinct for people than I do. Besides, remember Pearl? You were right about her, and I was wrong, and I swore I'd listen to you next time around. I admit my frailties and want your input on this. Should I pursue this?"

"It's definitely enchanted." Andrew breathed in and out before continuing, taking a deliberate slow breath through his nose. "I didn't get much of a chance to see her, but she definitely didn't choose the bar by accident."

"Do you think she's trouble?"

"I didn't say that. But she knows what she wants and isn't afraid to pursue it." Andrew set down the matchbook. "That's not necessarily a bad thing."

"Hmm. It would be a relief to have a relationship where I didn't constantly lie about what I was doing. I think Kayla thought I was in the mob."

"Lila just thought you were cheating on her."

"Ann thought I had embarrassing digestive issues."

"Didn't Octavia try and follow you once?"

"Yeah, I had to convince Scaevola to promise not to bring her in for interrogation." I sighed. "I just want a normal fucking long-term relationship. I want to get on with my life. I mean, she knows about the Chosen One thing, it would be good not to hide that half of my life from her, you remember how things went with Holly." Andrew snorted, but still didn't talk. "And she might have a sense of the limitations I have. So, she won't worry as much about waiting for things until...well, everything's settled."

Andrew nodded his head to the side. "I did get a read on her friend. Definitely privileged, with a lot of the baggage that goes along with that."

"Yeah, I caught that whole burial ground thing." I shook my head. "But that doesn't necessarily mean Jennifer is prejudiced. I mean, we can't always choose our childhood friends. And I can't really judge without giving her a chance. Sure, if she's like her friend, it's a no go, but I don't want to jump to conclusions based entirely on association. Plus, she was hot."

Andrew smiled and shook his head. "I'm not going to talk you into or out of this. I will say this," as he tossed the matchbook to me. "She came looking for you and enchanted that matchbook to stay with you as a reminder of her. It's subtle, but it's there."

I caught the matchbook. "I need to do some research, but who knows. Maybe this'll be the year it all happens, and I die saving the world. That would solve my problems."

"Well, some of your problems." Andrew smiled gently. "But hey, you're not a stupid kid anymore, maybe you've learned enough to survive."

"That's what I like about you, Andrew. You recognize that I'm not an idiot." My watch beeped and I sighed. "Well, duty calls."

"Second Wednesday?"

"Second Wednesday."

Chapter 3

I adjusted the hang of my long velvet robe, waiting in my personal antechamber. I'd worn it at least once a month and for over two decades, ever since my initiation, but time hadn't made it less awkward and scratchy.

There was a knocking at the door, three firm knocks with equal pauses between them. I opened the door in front of me and stepped into the room as the seven other doors on the walls of the chamber opened in unison to reveal the members of the Chicago Conclave of Keepers, Ascendant Conclave of the Grand Esoteric Order of Keepers.

I mean, most people just call them Keepers, though that term technically only refers to the highest members of the Order in a given city. There are a lot of people within the Order who aren't technically Keepers, if you get into the deep levels of technicality, but that would actually require revealing the deeper mysteries and I can't do that. Like, if I do that I die kind of thing.

Anyway, when I was just a trainee Chosen One, my fellow initiates and I started calling them the Avuncular Order, because we were nerds who were forced to study way too much Latin and because we all had to be sponsored by an uncle. Years later, anything that was seemed really on brand for the Keepers would get a quiet 'A-O' between us and a quiet smile.

The seven old men gathered here were the leaders of the Keepers in Chicago, which, because it was the location of the one and only Chosen One, was the most important Conclave in the whole worldwide order. Which is to say that even though we did this every month on the second Wednesday, it was chock full of pomp and circumstance.

Each of us moved into the room, taking the magically significant three steps to reach the magically significant eight-sided table in the center of the room before sitting in our magically significant prescribed seats. The Keeper of the Laws sat first, and the order passed to the right, with the Keepers of Guards, Flames, Keys, Books, Coins, and Keepers sitting before I took my seat at the right hand of the Keeper of the Laws, my great uncle Casimir. I swear, I've spent days of my life watching old men sit down in order.

For the next twenty minutes, we intoned the calls and responses, the mystical rites of safety, direction, mission, mystical secrecy and health, invoking the secret names of ancient spirits to protect and bless the gathering. I knew every word by heart, stood when needed, kneeled when needed, produced all necessary artifacts and made every intricate gesture from muscle memory. Years of practice had turned this all into rote, so my mind often drifted during the ritualized opening. Today, it kept drifting back to Jennifer. To call or not to call. She had been interested in me, enough to work the smallest of magics on a matchbook. But was that interest suspect? She wasn't the first woman to be interested in the Chosen One, after all.

I mean, I didn't exactly keep a low profile these days. Nothing nearly so public as my early 20s, looking for leads on the Prophecy by day, partying by night, sleeping way too little, drinking way too much. I was subtle enough nowadays, but it wasn't exactly a big secret that I tended bar at Brando's. Still, something about this made me uneasy, call it a habitual overabundance of caution. The ritual chanting rose to its climax and then came to an end, and I left my daydreams to return to reality. We'd have official reports from the Conclave, we'd have dinner, then I could head out.

Casimir cleared his throat, "Well now, we are met here in conclave, let us share what needs to be known." Casimir wore his typical frown, well-aged into his face from years of practice. "As Keeper of Laws, I can report the results of the trial of the nihilist Adam Summers. For his plot to destroy the Sacred Flames, I have pronounced anathema upon him and bound a vengeful Jinn to his spirit. Should he make further moves against us, he will be destroyed utterly. There have been lesser trials of his associates, they are on record with the Keeper of Books, as are some fresh reports from the Conclaves in Rome and Singapore. Keeper of Guards?"

Beside Casimir, the Keeper of Guards leaned forward. Clark was stiff-shouldered under his robes, his beard closely trimmed and still more black than gray. The head of the Praetorians had come to Chicago fifteen years ago from New York and brought military discipline to the Conclave's Praetorians. "We have reports of a new cult operating in the greater Chicago area. Some troubling information coming out of South Shore and Hammond in the port areas. My men are following up on leads, we'll report further developments." I made a mental note to follow up with Clark, new cult activity could be nothing or it could be something. A few years ago, Clark had me run down a tagger named "Weed Wolf" on suspicion he might be binding wolf spirits into herbal poultices for nefarious purposes. Long story short, he wasn't, but I did get a new source for certain products. This sounded a little different than some random tags, but I couldn't be sure without talking to Clark.

There was a pause before the next report. Ephraim sat back in his chair, his hood obscuring his face. He was the eldest of the Keepers, and I wasn't the only one worried he'd fallen asleep. But before anyone could lean in for a subtle nudge, he began to speak. "The Sacred Flames are high. Storm clouds gather at the edges, we must watch for floods." The room grew silent after his pronouncement. Ephraim watched the sacred prophetic flames for portents and the mention of floods caught everyone's attention, touching as it did on the prophecy that had brought this Conclave to Chicago. Of course, follow up wouldn't exactly clarify things, years of practiced magical engagement with entheogens, and not like beginner stuff like ayahuasca or LSD but heavily engineered Keeper shit, meant Ephraim wasn't always a fount of coherence when talking about his visions. But still, he was my favorite 'uncle', so it couldn't hurt to stop by some time this week, there would at least be some good conversation and maybe some time for fun.

As the silence settled after Ephraim's pronouncements, Master Tangherlini, the Keeper of the Keys, spoke up. I knew that by this point I could call him Prospero, but he had been our teacher for so long, that my first instinct was still Master Tangherlini, even two decades after graduation and full initiation into the higher mysteries. "Well, with increased activity on the South Side, I thought it prudent to cultivate a new ritual space closer to any local problems. I have finalized acquisition of a former church on Blackstone and 57th. It has a dome already, so we should be able to easily incorporate it into protective designs." I knew the building he was talking about, so I made a quick note of it in my mind. This wasn't exactly news, as a Chicago local, Master Tangherlini had been looking at the place for years, but now it was apparently final. "I'm beginning this year's audit a little early, so let me know if you know any spaces that need wards renewed so I can make sure to send someone around."

My uncle Anthony, the Keeper of Books, was next. He was my mother's brother and technically my only actual uncle here, though tradition allowed the term to be used more liberally. "Nothing of note from the library. We're finished with the book sale, which went well. An ARC of Game of Thrones went for 9000, which is pretty nice. With that out of the way, we're working on some enhancements for the special collections area, should be done fairly quickly, but we had some worries about fire, flood, etc." He smiled in my direction as he finished. Anthony and I shared a love of books, though that wasn't exactly unique among the Avuncular Order. Anthony's news hadn't caused much of a stir, and everyone's eyes moved along to the next of the Keepers around the table.

Simon jumped in quickly, "I could bore you with lots of numbers, but I'll keep it short and sweet. We're still quite rich." A few of the others chuckled as the Keeper of Coins sat back in his chair, spreading his hands to indicate that he'd said all there was to say. Simon had a head for numbers, he joked he snuck onto the trading floor of the Board of Trade in high school and had made ten thousand dollars in corn futures before they kicked him out. He had been thrilled with the ascendency of the Chicago Conclave, as it had given him access to a lot more resources, but he was happy to spread the wealth.

All eyes then turned to the last member of the Conclave. Scaevola was the Keeper of the Keepers, the one who watched the others for signs of treason, mystical corruption, or disloyalty. He drew himself up, which only highlighted his twisted shoulder. "I have concluded my annual investigations. As this was the 168th year of the Conclave of Chicago, I conducted deep investigations into the first, second, third, fourth and sixth chairs of the Conclave. Such a year required significant additional investigation and travel." He paused as everyone looked around the table to the indicated chairs. Everyone except Anthony, me and Scaevola himself. "I am pleased to report that no one has violated the sacred trust of our order." Scaevola smiled as everyone relaxed. "I trust you will all stay loyal? Keep my job easy?" The laughter around the table was thin and nervous. "My reports have been filed with the Keeper of Books."

Casimir nodded, "Well then, unless The Chosen One has anything to add…" I shook my head, "then I suggest we adjourn to dinner. Let the circle be closed."

Chapter 4

Wednesday, June 10th

I poured another glass of port for myself at the bar in the Keeper's lounge as Uncle Casimir walked over to me. At his gesture, I poured one for him as well, extending it as he approached. "Here you are, sir."

He took the small glass in his pudgy hand, delicately holding it by the stem. "Thank you, Joseph." He took a noseful of the bouquet before sipping the port with a slight slurp, aerating it as he'd taught me years ago. "The Summer menu just went up at North Pond, Joseph. You must join me for dinner sometime soon."

I nodded to him, "That sounds excellent, sir. Just let me know when."

Casimir pulled a small notebook from his pocket and flipped through. "Perhaps next week Saturday, the 20th?"

"I was going to be having a get together for my birthday that night, sir."

"Ah, of course, wouldn't want to spoil your fun. Let's look at three Saturdays from now, the 27th." Casimir smiled as Anthony approached us. "My treat, of course."

"Thank you very much, sir." I nodded to Anthony as he drew near, and Casimir did the same.

Casimir patted me on the shoulder, "The two of you must excuse me, port just goes right through me." We all chuckled politely as he left.

"Joe." Anthony gave me a hug, made slightly awkward by the obviously book shaped package in his hand. As he broke the hug, he handed me the package. "A little early birthday present. I came across it during my preparations for the vault audit and thought it might be of interest." He gestured to the package, indicating that I should open it.

I pulled off the somewhat sloppily applied wrapping paper and uncovered the heavy leather-bound volume. I turned the spine upwards and read aloud. "Maxwell's Lives of the Chosen."

"We had a third copy and I thought you might life one in your collection. I particularly like his account of Balian of Ibelin." Anthony smiled, "Much more detail than Archer and Kingsford. Of course, our records of the period are much better than the public ones, so you can't fault mundane historians."

I felt the arm around my shoulder before I heard the voice and turned to see Prospero. "If you want him to actually read the book, you better have hidden some pornography in there." My old teacher laughed, though Anthony blushed. "I'm only joking. If by 37 you haven't figured out how to find your own pornography, then I despair for today's youth."

Anthony was a bit tongue tied, so I jumped in. "Master Tangherlini, I swear, I really was interested in classical imagery in fin-de-siecle portraiture." I smiled and raised my hand to my chest in mock offense. "I was just a budding art lover."

Both men laughed at my comment as the tension diffused a bit. Prospero continued. "I'll only interrupt for a moment. Daniel will drop by on Thursday with the plumber to look at the sink. You don't have to be around if you have plans, Daniel's got the keys." He shook my hand and grabbed a bottle of scotch from the bar then headed over to Simon and two bureaucramancers sitting at one of the low tables with some books laid out before them.

Anthony looked quizzical, "Trouble at the apartment?"

"Nothing serious, just the sink running slow. Thank you for the book, Uncle Anthony, I look forward to reading it."

"Well, happy early birthday to my favorite nephew."

"Your only nephew." I smiled as Anthony patted my shoulder and moved away into the room. Three down, four to go, I thought to myself. The after-dinner portion of these meetings was almost as complex and tedious as the ritual. Years of practice had taught me that I needed to talk to each of the Keepers at least once before going. Anyone I didn't talk to would take it as a snub or worse, see weakness elsewhere. Not that it was always a trial. Anthony was nice enough and Ephraim was always good for some unusual insights. Outside of the inner circle of the Conclave, everyone else at the reception was optional. There were usually a number of others around, some of Clark's Praetorian guards, some trusted members of the Atlantans and some wives and aunts from Kappa Tau Omega, the occasional Bureaucramancer or visiting member of the Order of Usnard. I could speak with them if I wanted, but nobody would take it as a loaded political statement if I didn't.

Looking around the room, I saw Ephraim sitting alone in the corner and decided to take the opportunity to have a quiet word.

"Ah, Zar-Ptak," Ephraim gestured to the chair beside him as I walked up. He had always used this pet name for me since our first entheogenic journey as part of my advanced training. We had set out to examine the flames of prophecy and I had seen/become a bird, so from then on, I was the firebird.

"Hello, Ephraim." I sat in the chair beside him, he opened his coat and offered me a cigar. "No thank you, sir, I'm still quit."

Ephraim nodded, "It's gotten much easier to get good Cubans lately. Not that I had much trouble before. Has your Indian friend seen much business in them?" Ephraim pulled one from his pocket and began the slow ritual of trimming and lighting it.

"Andrew really prefers the term Native American or Lakhota, but yeah, he's seen a brisk trade in them. He mostly focuses on the traditions that need sacred tobacco, but good Cubans help pay the rent on the store."

"That's a good service he provides." Ephraim took several savoring puffs. "Have you been communing with the flames recently? Looking to your future?"

I shrugged, I had some training in prophecy, but mostly for other people. Searching out one's own future is always tricky, it's like looking at yourself in a mirror, most of what you see is yourself looking back. "I've looked some, but I've been a little busy. I had to wrap up some of the aquatic training refresher and there's been an increase in ley line instability with the change of season, so the Conclave has me doing some charting. "

"Zar Ptak, you need to be mindful of time. You'll learn that when you grow older. I see you so rarely, one of these times it will be the last time." Ephraim shook his head.

"Hopefully not for a long while, sir."

"You young people, always so optimistic." Ephraim looked thoughtfully at the glowing tip of his cigar, then turned to me, his eyes clear and intense holding the glow of the cigar in his dark pupils, a reflection of the sacred flames whose names only he knew, "We will see each other twice more, once before it happens and once after. I will tell you what is to come, but you won't understand, and I will tell you the truth, but you won't like it. But both must come to pass for you to follow your chosen path." The intensity faded from his eyes, and I shivered at the statement.

"What do you mean, Ephraim? Twice more? Before what happens? After what?" I looked at him, incredulous, trying to keep my voice calm, not to bring attention from the people around us.

He waved his hand to quiet me, then patted my hand. "This is not the time. I wish to enjoy my cigar and brandy and you need to make with the niceties. It won't be much longer and nothing we say today will change that. All needful things are already in motion." Before I could say more, he waved Simon, who was standing nearby, over to us. "Simon, Joseph here is looking well, is he not?"

Simon stepped over, "He's looking a bit peaked, to be honest. Whatever did you say to the boy?" Simon's tone was joking, I imagine he thought Ephraim had made some off-color joke or mysterious comment.

I recovered my expression a bit. Ephraim shook his head tersely as I glanced at him, what he said was for me alone, as troubling as it was. "Nothing, he offered me a cigar and I was trying to resist the temptation. I've been quit two years at this point and I'm trying to stick to it."

Simon nodded, "That's downright wicked of you, Ephraim, tempting the boy like that." He turned to me "I had just come over to ask how the chapbook was selling."

"Great, for a poetry chapbook." I reached into my pocket and pulled out my checkbook. I had come prepared. "I should be able to pay you more today, the last half will take a little bit."

Simon shook his head. "No rush, Joseph. Just pay me back when you can. Come on, let's leave him to his nap." Simon gestured to Ephraim, who had begun to nod off in his chair.

I got up reluctantly taking Ephraim's cigar from his sleeping hand and placing it in the ashtray beside him. Simon and I were crossing over to the bar when the flow of people brought us together with George. George Pullman Green was a member of the Atlantans, an affiliated order of African American practitioners. He ran an antique shop in Old Town that specialized in the restoration of mystical objects. Many of the Keepers frequented the shop, though my own taste for 20th century retro was more kitschy than classy.

George greeted Simon first, "Keeper Smith, I just finished restoring a Bourbon era alchemical supply cabinet. You should drop by the shop and take a look. I think it would be just right for you."

"Ooh, color me intrigued. Do you think it might be an authentic Desgraces?" Simon rubbed his palms together; he was an eager collector of alchemical ephemera. Modern techniques were much better, but like so much of the Conclave, Simon loved the archaic trappings of the glorious past.

"It doesn't have his mark, but it does bear some of his characteristic flourishes, it could be an early piece, I haven't had a chance to trace the psychometrics, yet."

"I have a scrying basin table of his, exquisite channeling of mystic currents. Joseph, have you seen my collection of classic scrying basins?" I realized my peril too late and was stuck for the next 20 minutes in a lengthy discussion of historical divinatory furniture and the role of psychometry in tracing chain of custody. Every time I tried to make my escape, one or the other would ask my opinion on lead lining or on the five/six leg debate. Finally, Simon's phone rang with an important business call, and I was left alone with George.

"Master Palevsky, Keeper Lloyd says you're having a birthday soon." George and my Uncle Anthony were good friends and often had lunch together, as George's antique shop was near the library. "Any big plans?"

"Please, just Joe. I'm having a little party, nothing huge, just a get together at my apartment, everyone dressed up as a favorite literary character."

"Oh, that sounds very nice. I remember some of your birthday parties with the rest of the candidates, back when you were kids. There was the year you got that new bike and Ellis nearly fell in the lake." George smiled at the memory. "Do you see Ellis much, nowadays?"

George's son Ellis and I had known each other much better when I was still a teenager studying with the other potentials and Ellis was a little kid who tagged along with us. He was a fair bit younger than I was, but he had been a nice kid, though I hadn't had much time for him, and I knew that he didn't have much time for his father nowadays. "I don't see him much. We occasionally cross paths, this is Chicago after all, but we mostly run in different circles." Honestly, I hadn't seen Ellis for a few years, but that's not really comforting to an estranged father. I didn't see much harm in the lie.

"Ah, Okay." George was slightly crestfallen but hid it well. "Next time you hang out, could you ask him to get in touch with me?"

"Sure thing George," I added a comforting nod, "I'll let him know the next time I see him."

"Thanks, Joe." George smiled, "Drop by the store any time."

I nodded and broke away from the conversation as Simon came back from his phone call. I looked around the room, it had cleared out some, but the last two members of the Conclave still sat in one corner, talking quietly.

I looked around before I headed over to them. Ephraim's comments had worried me, and I looked to see if he was still around, but his chair and ashtray were empty. Oh well, time to do my duty and talk to the last few Keepers, I walked over to Clark and Scaevola. They were deeply engrossed in conversation and looked up only as I drew near. On the table between them was a napkin with a symbol drawn on it. I didn't recognize it, a stylized cityscape under a stylized wave.

"Joseph!" Clark's exclamation on seeing me surprised me. I thought at first I had upset him by intruding and began to apologize when he stood up and clapped his hand on my shoulder. "I understand you met my niece!"

"Your...niece? Jennifer is your niece?" I stumbled through the sentence as pieces fell together in my mind. "Right, yes, she would be your brother Thomas Jefferson Davis' daughter?" Five years of mandatory genealogy lessons clicked into place.

"Yes, she's Tommy's little girl. Not so little anymore, though." Clark smiled.

I weighed my options. Complimenting the attractiveness of a man's niece was not a safe passage. You could easily run aground on avuncular protectiveness or end up insulting a man's family, a regular social Scylla and Charybdis. But Clark had obviously told Jennifer about me, so he didn't entirely disapprove.

Clark and I had never been close. There was a certain disciplined distance between someone and their military trainer that was normal. He had never been mean or anything, just strict. I realized that I'd been pausing for way too long at this point. I leaned into the pause, playing on my thoughtful expression and cracking an awkward smile. "She is a... well-spoken young lady and... presents an...attractive figure."

Clark laughed, though Scaevola, still seated, only rolled his eyes. "Don't worry, Joseph," Clark patted my shoulder with his strong hand. "I'm not trying to ensnare you. Jennifer is her own woman and said she's not interested in an arranged match. You can wipe that cornered animal look off your face."

Scaevola stood, looking at me closely. "I hope you apply yourself equally to maintaining your training regimen as you do to flirting with Clark's niece. It is your actual job, after all." He picked up the napkin. "I'll look into this." He nodded curtly to both of us and walked away.

"Sorry about that." Clark's smile faded a bit. "You know Scaevola. Takes his job very seriously. I know it's important, but would it hurt to smile?"

"With him...I suspect it might." I waved away the concerns. "What was the symbol?"

"Something my men came across down in South Shore. I think it's related to the new cult activity down there, I thought Scaevola might know of any secret organization that may be using it." Clark sighed, "I didn't mean right this second. He could have taken a moment to discuss something not job related. That's part of the point of the meal afterwards."

I thought back to my meetings with the Keeper of Keepers. Scaevola was not a pleasant man. His job consisted of investigating his colleagues for signs of internal corruption, never a crowd-pleasing profession. "Scaevola's had a hard year. It was year 168 of the Chicago Conclave, right? That means investigating pretty much everyone at once. Lots of travel and business. All work and no play, am I right?"

"And I'm sure Casimir's official investigation of Scaevola's own loyalties must be a burden too. At least he gets a slow year this year." Clark shrugged, "Well, if he's going to go right back to work, then I guess I should too." He stood up. "You know, Jenny is new here in Chicago. I'm sure she'd be happy for a friendly face to show her the sights." Clark smiled and patted my shoulder before departing. I saw him stop and talk with Austin and Francisco, two of his Praetorian guards, and they all left together.

I pulled the matchbook out of my pocket and opened it. Well, she had come to the bar with an agenda, but at least now I knew how she knew where to find me. I figured I'd call her, tomorrow or the next day, when I wasn't tipsy on port and light-headed from cigar smoke.

Chapter 5

Friday, June 12th

I practice conversations. Not every conversation, I don't write out scripts or anything, but I do practice. It's a habit I picked up from my schooling. It's not like I had a class called Inspirational Speaking for Destined Heroes, but I was taught to communicate strategically. A good inspirational speech can be the difference between life and death in some situations. My favorite time to practice conversations is while running. It serves a few purposes. One, it keeps people from bothering me. You'd be surprised how many people will avoid you if you seem like a crazy person talking to nothing. Two, it helps me regulate my pace. Too fast to talk is too fast to build endurance. Three, it distracts from the tedium. I hate running, but it's a necessary and functional skill if you are expected to one day fight off a great evil or save the world from disaster.

Today, I was running in Lincoln Park, around the lake next to the Peggy Notebaert and practicing my impending phone conversation with Jennifer. "Hello, this is Joe. From the bar. The Chosen One." "Hi, it's me, Joe, I'll be your destined savior this evening." "Come with me if you want to live." Okay, that last one probably wouldn't work over the phone.

I gave some ornery looking geese a wide berth. "So, I was thinking.... No, that's not unusual for me.... Well, that's just mean and I think uncalled for." Practice conversations often went in directions that normal conversations never approached, but it didn't hurt to be ready. I mean, as the great philosopher Calvin said, 'what if someone called us a pair of pathetic peripatetics?'

"So, you're new in town. I could 'show you the sights'" No. "Let me show you some of my favorite things." You're going for non-creepy, Joe. Start over.

"Hey Jennifer, it's Joe."

"I thought it was." I skidded to a halt, startled by the interrupting voice. My skid was not nearly as graceful as I hoped and quickly turned into a tumble. The geese nearby raised a ruckus as I came to a halt on the ground.

I looked up as soon as I figured out where up had gotten to. Jennifer was standing there, coffee in hand. Her other hand was over her mouth, as concern over my fall turned into trying not to laugh. I stood up, wishing with all my might that I didn't have goose poop in my hair. "Hey, Jennifer, right?" Great. Real casual, Joe.

"Yeah, from the bar." She looked me up and down. "You okay there?" She was dressed casually, tank top and jeans, sunglasses, her hair pulled back into a ponytail.

"Yes, I'm fine. I've done enough Aikido to know how to fall down without hurting myself."

"I'm sure that's a valuable life skill." Jennifer gave a smirk that settled into her enigmatic smile as she quipped.

"Don't knock it until you've tried it." I smiled, "So, how long have you been watching me?"

"Just one lap, long enough to hear you muttering like a crazy person."

Wonderful. "Ha, I was just…"

"Practicing asking me out?" Her enigmatic smile remained steady and with her sunglasses, it was hard to read whether it was disdainful or amused.

I decided to just go with confidence. "I was going to give you a call. See if you wanted to see some of the city. You're new here, wouldn't want you to accidentally go to one of the wrong brunch spots. There's some serious hipster/yuppie conflict on the Uptown/Edgewater border. Nothing ruins brunch like watching a man with an ironic mustache get impaled on an artisanal baguette."

Jennifer chuckled, then her smile faded a bit. "Why do you think I'm that new? I said I was newly local, not fresh off the farm."

"One, you have a Texas driver's license. I carded you, remember? The picture was decent, but not such a miracle DMV shot that you would hold onto it. Two, you have an out of state phone number." I pulled out the matchbook from my pocket. "Sure, that doesn't mean as much nowadays, it's pretty much wherever you were living in 2004, at this point. Three, I saw your uncle last night. He said you'd just moved here. I'm not a stalker, I'm just highly trained in investigation"

Jennifer's smile returned, "Ah, right. Well, I haven't had a chance to hit the DMV yet."

"Go to the one in the Thompson center, they're used to crowds and there's a decent sushi place for afterwards."

"Are you asking me on a date to the DMV?"

I laughed, "No, I'm just passing on some of my vast Chicago expertise. I was planning on asking you on a date to one of my favorite spots in Chicago."

"Aha, your secret agenda is revealed." She was smiling at this point, so my hopes were high.

"You've got me." I smiled back, playing it as cool as I could with an unknown quantity of goose poop on me.

"Alright, when do you propose to do this?"

"I was thinking Sunday. We can meet outside the Roosevelt Red Line. You know how to get there?"

"No need to be patronizing, Texas does have trains." She protested playfully.

I held up my hands in a mollifying surrender, "I wouldn't know. I haven't left Chicagoland for the last two decades."

"I... I hadn't realized." She seemed abashed.

"It's the nature of the job." I shrugged, "I need to be here and ready for when disaster comes and that could be any time."

"Well, I agree to this proposal then. What time should I meet you?"

"Shall we do 10:30? We can get some brunch beforehand. No baguette stabbings, I promise."

"Okay, see you then." She brushed some goose poop off of my shoulder before she walked off, sipping her coffee.

I spent the next few days a bit scattered, doing all the normal things while not really able to concentrate on any of them. I worked my shift at Myopic, pricing the incoming used books. I had lunch with Andrew, who nodded his typical taciturn approval at my love life.

I got a haircut, dropped off some dry cleaning. I made sure my apartment was clean, not to assume anything, but better prepared than not and even if it didn't work out, I had a clean apartment. I finished attuning myself to the seasonally reconfigured lines of mystical energy running through the city, y'know, normal stuff.

Kept up with running, picked up and sent out invitations to my birthday party. Worked at Brando's, pouring drinks for the South Loop karaoke crowd. Read the book Anthony had given me, dropped in on a queer poetry slam Andrew was performing at. But mostly, I found my myself thinking about the upcoming date and about Jennifer. I don't really know in retrospect how much of that was lingering energies from her spell and how much was just genuine anticipation.

Chapter 6

Sunday, June 14th

"Palevsky for two." I held up two fingers, Eleven City Diner was always loud on the weekends.

The host nodded at me and looked down at his clipboard "It'll probably be about 15 minutes, unless you don't mind the counter."

I turned to Jennifer, "Up to you, It's a more authentic diner experience, if you daaare." I made the last part a little spooky sounding, then inwardly kicked myself.

"I'm game." Jennifer's smile still had a bit of a twist to it, cunning in some way, but nothing gave the lie to her words. I looked from her to the host and nodded. He grabbed two menus and escorted us the 20 feet to the end of the counter. I waited for Jennifer to sit before joining her. "So, what's good here?" she asked.

"It all depends on your preferences, but pretty much everything. Besides, what you order on a first date can tell me a lot about you. I wouldn't want to think you were ordering something just because I recommended it. Those are important clues for my investigation."

"Some help you are." Jennifer's expression less vexed, more playful.

"I just try not to presume universal taste. Some people despise pickles, some love them. I wouldn't want to get a reputation for being the Chosen One who forced everyone to eat pickles. People remember these things. I mean, there's still a Peter Massey special at Wolf's Delicatessen if you know who to order from Or so I hear from my Uncle Casimir. I haven't ever been. Anyway, all I know so far is your taste in beverages."

"What is it?"

"Well, specialty aged bourbon, as far as I can tell."

"No, the Peter Massey special." Jennifer quirked an eye

"Oh, Pastrami on Rye with extra brown mustard and slaw."

"So, food recommendations aren't your specialty?"

"Nope, I'm trained in offensive and investigative magic. I can manipulate all sorts of elemental spirits and do some decent psychometry and a bit of localized prophecy, but I'm not great at the mental stuff. My friend Andrew, he can look at someone and tell you what they had for dinner the night before, not me."

"That's your friend from the bar?"

"Yeah, he's a regular, he's got a knack for naming."

The waiter came over to us and talked over the counter. "Can I get you started with a drink?"

Jennifer looked at me. "How's the coffee?"

"Excellent. Chicago's a great coffee town. Maybe a little later we can stop by Intelligentsia, they have great single origin espresso."

"I'll have a coffee then." She looked briefly over to the waiter who nodded and looked to me.

"Bottomless root beer for me." The waiter left to fetch the beverages.

"Root beer?" She raised one eyebrow in a skeptical expression.

"They make it here. It's a quality beverage, not just sugary junk."

"I'll have to try it some time."

"Well, if you're nice, you can have a sip of mine."

"If I'm nice. What if I'm naughty?" Jennifer smiled a flirtatious smile.

"Well, we'd probably get thrown out of the restaurant," I bantered back, "and that would seriously impact my root beer supply."

"I'll try to contain myself." As she said it, the waiter returned with our drinks and departed with our orders, a lox plate for her and a waffle for me. Look, it may seem weird that I always remember what people order, but I do. I know it's not something that everyone pays a lot of attention to and for most people, it wouldn't matter. I learned to do it years ago from Scaevola. Sudden changes in eating habits are one of the surest warning signs for potential possession, so I basically have this mental file of what people like and don't like to eat. It makes planning dinner parties easy but takes up valuable mental space.

We paused as a brief struggle for conversation topic broke out. Out of the silent depths, I opened, "So, what brings you here from Texas."

She paused for a moment, thoughtful. "My license, right."

"That is correct, Jennifer V. Davis."

"Do you memorize everyone's information or just attractive women's?" She smiled a wicked smile.

"I've got a good head for details, but if I'm honest, it's because I wasn't sure about you. I've had people come looking for the Chosen One for less agreeable reasons. I wanted to make sure you weren't dangerous and if you'd been really shady I would have had to investigate you." I shrugged. "Had I known you were Keeper Davis's niece..."

"Can't a girl try and maintain a little mystery?" She smiled, slightly abashed. "Sorry about that. I guess I don't know much about what it must be like to be the Chosen One. I didn't know there were people who would come after you."

"Nihilists, mostly. People who want to see the world burn."

"They mention them in Kappa Tau Omega training, but we're not really trained to deal with them ourselves."

"Yes, Kappa Tau, I have a cousin in Kappa Tau, in the Washington D.C. house. She said she mostly learned domestic magics, tapestry weaving, house spirit summoning and so forth." I left the statement open ended.

"Those are the basics, though each house has its own secrets. We do learn some self-defense, basic wards and precautions, not to share your true name and so forth. We don't learn much about actually fighting Nihilists." She shuddered a bit as she finished.

I patted her shoulder beside me "No, that makes sense, it takes a certain type of insanity to want to tear down the whole magical world order. People like that always think they'll end up on top when the dust settles, that's not just insane, but really poorly educated in statistics." There was a moment of awkward silence between us. "Okay, my list of things not to talk about on a first date now includes Nihilist ideology."

"Well, fair's fair. Tell me something interesting about y'all's training." She straightened up as she asked this, brightening her tone, a bit of accent creeping in playfully.

The abrupt shift in tone took me by surprise, so it took me a moment to respond. "Okay, well, it was partially just normal schooling. I went to Boys Latin and then UofC. Right, University of Chicago. You'll get the local lingo down." I corrected myself based on her quizzical expression. "During that time, we had several independent studies with various tutors."

"Like my uncle Clark?"

"Like your uncle Clark. He was our martial studies instructor, he taught us martial arts, battle magics and combat strategy."

"You said we and our? Who else was there?" Jennifer looked interested. "Are there other Chosen Ones out there?"

"Oh, yeah, I guess even that people in the know don't necessarily hear all the details. Right, while there is only one Chosen One, hence the term, there are a few of us who were considered potential candidates. The ones who were born within a month before or after the previous prophecy was fulfilled. The Chosen One is determined quite early, but the members of the cohort train alongside him through the years. It actually goes back to the Alfarero twins from Madrid back in the 15th century. They weren't sure which one was the Chosen One, so they trained both."

"I had heard some of that. My uncle was a friend of Peter Massey's back in '77."

"That I knew. Though he doesn't talk much about it. I wasn't sure if he'd mentioned it to family."

"I've never heard him talk about it personally, but my mother has mentioned it before. Peter and Clark were good friends, but she won't say much else." Jennifer's smile had faded at this point.

"Well, that's more than I got out of him. Anyway, Prospero Tangherlini was our main tutor in mystical subjects, and my great Uncle Casimir was in charge of training in the grand traditions of the Order."

"That's Casimir Palevsky, he's the head of the Keepers, right?"

"Yes...ish." I waggled my head to express the ambiguity. "He is the head of this Conclave, which is in ascendancy because of the Prophecy of the Chosen One. Once the prophecy is resolved and there is a new Chosen One, ascendancy will switch, and some of the Conclave will move based on local needs. Sometimes, things can be tricky with that. Back in the late 19th Century, there was a territorial dispute over the Chosen One in China. The prophecy foretold the upcoming Boxer rebellion and German Keepers in Qingdao and British Keepers in Hong Kong disputed who was better able to serve the Chosen One and be in ascendancy. But, you didn't come here looking for a history lesson." I quickly added as I saw her eyes glazing over.

Fortunately, the waiter arrived with our food, saving her from protestations of interest and me from awkwardness.

"So, where is this place you're taking me?"

"It's a closely held secret." I smiled at her as we walked north along Wabash, moving at the awkward pace of the first date. Slow enough for conversation, slow enough to catch nuances of reactions, slow enough to occasionally get frustrated looks from city native pedestrians just looking to get where they're going.

"Is it one of those mob speakeasies? Are you going to ply me with bathtub gin and sinful jazz?" Her tone was joking.

"Not today," I smiled, "Vaudeville makes a much better second date."

An Orange line train passed overhead as we crossed beneath the tracks on Harrison. Jennifer flinched slightly at the noise. "I thought y'all had trains in Texas." I said flirtingly after the train finished going by.

"We do." She artfully enhanced her drawl, "We just keep them in sensible places, down on the ground."

"Well, Chicago is the city on the move. We've even got them new-fangled skyscrapers." I faked a drawl of my own.

"You think Dallas is nothing but sod homes and cattle pens?" She played at being offended.

"No, I'm sure there are oil derricks, too." That earned a playful slap on the shoulder. "Speaking of Chicago, what brought you here? Dallas winters not brutal enough?"

"I wanted a change of scenery, all of Dallas society knew me since I was a gawky debutante with braces and pimples. I figured Chicago was somewhere I could make my own way."

"Tell me about it, my middle school teacher is my landlord."

"Plus, I have family here, and I heard Chicago guys were cuter than Dallas guys." she looked at me playfully.

"Anyway," I said, gesturing widely, a little flustered. "Here we are." The building across the intersection was large, taking up an entire half-block of the city with its red marble stone, its Romanesque arched windows and its sweeping green and glass roof, complete with looming owl statues. "The Harold Washington Public Library."

"Your favorite place in the city is the library?" She smiled, not mean, but a bit skeptical.

"Wait til you see the inside." We crossed the street, waiting as three number 6 buses in a row crossed in front of us.

"Ugh, is that some sort of sign?" Jennifer looked at the buses.

"Just that the CTA is running normally." I shrugged. "Buses bunch up like herd animals in this city."

We walked along the sidewalk towards the entrance, but as we drew close, I stopped short. Jennifer was surprised and stopped alongside me. "What's wrong?"

"Nothing's wrong, just a surprise. Someone I haven't seen in a while." I stepped forward and called out. "Ellis." I waved as he saw me and walked over. I turned to Jennifer as he approached. "He's a childhood friend, I'll introduce you." Ellis pulled out his earbuds and tucked them into his pocket. He was wearing green slacks and a white sox t-shirt. His hair was done in a short natural style cut that was new since I had last seen him, but the Malcolm X glasses had been the same since high school.

I walked over and extended my hand to shake. Ellis gave me a short uncertain look and took my hand in a quick handshake. I smiled as I spoke, "I saw your dad just the other day. He asked if we'd been 'hanging out'."

"Yeah," Ellis sighed, "Pops doesn't keep track of who I see in the day-to-day." There was a brief pause.

"What are you up to here?" I gestured at the doors to the library.

"Volunteer weekends at the YouMedia center. Working on a project on Silenced Voices of Minority Youth."

"Nice." I nodded my approval. "This is Jennifer," I presented her with a simple gesture, "Jennifer, this is Ellis Green. His father has done a lot of work with my Uncles. We used to hang out when we were younger."

"More like you babysitting me." A quick smile flashed on Ellis' serious face.

"I was just going to show Jennifer the Winter Gardens. She's new in town."

"Joe says it's his favorite place." Jennifer smiled and nodded to Ellis, "Nice to meet you."

Ellis returned her nod then gestured to the doors. "I better get in there before the kids burn the place down."

As he moved away, I spoke up, "If your dad asks again, anything should I tell him?"

Ellis stopped and turned. "Tell him we ran into each other on the street, but I had to run because I was on my way to an interview for a nine-to-five followed by a date with a respectable girl and an appointment with the most boring tailor in Chicago for some professional clothes." He gave a sarcastic smile.

I gave a brief smile and nod. "I'm having a birthday party next Saturday, you free?"

Ellis shook his head. "Can't...I got some stuff going on, might be in jail. You know how it goes." He smiled and went into the building.

Jennifer came up beside me, taking my arm. "Well, he's a character. In jail?"

"He's kidding. I think." I shrugged it off. "We used to hang out some when I was a teenager, but we were a little far apart in age. I mean, I don't think he's up to anything criminal or anything like that."

Jennifer nodded and I opened the door to the library for her. "So, this is the crown jewel of the Chicago Public Library system." Jennifer smirked as she looked at the bare marble walls. "Chicago couldn't afford any books?"

"Y'know, there's actually a funny story about that." We walked into the central lobby and began to ascend the escalators as I talked. "Back in 1871, Chicago burned down. Big news, you might have heard about it. Well, in the aftermath, all these European cities, London, Paris, Berlin, etc. started sending boxes of books. They all came with the same message. Sorry about how you lost your city, here's some books to help you rebuild your library."

"Now, by 1871, Chicago wasn't a wild frontier town or anything, but it was more or less just a big slaughterhouse with a city around it. We'd only had a fancy hotel for a year or two. There wasn't a library to speak of. But Mayor Mason wasn't about to miss the chance to build up his city, so he thanked them kindly and promised the library would be even better than before with their kind help."

We had come to the fop of the escalators as I finished. Jennifer smiled, "Well, he wasn't technically lying, it was better than before."

I pointed at her, smiling. "You'll make a Chicagoan yet." As we entered the library lobby on the 3rd floor, I swept open my arms. "This is the result of all that. Many years later."

"Okay, not bad." Jennifer nodded.

"There are four more floors of materials, plus our main destination." I led her over to the elevators at the back.

"So, this library is one of your favorite places in Chicago?" She asked as we waited before the elevator doors, smirking slightly.

"Yes." I nodded my head in mock shame. "My Uncle Anthony is a librarian. He loved to bring me here." We both got into the elevator, and I pressed the button for 9. "I have a lot of fond memories. He had friends in various departments, so I got to see behind the scenes. There are a lot of amazing historical pieces here." The elevator doors opened, and we stepped out. "Plus, there's this."

The Winter Gardens of the Harold Washington Library are a two-story grand lobby at the top of the building, complete with a massive skylight. All around the walls are plants and spread through the middle of the lobby are tables and chairs. These were sporadically filled with people reading, conversing and playing games.

Jennifer was taken aback for a moment, looking around. She briefly touched the small gold cross at her throat and murmured quietly. "This is quite a place of power."

I nodded, "Public space, devoted to knowledge, complete with a shrine to a hero of the city." I gestured toward the gallery space, with its large picture of Harold Washington.

"Wow." She looked at me, "Impressive."

"There are some nice views as well," I gestured to the large picture windows to the east, the large curtains barely parted. The two of us walked over in respectful silence and for a few minutes, we looked out at the buildings and the sky, light glinting off of the windows.

Jennifer broke the silence, "Alright, Chicago's pretty, I'll give you that."

I turned towards her. "The rules of banter dictate I should say something like 'not half as pretty as you,' but I fear being quite that corny on a first date." I smiled.

She returned the smile with a crook of her lip, "well, nothing ventured, nothing gained."

I was about to respond when my phone buzzed. I held up a finger and frowned as I pulled it out. A message from Scaevola <*ASAP 557W 1100S*>. I sighed loudly and looked at Jennifer. "I have to go. I can't really explain, except to say that it's a Chosen One emergency and I don't usually do this."

Jennifer looked at me, scrutinizing my face. She nodded and leaned in, giving me a kiss on the cheek. "Go be a hero. You'll just have to make it up to me."

I thought briefly. "Tuesday night?" As she nodded, I jogged towards the elevator. "I'll call you."

"You better."

Chapter 7

Maxwell Street Market was still crowded in the early afternoon. I made my way up the street taking a slightly roundabout route from where the cab dropped me off. I passed the rows of industrial size pipe wrenches, the knock-off toys, the paleta vendors with their giant bags of orange snack things, and the stalls playing bootleg CDs and took my short detour to the parking lot overlooking the Dan Ryan expressway.

Pilar's booth was in her normal spot near the northern end of the lot. She was seated behind her table in her folding camp chair, fanning herself against the summer heat as people perused the oils and charms adorning her table. She waved as she saw me. "Joseph, what brings you to Maxwell street today?"

I smiled and leaned over the table to kiss her on the cheek. "Trouble, unfortunately. I need to assemble a few things for an investigation. I left my kit at home, didn't have time to go back there and then make it here."

Pilar looked at me over the table, "Joseph, that is not very good for my confidence in you." She playfully scolded, "You are the Chosen One, you have to keep your head in the game."

"I am sorry, ma'am." I raised my hands and shrugged, "I was on a date."

"Oh, well that's different. Give me a second." She lifted herself awkwardly out of the camp chair. Pilar wasn't old, but she was quick to remind me she wasn't young and that the aches in her joints proved it. She shuffled over to the plastic tubs behind the stall. "Nice girl?"

I shrugged, "I'm not sure yet. It was just a first date. And running off to secret emergencies doesn't lead to many second dates in my experience."

Pilar clucked at me as she sorted through the baggies within the cases, "Is she an hechiciera?"

"Si, Kappa Tau Omega."

"Ooh," Pilar sucked her teeth a bit. "You gotta be careful, my friend Paula says they have secret tricks for snaring men. You need some sort of protective charm?" She gestured at the rack of hanging pendants.

I laughed. "No, I'm fine. And you can tell your friend Paula that the only tricks they have are arranged marriages and family money. Lots of people would be snared by a housewife that comes with her own house."

"Well," Pilar drew out the word, "If that's how it is, she'll be happy to sit at home and raise some babies."

"She doesn't seem the type. And you know I can't be having babies yet." I smiled. "I've got the world to save."

Pilar put a plastic bag on the table. "What do you know. It's only your first date. I put in some sand, some chalk dust, incense, holy water and a dandelion. You need anything else?"

"Yeah, something for a pendulum..." I pulled down a glass bead pendant for evil eye protection from the rack. "And do you have any mirrors?"

Pilar pulled a few small hand mirrors from beneath the table. "These should help."

I looked in the bag, "Muchas gracias, how much do I owe you?"

"Oh Joseph, I can't take your money. You're out here protecting us, every day."

"I'm glad you're thankful, but I don't want to take advantage. What would you charge someone else who got all this?"

Pilar scrunched up her mouth a bit, "15, but you don't have to."

I pulled a bill out of my money clip. "Here's 20. Keep the change. And tell Miguel I say hi. How's he doing?"

"He's just fine, you be careful out there," she thumped me on the elbow with her fan.

"You mean with the girl or with the emergency?" I smiled at her as I walked away.

It took me a minute to find Scaevola, even after I found the intersection from the text. Our method of navigation was a relic from the days of pagers and hadn't really gotten easier. I'd mastered the basics pretty quickly, the Chicago grid is easy once you learn it, but there's no nuance in the system. For an obvious building, I sometimes get a room or floor number, but things get complicated with anything beyond that.

I finally found him around the back of the Chicago Fire Department training building, standing by a large brass sculpture, it's three twisted prongs twisting upwards, reaching for the sky.

Scaevola stared at me as I approached, his expression stern. "Joseph Samuel Palevsky. I trust everything is alright." I shuddered a bit at his use of my full true name. Scaevola always started clandestine conversations like that, worried people were using glamours or mind controlled. Using the true name is a bit of a brute force test, but it is a certain one. I was warded against attacks using it, but it always shook me up a bit, given that he could follow it with powerful magical words. He looked down at my bag, then back up at my eyes, suspicion plain.

"I was out of the house. I needed to grab some quick supplies." I always felt defensive in front of Scaevola. He looked at everyone and everything as if they were guilty of something and it could get to you, especially if you were out doing something frivolous like having a love life. I played contrite, "I'm sorry, sir. I assumed speed was the priority, here. Better here and short on preparation than late and fully equipped. As you always say, the enemy doesn't just wait for you to show up."

Scaevola narrowed his eyes, but then he waved his hand. "Very well. Do you know this monument?"

I looked at the statue. Scaevola treated everything like it was a pop quiz and I hadn't been studying. Except I'd spent the last two decades learning the ins and outs of Chicago, while this wasn't the Picasso or the Bean, it had enough symbolic importance for it to have been on my radar. "The Fire." I said clearly and nonchalantly. If this was some sort of test, I didn't want him to see me sweat.

Scaevola nodded, "Yes, this was the starting point of the Great Chicago Fire. I was walking through Maxwell Street Market, making sure nobody was selling anything on the anathema lists, when I sensed the energies." He pulled his hand from the pocket of his suit and dangled a highly ornamental pendant from a chain. As he whispered to himself (I could just make out the name of fire on his lips), the pendant snapped towards the statue, pulling taut.

"Well." I tensed involuntarily. "That's unusual."

"Yes." Scaevola's response was followed with a long stare.

"I'll look into it, sir." I sighed, inwardly.

"Good. With increased activity in the area, we can't be too careful." Scaevola moved towards the curb. "I want a full report on all ignotic sites in the city in 48 hours."

"All ignotic sites in the city?" I groaned to myself; this would take up the next two days. So much for the idea of trying to get Jennifer with a surprise make-up date. As Scaevola hailed a cab, I decided to ask. "Sir, is this some sort of test?"

Scaevola turned to me as he opened the door of the cab that pulled up. "Would it matter if it was, Joseph? You have a duty to follow orders. Whether that's investigating a perturbed fire spirit or proving you have absorbed your lessons properly. Either way, you have 48 hours." He got in the cab and left. I cursed to myself and began to unpack my makeshift kit.

I had been at my examinations for about an hour when the police car pulled up. I had already spread out a lot of my materials, a circle of sand around the statue, a number of items spread out around the circle, and I was just getting ready to set up the mirrors and light the incense to check the condition of the fire spirit contained within.

"What's going on here?" The officer was a Black woman of middling height, about 30, if I were to guess. She walked over from the car as her partner, a Hispanic man a few years older and a few slices of Lou Malnati's heavier exited the driver's seat of their SUV. Her approach was authoritative, but not threatening. She was cautious, but also curious and didn't see me as a threat.

"Hello, officer." I stood up from where I was crouching by the incense. "I'm just doing a bit of public performance art, here. I have all my permits in order." I said, reaching into my wallet and pulled out my card for these situations.

"What about all this mess?" She gestured at the empty bag of chalk dust and the discarded water bottle.

"Here." I handed her my card. "Just check with the office, the number is on the back."

The officer looked skeptical and signaled her partner over. After a brief consultation, he waited with me as she moved away to make the call. I wasn't worried. We had several bureaucramancers on Keeper payroll working in City Hall. Their entire job was to smooth over these kinds of situations, magically backdate paperwork, get investigations transferred, the normal stuff."

"So, what's this all about?" The older cop nodded towards the materials laid out around the statue.

"The art?" I paused for a moment, but I could bullshit about art as well as anyone with a prep school education "It's about the illusion of safety. It's easy to capture something as powerful as the fire in something as peaceful as bronze, but people forget the real thing was a thing of smoke and flame. That's what the incense is for. The chalk dust represents the ash, and the sand is just to keep people from coming too close and knocking things over."

The Policeman nodded as his partner returned. She looked at me. "Okay, you can carry on. But be sure not to leave a mess." She handed me my card back as she and her partner went back to the car. "We'll be back later to check."

"Of course, officer." I smiled as they drove away and returned to my investigation.

Chapter 8

The knock on my door surprised me. I looked over to my stereo, the music wasn't too loud. What time was it? The clock said that it was barely 8pm, not even remotely early enough for Matron Bielski to complain, even on a Monday night. Nobody had buzzed in; I wasn't expecting anyone. I moved quietly to the door, picking up my shillelagh on the way, whispering awake the war spirit bound within as I crept close.

As I neared the door, the knocking came again, and a voice yelled through the door. "Joey, I got pizza, put on your pants and get out here." I dropped out of the sneaking crouch, whispered the spirit back to sleep in the short club and took the last few steps over to the door. I opened it to see Daniel Derita standing there, his suit looking rumpled from a day of work and a large box from Gino's East in his hand. He eyed the club in my hand. "I can go grab Lou Malnati's if you feel that strongly about it." I waved him in with the club and he moved past me as I closed the door.

Now, when I'm on a research binge, my apartment is usually a combination of stacks of books, empty Dunkin cups and the occasional map or diagram on the tables or desk. Today, the dining room table had a large map of Chicago mounted on a cork board, a few fresh pins in it along with the remnants of a quick takeout lunch from Sultan's Market.

Over the desk, one of the large white boards around the room had a number of equations and diagrams, some crossed out, some with large question marks. Daniel looked around and headed over to the small kitchen with the pizza box. "Prospero said you were doing some research, so I thought I'd bring some vital supplies." He pulled out a small bottle of whiskey from his suit pocket and set it on the counter next to the pizza. "The finest 7-11 has to offer."

"Why yes, Daniel. Please come in. Make yourself at home." I said in a sarcastic deadpan I've known Daniel for over 25 years, and he honestly hasn't changed much since we were 13. I walked up next to him and pulled down paper plates and plastic cups. I passed him the plates and took the whiskey and cups over to the coffee table, clearing away space between the stacks of books I had pulled off my shelves for research purposes. Daniel came over with two slices and my finest plastic silverware. The next few minutes, we just ate, occasional sounds of satisfaction the only thing that disturbed the musical stylings of John Coltrane.

After two slices, Daniel sat back, patting his stomach. "Nothing like deep dish, am I right?"

I sat up from my own post pizza reverie and took a sip of whiskey. "It does hit the spot."

"Good thing you have me bringing you food, you'd starve. You need to find a woman; you can just yell out 'bring me a sandwich' and boom." Daniel laughed.

"Dude. You know I don't find that shit funny." I looked at Daniel seriously.

"What? It's just us guys, what's the problem?" Daniel got defensive. "C'mon Joey, it was just a fucking joke."

I sighed, "fine, whatever. I'm just kinda sick of it."

"Guess I hit a little close to home." Daniel sipped his whiskey and gestured at the books and papers, dropping the topic. "What do they have you researching?" He idly picked up one of the books, a special reprint of some of Newton's secret alchemical work.

"There's some sort of elemental disturbance down at the Fire monument down in the South Loop. Scaevola noticed it and dragged me out of a date to investigate." My voice was full of disappointment.

"Oof. Just cause he decided life shouldn't be fun doesn't mean the rest of us shouldn't get to have some." Daniel imitated Scaevola's stern manner. "Constant vigilance, Joseph. Getting laid is an unnecessary frivolity."

I gave a desultory snort. Daniel wasn't as funny as he thought he was, but if I didn't laugh, he'd just repeat the joke as if I hadn't understood it. "It is a little unusual. Something stirred up the spirit of the Chicago fire, at least the fragment in the fire monument. But I've checked a few other locations around town to see if there's some sort of general upheaval."

I went over to the dining room table and pulled out my map, gesturing to some other locations and my notations from yesterday's research. "If there were some sort of actual disturbance in the overall spiritual landscape, some sort of imbalance getting the spirits agitated, there would be resonances here." I indicated the Water Tower, "here," I indicated the Stockyard Fire Memorial, "or here," I indicated the location on the UofC Campus.

"Remember back in school when we convinced Crazy Matt that the best reagent for summoning naiads was his own piss." Daniel nodded at me from the couch.

"And he saved up three jars before Prospero found out." I finished the anecdote. "You know, I hear he still swears by it." Daniel laughed out loud, and I smiled with him. "Anyway, I have one more location to check and rule out."

"Man, so you're not free yet? I figured you'd be done by now so we could go hang out on the boat tonight." Daniel had gotten a boat last summer. The way he lovingly described it, I'm sure I'd be impressed if I had any clue about boats, but he spent most of the summer either out on the boat or trying to talk me into going out on the boat. He spent most of his time just sitting in the area just north of the curve on lake shore drive, drinking with the crowd that hung out there.

"Sorry, I should be done by tomorrow, but I have a date. I'm lucky she didn't freak out after my emergency call." and I held up my hand before Daniel could follow up. "And I'm not taking her out on your boat for our second date. I'm not really ready for her to meet you yet."

"Afraid she'd see what a real man looks like?" Daniel joked as he flexed his non-existent muscles.

"Afraid she'd realize my friends are assholes and move back to Texas." I shot back.

"Alright, but we gotta celebrate our birthdays, bro! Boozy brunch out on the boat next weekend?"

I threw my hands up. "Twist my arm. I'll bring mimosa stuff."

Daniel grabbed the plates and headed over to the kitchen. He tossed the paper plates in the trash and began looking over the sink. "Everything working well here? I was trying out a new plumber."

I looked over. "Yeah, everything's working just fine. Drain's flowing much better. Not that I get much chance to use it, between work and Chosen One duties, I can't remember the last time I got a chance to cook for anyone. But yeah, everything's much clearer."

"Great, Prospero has been letting me do a lot more independent stuff, making the hiring decisions."

"That's great." I poured a bit more whiskey and started looking at one of my maps.

"Who'd a thought, y'know." Daniel finished the whiskey in his cup. "If you asked ten-year-old Daniel where he'd be now, I don't think he'd say deputy chief property manager for the Conclave in Chicago."

I put down the map. Daniel was obviously getting introspective, a serious risk when he had whiskey. This required subtle action if I didn't want to spend my evening alternating between being nostalgic and maudlin. "Look, none of us knew back then. We all thought we might be dead by now. At least, I did."

"Do you hear much from the guys?"

"Some of them. I write sometimes with Gunter. He's all tied up in the Greek financial business."

"What about Bertie?"

"His lordship is busy living the high life in the English Countryside. Last I heard, he was appointed to the High Allthing, supervising magical practice for all of Northern England. Oh, and he and Kathleen had twins." I shrugged. "How about you?"

"I had to block Crazy Matt on Facebook. He's gonna get himself in trouble if he keeps on like that. I still write some with Underwood's sister. I haven't seen her since Arlington, though." Daniel poured some more whiskey, looking maudlin.

"I was sad I couldn't make it. I appealed to the Conclave, but you know how they are about travel." I took the whiskey from Daniel and poured some in my own cup. "To Underwood." I raised my cup.

"And Trevor." Daniel raised his own in response. We both winced a bit, mostly from the burn of the cheap whiskey. "Y'know, before the accident, I thought he might have been..."

"You and me both." I shrugged. "But destiny is funny that way. Anyway, he would have hated the paperwork." I gestured to the spread of books and papers.

"Right, yeah, you get back to that." Daniel rose and moved to the door. "See you Saturday for the party." As he left, the room was still, only music disturbing the silence as I sat there, lost in might have beens.

Chapter 9

Tuesday, June 16th

It was mid-day when I showed up at the Conclave building. I was a few hours before Scaevola's deadline, so I figured it should be fairly empty. I hadn't gotten much sleep putting things together and had two days of stubble. I hoped Uncle Casimir wouldn't be around to see me this disheveled. I didn't quite feel like a lecture on presentability after 40 hours of fruitless research.

When the attendant brought me up to the lounge area, I moved slowly, wary of unpleasant confrontations, but the room was nearly empty. It was a Tuesday afternoon and most of the Keepers found things to keep themselves busy, even if they didn't need to work for a living. I was actually beginning to worry I wouldn't be able to find anyone to turn in my report to when I heard a cough from the direction of the fireplace. I would my way through the high comfortable chairs and saw Ephraim stirring in front of the fire.

I was pleased to see him, but hesitated before approaching him, as our conversation from the other night and its terrible implications came to mind. Ephraim looked up before I could move away. "Zar-Ptak. What are you doing lurking there? Come. Sit." He gestured to the seat beside him in front of the unseasonal fire.

"Of course, sir." I sat at the edge of the chair. Not sitting back, my report portfolio on my lap.

Ephraim reached out and patted my knee as I sat there. "Joe, relax. You seem all wound up." I let some tension out of my posture at his words, "why are you so worried?"

"Sir, the other night...You implied that we would only...speak twice more. I guess I'm a bit nervous about that."

Ephraim nodded, "You are still a young man. When you get to my age, you wonder about everything. Will this be my last cigar? Will this be the last opera I see? Will I make it to another springtime?"

"Sir, you said we would only speak twice more. Does that mean I am going to die? That I am going to leave? Are you..."?

"The flames show me things. I saw two conversations, this one today, and one more. Both are important, but the flames showed our paths parting after that. If it worries you so much, I could do a reading for you."

I considered my fatigue, my need for a nap and a shower before my date tonight. But compared to my uncertainty, I couldn't pass this up. And if it was my next to last conversation with Ephraim, I wanted to take advantage of his wisdom. "Yes, sir. I would like that very much."

Ephraim smiled, "Alright, Zar-Ptak, your choice. Though I would take it as a courtesy if you did not choose tea leaves. I already have to pee every five minutes; my knees can't stand getting up more often."

I laughed. "Let's go with a simple tarot spread, then. I do have to go get ready for a date after this." I smiled back at him and brought over a side table as he pulled a deck and cloth from the pocket of his brocade vest.

"Very well," he riffled the worn cards with a practiced ease. "Focus on the dilemma in your mind," He spread the cards in front of me, "Draw the first card."

I reached to the spread of cards and pulled one from the fan. Ephraim took the card from my hand and laid it on the cloth, flipping it to reveal the Fool. "That is a beginning." Ephraim nodded slowly. "You weren't perhaps thinking about your romantic history, eh?" He gave a wicked smile. "I joke, I joke. You stand at the precipice, about to begin something unknown. It yawns before you. It is an auspicious start." He spread the cards again.

I reached to the spread cards again and pulled another from the fan. Again, Ephraim took it and laid it on the cloth as he flipped it, I recognized the Hierophant, reversed.

"Hmmm." Ephraim contemplated the card. "Opposition from a spiritual authority. One who is outside his normal scope of power, unsettled from his position. You face power, Zar-Ptak. Twisted power."

I took this in as he shuffled for a third time and spread the remaining cards before me. Once more I drew and once more Ephraim flipped the card, the ten of swords was revealed before me.

Ephraim and I both looked long and hard at the figure on the card, lying on the ground, pierced by swords. We both knew the implications, Ephraim had taught me well, but we both paused. "Betrayal. One you believed to be an ally will reveal themselves to be an enemy." He looked up as he scooped up the cards to lay out the last spread.

As he spread the cards out before me, I hesitated. Given the reading so far, I wasn't sure what I wanted from the final card. I took a deep breath and pulled a card from the deck. Ephraim took this last card and flipped it, laying the reversed Judgment card beside the others.

Ephraim took a deep breath and looked me in the eye. "Well, I have good news and less good news. The less good news is that it's almost time. The day of judgment looms ahead. The good news is that the future is not set in stone. Your decisions can still influence what is to come. Do you understand?"

I looked over the spread of cards, "So I, the Fool, unknowing hero setting out for adventure," I pointed to the cards in turn, "crossed by the displeasure of a spiritual mentor, the reversed Hierophant, I will be dramatically betrayed, ten swords in my back, and then, it all comes to a head in uncertainty?" I kept my finger over the reversed judgment card, looking at Ephraim for guidance.

Ephraim nodded, "You have it up until the end, then you lose the thread." He picked up the card. "Your choices will determine how things turn out. The unexpected choice is the hinge on which the world opens." Ephraim sat back and picked up a half-smoked cigar from the ashtray beside him. He looked through his vest pockets for a match for a few moments, coming up empty. I reached into my pocket and offered him Jennifer's matchbook.

Ephraim took the matchbook from my hand and turned it over in his fingers. He opened it and lit the cigar with a single match, watching the flame as he puffed. After a moment of concentration, the fire flared up in his hand and the match was consumed. He turned his gaze to the matchbook, looking over the number. He looked at me and smiled as he handed back the matchbook, his prodigious eyebrows waggling.

"That's actually why I need to get going, sir." I returned his smile and rubbed my stubbly chin. "I have a second date this evening and I could use a little cleaning up after my recent research binge." I gestured with the portfolio in my hands. "Could you make sure this gets to the rest of the conclave?"

"Well, at least years of training haven't entirely messed up your priorities. " Ephraim took the report in his hand and set it on the table in front of him. "Go, enjoy yourself. Before all this," He gestured at the cards, "gets in the way."

"I will, sir." I answered with mock solemnity. I even threw a mock salute. Ephraim chuckled as I walked toward the door in my pretend military posture.

As I reached the lounge door, he called out. "Zar-Ptak, when in doubt, listen to your friends and remember, our next conversation is the important one. Don't miss it." His words rang in my ears as I left.

Chapter 10

I waited outside the Green Door Tavern, occasionally checking my watch. I'd sent Jennifer the address and the time, but I hadn't told her more about the agenda for the evening. She was a bit late at this point, but I tried not to worry myself too much about it. At 7:15, a cab pulled up and Jennifer stepped out, wearing a simple summer dress in black with the same cross necklace.

I doffed my hat to her, bowing slightly. She smirked at the affectation, "I'm sorry I'm a bit late. Is traffic always so bad here?"

"I'm afraid so. But you do eventually get used to it and figure out tricks to get around more quickly." I gestured to the door. "Shall we?"

She looked over the building and smiled a weak smile. "Alright." I opened the door to the bar, and we went in.

The inside was nice but not notable, a typical Chicago tavern, bottles on display behind the bar, colorful tap heads at the front, the ubiquitous televisions showed the Cubs, doing their best to overcome their ancient curse. Jennifer took it in as we entered, somewhat skeptical. "Follow me," I gestured and reached out my hand. After a moment, she took it and I led her back into the bar. We passed the dartboards and the bar and were through the pool room and the stairs when she stopped. I saw her looking at the restrooms sign with some skepticism. "Trust me." I smiled and tugged lightly on her hand.

At the bottom of the stairs, she looked around at the short hallway with cluttered shelves and two restroom doors. "If you are going to show me your favorite bathroom in Chicago, thanks, but..." I held up one hand and with the other turned the concealed knob within the shelves, opening the hidden door.

The door opened onto a dimly lit room with booths just visible. "The Drifter," I said as Jennifer followed me in and took a moment to take in her surroundings.

The room was small, but elaborately decorated. On one wall were a series of half-booth tables running back to a curtained off area. The other wall was dominated by a large antique wooden bar, its ersatz proscenium framing a collection of obscure spirits. The light in the room came from dim bulbs hanging down within archaic decanters and from the silent movies being projected onto a sheet covering a stage area. The room was not quite full, but most of the tables had a few people in them, deep in conversation, quiet enough not to overwhelm the sound of antique jazz playing on the speakers.

Jennifer turned back to me. "Okay."

"Okay?"

"Yeah, this'll do." She wrinkled the bridge of her nose in a slight sarcastic gesture. "I suppooose." She smiled as she drew out the vowel sound.

The host approached us as we stood there. "Joe, how are you this evening?"

"Hey, Tony. I'm doing well. I should be on the list this evening with a plus one." I smiled at Jennifer as Tony checked the clipboard and nodded, gesturing to one of the booths further back. We walked over to the table near the stage and slipped into the seats. She sat gracefully and I slipped into the seat across from her beneath the large antique circus banner, even here sitting where I could keep an eye on the entrances.

"Okay, I'm impressed. I thought the whole second date speakeasy thing was a joke, but I'm glad it wasn't."

"Well, it actually started as one, but a perk of being a bartender is that I know a lot of the different places around the city. Professional curiosity, mostly. Plus, I have a friend performing here tonight."

One of the servers slipped from behind the bar and came over to the table. "Hey Joe, who's your friend?"

"Leslie, hey. This is Jennifer. Jennifer, this is Leslie, one of the mixologists here." Leslie and Jennifer exchanged introductory nods.

Leslie reached down and laid a set of Rider-Waite tarot cards on the table. Each had a drink recipe written at the bottom with the name at the top. "Here are our specialty cocktails for the evening." She set a piece of paper on the table between us. "Our beer and wine are on here as well as some snacks at the bottom."

I looked over at Jennifer, "How do you feel about olives?"

"Is this some sort of test? A compatibility thing?"

"No, I was going to order the olive plate, but if you don't like them..."

"Ah, yes, I like olives." I nodded to Leslie, and she left to grab the food. Jennifer continued. "You haven't seen How I Met Your Mother?"

"I don't watch a lot of TV. I wasn't allowed one during my formal training, and the ones at the bar are always on sports. So, I never really got in the habit."

"I had some sorority sisters at SMU who were *obsessed* with it." She put extra emphasis on the word. "I couldn't avoid it. There's a whole thing about olives and romantic suitability."

"You'll have to show me some time." We looked over the drinks until Leslie returned. I ended up ordering a "Same Difference" off of the Magician card, which she went with the Two of Cups, a "Pistol Packin' Mama". We settled back in with our olives.

"So, what do you do for fun if not TV?" Jennifer smiled as she ate an olive.

"I read, short stories and poetry, mostly. Sometimes I go to poetry slam or live lit shows, there's a great scene in Chicago. Andrew and I do the crossword most days." I thought about it, "I go to movies at the Music Box or the Gene Siskel when there's something classic playing. Oh, and museums, I go to a lot of museums. I had actually been planning on taking you to the Art Institute on Sunday when we were interrupted."

"How did that turn out?" Jennifer looked up, a little surprised. "I meant to ask."

I paused as Leslie delivered our drinks and waited for her to go. "I can't really talk about details, but it went fine." I smiled reassuringly. "Only about a three percent chance of fiery doom."

"Is that a lot?" Jennifer seemed inquisitive. "I mean compared to normal."

"No, that's just a bit over normal. I'd say most of the time we're closer to 1.5." I smiled reassuringly. "So, what do you do for fun?"

"Well, I watch TV, some. I also read. And I sew. I made this dress myself." She gestured to it.

"Very nice." I cast an appraising eye on the craftsmanship.

"Thank you. I learned back in college doing theater. One of the girls in the theater department showed me how to sew and I realized it was something I could do during vigil nights. Which is something *I* can't really talk about."

"Ooh, mysterious." I smiled. I was about to continue flirting, but the music went silent, and Tony came up on the stage, pulling back the sheet that had been used as a screen, revealing a simple tableau. A young woman with a forties style twist updo wearing high waisted pants and a modest tank top walked out onto the stage carrying a stool and a ukulele. "Hello everyone, my name is Samantha and I'll be playing a few songs for you.

The bar grew silent around her, a dozen muted conversations ceasing as she strummed and plucked her instrument to life. She sang a stylized rendition of 'God Bless the Child,' followed by a nearly acapella version of 'Dream a Little Dream'. I took the opportunity of the songs to watch Jennifer watch the performance.

She was lovely. Well-arranged and put together, her hair cascading in artfully arranged waves, her hand resting against her delicate throat, gently touching her necklace. But what struck me more than that was the intensity of her attention. She watched Samantha perform, taking in the nimble motions on the uke, the nuances of the lyrics, the variations in the familiar songs. I watched her watch the show and admired her as she did it. As the set ended, we both applauded, but she did so with an expression of genuine appreciation, smiling as she looked to me and nodded her satisfaction.

"That was very nice." She took the last sip of her drink and set it on the table.

"Yeah, Samantha really knows how to play." As I said it, Samantha dropped into the booth beside me.

"Joe, you came." She gave me a quick hug.

"I said I would, didn't I?" I returned the hug and Samantha sat back. Jennifer was looking at the two of us, a look of uncertainty on her face. "Samantha, this is Jennifer, Jennifer, Samantha."

"That was very nice up there." Jennifer reached out a hand to shake Samantha's. "How long have you been playing?"

"Thank you. I only started the ukulele a few years ago, but I've been playing guitar since I was 13." Samantha tipped her head to the side. "The Uke is much more portable, and I can get a whole Zooey Deschanel thing going." She turned to me. "I just wanted to say hi. I won't interrupt anymore. Looking forward to Saturday!" She hugged me again as she got up. "Nice to meet you."

Jennifer smiled as Samantha left. She looked back at me, a curious expression on her face. Before she said anything, I spoke. "Samantha's a friend. I met her girlfriend Amanda at an arts and crafts fair almost ten years ago. She's a really skilled weaver, you and she might chat about fabric arts." Jennifer's expression shifted as I spoke, softening a bit.

"What was that about Saturday?" Jennifer looked a little bit sideways at me.

"Actually, I was planning to talk to you about that." I nodded, "I'm having a birthday party this Saturday. I know we haven't known each other long, but if you'd like to come..."

Jennifer tilted her head back and made a thoughtful noise, "What are the details?"

I reached into my vest pocket and pulled out an invitation, sliding it across the table to her. "It's a literary character party. No gifts necessary, any bottles for the bar are welcome. You come as a favorite literary character. What do you think?"

Jennifer thought for a moment, then smiled. "I'm just thinking what I have that will work for that theme and if I have time to do some sewing."

"Excellent, I'll see you there. Oh, and if you want to bring along Miriam, the more the merrier."

"Okay," Jennifer took the invite and pulled a pen from her purse. She wrote Jennifer Davis +1 on the back in an elegant hand and slid it back to me.

I smiled at that and signaled Leslie for another drink.

Two hours, three drinks and a few small plates of food later, we found our way up to the streets, a bit tipsy but none the worse for wear.

"Well Joe, you certainly know how to bring a lady to a bar basement and impress her."

I took a mock bow. "I aim to please." I offered my arm, "it's a fine night, would you care for a walk?"

Jennifer looked at her watch. "I can't stay out all night, but a short walk could be nice. I do have work tomorrow."

"A short walk then. What can I show you in a short walk?" I thought to myself. "okay, come with me. I'll show you the river."

We set off down the street, Jennifer on my arm, the scent of her perfume elusive and intriguing in my nostrils. "So, I realized I didn't ever ask what you do for work?" I said, "I just assumed you..."

"You assumed I what?" Jennifer tossed her hair and looked at me with a sly smile and a look of faux indignance, "Go on, I want to hear this."

I was unperturbed, "I simply assumed a woman of your wit and poise must be exiled royalty or the oldest of old money."

Jennifer shrugged, "well, you aren't completely wrong. But being old money isn't easy. I manage my family's charitable foundation. That's what I went to school for."

"Oookay, that makes sense." I nodded, "I guess that's part of why you haven't gotten betrothed? Finishing your schooling and all that?"

"that's part of it." she fell silent.

I paused to let her continue, but she remained silent as we came up to the park. "Well, here we are. Montgomery Ward park, one of the only parks right by the river."

I led her down the stairs towards the river as I swept my free arm wide, presenting the city. There's a great view of the Sears Tower from here."

"I thought it was called the Willis Tower now?"

"Only for tourists." I smiled, "surefire way to out yourself."

"How about you, Joe? Do you have a betrothed somewhere? Some nice girl your parents promised you to when you were young? Some secret love somewhere?" Jennifer seemed almost shy asking me.

"No. Actually not allowed to get married or have kids until my destiny is fulfilled. Plus, most women don't really deal well with the whole running off after emergencies thing. So, nobody for me." I shrugged, "Peril isn't great for the love life."

She looked sad for a moment, "Joe, what is the survival rate for Chosen Ones?"

I sighed, "Well, like everyone, the death rate is 100%." I smiled wanly, "But seriously, it's not very high. Most who die do so before they're 20, facing their prophecy. But I obviously missed out on that."

She looked at me straight in the eyes. "Well, then you'd better hurry up and kiss me before the odds catch up with us."

Chapter 11

I was halfway through a bag of graphic novels when Anthony walked in. He wasn't exactly a rarity here at Myopic, he had brought me to the used bookstore the first time back when it was down on Division, so I nodded hello and went back to sorting. 90's X-Men graphic novels weren't flying off the shelves, but we'd probably take them anyway. Graphic novels weren't hard to store, and nostalgia would carry them out the door at some point.

Anthony came down the counter directly rather than his accustomed browsing meander across the different floors, so I knew something was up. "What's going on?" I set down the comic I was examining and looked up.

"I know I don't usually discuss Keeper business out and about, but Casimir needs to discuss your report." Anthony looked abashed as he gestured to his car in the waiting spot out front. "Now."

"I'll grab my things." I tapped Ken on the shoulder, "Hey, can you finish these up? This pile is yes, this one is no." I gestured to the books.

"Yeah, no problem. Family emergency?" Ken was nice, but wasn't in the know, so he only knew the cover story of a sick uncle.

"Yeah. I'll see you Saturday, right?" I patted his shoulder as I moved over towards the register where Anthony was already chatting with my boss David. I coughed to get his attention.

"Joe, what's up?" David looked over to me.

"Family emergency," I gestured to Anthony, "I have to head out a bit early."

David nodded, "That's fine. I hope everything is okay." I never really knew how much David had learned from Anthony. The two of them were friends from library school years ago, but I wasn't sure if Anthony had ever told David he practiced magic. I'm sure he never shared that he was part of a globe spanning organization devoted to preserving the world. So, I stuck with the cover story. Anthony had gotten me this job for its flexibility. I could earn some money while still being at the beck and call of the Conclave.

I grabbed my stuff from the staff area and took the chance to confirm a few RSVPs from coworkers before running out to meet Anthony at the car.

"How are things going, Joe?" Anthony inquired as he pulled out onto Milwaukee Avenue. "Read any good books lately?" Anthony was a voracious reader and was always looking for recommendations. "Have you had a chance to read 'Go Set a Watchman?' I am itching to talk to somebody about it."

"Sorry, I have been a bit preoccupied lately, between the investigation and... other pursuits."

"Ah, you mean Clark's niece?" Anthony's inquiry was friendly, though a bit loaded.

"Yes. We've been spending some time together." I had to be a little careful. As my maternal uncle, Anthony was technically responsible for any marriage arrangements that might be made for me, so I didn't want him to get the wrong idea.

Anthony looked over and smiled. "You make it sound like she's your parole officer. I hope you're having some fun."

"Yes. We are. I'm not really ready for anything more, I don't want to overstate things, but yeah, we've had two nice dates. Well, one and a half."

"Don't worry Joe, I'm the *last* one to push you into an unwilling arrangement. Think of me as Uncle George, not Aunt Agatha." Anthony nudged me to drive home the reference.

"That's lucky, as I don't have a polymath valet to help extricate me." I needled back; I could give Wodehouse as good as I got.

The car trip from Wicker Park down to the Loop was quick, by Chicago standards. Mid-day weekday Chicago traffic wasn't too bad, not like rush hour, and before long we reached Russian Tea Time. Anthony dropped me off at the front door before heading off, back to the library.

A brief trip upstairs and I was in a private dining room with Casimir and Clark, two Praetorians standing guard outside. I had arrived simultaneously with a server bearing a multi-tiered tray of pastries and another bearing a samovar of tea. I bowed briefly to the Keepers, if this was serious, I wanted to observe formalities.

"Joseph." Casimir said, his tone neutral. "Have a seat. We're still waiting for Scaevola. But in the meantime, we can enjoy some tea." He gestured and the servers poured a mixture of concentrated tea and hot water from the samovar and passed it around.

Scaevola didn't arrive for another fifteen minutes. Long enough for us to finish our first cups of tea and for Casimir to take the finest selection of tea cakes. Scaevola was sweating when he came in, breathing heavily. He bowed formally. "Master, I apologize for the delay." He waited in his bow for Casimir to acknowledge him.

"It's alright, Keeper Fortier. You were the one who felt the matter so urgent." Casimir gestured to the empty seat and dismissed the servers.

Scaevola sat and took a breath before starting in, placing a copy of my written report on the table. "I have been following up on this report of yours and I don't know whether you were careless or lazy, but the sites that you *indicated* that you investigated are active. Very active."

I tensed at his accusations but kept my voice cool. "I'm not sure what you mean, sir. I measured the dormancy of the spirits myself. The wakefulness was within normal limits by LeDuc standards."

Clark interrupted, "What are you saying, Scaevola. That the report was inaccurate?"

Scaevola glared at me, then looked to Clark. "Yes. The measurements reported by Joseph are inaccurate, highly inaccurate. The Water Tower and the Stockyard Memorial are both highly agitated, their fire spirits awake and active, not dormant as Joseph indicated."

Casimir held his hands up. "Could there have been some change? Joseph, when did you take your measurements?"

"I don't have my notebook handy, but I took those on Sunday." I gestured to my table of contents, "About 2pm at the Water Tower and 4pm at the stockyards. I didn't check out the University site until eight and I checked the St Mary of the Angels site on Monday morning."

"When you arrived at the Chicago Fire Memorial, you were using rudimentary materiel. Perhaps you were simply ill prepared to deal with serious magics."

I kept myself composed. "I picked up my regular equipment after examining the Water Tower. So even if, as you claim, I was hampered by my tools, I still should have gotten accurate measurements at the stockyards."

Scaevola seethed, "The fact remains, there are disturbing readings at multiple ignotic sites. You need to do something about it." Scaevola looked to Casimir.

Casimir contemplated and then nodded. "This may have been something that happened after the first check or something that was hidden at the time. Regardless, it demands a second check, Joseph."

I bristled, "I... will go get my equipment. Wouldn't want to work with inferior tools." I bowed to each of the Keepers and started for the door.

Clark rose before I could leave. "Hold on. I can give you a ride back to your apartment." He rose and picked up a small scone from the table on his way to the door.

We were quiet as we got into Clark's truck. As we pulled into Michigan Avenue traffic, Clark spoke. "You'll figure it out. Don't mind Scaevola. He has good intentions, just bad at expressing them in ways that don't invite punching."

I snorted. "I know. I hate how he treats me like I'm still a kid. He thinks I'm some idiot teenager. It's been 20 years since I was that young and I hope I was never *that* stupid."

"yeah, he can get pretty set on things."

"I just wish he'd treat me more like a colleague than a student."

'Well, I can have some of my men conduct a search for the stick up his ass, but I imagine it's a dangerous extraction." Clark smiled as he pulled out onto LSD.

There was some silence as we passed Navy Pier and the curve, then Clark spoke up, his bright tone heralding the change of topic. "How are things going with Jenny?"

"With Jennifer?" I paused, switching mental gears. "They're going well. We were out together last night and she's coming to my birthday party on Saturday."

"She mentioned that. "Clark nodded as he maneuvered to the exit, "So things are good?"

"Yeah, we had a great time. I assume she got home okay from the bar? I put her in a cab myself."

Clark laughed, "for God's sake, Joe. I'm not her father, or yours. I'm just checking in. She's a grown woman with a master's degree. She can handle her dating life without adult supervision."

'Yeah." I was a little surprised, but Clark being happy was the opposite of a problem.

"Besides, I know how ladies in the trade react to the Chosen One. It was like Studio 54 some nights with Peter and the guys."

I was silent for a moment. Clark didn't talk much about his time fighting alongside the previous Chosen One. Plus, talking about wild sex clubs with the Uncle of the girl you were dating, I'm not gonna fall for that trap.

"Not that I'm suggesting that, mind you." Clark pulled the car up in front of my building. "Just encouraging two nice people to...I don't know how to say it without sounding like a jackass."

"Be fruitful and multiply?" I offered.

It was Clark's turn to laugh. "No multiplying until at least the fifth date, hear me?" We both laughed for a minute before I got out of the car.

"I'll send along the info as soon as I have it. And I'll try to quiet things down or see what's doing this."

Clark nodded. "Stay safe. With everything going on, I'd hate to see something happen to you." He waved as he drove away.

Chapter 12

I pulled the van up to the curb and put on the flashing lights. The city parks logo 'hortus in urbo' kept the overly curious away, and hopefully nobody would think too hard about why a city park worker was doing maintenance on the UChicago campus on a Friday evening. I pulled out some cones and marked off the front and rear of the vehicle and pulled out my phone. The Bureaucramancer hotline was second on my speed dial.

"Chicago department of esoterica, Kennelly speaking."

"Hello, this is Joseph Palevsky, I have van #2 in position down at 57th and Ellis. I could use some interference with local PD, a little uninterrupted time."

"What is your operating number?" The Bureaucramancer's affect was flat and unemotional.

I sighed. "Joseph Palevsky, 001." Bureaucramancers magic required the precision of minutia, but it got boring.

"Confirmed, Joseph Palevsky 001. Request received, UCPD distraction required. Preferred approach?"

"Nothing too flashy, maybe a little random noise?"

"Checking...We will deploy car alarm protocol at 60th and University. Estimate 20-minute patrol disruption."

"That will do. Thanks." I hung up and grabbed the low screens out of the back of the van. They didn't actually block out people's view, but they did keep folks from paying much attention. Years of practice has taught me that the more you try and hide something, the more people get curious.

The Nuclear Energy statue was my third ignotic site of the day and I was annoyed by my lack of progress. The other sites had offered very little information, their spirits were not very inquisitive and had been cleared of recent psychometric material. There weren't even signs of recent burning, which pointed to some sort of portable container to avoid leaving evidence. Whoever was doing this was being secretive. Fortunately, this spirit was a bit more intelligent and might have a few answers.

With the screens set up, I pulled out my material. I wanted more answers, so this spirit would need more offerings. It wasn't my first time talking to the spirit here, so I knew what to expect. First, I pulled out the incense burner and shook the shavings into it, recovered wood from the Stagg Field bleachers had been hard to come by, but I only needed a bit. "I offer here evidence of fire's mastery over air." I said as the smoke rose thickly. I pulled out a small bottle from my case. I had mixed a bit of chianti in with a pure grain alcohol to make it burn. Fermi had toasted with Chianti, and this resonated with the spirit. "I offer here evidence of fire's mastery over water." The spirits burned with a blue light in the small dish. Finally, I pulled out a small lead box. This was the big piece, a chunk of depleted uranium. "I offer here evidence of fire's mastery over earth." As I opened the box and placed it beside the other offerings and spoke the name of the spirit aloud.

My perceptions shifted and I saw before me the spirit of Chicago Pile-1, simultaneously a nondescript stack of bricks and a towering mushroom cloud. I could tell from seeing it that it was active, more awake than normal. I'd have to check my readings later, but it was certainly no longer somnolent. It spoke in my mind. "Chosen One. Your offerings do me honor. What do you ask of me?"

"Questions, one for each offering."

"I accept your exchange."

"Why have you awoken, what disturbed you from your rest?"

"A visitor came, made offerings to my glory and requested I be ready for what is to come." The spirit intoned.

I went back and forth, I needed to save my final question, and so I had one left. I knew someone had come, but also that there had been some sort of prediction. Who or what?

"What is to come that might concern a spirit of your dignity?"

"A great ritual will bring fire together with water, bringing the uprising forth into the city."

This was concerning. It might not mean anything, but it was more than I had gotten at other sites. That was going into my report, though I was sure Scaevola would have something to say about not asking about who the visitor was. He was always more focused on who was behind things as key, who his enemy was.

I asked my final question. "What boon would you ask for a return to somnolence?" I needed to settle the spirit first, then move on to the remaining ones.

"I ask that you tell my story to one who has not known it."

"Very well, I thank you for your answers."

I gathered up my materials and put them in the van. Where could I find someone who hadn't heard about this, and fairly quickly? I had more sites to settle and a few errands for tomorrow's party. Who would even be around at 8pm on a Friday?

I showed my alumni card at the library desk. I wasn't technically a full alumnus, but a few strings and Keeper contributions got me library access.

The lobby area was pretty full for a Friday night during the summer, which meant about half a dozen students studying around the first floor. I surveyed the scene. Who was likely not to know? I didn't want to come across all creepy, so ideally, I wanted to talk to as few people as possible. The reference desk was empty, but there were a few folks at computers. I saw one young guy, are college students really that young now, reading a medical textbook. Alright, time to try lost tourist.

"Excuse me, do you know where the nuclear energy statue is around here?" I moved quietly beside his chair. "I'm an alum visiting from Wisconsin, but I guess with all this construction I'm a little turned around. I know it's near the library, could you help me out?"

The guy looked me over but didn't seem worried. "I'm sorry, I don't really know what you're..."

"Oh, no worries, no worries. Could you google it for me? I don't have a login and just an old person phone." I waggled my flip phone from out of my pocket.

"Yeah, sure." The guy opened a new window. "What's it called?"

"Nuclear energy. It's the site of the first sustained nuclear reaction, back during World War 2, Enrico Fermi and some folks made a nuclear reactor back in a squash court in the old football field, back before they bulldozed it. Real landmark moment in human innovation." I felt the energy of the spirit flow through me briefly as its binding released and it slipped into dormancy."

"That's cool. I think it's just out to the west of the library. If you go out front and turn right, it should be behind the Mansueto. That's the big glass dome."

"Right, thanks. I knew it was something like that." I patted him on the shoulder, "Thanks, good luck with your studies." One site down, just a few more to do.

Chapter 13

By Saturday morning, I had a report on my examinations and activities related to the rest of the sites of fire spirits in the city. All the ones Scaevola had mentioned were indeed stirred up and had been in the last few days. There was a surprising lack of psychometrically readable material near all of them, as if every piece of trash had been specifically cleaned up. I settled the energies of the sites, the restless fire spirits charmed back to dormancy, and I'd even bound some minor spirits of watchfulness to report any additional activity at each site.

I'm not completely sure I slept in those few days, but I must have at some point. Regardless, by 7pm Saturday, I was ready at the door, dressed and pressed as I greeted my first guests. A good party includes the occasional person who actually shows up on time, a virtue that I didn't really know the value of until I spent several stressful parties in my 20s sweating out the first two hours waiting for the laxly punctual.

Kim and McNealy from work filled that role for me for the party, showing up right at 7, arrayed as street urchins. McNealy was easy enough to guess, he was a huge Dickens fan, the Artful Dodger was an obvious choice. It took me three guesses and a bit of wracking of the brain to figure out Kim's, though I finally remembered she had been carrying around a copy of Neverwhere a few weeks back and I was able to identify her as Lady Door.

Once I'd poured some drinks, we sat and swapped work stories, McNealy had apparently come across a couple of ardent teenagers near the astronomy section that afternoon and actually had to throw a book at them to get their attention. Of course, book lover that he was, he'd headed back downstairs to grab a paperback copy of Twilight rather than risking something more valuable.

Kim told about her miracle shelf pick. A customer had come up to her while she was shelving and asked if she could help locate a book that was "blue-ish". Exasperated, Kim had grabbed the nearest one that caught her eye, and it was apparently the exact right book. We had both heard the story before, but Kim never failed to do it justice in the telling.

David showed up partway through my own story about the guy who brought a bag of poetry journals in, self-written poetry journals, in composition books, to be clear, and was offended when we didn't want to buy them, and after David, the flood of people began.

The party was hopping by 9, Andrew was in the corner, sipping his ginger beer straight from the can while he talked with Kim about Donna Haraway and intersectional feminism. He had stumped me on the way in, though I contended that Victor Joseph from the Lone Ranger and Tonto Fistfight in Heaven was a stretch as he was basically an author surrogate. But he was able to get my costume based purely on my rolled white flannel trousers, so I gracefully conceded his superior literary expertise.

Sullivan from the bar, dressed as Bernard Mickey Wrangle from Still Life with Woodpecker, complete with pack of camel cigarettes and what I hoped was a fake stick of dynamite in his pants, was chatting with Patrick, a buddy from college and my current purveyor of entheogenic supplies, who was dressed as Harry Dresden, though I knew for a fact that he had been wearing that leather duster for over a decade.

Samantha and Amanda had just arrived and earned a combination laugh/groan from the group for their combination of Penelope, resplendent in Ancient Greek Dress and Penelope's loom, with a half-done tapestry converted into a poncho. I welcomed them in and pulled David over, briefly explained his outfit of Bill Bryson from Notes on a Small Island to explain the underwear on his head, and introduced the shared subject of ukulele music, sending them off to converse. I was about to close the door when I noticed Jennifer and Miriam approaching down the hall.

Jennifer looked...resplendent? No, her outfit was too simple for resplendence. Elegant? No, that implies an aloofness. Effulgent. She was in white, a diaphanous two-layer flapper dress and simple flapper bell hat with a long string of costume pearls. She seemed to literally glow, which the intellectual part of my brain presumed was a minor light spirit bound to the garment, but the non-intellectual part attributed to being some minor choir of angel. The outer layer of the dress seemed to flow around her. I was lost for a moment but recovered quickly.

"Mrs. Buchanan, how lovely it is to see you."

Jennifer's face curled into her peculiar smile as she looked at me. "My, aren't we quick."

"Do come in." I turned to Miriam as I extended my hand to Jennifer. Miriam's elaborate antebellum dress and curls were easy to identify. "I see you've brought Miss O'Hara. Or was it Mrs. O'Hara Hamilton Kennedy Butler?"

Miriam fanned herself demurely. "Scarlett will do just fine." She drawled.

I escorted them both inside and began to make the rounds of introductions. The night became a bit of a blur after Jennifer's arrival. My eye was continually drawn back to her, and her occasional smile quickened my pulse like I was still a teenager.

It was another hour before the last guests arrived with a surprise. I was engaged with a spirited discussion with Jennifer and McNealy about whether Dickensian names were genius or nonsense when the door opened. I was surprised for a moment; sure it had been locked. Daniel came in, his super's key in the lock.

"Daniel. You could have knocked." I walked toward him.

"That would have ruined my surprise." Daniel stepped aside, revealing a tall man dressed in 18th century gentleman's wear. It only took a second for me to recognize Gunter, one of my cohort from my training days.

"Joey." Gunter stepped inside, bowing like an actual 18th century gentleman and offering me a bottle. "This is from my family's vineyard. It took some work getting it through customs, so you should truly savor it."

I pulled him up and gave him a hearty hug. I looked over to Daniel, who smiled. "Happy Birthday. I thought a familiar face would be welcome."

"You thought right." I enthused. "I thought you were tied up with the Greek debt deal."

"I was, and I will be again on Monday, but they have these things called airplanes." Gunter's English was nearly flawless, just a hint in the vowels that it was his second language. "Daniel and I put this together. I'm flying out in the morning, but a day of good Chicago food followed by a night of partying is worth a little lost sleep."

"We'd hoped to kidnap you earlier, grab some Alinea." Daniel smiled.

"Sorry, I was running all over the place." I dropped my voice slightly. Not everyone at the party was in the know. "Conclave business."

"Not a worry." Gunter waved his hand. "Besides, I had the phone number for a stewardess with a lonely roommate."

"Well, let's make up for it." I took Gunter and Daniel by the shoulders as I turned. "Ladies and Gentlemen, this is my good friend Gunter from Munich. He officially wins the 'came from the farthest away award' for the night. Sorry Sullivan, Hyde Park doesn't take the prize this time around." Everyone chuckled, including Sullivan who snapped his fingers in mock defeat. "Let's show him that we can celebrate on this side of the Atlantic."

I broke out some backup drinks and switched the playlist to electro-swing as Daniel and Gunter made their way around.

Jennifer came up beside me as I was finishing with the music switch. "Hey." She smiled.

"Hey." I returned, "what's up?"

"Tell me about your friend Ken." Jennifer looked at me slyly.

"Ken?" I looked around and Jennifer pointed over to one of the bookshelves where Ken, dressed as Bobby Shaftoe in a WW2 marine sergeant's uniform leaned in towards Miriam, who demurely hid her smile behind her fan. Jennifer raised an eyebrow as she saw me take it in. "Ken, right. Ken's good folks. He works at the bookstore with me."

"Is he in the know?" Jennifer's question was direct, but not rude.

"No, he's not." I kept my look neutral. "Is that an issue?"

"Oh, no." Jennifer looked a bit shaken by my question. "I'm just being a nosy friend."

"Ken's a nice guy. He's single and he owns a very friendly belgian shepherd named William Rufus." I pointed over to him and gave a thumbs up. "Miriam's in good hands."

"Good." Jennifer smiled. "Though if she heads out with him... I may need an escort home."

I hoped my smile wasn't too dopey as I nodded back. I was saved from a reply as Daniel and Gunter came over. Daniel was dressed in fairly archaic business wear, and I was going to ask about his costume when he thrust business cards into our hands. A quick look made things clear.

"Do you have any Huey Lewis and the News?" Daniel smiled a toothy grin.

"Sorry Mr. Bateman, we have good taste here." I needled Daniel. "Jennifer, meet Daniel and Gunter. They were part of my Keeper cohort."

"Actually, we've met." Gunter smiled as he kissed her hand, "At the conference on trust management, in Zurich."

"Yes." Jennifer smiled, "I thought you looked familiar."

"I was dressed a bit more modern. No wig."

"I was going to ask about that. Who are you supposed to be?" I asked.

"Ah, I am so sorrowful that you don't recognize me." Gunter put the back of his hand against his forehead, looking despondent. "Sorrowful. Sorrows." Gunter remained in position as he prodded us in vain.

"Sorry. I have no idea." I gave up as Jennifer shook her head in unison with mine.

"You Americans. No appreciation for German literature. I am Werther. The Sorrows of Young Werther?" At our expressions, which ranged from Daniel's blankness to my vague recollection, Gunter threw up his hands. "Heathens, all of you."

"I think I saw the opera once?" Jennifer looked doubtful. Gunter shrugged.

"It'll be next on my reading list." I jumped in, putting on a serious expression. "Is that with a V or a W?" Gunter made to grab me into a headlock and some laughing struggle back and forth ensued, with Daniel ending up with Gunter's wig and the peach I had been holding ending up squished. It was hard to believe that we were two decades out of high school, the way we were acting.

After that, Gunter demanded we take apology shots, and the party got a bit more lively. Some dancing started up, the lights got dimmed and the party picked up, there was even some canoodling if you can believe it, and the rest of the night blurred into a warm glow of dancing, drinks and effulgent smiles.

Chapter 14

I had just put Daniel and Gunter into Daniel's excitedly-summoned Uber, with hearty embraces and oaths sworn that we would see each other much sooner next time.

Jennifer had seen off Miriam with Ken, after a friendly check-in, into the cab whistled down by the doorman. That left just the two of us alone in front of my building.

"You promise he's a good guy?" Jennifer said, looking at the cab.

"I'd trust him to date my sister." I raised my left hand, placing my right upon my heart. "I mean, if I had a sister."

Jennifer cocked her head, "Any siblings?"

"No, my parents had just the one. They figured they got it right the first time. You?"

"I have a very protective older brother." Jennifer smiled, "But you don't have to worry. He'll like you He's a Praetorian down in Dallas."

"Good to know." I extended my elbow to her, "You said something earlier about an escort home?"

Jennifer looked me over, her expression enigmatic. "I'm just trying to decide if you're making fun of me."

"I would dream of it." I gestured inside to the lobby attendant. "I could have Eileen call you a cab."

"No." Jennifer stepped up beside me, slipping her arm into mine. "Let's take a nice walk." We set off towards Clark's place, taking a more scenic route through the park, near the lagoon and nature center. "You've got a peculiar group of friends."

I shrugged, "Yeah, there are some I have managed to hold on to, some who haven't realized how flaky I have to be because of my duties, and one or two I haven't been able to shake, no matter how hard I try." I let the sarcastic tone creep into my voice for the last bit.

"Oh, and these two weird women who tried to pick me up in a bar." That one earned me a playful nudge. "I haven't had the most normal life." I shrugged, "Being the Chosen One means being at the beck and call of the Conclave. It's not every day or even every week, but things come up. I have trouble holding down a real job with regular hours because I might have to drop everything to go save the world and I can't tell anyone."

"I never really thought about it that way." Jennifer spoke quietly, "I grew up hearing about the way the Chosen One kept us safe from threats. But I guess I always thought about it as someone young, not someone with a job."

"Yeah, most previous Chosen Ones faced their big trial when they were younger, some as young as 13 or 14. When I was young, I figured it would be the same with me, but no."

"Well, I think it's very brave." Jennifer sounded sincere. "You've had to do this for so long, just waiting for things to happen."

"Yeah, I won't say I haven't been tempted to run away once or twice, but there are lives at stake." We walked in silence for a bit. "I hope it happens soon, even knowing the odds. Part of me is afraid, but most of me is relieved. It'll be done. One way or another."

"Hey." Jennifer sidestepped the topic, brightening up as we approached the corner of the park. "How about you tell me more about this city. Pop quiz, who's that statue of?"

I didn't even have to look. I ran by here all the time and the Keeper's headquarters was across the street. "Gunter would be proud of me for this. That is Johann Wolfgang von Goethe, great German Author. I think normally he wore more clothes and didn't carry around an eagle."

"Wow, you get 100% and an A+ deserves a kiss." Jennifer turned to me, and we kissed beneath the statue. The world faded around me for a moment as I savored the feel of her close to me, her smell, the sound of her breathing, shallow and nervous.

I was brought out of my reverie by the squealing of tires. Two vans had pulled to a sudden stop at the corner of the park. "This doesn't look good." I held her close to me briefly as I looked over the vans. Rentals, unmarked. "You aren't trained in combat magics, are you?" Jennifer shook her head. "Stay behind me. If you get the chance, run."

Six figures emerged from the vans' side doors, all of them wearing robes. As they passed beneath the streetlamps, I could see they were a dark blue. They had fitted hoods with tight mesh masks, obscuring the wearer's faces.

As they drew closer, they pulled short focusing cudgels from out of their sleeves and began to circle around us. I drew a deep breath and touched the tattoo over my sternum, whispering the name of the guardian spirit bound within the Gorgoneion. I felt resilience pass through me, and I moved into position, dropping into an Aikido stance. I had to hope they weren't good at asymmetrical skirmish tactics; I didn't want to break out serious magics in public.

A glance over my shoulder showed Jennifer cowering against the base of the statue. Her wide eyes drove home that she was not accustomed to violence, not many people are, and few realize how unprepared they are until it's too late. There wasn't time for reflection as the first of them came close. He swung his cudgel down at me, a sidestep and a quick move and I'd tossed him aside towards one of the curved hedges.

Two of them came at me next from different sides. I cursed at their coordination and rolled between them, coming up in front of another and snatching his cudgel with a twisting disarm. He seemed taken aback and I took the moment to crack him hard in the knee. He went down screaming.

I turned to see the two who had come at me change direction and head for Jennifer. She tried to circle the statue murmuring a protective incantation, but another one had gotten around the other side and grabbed her from behind. One of the two I'd rolled past made a grab for her neck and came up with her cross necklace, snapping it from her neck and casting it away into the grass. The other spoke forcefully and I heard the thrum of a true name and Dee's imperative inflection. "Jennifer Varina Davis, Sleep." Jennifer slumped into the arms of the one behind her as the other two turned back towards me.

I dodged several blows from their cudgels, taking a few blows to my spirit-strengthened skin as they coordinated their swings and I had to choose what to dodge. As one came down with an overhand swing, I knelt, touched the ground with my palm and spoke the name of the earth. The ground rippled out from me, knocking him off balance and making him swing wide.

I shoved him backwards and lunged towards Jennifer only to find her gone. Two of the hooded figures held her between them and were halfway to the van. I began to lunge after them when one of them grabbed my loose-fitting shirt and pulled me back, throwing me into a hedge.

As I pulled myself up, the rest of the robed combatants were fleeing towards the vans as the sleeping Jennifer was put into one of them, the door closed behind. One was lagging behind, limping from his knee wound and I swiftly caught up with him, pushing him to the ground. I bellowed at them "Let her go or your friend gets it!" I raised my cudgel, but they just glanced back, slammed the van doors and peeled out.

I turned to the fallen man and yanked off his mask. "Who are you?" I yelled in his face. "Where are they taking her?"

I was taken by surprise as he pulled a gun from his sleeve, a small pistol. I dropped him and pulled back my hands to try and conjure a shield spirit.

He looked at me and said, "I am only one wave in the coming Deluge that will wash your world away. You won't take me alive, Keeper Scum." He took the gun, placed it behind his ear and pulled the trigger, ending his life and splattering me with blood as I gaped in shock.

End Act I

Chapter 15

Sunday, June 21st

I stood in the corner of Lincoln Park; my white flannel trousers stained with the blood of the suicidal cultist whose compatriots had just kidnapped my date as I attempted to walk her home. I was still reeling in shock, the loud gunshot ringing in my ears as I looked at the dead body. This was bad.

But this wasn't my first emergency. Between adrenaline and training, I jolted myself from panic to crisis. I looked around. The vans had left to the north, probably headed for Lake Shore, no chance to catch up on foot, that would be a waste of time. The area was clear, no bystanders to witness, no backup cultists waiting to ambush. No nearby police, either. I had two minutes, maybe three before unwanted attention.

I pulled out my phone and speed dialed the Conclave's emergency line. it picked up immediately and I launched into talking without waiting for the cover phrases. "This is Joseph Palevsky, pass phrase Kwisatz Haderach. I've been attacked by a small group of unknown affiliation."

The operator jumped in. "Pass phrase confirmed. Details?"

"I'm at the corner of Lincoln Park. Lakeview and Diversey. I have one enemy fatality, self-inflicted, and one ally captured. Kidnappers fled to the north in white rental vans. I need extraction and cleanup, no authorities on the scene so far, and get someone tracking those vans." I kept an eye out, looking to make sure no one was taking an interest in my altercation.

"Message received. Help is on the way." I shut my phone. My hardened flip phone took a beating much better than a touch screen and for once I was glad I had one, as one of the cudgel blows had glanced off the edge. I looked around on the ground nearby. Jennifer's purse lay on the ground next to where they'd knocked her out and grabbed her. I grabbed it. Off to the side of the hedged in area, I saw a glint of gold, Jennifer's necklace. I moved quickly and grabbed it up.

I looked at it as I considered the attack. There were mystic etchings on the fine cross, it was obviously part of Jennifer's magical defenses. And they knew that. They knew her full name, they knew her defenses well enough to neutralize them and they coordinated their assault to grab her. She must have been their target, but why? And why do it while I was there?

I didn't have long to contemplate. Several of the Praetorians in plain clothes had arrived at the corner and I waved them over. As they approached, I pointed out the body. "This is the important thing. There was a gunshot, so we might have to deal with police attention. No witnesses visible, I recommend backfire protocol. Get him off the street and back to the lodge." They nodded agreement and got to work. I took one last look around and jogged towards the Keeper's HQ.

Fifteen minutes later, I emerged into the meeting room. My clothes were bagged and tagged for any potential psychometrics, and I had cleaned off the blood and brains with a quick shower, which left me dressed in plain gray training sweats from the Praetorian gym. Several members of the Conclave were gathered around the table, maps and papers were spread out and their overlapping conversations made the room a messy cacophony. Simon typed on his laptop. Clark was conversing with the patrol squads over long range walkie-talkie, checking the results on the local maps and directing searches, Casimir was yelling on his phone in Polish so fast I could only get every third word. Prospero was closest to me and was cross checking some papers with the local map, he saw me enter and gestured me over.

"From what you said, it looks like they must have exploited a gap in the security patrols to have struck so close to the headquarters." Prospero gestured at the map he had diagrammed with patrol diagrams. The sentries on duty were shot with a tranquilizer, we're not sure if they'll make it."

I nodded, absorbing the information, then shook my head. "This was not an attack of opportunity. This was planned. And I wasn't the target!"

Prospero looked puzzled, "What do you mean?" Clark shut off his radio and came over to us, his expression steely.

"I mean, they were there for Jennifer. They distracted me, kept me engaged while they grabbed her. They immediately disabled her protections and grabbed her."

Clark spoke up, "That could be a coincidence. Pendants are common protective charms."

"They used her full name, Clark. A sleep command using her true name. This was planned." Simon and Casimir were looking at me as my voice rose.

"Start from the beginning, Joseph." Casimir was direct, his phone went back in his pocket.

I recounted the full events of the attack to them more thoroughly than my initial debrief, describing from the end of the party to when I called the emergency line, trying to recall every available detail. Anthony came in as I was finishing the description, his eyes still groggy. Everyone was quiet for a moment as I finished.

Casimir broke the silence. "This could be part of a coordinated attack. We need eyes on everyone."

Clark replied, "Scaevola and Ephraim haven't checked in yet. I'll send some guards to check on them. Everyone should take protection with them." He looked around as the Keepers acknowledged his order.

Casimir continued. "Anthony, see what you can find from the body. It's downstairs, cross-check any identifying cult information. If this is a Nihilist attack, I want to know." Anthony blinked his eyes sleepily but nodded. "Prospero, make sure our safe houses are stocked and ready. Simon, get the bureaucramancers working, we don't want any undue attention and we need official surveillance access, and make sure everyone has cash. I don't want anything as ridiculous as a blocked credit card slowing down our response." Prospero and Simon moved, pulling out their phones as they left the room.

I looked at Casimir as he paused. "Sir?" He looked at me, "What should I be doing?"

"You get Clark all the information you remember, and then rest up, wouldn't want you getting sick now that your moment has come." I was a bit surprised at the specificity but didn't say anything. "Keep your wits sharp, keep your equipment at hand." He walked over and clapped his large hand on my shoulder. "The day of your crucible has come, Joseph. Make us proud."

Chapter 16

I was awoken by a firm hand shaking my shoulder. I jolted awake but held myself back from any sudden reaction. Andrew's face loomed close to mine; a concerned look evident on his face even through the morning blear. "Joe, what are you doing on my couch?"

I shook myself physically, trying to get rid of the sleepiness and soreness. "Sorry, I... I had to make sure you were okay. You weren't answering your phone."

Andrew's face expanded in a smile. "I was a bit busy last night. I had my phone turned off." The smile faded as the gravity of my statement combined with the look on my face to cut through the morning after bliss. "Why wouldn't I be okay?"

I stood up, wincing slightly as I shook of the stiffness of last night. At 37, wait, no, 38, most mornings were a little rough, but the combination of hangover, post adrenaline crash and nightmare filled couch sleeping all added up to a stomach that couldn't quite handle standing without a reaction.

Andrew was standing outside the bathroom as I emerged. "Joe. Why would I not be okay?" His expression was serious and concerned. He handed me a glass of water.

I took a sip and pulled myself together a bit more. "I was walking Jennifer home from the party when we were jumped by a bunch of weird cultists." I paused and breathed out. "They took her. They planned their assault to take her and kept me occupied just long enough to do it."

Andrew's expression had gone from serious to grave. "Are you okay?"

"One of them killed himself right in front of me rather than be captured." I looked at him. "I was worried they might be targeting people close to me, so I came over here."

"Are you okay!?" Andrew was insistent.

I paused and collected myself. "I am not in a great place right now. But I think what I need is to figure out what's going on. Where were you?"

Andrew gave a slight smile. "I was over at Kim's place, so if they were looking for me here, they would have been out of luck."

I grinned slightly through the stress, "Your luck with women."

Andrew shrugged, "If I'd known…"

My grin was a bit manic, "I mean, how could you have. Kim's just your type, smart and cute. Gender Studies major, doing some sort of work on Kristeva's abject…"

"Joseph, we can talk about her later." Andrew put a hand on my shoulder. He returned my smile then grew serious again and I could feel the pull of stabilizing name magic, recentering me in myself. "Tell me about these men who attacked you." He gestured over to his table. There was a large puzzle on it, an image of a Georgia O'Keeffe flower half completed, sitting on a green felt mat. He slid it aside as we sat. "Let me help."

"They aren't from any group I recognize. The one who killed himself said something about a Deluge and implied he's been a Keeper prisoner before." I ran my hand through my hair, then leaned on the table, my hand on my forehead. "My uncle Anthony is doing the research on the cult."

"When you get more information, let me know. I have a customer, well, more of a friend, who is an expert on secret magical societies. She might know things your uncles don't." Andrew put his hand on my shoulder. "Just let me know what I can do to help."

I looked up at Andrew. "Thanks. For now, just keep an eye out for danger and keep your ear to the ground." I got up and began patting my pockets. "I should get home. There might be news."

Andrew got up and handed me my bag from beside the couch. "Don't worry, I can handle myself in a fight."

"Well, there might be one coming. I'm not sure what my uncles would say, I'd like to have you with me if things get crazy but…"

Andrew nodded. "Of course."

"Y'know what, fuck what they'd say. You and me, right?" I reached out my hand, Andrew took it and I pulled him into a quick hug.

My phone buzzed as we broke apart and I pulled it out to see a text from Clark. <911 1800 N. Clark>. "That's an emergency at Scaevola's place. I gotta go."

Andrew opened his door and gestured me through it. "Keep me informed, Joe. I'll be at my shop. If you need somewhere safe, my doors will always open for you." The words of his sacred pronouncement echoed as I made my way downstairs.

Chapter 17

The cab pulled up to Scaevola's house and I slipped the driver a twenty from my emergency cash. I hefted my pack, full of magical supplies, and walked towards the stairs leading to the door, keeping an eye on Clark street for vans.

Scaevola lived in an immaculately kept house facing Lincoln Park, near the base of operations for the Conclave. I'd been over maybe a dozen times over the years, always for training or other official business. Scaevola and I had never been close, if he threw parties, I was never invited. I had never taken that as an insult. Scaevola was not a party guy. I knew immediately that something was wrong as I walked up. The front steps were scattered with broken pieces of pottery and the remnants of Scaevola's plants, a stark contrast with his usual neatness.

The door was partially open, and I entered, knocking. I kept a cool demeanor, but one hand hovered close to my protective tattoo, the other gripped my shillelagh in my satchel. Clark emerged into the destroyed foyer from the back room, and I relaxed a bit as he beckoned.

"Joe." Clark's manner was strained and serious. "I'm glad you could make it here so quickly." He gestured to the broken furniture around the room. "We have a situation."

Clark led me through the ground floor, past Scaevola's destroyed living room and kitchen, back to what was clearly his study. In the center of the room, there was a shimmer of energy bound within a chalk circle. I looked over the circle and drew out my spirit glasses from my bag. A chaotic shape writhed within the circle, a spirit of destruction. I shuddered briefly as I looked at it. "Did you capture this here?" I looked to Clark.

Clark shook his head. "Some of my Praetorians did. I was arranging things with Simon for the police investigation while Austin and Francisco were checking things out here. They ended up luring it into the study with some Swarovski crystal as bait. Even with that, Austin might have broken his arm. They're at the hospital now." Clark moved around the circle carefully, avoiding the chalk lines. "It destroyed nearly everything in the house. I think whoever took Scaevola must not have wanted to leave anything intact that we could get a reading from."

"They took Scaevola?" I looked at Clark, my tone rising.

"That's what we think, given the… other kidnapping. Simon's bureaucramancers at City Hall were able to procure some footage from nearby traffic cameras that show the vans you describe." Clark walked over and handed me a large envelope from his own nearby satchel. Within were several grainy image printouts that showed two vans driving through the intersection at Clark and North. "We think they might have grabbed him before they grabbed Jenny." Clark's voice cracked a bit as he said her name and he coughed away the emotion.

I put my hand on his shoulder. "We'll find her. What can I help with here?"

Clark nodded, "I need your help moving a piece of furniture. There's one piece that wasn't completely destroyed, an antique scrying table. It had a strengthening enchantment on it that stopped the worst of the damage. It might be recoverable, at least enough to get a reading, but I can't quite get it downstairs by myself and with Austin and Francisco at the hospital and the rest of my men out looking for vans, I thought you could help."

"Well, Chosen One furniture moving at your service." I fished out some gloves from my bag. "Do you need a pair? Maintain the resonance?"

Clark pulled a pair from his own bag and put them on as he moved upstairs. We came to Scaevola's bedroom, clothes in tatters and his elegantly simple bed frame in flinders on the floor. Everything in the room was covered in the fluffy remnants of his mattress, which made the room oddly cloudlike. Clark gestured to the scrying table in the corner. A large crack moved down most of the middle of the table, nearly bisecting the wood.

It ended up taking us about an hour to move the table down to Clark's truck, moving slowly and gently, improvising cushioning with tattered clothing. "What next?" I asked as I drank from my water flask and wiped sweat from my forehead.

"I've got George Green down at the lodge, he's got some skill with antique restoration, so hopefully he can patch it up enough for us to get some answers.

I crooked an eyebrow "Doesn't he mostly do specialty resale?" I realized I hadn't ever thought about George working with the Conclave.

"He's one of our only allies in the area who can do it at short notice." Clark tucked his work gloves into his back pocket and pulled out his keys. 'This thing is way too fragile to ship elsewhere and we might not have time to bring someone in from out of town."

"Right, then." I smiled as I got into the passenger seat of the truck. "Let's go.

Clark and I headed North towards the headquarters, but I could tell something was off when he skipped the first turn, continuing up Clark street. I was going to say something, but when he turned down Fullerton, I figured he was just taking an alternate route. But when he rolled through the park, I knew something was wrong.

As I looked over at him, he spoke, "You said the people who jumped you last night were in white vans?" He gestured to the rearview mirror with his chin. "How well is the table secured?"

"I strapped it down pretty tightly." I looked at the side mirror. "It shouldn't move much."

"Good." Clark gunned his truck through the red light in front of the zoo entrance, swerving through traffic towards Lake Shore Drive. I heard the sound of horns and squealing tires and turned to see the vans trying to follow us through the intersection. Clark turned onto the southbound entry lane and dodged around a few slower vehicles to get onto LSD.

Behind us, the vans swerved onto the entry ramp, one of them scraping alongside a guard rail to get around a sluggish minivan. Clark looked in the mirror as he sped southwards. "Damn. Joe, can you whip up some kind of cover? set up an escape?"

I looked around, getting my bearings. "Okay, yes. Head for the curve, get in one of the left lanes like you're headed through but be ready to do a quick turn to the exit, then a quick U turn in the tunnel off under Michigan, got it?" Clark's nod was quick, and I got to work as he shifted into gear. The waves were already high near the curve, it was a windy day and they already splashed dramatically over the joggers brave or foolish enough to run in such conditions. I drew in a deep breath and leaned out the window, bellowing the name of water, intoning it to the spirit of Lake Michigan. The next wave crashed hard against the side of the embankment and sprayed high into the air. The drops cascaded downwards in a fine mist, sunlight glinting off of them and temporarily obscuring vision.

Clark gunned the engine and swerved across four lanes of traffic to a symphony of horns into the Michigan Avenue exit. At the bottom, he executed a screeching U-turn and slowed down to move slowly through the underpass taking us back onto Lake Shore heading north.

I watched behind us, scanning for signs of the vans in pursuit, then caught sight of them as we emerged onto the Northbound drive, they were still stuck trying to get off on the Michigan avenue exit. I turned to Clark, "I think we're clear."

Clark was smiling, "That'll get the blood pumping." He breathed out slowly, losing a bit of the manic enthusiasm. "Whew, good work with the cover back there."

"No problem, it's something I do for meditation exercises sometimes. The lake wants to flex its muscles, I just give it permission." I looked back as we emerged. "They look like they're stuck in traffic back at the curve, we should be able to get back to the lodge before they get turned around."

"Call the switchboard, have them send anyone available, track them while we can." After I hung up, Clark looked to me concerned. "Why were they there? Do you think they followed you?"

I thought back. "No. I've been doing a lot of anti-pursuit stuff. I got off the red line a stop early, grabbed a cab, and I've been watching for any tails. Maybe they were watching the building?"

"Why didn't they attack earlier? When I sent Austin and Francisco away, it was just me. They could have just taken me out." Clark slammed his hand on the steering wheel. "This whole thing just…"

"Let's get this back to the lodge. There's obviously information they don't want us to have." I put my hand on Clark's shoulder. "I'm sure she's still safe. We'll rescue her."

Clark nodded and breathed slowly through his nose, his jaw set. "She'd better be. Or I'm going to fucking destroy whoever harmed her."

We silently pulled into the garage below the lodge, neither of us ready to voice the fears that lingered in the cab.

Chapter 18

George bent over the damaged wood, leaning over to place a tuning fork on one side of the long split. He whispered to the wood and watched the vibration of the fork and then repeated the process on the other side of the split, testing a few locations. Anthony and I watched him work, silent to avoid disturbing the delicate process. Clark had gone off to coordinate the Praetorian Guard and hunt down the vans that had pursued us.

George walked over, tuning fork in hand. "Well, there's some good news. The wood still thinks of itself as one piece. I should be able to fix it, given some time."

I nodded. "We just need it strong enough for one good psychometric reading. How much time do you need for that?"

George contemplated. "I think that should be doable, but it will take at least a day. I need to reinforce the harmonic bonds and set up a resonance sink to make sure it doesn't vibrate itself apart."

"Let me know as soon as you think it's ready." I hurriedly appended, "Keeper Davis and Keeper Palevsky as well. Is that okay, George?"

"Of course, sir." I flinched a bit inside at George's deference. It always felt weird when someone 20 years older called me sir. "It's not my specialty, but I'm always happy to help the Conclave."

"I'll let you get to work. Thanks." I looked over to Anthony, "Can I have a word, Uncle?"

Anthony and I exited the workshop together as George began pulling tools from his toolbox. "What do you need, Joe?" Anthony was nervous.

"You've been doing the research on the guy I brought in, right?" Anthony nodded at my question. "Do you have anything yet?"

Anthony shook his head. "I've only just finished documentation of the various symbologies and markings on the tools and the...body. I haven't had a chance to do a full archival workup yet." Anthony seemed a little shaken, but apologetic.

"That's okay." I put a hand on his shoulder and gave a sympathetic squeeze. "Could I get a copy of what you have so far? I want to see if I can prepare some defensive incantations and I can do a little work in my own library. I can at least check Tobin and Roylance, see if there's anything in Nutter's prophecies."

"Of course." Anthony nodded. "I'll give you everything I've found. Though I wouldn't put much stock in Nutter."

"I take it with a grain of salt." We went down into the basement work area the Keepers had set up when the lodge was built out in the 80s in preparation for Conclave Ascendancy. The morgue area was understandably cold and sterile, and the body lay under a sheet on the examining table.

Anthony went over to a copy machine in the corner and pulled a stack of papers out of a folder, feeding them into the top of the machine. A minute later, he handed me a folder. "I can walk you through what I found on the body." He looked uncomfortable as he gestured towards the table.

"That's okay. You can get back to the books, I'll call if there's anything unclear. Besides," I chuckled. "You're a librarian, not a coroner."

"Well, I hadn't realized that autopsies were a required skill when they invited me to be part of the High Conclave." Anthony's face had paled, but color started to return.

"It's my fault. As my sponsor in the order, you had to be part of the ruling council." I shrugged. "Or, I suppose you could blame Lord Booth and the Cavalier Conclave, but as they've been dead three centuries, they're less likely to respond."

"It's okay." Anthony smiled. "It's just that library school didn't have any courses on corpse examination. I could have gotten a joint degree if I'd known."

We both laughed a bit weakly. "Thanks for this, Uncle Anthony." I waved the folder." I'm going to go get some coffee and dig into it." I left him there in the morgue looking ruefully at the body.

Chapter 19

My apartment was the cleanest it had been in years. Andrew was going to come over once he closed his shop and I had nothing else to do. I had checked out Anthony's evidence against the symbologies I had handy, but my collection wasn't really set up for secret society research, so I had hit nothing but dead ends. And all around me were the remnants of the party. Every cup and plate was a pang of guilt. I'd failed to protect Jennifer.

So, I cleaned. I washed and dried dishes. I organized notes. I cleaned irrelevant scribbles off of my white boards. When I ran out of reasonable things to clean, I began to clean unreasonable things, breaking every five minutes to check my phone, just in case some vital text or call failed to make a noise.

I had my couch half-propped up on a stack of encyclopedias when a knock came at the door. The sun had started to set, and the apartment was darkening as I went over.

"It's Andrew." The voice through the door had the recognizable cadence of the Northern plains and Andrew's carefully low tone. I looked through the peephole and he was there.

"Come in." I opened the door and gestured him inside. He looked around at the raised couch and the tables, so often cluttered, now bare except for a vaguely marked map. He looked back with an expression of concern that I waved off. "I am not the greatest at waiting. And I figured it might make things easier. And I found my divining rod, so hey, that may come in handy." My casual laugh betrayed me, turning slightly manic.

Andrew nodded, "Mind if I grab a drink?"

"Of course." I moved to fix the couch as Andrew went to the kitchen. The couch was back on four legs when he returned, can of ginger beer in hand.

He looked from the couch to the folder on the table. "Is that what you have on the attacker?" I nodded and he sat down and leafed through the papers. "Good. I spoke to my friend. She's an expert on the genealogy of secret societies and she's willing to spend an all-nighter or two to help out."

"Is she..." I hesitated, unsure how to ask the question. "Friendly?"

"She's a witch. From one of the neutral covens." I'm sure a look of concern went over my face, because Andrew continued quickly. "She knows that lives are at stake, and I trust her."

"Alright." I sighed. "I trust you on that. Does she know what's she's doing?"

"She's a graduate student at the University of Chicago who's been studying the fringes of the magical community for over a decade. There are experts outside of your conclave."

"I know." I looked quietly at Andrew. "Just, this is very important." Andrew nodded, quietly.

Another knock came at the door. Andrew looked at me and I shook my head. I wasn't expecting anyone. Andrew moved quickly, taking position in the coat closet behind the door. "Who is it?" I asked casually.

"It's Daniel." His words were a bit sluggish, but it was definitely him. I checked the peephole and opened the door. Daniel came in, walking a bit slowly. He wandered over to the bar. "What do you have left to drink?"

I looked at Daniel, taken aback at his casual entrance. "What?"

He looked over, unconcerned and gestured to try and overcome my apparent thickness. "To drink? A little hair of the dog?" He saw me looking at him, open mouthed and then jumped slightly as Andrew walked forward with a stern expression, emerging from behind the door. "What?" Daniel looked between us.

I stared back at him. "What are you doing?" Daniel looked at me, confused. I continued, "you..." But I lost my train of thought completely and just stared at him, callously standing there.

Andrew broke in, "Daniel, do you know what's going on?"

Daniel looked at Andrew then at me. "I...am going to say...no." Andrew nodded to me as Daniel responded and I closed my mouth.

"Daniel, how do I put this...where the fuck have you been?" I held my voice down, barely.

"Well, I had to take Gunter to the airport, but we had a few hours until his flight, so we hit a few bars first."

I sighed, "Where is your phone?"

Daniel patted his pockets and looked thoughtful. After a moment, he had an apparent epiphany. "It's in the toilet at the Duke of Perth." He looked briefly confident then blanched at my look and winced briefly at the pain from the gesture. "I mean, it probably isn't anymore, someone probably..." he trailed off.

Andrew spoke up. "I'll take care of this." He went to the kitchen and was back briefly, with a bubbling cup of red liquid, with flakes of something on top. He handed it to Daniel, "Drink."

Daniel looked at the cup, shrugged and then drank it down. The effect was near instantaneous. Daniel snapped from hungover straight back to sober, and not gently. After a moment he ran to the bathroom, emerging after just a minute with a shell-shocked expression. "Well, that was horrifying." He said, holding his head.

"Alright, are you coherent?" I paused until Daniel nodded at my question. "Last night as I was walking her home, Jennifer and I were attacked by cultists."

"Holy shit!" Daniel's outburst was a bit surprising in its volume after the tense silence of earlier. "Sorry." Daniel's expression was sheepish in response to Andrew and I flinching. "What happened?"

"She was kidnapped. And it looks like they grabbed Scaevola at the same time. We're under attack."

Daniel processed what I said. "Shit. I'm sorry bro. They kidnapped your girlfriend and I'm sitting here like a drunken asshole." Daniel clapped me on the shoulder.

I paused after he said it, unsure how to respond. "Right...I mean..." I gathered in the thought. "Look, just to be clear, I don't want Jennifer to be hurt and I take rescuing her very seriously, but she's not my girlfriend. We'd been on two dates. We haven't even slept together. Shit. I mean, look. Don't get me wrong. I feel terrible that she was kidnapped, especially if it was some attempt to get at me, but I want to be clear with you guys, it's not that kind of thing."

Andrew and Daniel looked at each other and back at me. While they weren't really friends with each other, I'd talked with both of them about women over the years. I shook my head. "I feel like an asshole."

Daniel chimed in. "No way. You're cool, this isn't a rescue the princess thing, that's fine. Right?"

Andrew nodded. "You still plan to help, right? That's all that really matters."

"Of course. I feel like I owe her that even more." I nodded. "I just don't want you guys thinking this is something it isn't."

Daniel came up and gave me a quick manly hug, thumping my back for good measure. As he pulled away, he said "I gotta go. They probably think I was kidnapped too. Prospero is gonna skin me and make me into a hat. Give me a call if you need anything. I'll text when I have a phone again." Daniel nodded to Andrew and headed out the door.

Andrew looked at me. "Joe, I'm going to get this information to my friend, but you should get out of here. Take a walk, get some air. Clear your head. I'll call." Andrew patted my shoulder and left with the folder, leaving me alone in my apartment with my guilt.

Chapter 20

Monday, June 22nd

I didn't really sleep, though there were a few periods of unconsciousness between my periods of pacing and fitful self-examination. I had given up on sleep entirely and was making coffee and breakfast when my phone rang. I was surprised when I saw it was Casimir calling. Casimir always had someone else call, privileges of leadership and all that.

"Hello?" I answered tentatively.

"Joseph. It's your uncle, Casimir." Casimir's voice was tired and strained.

"Yes, sir." I tensed myself a bit as he spoke, waiting for bad news. Was Jennifer dead? Had I been lying around while some deranged cultist murdered her?

"You'd best hurry to the sanctum. We have something you need to see." The phone went quiet as he hung up. I was out the door with a fully packed satchel and a mug of cold coffee within a minute.

One quick cab ride later I was in the lodge. The club area was busy, Keeper members and allies working on different tasks, a low hum of whispered conversations as plans were made and contacts were contacted. One of the club attendants saw me enter the room and came directly over to me. "Excuse me, sir. The Keeper of Laws is waiting in the workshop area." I followed him through the room towards the Inner Sanctum.

As I entered the workshop, I was struck by the group that was present. Casimir and George were standing near the worktable, the restored scrying table upright beside the cleared surface. Clark paced furiously on the side of the room, and Daniel, looking cleaned up and chastised was standing a little too erectly against one wall. At my entrance, Casimir looked up. "Joseph. We have more information, something that must alter our strategy." He gestured to the table. "George here was able to restore the table enough to get a psychometric reading and, well, the news isn't good."

"What is it, sir?" I looked around, Clark and George's expressions were grim, but Daniel seemed not to know what was coming.

"Best see that for yourselves." Casimir gestured and George began setting up the psychometric ritual, laying out a circle of fine sand around the scrying table and placing a crystal prism set inside an ornate planchette alongside an old phonograph style horn on the table itself.

A ghostly image appeared in the center of the room and George moved to adjust the crystal and bring the image into better focus. He placed the needle of the psychometric audioscope against the table and sound began, echoing in the empty workspace.

Two figures stood in a ghostly version of Scaevola's bedroom, unruined at this point. They wore robes similar to those worn in the attack in the park, but without the concealing masks. The figure on the left was a woman, short and slightly built with very short dark hair, the other was a tall Black man. As he spoke, I could tell by his inflections that he was from South Africa. "I searched the study; the book isn't there."

The woman gestured around the bedroom. "It's not in here, either." She seemed deeply frustrated, but the next sentiment was cockier. "I'm just saying, if we have to break into a Keeper library, I would have appreciated some notice."

The African man nodded, "We'll see if the Master had better luck downstairs." Looking off the side, he watched the approach of another figure.

From the doorway walked Scaevola, wearing a cultist's robe. Daniel and I both gasped, while Clark, George, and Casimir all looked varying flavors of angry and upset, they had seen this before, they knew this was coming. Scaevola walked up to the other figures, "It's not here, but it doesn't matter. They won't have time or the wits to stop the Deluge. Release the spirit, they should think this a second kidnapping." The image faded as George released the energy of the projection.

Clark spoke first. "That sneaky bastard. Investigating all of us while he..." He punched the wall as punctuation.

"We're working on identifying the other two, but it's clear that Scaevola has betrayed the Conclave." Casimir's voice was stern and collected, but anger seethed beneath the surface.

I didn't have anything to say. Scaevola was unpleasant and direct, but I never thought he would have betrayed the Conclave. Scaevola was the one who watched for betrayal, how long could he have been involved in this sort of thing? How much damage could he have done?

Everyone was looking at me, so I roused myself from my reverie. "So Scaevola was involved with...wait a minute. The fire spirits. Do you have my case report handy? What if he was the one stirring them up in the first place? Kept me running all over the..."

I stumbled, actively tempering my language before Casimir, who would scold me for anything stronger than hell, "dang city the whole last week while he was up to who knows what."

Casimir nodded. "We'll have someone look into that. Clark, get the report from Anthony and have one of your men look into it."

I paused for a moment. "They said something about a book?"

Casimir nodded. "Ephraim and Anthony are looking into that. We need you to be ready. Any clues that come in might call for immediate action." Casimir walked over to me and took me by the shoulders. "We knew that someday you would be called on to save the world, now we know how. I'm sure you're ready, Joseph."

A few minutes later, Daniel and I sat in the lounge, facing a cold fireplace. I was sure my own expression matched his, a face full of shock and betrayal with a dose of exhaustion. One of the club attendants came over with a tray with two cups of coffee and the accompanying trimmings.

Daniel pulled a flask from his suit coat pocket. He offered it up to me. I held up my hand, "No, I have to keep my wits about me."

Daniel nodded and looked at the flask and his coffee. "Me too?" He looked at me questioningly. I shot him a look and he slipped the flask back in his pocket and picked up his cup. "So. What's the plan?"

"Are you in?" I looked at him. "This could be really dangerous."

"Are you kidding, bro? I've been here since day 1. We all got the same speech about responsibility and the sacred unity of the Conclave and all that shit. I'm in. Besides, after cellphone-in-toiletgate, I am not sure I could survive backing out."

"Well, that's something." I shook my head as we sipped our coffee. "I don't know. Scaevola a traitor. That just seems wrong."

"It is wrong. That fucker screwed us all over." Daniel's passionate words were slightly undercut by the delicate china in his hands.

"No, I mean it feels really weird. Has he always been a traitor? He was the main line of defense for us. Has he been betraying us all along? Like, three years ago, when he was instrumental in rooting out that Nihilist cell that was going to assassinate Casimir we hosted the G-8 shadow conference. Why did he do that?"

"Maybe he has some grand plan. Or maybe he just went crazy. Or hey, maybe he's possessed." Daniel reached across and punched me lightly on the arm. "But hey, now we finally know what you'll be facing."

"Sort of." I sighed, "I hope he hasn't done anything to Jennifer."

My phone buzzed before I could continue. I pulled it out of my pocket and saw a text. 'Meet at Medici in Hyde Park at 6:30.' Andrew's number at the top. I texted a quick 'okay' back, then tucked my phone away.

Daniel looked over, expectantly, "What's up?"

"Andrew is running down a lead for me. He's got some information and a place to meet."

"Right." Daniel looked apprehensive. "You need some security backup?"

"To meet with Andrew?" I looked at Daniel skeptical.

Daniel gave an expectant shrug, "Yeah. Are you sure you can trust him?"

"Yes." I didn't hesitate. "Andrew is neutral in magical politics and has been helpful in more than one investigation."

Daniel nodded and raised his hands, "Alright. It's your rodeo. What should I be doing?"

"First, make sure you have your kit together. We might need to go at a moment's notice. If you need anything from stores, requisition it. And get stuff for me too, first aid, lethal and non-lethal, reinforced clothes." Daniel nodded at my instructions before I continued. "Second, stick around here and listen." Daniel started to object, but I cut him off. "A. I need you to get word if things begin to move. B. Scaevola might not have been acting alone. See if anyone else is acting funny."

Daniel nodded, "Sure. You can count on me."

"And stay sober." I looked at him seriously, "the drinks are on me after this, but I was addled when they took Jennifer. I don't want that to happen again."

Chapter 21

Monday, June 22nd

I got off the 6 bus west of the Museum of Science and Industry. I had taken the CTA down to give myself some introspection time before the meeting. The bus could be crowded, but I liked the chance to be alone in a crowd. Good for thinking, even though it was mostly strategic second guessing. Maybe if I'd gone right instead of left, maybe if I'd kept Jennifer back to back with me, no, that kind of second guessing gets you nowhere...

I was running a bit early, so I stopped in briefly at 57th street books and browsed a few blank notebooks. I grabbed one and hit the counter, exchanging familiar pleasantries with the manager Ted, a former college friend who'd put down roots in Hyde Park.

Even after half a dozen stories about Ted's new puppy. I was still early when I got to the restaurant and after a quick look around, I assured myself that Andrew wasn't present. I grabbed a table for four up on the balcony and began breaking in the notebook as I waited.

I turned to the first blank page. 'Notes on Investigation.' Beneath that, I wrote a few subheadings. 'Jennifer'; 'Scaevola'; 'Cult'. I stared at the page, thinking back over the events of the past few days, focusing on Scaevola's name on the page. It just didn't make sense.

Scaevola had been brought into the Chicago Conclave aback in 86, taking the keeper position from his retired predecessor, Adam Philips. He had been doing cultist investigations in Western Europe, mostly France and the low countries and was highly recommended to the greater community of conclaves by Paris and Brussels, with concurrences from a number of other cities. He had been injured in an assault on a Nihilist chantry in Amsterdam shortly before his assignment here and had come with his slight limp and twisted shoulder to an unfamiliar city.

He excelled at his work. When David Noyes, one of Clark's lieutenants had been taking bribes from a group of Princes of the City looking to set up on the south side, it was Scaevola who investigated and revealed the treachery.

He and Clark had uncovered an attempt by the Rising Sun to subvert Chicago's bureaucramancers and had rooted out the conspiracy. That was just eighteen months ago. I had joined in the assault on their rooftop temple. Scaevola just didn't seem the type.

I wrote under Scaevola's name simply "Why now?"

I looked at Jennifer's name on the page. Who was she to be kidnapped? I'd only had a little time to get to know her, but I didn't get the sense that she was that powerful a practitioner. The cultists had been ready for her to be there, had known her name. Was she the actual target and was I an inconvenience? Was she a known obstacle in a failed assault on me? Was she a hostage? Did they have demands?

I wrote under her name simply, 'Why Her?'

I was looking at the heading of Cult on the page when Andrew and his friend arrived. I saw Andrew coming up the stairs from my vantage point and I waved to get his attention. Beside him was a woman, slightly taller than he was, long black hair collected into a braid down her back. She wore thick framed glasses, a UChicago 'where the fun goes to die' t-shirt and jeans with worn Doc Martens and carried a heavy backpack. As they approached, I shut the notebook and put it aside, rising to meet them.

Andrew came over first. His opening question was more than just a formality, "How are you doing, Joe?" I nodded and waved off his concern to he continued. "Joe, this is my friend, Boudicca Esthersdottir. Boo, this is Joseph Palevsky, the Chosen One."

I extended my hand and Boudicca shook it. "Nice to meet you, Boudicca. Andrew says you're an expert on cults."

Boudicca smiled a tight smile. "I don't really like that term; it carries way too much pejorative baggage. But yes, I literally wrote the book on peripheral magical movements. Oh, and call me Boo."

I couldn't help my smile. "Boo? Like a ghost?"

"If you want to think of it that way, sure. I like to think of myself as a postmodern Boo Radley with the Regenstein library qua creepy old house." She smiled and shrugged. "With a name like Boudicca, you don't have a lot of nickname options. I'm sure as shit not gonna call myself Dicca." That drew a chuckle out of me and a snort from Andrew.

"Fair enough. Boo it is." I gestured to the chairs, and we all sat. "Andrew shared the photos with you? I'm sorry that all we had are shots of a dead body, but, well, he killed himself right in front of me." I shuddered.

"It's alright. I've seen worse in my field work. Have you ever interviewed a zombie? Try figuring out the etiquette for when your interview subject's nose falls off and they don't notice." Boudicca began pulling books and papers out of her bag. "Anyway, I've gone over a number of books and found some interesting information."

"That was fast." I looked over the collection of materials. "You searched all these?"

Boudicca looked at me over her glasses. "These are the relevant ones. I searched a lot more than just these." She smirked as she sorted through the stack.

Andrew spoke up. "Boo specializes in magics related to information retrieval. She has a number of spirits dedicated to helping her efforts."

"My uncle Anthony would be fascinated by that. He is much more hands-on with his search methods." I noted Boo's expression and quickly appended, "Sorry for the interruptions, please continue."

"Thank you. Now there's some interesting concordances in the symbolism of Mr. Holmes' tattoos and gear."

"Mr. Holmes?" I asked quickly.

"The deceased is Eliot Holmes." She pulled a photograph out of a folder. The photo showed the dead man, ten years younger, in a desert landscape wearing a respirator around his neck and goggles on his brow. Beside him were two others similarly dressed, all flashing the matching tattoos on their forearms, an eye with flames instead of eyelashes. "This is from his time with the Burning Eye movement, shortly before their attempted temporal psychic incursion in San Francisco. His friends there died when you stopped that plan." She looked at me accusingly.

"I haven't even been to San Francisco." I said defensively.

"I don't mean you personally. Keeper forces." She pulled out some additional pictures. "These markings tie to the Burning Eye, but these others are more recent." She pointed to some tattoos darker in color. "That's where this gets interesting. These new symbols are different from the others. They don't correspond to any cataloged peripheral magical movements."

"What does that mean?" I looked at the photos of the tattoos. "They look like normal cultist tattoos to me." I caught a look from Boo. "Sorry."

"I'm not entirely sure." Boo exhaled and then continued. "It's hard to draw conclusions from a single example, but this is not from a known group or a splinter of a known group. You rarely see completely new symbology. Most symbols speak of ancestry and connections claims to political or spiritual legitimacy. You know, the Roman Eagle becomes the American Eagle, Athena becomes Minerva becomes Britannia, et cetera. This has none of that."

"Couldn't it just be something secret?" I looked at the central image, a wave within a circle, a star above it and a city skyline below. "Something you don't know about?"

"That's a good question. It's certainly possible." Boo nodded, "But I don't think so. Secret societies can only be so secret or else it's self-defeating, you know?" I looked at her skeptically. "Alright, I call it the Shaker problem. The Shakers had passionate believers once upon a time, lots of converts, but they decided not to reproduce and not to proselytize, so they died out. Secret societies need some way of recruiting, so they exist in rumor or implication. So, people hear of them and seek them out, or information slips out and something becomes known. This is not that. Anyway. A group that inspires suicide before capture doesn't seem like a casual hobby."

I took this in, Scaevola consorting with cultists, new cultists. It didn't make a lot of sense. What the hell was he doing? "Thank you for all this."

Boo smiled, "Andrew said there were lives at stake, I'm happy to help."

"If I get any more information, can I..." I let the question drift off.

"Absolutely!" Boo jumped in, "I'm eager to help." She handed me a business card with her phone number on it. "Plus, having this kind of access to an inter-group conflict at this scale is a rare opportunity, I can probably get a dissertation chapter out of this."

We sat for a moment in silence, and Boo broke in. "So, I'm sure you have to get back to stuff, but can I ask you a few questions while we wait for food?"

"Questions? Like about the case?"

"I was actually hoping more about being the Chosen One and stuff. It would really help my research."

"Don't you research...Peripheral magical movements? I would really call the Keepers peripheral."

"Oh no, of course not. The opposite, really. But so many movements define themselves based on the keepers and by extension the Chosen One that it would be incredibly valuable, I mean, you have groups like the Atlantans and the Order of Usnard who trace their founding to the actions of particular Chosen Ones on the one hand, and on the other hand you have entire movements that define themselves based on their opposition to everything the Keepers do."

"Nihilists."

"That's certainly one way of talking about them. A heavily biased, unnecessarily reductive way, but yeah, 'nihilists' owe as much to the Chosen One as anyone out there. So, can I ask you a few questions?"

"I can't reveal any secrets, just to be clear."

"Oh, of course not. I'm way ahead of you." She reached into her bag and pulled out a file folder. "Normally, I'd offer an informed consent compact with standard options for pseudonymity and data protection, but I can't just quote 'an anonymous Chosen One', now can I?"

I snorted; Andrew smiled.

"So, I have a modified version just for you. It's a standard information masking compact, binds me from distributing information gained from our research without explicit prior consent. I won't be recording; this is just some background information to give me a sense of your world." She passed over the paper. "I meant to pull this out before, sorry, I got a little into things."

I gave it a read and passed it to Andrew. After a moment, Andrew passed it back to me. "It is exactly what she says it is."

"I'll sign first, and this applies to the other research too." She patted her bag where she'd put the file on the cultist. "You would need to give explicit consent to release any of it. I had this for you regardless. Research ethics are kinda my jam." She signed the paper and passed it over.

"Alright, but I can't tell you everything, even with this." I signed and returned the page.

"Of course, just what you're comfortable with." Boo placed the page in the folder, then tied the folder shut with a peculiar ribbon that had a long word written on it. She whispered to the folder, there was a brief puff of air, and she untied the folder, handing me a perfect copy of the document. "This is your copy. For your files."

I folded the paper and slipped it into my new notebook.

"So, let's start general. What does the Chosen One do?"

"That's a pretty broad question. I protect the world from a coming disaster foreseen by the elder prophets of the Conclave of Keepers. If that's your level of question, then you aren't exactly filling me with confidence in your ability to help."

"I just want to understand from your own perspective. The words you choose tell me a lot. For instance, you say protect, not save, not defend, not destroy. You talk about a disaster, not a danger or a threat. Those are meaningful distinctions. I would have very different follow up questions if you had talked about ending threats."

"I mean...huh...yeah, I am here to put myself between the world and danger, but I have the tools to do it. To me, that's protecting. If the world were broke and I was questing to fix it, that might count as saving the world, but I feel like my role is more about seeking out things that aim to do harm and stop them. Keeping the peace."

"Do you work all alone? I mean, there's only one Chosen One, right? It's not a wildly misnamed job?"

"Ha. There's just me, but I have a tremendous amount of support from the Conclave, magical and logistical. They know the scale of the danger, so they make sure I'm equipped to confront it."

"Doesn't that make it a bit of a self-fulfilling prophecy?"

"Causality is a tricky thing to debate when it comes to prophecy. There have been past Chosen Ones who have succeeded with almost no support or with ineffective support, so it's not just the Conclave."

"Ineffective support?"

I waved my hand a bit. "Not incompetent, just sometimes prophecy can be slippery."

"Fair point. So, about the disaster?"

"Let me stop you. I can't actually tell you anything about that, even on deep background. Once it's passed, yes, but there's too much danger of nihilists seeking to aid the destruction of the world."

"Of course." Boo waved her hands a bit. "That makes sense why I've seen past prophecies but nothing current. It makes sense not to mention ahead of time. Plus, that way if you fail, nobody is the wiser."

The bags of food arrived, and I paid for the dinners. "No Chosen One has ever failed, the world is still standing." I smiled with a confidence I didn't fully feel. "Thank you for your help on this."

"Thank you for your perspective. Please send me any more information you need help with and if you need a hand, I'd love to come along. Keep the world on its metaphorical feet."

"I will keep that in mind."

Chapter 22

The lobby of the Newberry was empty as I came in, my steps echoing in the marble foyer. As I headed towards the stairs, I heard someone call my name through the silence. Startled, I jumped before I recognized Chris, one of the regular security guards. "Joe, hey, whoa, sorry for startling you."

I looked at myself, standing ready for a fight and relaxed my pose. "Ha, you really got me there, I was all up in my thoughts. How are you doing?"

"Can't complain." Chris walked stiffly over towards the security desk. "Happy Birthday."

"What?" I paused for a moment, "Thanks. How did you know?"

"Anthony was talking about it. Said he got you something nice." He sat down in the chair behind the desk. "You here to see him?"

"Yeah, a bit of family business."

"He should be back in the closed stacks; you know the way."

"Yup, thanks. And thanks for the birthday wishes." I waved as I took the steps two at a time.

I found Anthony in one of the reading rooms tucked into the basement level of the closed stacks, surrounded by a pile of open books and photographs. He looked up as I came in. "Joe, it's good to see you but I don't really have much more for you."

"I have some things for you, actually." I pulled out the folder I had gotten from Boo. "Have you heard about the Burning Eye movement?"

Anthony flipped through the pages. "This is impressive. Where did you get this?"

"Andrew has a friend who does freelance magical research."

"This is very sensitive stuff, Joe. This freelancer, is he someone you can trust?"

"I think so. She got results and Andrew practices naming magic, so he's VERY good at finding out deception."

"And you trust him?" Anthony was still looking through the folder but looked up as he asked.

"With my life." I locked eyes with Anthony as I said it. He nodded and smiled.

"Well, there's some good information here. I'll need to consult a few specialized texts." He moved a few of the books around, searching. "Where is…"

"Can I grab something for you?"

"No, I think it's in my personal…Oh Lord! My personal vault!"

"What's wrong with your personal vault?"

"No, not mine, Scaevola's! There were some items placed there recently, but they couldn't be paged because Wallace was out sick. I think we only brought out half of what was requested, there might be evidence in there, but…"

I was running before he finished, opening the key box on the wall and grabbing the master key. Anthony pulled his key ring from his belt and together we unlocked the dual locks that leading to the room with the Conclave's private vaults.

Each of the High Conclave had a vault where they could store things most valuable, secretive, or dangerous. The Keeper of Keys officially oversaw them, but the Newberry vaults had the best security, so Anthony had emergency access after they were built out in the 90s.

When we entered the vestibule, I could tell that something was wrong. A crackling energy suffused the area, and I could feel it emerging from Scaevola's vault. "Open it quick and be ready."

Anthony used his key to open the door as I readied myself for whatever was within. As the door opened, a humanoid figure made of warped lines of heat began to manifest and burst into flame. Anthony fell back with an undignified squeak as I moved between him and the creature. "Anthony? I will try and keep it busy and keep the damage down, but I need its name and some sort of fireproof vessel, quickly!"

The figure looked around the inside of the vault, seemingly oblivious to Anthony and me. It reached out with the flaming tendrils that passed for fingers towards a shelf of books.

I screamed out the name of ice and the moisture around the shelf congealed quickly into a cloud of mist. Not enough humidity in library storage to encase a shelf in ice, but enough to surprise the thing. The creature recoiled and turned towards me its face full of rage and pain. "Well, I have its attention now."

Anthony was fumbling with his keys, looking back and forth at the thing. "I think it must be one of the kings of the Jinni, the shape of the head…I think it's connected to destruction or war." I dodged a few exploratory lunges as Anthony opened his vault and disappeared within. "Maybe Murra? Who rules over the domain of Mars?"

"Wait, did you say Murra?" A flash from my school days came suddenly and I spoke the name of ice again, enough to coat my left forearm before blocking its lunge, directly towards my…well, let's just say it would have really hurt.

"You remember him?" Anthony called from the vault.

"He's an aggressive monster that attacks the groin. There was a month where anyone not paying close attention got punched in the crotch by Daniel yelling 'Murra strike!'"

"Oh yeah, I had forgotten that. You boys were a handful." Anthony emerged from his fault, opening a velvet lined box and pulling out an ornate brass decanter. He tossed it to me as he pulled a ball of wax and an ornate seal from the box.

"Al Ahmar, Lord of Ifrits, Ruler of Mars, I bind you in the name of Seth. I bind you in the name of Solomon, I bind you in the name of the Conclave." As I intoned the words, I forced my will into the incantation and focused on the emptiness of the bottle. The Ifrit's shape twisted into impossible dimensions and folded itself into the decanter, heating the mouth and becoming a shimmering distortion. Anthony put the ball of wax onto the top and pressed the ornate seal over the softening wax, which hardened instantly into a six-pointed star with a circle of binding written around it.

The fire alarms were going off, but Anthony hit some buttons on the wall that prevented the fire suppression system from going off. I took the sealed bottled and placed it gently back in the velvet box. I handed the box to one of the clerks who had come in response to the commotion. "Secure that somewhere. Let's see what it was sent to destroy." In the center of the shelf, on the lectern, sat a book, old looking and mysterious. "Not precisely hidden. "I moved back to my satchel that I had dropped preparing for the fight and pulled out my prismatic lenses.

There were a few protective enchantments on the shelf, Dee's non-detection, Landsman's thief's surprise, one of Scaevola's own alert spells. All of them were easy enough to unweave and I was lifting the book from the shelf when Anthony returned, handling it delicately with freshly gloved hands.

"It's lucky you were here, Joe. I don't know what would have happened if this had been released with just me here. The whole vault might have been destroyed." Anthony picked up the fragments of the clay seal that had bound the spirit. "Scaevola must have left this here to destroy any evidence."

"Lucky." I let out a desultory snort and Anthony gave me a quizzical look. "Scaevola always told me the man who relies on luck is bound to lose."

"Well, that's...I don't know if it technically meets the definition of irony, but it's close." Anthony came up to look at the book. "That looks old and... complex." The interior was a combination of ritual designs and coded writing. "The cover, is that...human skin?" Anthony touched the cover before turning pale and fleeing in the direction of the bathroom.

When he emerged, I had the book on the table with the other research materials. Anthony grayed a little looking at it. "You have enough to be researching right now." I patted the book as I looked at him. "Let me take a crack at this one."

Anthony smiled weakly. "That's smart. I can keep looking into the people in George's vision and into the material you brought me."

As I rose to go, I turned back to Anthony. "When did Scaevola put this in his vault?"

"Well, I can't say for sure, but it must have been about a month ago, when he came back from Los Angeles."

"It... just seems like an odd place to hide a secret tome, is all."

"Never underestimate the hubris of the wicked." Anthony smiled, "Another of Scaevola's sayings."

I left with the words bouncing around my head.

Chapter 23

Monday, June 22nd

I had been jerking awake so much I was beginning to be afraid of whiplash. The clock on my wall said it was nearly 3am and my research into the book was moving unbearably slowly. I had barely finished translating the first page of 'the ancient and eternal rites of the Deluge'. Skimming the book hadn't helped. The binding was tight enough and the pages stiff enough that I couldn't flip through quickly. I needed help, but Anthony was neck deep in cult research with Boo's notes. Boo, right. She's been able to do that all so quickly, maybe she had some tricks that could speed things up.

I pulled out my phone. She'd given a cell number. It was too late to call, but I could send a text and see if she could help. Probably wouldn't help until morning, but it wasn't like I was making any progress now.

<hello Boo, it's Joe from earlier. Do you have a way of translating a book super quick? Call or text when you wake up. Sincerely, Joe>

I set down the phone and went to brush my teeth. I could get some sleep while I waited. I came back to three messages.

<when I wake up assumes I sleep like some sort of normal person. When else I am gonna get in all my milk curdling and crop ruining?>

<Which is a joke, in case that doesn't translate over text. #notallwitches #alsoajoke #3amBooisLoopyBoo>

<Meet tomorrow noon?>

I stared at the phone for a moment, strange woman. I couldn't tell if it was late night punchiness, but i did chuckle a bit. <Noon is good for me. Meet at Andrew's shop?>

<Roger. 10-4. Five by Five. Over>

With that arranged, I set a quick alarm and passed out unceremoniously on my bed.

My cab pulled up at Andrew's at quarter til, bearing 24 ounces of the strongest coffee Corbel had to offer. Andrew looked up from the Red Eye and nodded to me. "Not here yet. Got a few minutes?" He pulled out the crossword.

"More than a little bleary, but I'll give it the old college try." I replied as I sipped from my cup.

"Happenings of Exodus 7-12, seven letters, ends in an s"

"Hmm, that's the plagues. Does that fit?"

"Let me cross check a bit...looks like it fits." Andrew scanned around the puzzle, "Vesper adornment, middle letter is i."

"Ask the bartender. Vesper is a vodka martini with Lillet, garnished with a twist of lemon, shaken, not stirred."

"That fits, which makes legless dragon start with wyv?."

"Wyvern, it's a whole heraldry thing, don't get me started."

As Andrew finished writing, the door dinged as it opened, and Boo walked in. She wore a long flowing skirt, a tank top reading [insert pithy phrase] and a pair of oversized sunglasses, though her boots remained unchanged. She carried a similarly large coffee and pointed at my cup. "Coffeebros!' extending her fist out toward me. She held it still until I realized I was supposed to give it a bump, which took an embarrassingly long time.

"Looks like 12pm Boo is loopy Boo too."

"That's my secret, Cap. I'm always loopy." Boo gave a sly smile and waggled her eyebrows. "You've got a book that needs translating?"

I pulled the book out of my satchel, giving a brief look outside and placing it on the side counter. Boo moved to it quickly.

Boo pulled a pair of cloth gloves out of her backpack and moved in hungrily. "Alright, this cover is unusual, definitely not cow leather."

I shifted uncomfortably beside her. "It's not...human skin, is it?"

"Probably now, human skill is really shitty book binding material at this size, and not just for the human. I can check on that." She raised the book up to her nose. "Hmm, not much in the way of vanilla, faint smell of tannins. Curious. She held the book open and peered through one of the pages into the light. "No chain marks, consistent weight, but the script definitely looks classic gothic blackletter. That'll make things easy, but this is a weird one." Boo looked over her shoulder at me, "Let's talk timing and needs. I can do a full SLP, but that's a bit time and material consuming, probably two weeks to write and de-ghost the incantation."

"I'm sorry, what now? SLP? I..."

"Supernatural language processing, using spirits to dive into a text and do all sorts of things. You ever seen a real physical word cloud? It's not super useful, but it's great at parties. Well, certain parties."

"I had no idea this was even possible." The notion intrigued me. "Is this like a hacking thing?"

Boo blinked at me, "You aren't very tech savvy, are you."

"I have email, I can google." I get a little defensive about tech stuff. "I wasn't allowed to do much tech stuff; the keepers saw it as a distraction."

"Well, I can forward my article from Witch Quarterly."

"Now you're just fucking with me."

"Yes, but in fairness, I didn't think you'd realize." Boo smiled.

Andrew laughed out loud and shook his head at us.

I turned back to Boo. "I don't have two weeks, what can you do fast? Like, tomorrow fast."

"Word frequency, rough translation, I can do hex decoding as long as it uses a standardized format."

"The diagrams are in early Plessis."

"Right, hmm, that would put it in the post-incunabula period, which makes sense for the paper quality, but the preservation...hmm. I can do it. Run it overnight, materials will probably be about a hundred, is that...." She paused as I had already pulled out a roll of bills.

"Here's 200, just in case."

"Great! I will dive right in and text you when it's done, 24 hours, tops." Boo scooped up the book and deposited it in a plastic treasure island grocery bag, which she wrapped around it before slipping it into her pack. "You bring me interesting artifacts and research funding; a girl could get used to that."

After she left, there was a moment of silence as I watched her head for the train. I looked back over, and Andrew was looking at me. "What?"

"Nothing. This is moving quickly, you have leads you are following?" His face turned serious.

"I think I do. It's already been two full days; they could be doing anything. But at least we know more than we did. Like the fact that Scaevola is involved."

Andrew's brow furrowed. "Scaevola Fortier? The Keeper of Keepers?"

"Yeah, he's apparently in charge of this cult. I should have seen it coming somehow."

Andrew remained pensive. "I met with him several years ago, after we began hanging out."

"I remember, he determined you were a 'benign influence with limited subversive connections'."

"I should put that in my author bio." Andrew snorted. "He was a man who defined himself by his role, by the trust placed in him. I did not see him as a traitor."

"Well, something must have happened between then and now. But that's just more that doesn't add up."

"Joe." Andrew's statement was firm. "I'm here for you, whenever this goes down, whatever happens, just let me know.

"Thanks." I gave him a tight hug and left the shop before I got too emotional. Too much still to do.

Chapter 24

Tuesday, June 23rd

How often do you think about meals based on the likelihood you'll go into battle? Probably never, right? In a crisis, I have to plan these things. I always carry some sort of quick calories, you'd probably guess powerbars or nutrigel, but I decided on Snickers bars when I was 13 and stuck with it. Protein and sugar, compact and tasty, usable as a makeshift weapon against the peanut allergic, alright, I don't do that, ever, but I could.

In an emergency situation, dinner can't be too greasy, that could interfere with grip on weapons, or with climbing, so pizza is out without extensive wet wipes. You can't eat something that has a strong magical taboo, I can't account for everything, but definitely no pork, no blood, of course no human flesh, though that doesn't actually change my diet. I even have to plan for stealth. Nothing too smelly, nothing that might be, well, noisy afterwards. Anyway, most of those things don't have filters on grubhub, so I was just sitting and staring at my computer screen, overcompensating for a bit of Luddite anxiety, when my phone rang, Clark's number.

"Joe, we have a lead on the cult and need your presence. Daniel is in a car and coming to get you. Meet him downstairs, bring your tactical gear."

When Daniel pulled up, I got right in. "Quick detour. I need food, fast as possible."

"I got ya. Whatya want, Jojo?"

"Sultan's market, that'll be fast." As the SUV turned, I pulled out my phone and quick dialed. "Sarah? It's Joe Palevsky. Usual for pickup, extra napkins." One stop, five minutes and an exorbitant tip later, I was eating shawarma and curry rice as Daniel sped down Lake Shore, the evening traffic light.

"Watch the upholstery, Bro."

"Drive better." I wiped my hands on the napkins. "Where are we headed?"

"Only the best named neighborhood in the city." Daniel looked back and forth between me and the road ahead.

I paused to think, but Daniel was nothing, if not predictable. I sighed to myself. "The Bush?"

"The Bush!" Daniel went up for a high five, I indulged him.

"What's the tactical situation?" I finished the last of the rice and stuffed the trash into the food bag as I pulled up my tactical bag, checking the straps and sheaths.

"I don't have the full sitch, but Clark mentioned a few things. There were some Praetorians doing spot checks on locations near the lake and some radioed in some suspicious activity. Apparently, there was some fighting, but I don't have more than that."

I searched my memory, "Down at the old steel works? Park...566?"

"That's where we're headed."

"I know we had some historical presence down there, but I hadn't thought we had anything active at the site."

"Prospero had me check out a decommissioned vault down there like five years ago, make sure it wasn't flooded or infested. It wasn't." We rolled past the Museum of Science and Industry and continued south. "I have the keys in case we need to disarm any of the defenses." Daniel patted his pocket with a heavy clank.

As we continued down, I pulled out my phone and dialed Clark. He picked up almost immediately, but I heard the open mic sound of speakerphone and road noise. "Go."

"Clark, it's Joe. We're a few minutes out, are we coming into an active fight?"

"Negative. There was a fight, but the area is secured according to Praetorians on scene. I think I'm just a minute or so behind you, there should be someone to wave you in."

"Thanks. See you there." I hung up and turned to Daniel. "We're safe coming in. Head right for the park."

We pulled in a few minutes later, as one of Clark's Praetorians waved us in using a flashlight. A few others were positioned around the scene, but the thing that jumped out at me was two white vans, parked side by side near the water. There were a few Praetorians moving around the vehicles with flashlights. Before I could make my way over, Clark's truck pulled up and he got out of the cab swiftly. He gave a loud whistle that got everyone's attention.

The Praetorians gathered around Clark and stood at attention. "Report." He looked around the circle. "First on scene?"

Praetorian Cumberland raised his hand and stepped forward. "Morse and I were closest down here, so we did the initial approach. When we arrived on scene, we spotted the vans and a number of people moving materials from the vans to a number of zodiac rafts in the dock area. We called in backup and continued to monitor."

"We were trying to get a better angle on the action, there's not a lot of cover, but we wanted to get some tactical positioning before backup arrived. That's when they spotted us."

"Were you able to capture anyone?" Clark looked between the two of them, who shook their heads.

Morse piped up, "We did kill two, but the rest that were still here got to their rafts and headed out to the lake."

"Did you see Jennifer? Did they have the prisoner?" Clark was livid, shaking a bit as he nearly yelled at the two.

They shook their heads and I thought for a moment that Clark was going to punch one of them, but he turned away and stalked out of the circle. I held up a finger to the guards and walked after him, catching up where he sat on a rock.

"We'll find her, sir. There may be information here and they may not be planning on harming her. If they knew about her relationship to you, they may want her as a hostage. That'll give us a chance to rescue her." I came up behind him and put a hand on his shoulder.

Clark's eyes glistened with held back tears. "I don't think.... Joe, they're going to kill her. Why else would they have kidnapped a Vestal Virgin?"

"I didn't...she never mentioned that."

"It's not a public thing, for exactly this reason. But I'm sure Scaevola knew. The asshole is taunting me. Even this place as a base of operations. You know the connection between this place and my family, and Jennifer's family! Now I have incompetent Praetorians blowing the only real lead we could have had here." He began to rise, as if to go back to the circle in anger.

I held up a hand. "Sir, let me take charge of the scene, I can manage this and find what we need. This is my mission, let me fulfill it." He sat back down and just nodded.

"Alright, spread out and scour, psychometry protocols in effect, but don't worry about this as a crime scene. We need things fast, bring it all back here. Cumberland, Morse, was there any flashy magic in your fight? Anything anyone local will get curious about?" Their tentative expressions told me enough. "Get out to the road and watch for cops, you're neighborhood watch and there were some punk kids setting off Indiana fireworks, they ran off south, got it? Next, you two get the vans, you two, dock area, everyone else? Spread out. Daniel and I will check the vaults." Everyone spread out around the park.

Daniel shook the ring of keys as he pulled them out of his pocket. "Vault is over here." As we walked away from the group, he said more quietly. "Way to fuck it up, Joe."

"What?" I kept my cool and looked over.

"You're supposed to end a speech like that by making a dumb joke and putting on your sunglasses."

"Daniel, the sun set an hour ago, I don't even have my sunglasses on me." I rolled my eyes at him, and we kept walking in silence. "So, like, get it done and don't miss the boat?"

"Come on, you can do better than that, bro." Daniel waggled his hand.

"These cultists are gonna get a shipment of whoop ass?"

"Maybe not so much with the boat puns."

"We'll catch those zodiacs so fast they think we own the horoscope?"

"We'll workshop that one." We arrived at the entrance to the secret underground vaults, installed back during the steel works days. Daniel's keys proved entirely unnecessary, the door was wide open, and the room was scattered with a wide variety of maps and papers, diagrams on the walls. "Whoa, this is gonna take a while."

"Get started in here, I'm gonna tell everyone to bring things in here and get us some more hands."

Casing the entire scene took a few hours, but at the end, we had a whole table of material laid out on a null energy cloth to preserve the resonance. Clark leaned against the wall watching as Daniel laid down the last item, a nautical chart.

"Okay, let me sum up what we have out loud. Let me know if I have anything wrong." I looked around to the gathered group.

I gestured at the astronomical diagrams on the wall. "We have a timeline. The calculations are based on tomorrow's positions, right?" I looked over to Praetorian Homan, who had the ephemeris in hand. He nodded. "We have a deck plan of a cargo ship with patrol routes marked on it, only partially scorched."

"The papers were too tightly packed, only the top layer really burned." Morse pointed over to the empty metal barrel and the pile of papers beside it. "There's some receipts in there too. They have supplies, mainly handguns, small ammo, easy enough to get down in Indiana, but nothing heavier."

"That's good to know. Nihilists who keep their receipts. You see something new every day." I quipped, there were a few chuckles. "And we have a chart. Can you read that, Daniel?"

Daniel was examining the chart and looked up at his name. "What? Yeah, I think so. The blood didn't get on the important parts."

"You think so or you know so? Our timing has to be right on this. We can't go chasing the wrong ship."

"I can be sure. I don't use paper charts usually, but I can put it in my navigation system."

"Good thing we have a boat then." I sighed, "We have a where, a when and a sense of the forces arrayed against us. That's...really lucky. You'd think a group this organized would have better information discipline."

"We caught them with their pants down." Cumberland smiled and nodded over at Morse.

Clark stepped forward. "Gather everything up and get the evidence back to Keeper HQ. We need to prepare for our assault." The Praetorians snapped into motion.

I looked at Clark, then pulled him off to the side. "Keeper Davis, I want to talk strategy for the assault. I think it's best if I keep the force small. I want to take prisoners, if possible, this group surprised us, I want to know how. And I think a smaller group has a better chance of getting all the way in and saving Jennifer before being noticed."

"Who knows how long Scaevola was hiding them from us. He had access to everything."

"I... guess I'm not quite sure of his motives. He could easily have killed us all without resorting to this ritual thing. It just seems sloppy and sudden. I want to take him alive if at all possible." Clark glared at me as I spoke. "So... I don't want you along on this. This is too personal for you. There's too much leverage against you. I will do everything in my power to save Jennifer, but I'm going in with a smaller team."

Clark glared hard and I thought for a moment he might yell at me, but he breathed in hard and contained himself. "It's your op. What can I do?"

"I need you in charge of the reserves. If things go badly, I need the Praetorians ready to go. I can't think of anyone more capable." I extended my hand.

Clark nodded and shook my hand hard. "We all believe in you Joe. We'll be ready. Save the world first, and Jennifer if you can."

Chapter 25

The Conclave's car pulled up in front of a house with a yard twice as verdant as those it bordered. Peculiar statuary dotted the garden which overflowed with various sprays of color. Boo had texted that there was some sort of problem with the book, so I had come immediately. The house itself was a three-story Victorian and Boo sat on the porch in the afternoon sun, wearing a pair of dirt stained overalls and a plain black T-shirt. The book was in her lap as she sat on a porch swing, a packet of multi-colored post-it notes at her side. As I got out of the car, she waved to me.

I approached the porch delicately, stepping around the flowers that spilled down onto the flag stones. "Nice house." I said, looking about.

"It's my grandmother's. She's lived here since the 1960's. I'm just staying here while I'm in school." Boo gestured to a table and chairs on the corner of the porch, and we moved there. She set the book on the table. "So, I've finished my analysis." She gestured at the book, which now had multi-colored post-its sticking from the cover.

"That was really quick! Thank you so much." The relief was thick in my voice. "Did you find anything I can use?"

Boo looked apprehensive, "Don't thank me yet." She paused. "So, there's something weird about this book. It's not real."

I looked at the book and instinctively reached out to touch it. It was warm under my hand. "Not real?"

"Alright. Poor phrasing on my part. The book is a real object, but it's not the tome of an ancient secret society. It's a fake." Boo looked excited. "Okay, so, I was doing the whole SLP thing, word frequency, ritual analysis and so forth. I had them looking for patterns, textual excerpts, parsing the book into different types of information." She pointed at the post-it flags. "They put these in here. Marking rituals and such. And they came back with some literal red flags"

"That's great." I nodded, looking at the flags. "But what do you mean by fake?"

"Okay." Boo tensed a bit, full of excited energy. "Here's where it gets weird. First, this is not actually an old book. The pages are wrong, they don't match the papermaking methods of the supposed era and the cover is actually pacific hagfish, which definitely wasn't available in Europe back when it says it was written."

"Couldn't it be a later copy?" I touched the cover, relieved to know that it wasn't human skin.

"Well, I considered that, which is why I ran some incantations on the second thing. This was written in Latin by someone whose native language is English. Modern English, at that." Boo looked at my skeptical expression and continued, "There are word frequency choices and some awkward phrases that indicate that the writer was attempting to adapt English phrasings into Latin."

Boo began to talk about non-native declension frequencies and tense structures my brain started to fog up, so I held up a hand to stop her. "I'll take your word on it." I nodded.

"Then there's the third thing. It's too consistent. I'd been searching for memetic traces, indications of where it might have come from. Y'know, is it a variation on Zoroastrian dualism or yet another attempted duplication of the Templars? Well, there aren't any. This was put together by a single person, all at once. I mean, not like, all in one sitting, but it's the work of a single person." Boo had been speaking quickly and was a bit out of breath. "Planned out and logical, that's just not how human belief systems work."

"Okay, what does that mean?" I spoke slowly, taking this in. "Is this not the real book?"

"Well, it's got working spells and rituals in it. I tested some and they work. Plus, the symbology matches what we saw from the suicidal cultist, Eliot Holmes. So, I think it's real, for certain definitions of real." Boo shrugged.

"Well, that's something. Does it have anything I can use?"

"There are a few things that could be useful. I could teach you a few unweavings with a few days practice." Boo flipped to one of the pages marked with a blue post-it, with an elaborate diagram.

"I don't really have a few days. They are planning the sacrifice tonight."

"Well, then I could come with you. I am quite good at hex deconstruction." Boo nodded. "And it could help answer some questions I have."

I hesitated before answering. "This is something really dangerous. It would mean coming into a combat zone."

"I know. I've studied Judo with my Grandmother and I'm as good with a bow as anyone who went through a five-year teenage obsession with Artemis." Boo spoke with a good deal of confidence. "Besides. If I'm reading this ritual right." She flipped to the back of the book. "Someone could be in serious danger."

"What's it do?" I looked down at the page and its diagrams.

"Well, it's pretty cliche, sacrificing a virgin to bring down a meteor." Boo shrugged. "And while I don't put much stock into the reification of virginity, I'd hate to see someone killed just because they bought into some patriarchal sex shaming bullshit."

"Right, that matches up some things I've learned." I nodded, "Okay. Meet at 8pm at the America's Courtyard statue near the Adler."

"Are they hiding in the planetarium? Those bastards!" Boo's anger came quickly but she still smiled through it.

"No. No. They're holed up on a ship out in the lake, we're getting a ride out there from Burnham harbor."

Boo nodded. "I'll be there." She flashed a smile. "This'll be fascinating. I can't wait to see what sort of things they've erected on an aquatic mobile temple structure. It'll be a great chance to see things in action. I wonder how they deal with directional drift."

"This may be an odd question, but what size bulletproof vest do you wear?"

"Well, it's been a while since my last fitting..." Boo shrugged and smiled, "men's medium, women's large?"

Chapter 26

I sat on the central stones in the granite circles that made up the public art installation called America's Courtyard. Beside me were my binoculars and a plain white paper bag, just showing hints of transparency at the bottom from the grease. I picked up the binoculars and took another look at the ship in the fading light. I would be out there shortly, fulfilling my destiny.

I set down the binoculars and opened the paper bag. Harold's Chicken was a guilty pleasure of mine, especially at my age. It wasn't the best fried chicken, but there was something perfect about its greasy, hot sauce laden succulence. If I was going to eat what might be my last meal, Harold's just felt right, that combination of nostalgia and guilty pleasure that you wanted to go out on, it was worth the cleanup.

As I worked my way through the meal, stripping the chicken from the bones, piling the fries covered with hot sauce and chicken grease on the bread and finishing with the cooling slaw, I reflected on how I'd gotten here. Here at the potential end of the world on the Eastern edge of Chicago.

I had been here for twenty-five years. First a student, then the Chosen One. Twenty-five years of waiting, never allowed to leave Chicago, once they'd determined that destiny would come to a head here. I'd seen every corner of the city, met thousands of people, hundreds of different magical practitioners. Now, I was waiting to confront one of my mentors over a kidnapped girl and a false book. What did it all amount to?

"Joe." Andrew had come up beside me as I watched the lake. He was only a few steps away when he said my name.

"Give me a sec," I said as I pulled out a stack of napkins from below my leg, wedged there to keep from blowing away. I wiped the last of the grease and hot sauce from my hands and tossed the napkins in the bag. I stood up and moved to Andrew and clasped his offered hand. "Good to have you here, friend." He nodded and had a seat on the stones, pulling out a rolled bundle of sage and lighting it.

We were in the process of a basic smudging as Boo walked up. She was wearing black cargo pants tucked into boots and had a bow slung over one shoulder alongside a quiver. On her opposite hip rode a satchel, out of which poked the book, it's post-it flags waving in the breeze from the lake.

Andrew looked up as she approached. "Boo. I hadn't known you were coming." He looked thoughtful for a moment, then nodded. "It is good that you are here. It is right." He looked to me and nodded.

"I'm glad she's here too. She's our expert on hexes and on this c...peripheral magical movement." I stumbled over the word.

Boo smiled. "Good catch. Though I think once you start sacrificing virgins, you can be called a cult."

"Whoa there, virgins?" Daniel came up from the direction of the harbor. "What's Joey been saying about me? I swear it's all lies."

Andrew sighed and rolled his eyes. Daniel was wearing a blazer and a greek fisherman's cap. I looked him over inquisitively.

"What? This is my boating outfit." Daniel smoothed his lapels and adjusted his cap.

'Daniel, this is Boudicca, Boudicca, Daniel." The two of them shook hands, slightly awkwardly as Boudicca shifted the bow out of the way.

I looked around at the three of them. "Okay. This is it. You still have the chance to back out. I know this is important and I know you all want to help, but I'm going to need you all to say yes again. I am here because my path has led me here, but you each have the option to leave. I want you here because you say yes, not because you didn't have a chance to say no. We are going into danger, while I don't want to kill anyone, we may have to, and I can't guarantee we'll all come out of this alive and safe. What do you say? Andrew?"

Andrew nodded. "I am here. We do this together."

"Boo?"

Boudicca's face was serious. "Thank you for asking. Consider this enthusiastic consent." She smiled.

"Daniel?"

"Hey, you couldn't get there without me, right?" Daniel smirked as he said it.

I looked at Daniel and sighed. "I could knock you out and take your boat keys."

"Whoa, dude, I'm only kidding. I'm in."

"Good. That out there is our target." I pointed out to the lake, toward the ship, shining in the light of the setting sun. "We'll discuss the plan en route." As I finished, my ragtag band grabbed their materials and we moved out.

End Act II

Chapter 27

Wednesday, June 24th

Distances always seem to close slowly over water. I watched the lights of the ship grow incrementally as the engine of the boat roared beneath us. Daniel sat beside me in his captain's chair, keeping the wheel steady as he watched his instruments. "I hope nothing is between us and the ship," he said, glancing at me, "with our lights off, we won't be able to see it."

"Well, keep her steady and..." I faltered, looking for something to say.

"Don't pretend to know nautical terms now. I'm just saying, this is already dangerous." Daniel slowed the engine. "We're getting close enough that sound might be an issue. I'm slowing us down and we should start whispering."

I pulled out my binoculars and scanned the deck. "Pull us quietly by the...stern? Where it..." I pointed, "that part, where that boat is." Daniel nodded and adjusted his course slightly. "I'm gonna need you to stay with the boat while we're in there."

Daniel paused before speaking, "I can watch your back."

"I know, but I hope to get out of this alive. So, I need to not have to swim to shore." Daniel smiled at the last part. "Okay?"

"Alright, but I'm gonna take the time to disable their boats." Daniel looked over. "Winona here is fast but running is easier if you tie some shoelaces together."

I smiled and patted him on the shoulder as I went past, heading down the ladder. Andrew was on the back, facing back towards the city. As I approached, he spoke softly. "I'm worried, Joe."

"I am too, Andrew. Anything specific?" I sat down next to him.

Andrew was silent for a moment, "There are spirits I could summon. Spirits who could help me in a fight. But I'm not sure if I should."

"Why wouldn't you?"

Andrew was quiet for a moment. "There are ceremonies. Ways in which warriors are invested by the tribe. These ceremonies are where the young warriors learn the true names of these spirits. I have not gone through them."

I was quiet, seeing if he would continue. When he didn't, I asked. "Are they still done?"

"Not quite the same way, but yes. You don't have to steal horses or count coup, but there is a ceremony." Andrew sighed. "When my uncle Albert went to Vietnam, some of the older men on the reservation did a ceremony for him. He did the same for my younger brother when we were teens, a rite of manhood."

"Oh." I understood. "But not for you."

"No, Albert was never...Albert never accepted me for who I am." Andrew's voice was tight. "I learned the names when my brother summoned them to demonstrate to me. I was never formally presented, but I could summon them, I'm sure."

"I get it." I put my hand on Andrew's shoulder. "Like I said, it's up to you, but if you want to hear my thoughts?"

Andrew thought for a moment. "Yes."

"I think it's a matter of respect. Your uncle never respected who you are, yet you still respect the traditions you both share. To me, that makes you the better man, more worthy of the rights of a warrior. Is your uncle still around?"

Andrew shook his head. "No. He died in a drunk driving accident twelve years ago. That was part of what brought on my moment of clarity."

I thought for a moment, watching the sunset behind us. "There's not really a non-corny way to say this, but what makes one a warrior comes from inside, not from a ritual."

"You're right." Andrew nodded. "There is no non-corny way to say that." He smiled at me while looking at me sideways.

"Fair." I shrugged. "Let me ask this. Do you feel this is the right time? I say trust your gut on that kind of thing."

Andrew sat quietly for a moment. "No. I have not trained with the spirits. They may change my approach in ways that leave unanticipated openings or cloud my perceptions."

"It's up to you, but I think I'd prefer not to have a partly cloudy Andrew." I jokingly pushed his shoulder. "There's something hinky about all this. You have the best bullshit detector I know. Keep it on and active."

Andrew nodded, thoughtful. "Thank you, Joe. I will." I patted him on the shoulder as I stood up and moved inside the cabin.

Boo looked up as I came in. She was seated in front of the book, reading by the faint light of an LED lantern. "Hey, just doing some last-minute cramming. Don't want to be naked at the exam."

"Have you found anything new?" I leaned against the countertop of the boat's small kitchen.

"I've been looking over the ritual, the sacrifice one, and I think I can contain or counterchannel the energy if we get there too late to stop it." Boo looked at the book, tracing some runic markings.

"Think or know?" I tried to keep the tension out of my voice.

"Think. I'm not entirely sure. Sorry." She winced slightly as she apologized.

"Well, let's hope it doesn't come to that. I cleared my throat. "For multiple reasons."

"Oh, yeah, of course. I'm just saying, and hey, worst case scenario, it'll probably take a few hours for something big enough to cause trouble to get here and destroy the city, so we can probably evacuate some people or something." Her smile faltered throughout and by the end she had a grim smirk.

"I'm not that hopeful. Chicago doesn't even have a plan for evacuation in the case of nuclear attack. Seriously, the futility is mentioned in the municipal code." I shrugged. "We have to stop things here."

A quiet knock came on the door. Andrew looked in. "Daniel says we're nearly there."

"Great." I pulled up my duffel bag and pulled out two bundles, handing them to Andrew and Boo. "Here. Kevlar vests, tasers and a bunch of police grade zip ties. We'll try and immobilize them quietly and quickly, but they are going to be too well defended for any sort of sleeping enchantment unless we soften them up first, so tase first, knock out with magic, then tie them up. No killing unless we can't help it. Everyone know how to put someone to sleep?"

Andrew nodded and Boo gave a patronizing smile. "They'll regret not inviting this witch to their baby's christening."

I rolled my eyes, then pulled out one more thing, tucking it into my satchel. "This is the emergency first aid kit. Just in case things go really wrong. And if they go really south, radio frequency 478.13750 code phrase 'Carthago delenda est.' that'll bring in the cavalry."

"That's what I like about you Joe, you aren't subtle with mission code words."

The three of us came on deck as Daniel pulled the boat up to the makeshift floating dock at the base of the ship. It bobbed slightly in the lake waves and two zodiac rafts with large outboard motors sat tied up beside it. I jumped out onto the dock and caught the line Boo threw me, tying it off loosely.

Andrew and Boo both joined me on the dock, and I signaled them to come close. I spoke softly, "There's probably a guard up top. I'm going to go up the ladder and subdue him, then lower him on that hoist." I pointed upwards, "Once you have him secured, follow me up. I'll drop a glow stick, if anything is coming."

They nodded their comprehension as I secured my backpack and began climbing, stopping briefly to check my equipment was secure. The climb was strenuous, but I spent enough time training on the rock wall at the gym that an unsecured ladder wasn't a challenge.

Near the top of the ladder, I stopped to catch my breath. It wouldn't do to reach the top and be too winded to overcome the guard. As I breathed, I whispered a soft incantation, invoking the names of wind and fire. Scrying had never been my strong suit, but I was excellent with elemental work, and I knew with a bit of work I could achieve some refraction, much easier than trying to balance one handed on a rope ladder while holding a mirror. The guard had her back to me, her thick robes blowing in the wind. She was a smaller woman, though it was dark enough that I couldn't make out features. Fighting women always required a bit of mental pushback against some of my upbringing. I pushed that down, she was part of a death cult, gender wasn't a primary concern. She was walking slowly toward the other edge of the ship, moving slowly between points on some sort of patrol. I swiftly finished my climb and vaulted the rail, being careful to land softly on my feet.

The guard paused and began to turn. In one fluid motion I ran forward and pulled my hand taser, flipping the switch as I leapt toward her. She scrambled with the air horn at her side, but I spoke the name of air and stifled the spirit within as I jabbed her with my weapon and spoke the word of sleep forcefully. She twitched as she went down and I stepped back ready to follow up if she began to get up, but she lay still, a few remaining twitches moved through her limbs as I bound her arms with a zip tie. I moved to the hoist. I pulled the bound and unconscious cultist over, listening for other motion. When none came, I wrapped ropes under her arms and began to lower her down, whispering a second suggestion of sleep to her spiritually weakened unconscious form. As I lowered her, I tried not to think about how they must have dragged Jennifer's unconscious form up this hoist just days ago.

As it reached the bottom, I let go and slumped against the side of the ship. The rest of the ship needed to be searched. Guards could be anywhere on it and time was not on my side.

In times of danger and stress, the mantle of the Chosen One sometimes pushes itself forward, taking me out of the present moment and into, it's hard to describe. It's kind of like a dream, in that it isn't a linear experience, but kind of all happening at once. It's not like accessing memories of the past, I can't replay the experiences of those who came before, just kind of experience the meaning of it, the sum total of their time bearing the mantle. There are meditation exercises I do to try and focus my own experiences for future Chosen Ones, it's part of how I have a good memory for events and such, but sometimes it happens, something touches some element of the mantle, and it rushes over me in a moment. That happened now, breathing heavily on the edge of the ship, I found myself connected to the image of Peter Massey, my predecessor, Chosen One from 1977.

Chapter 28

Wednesday, July 13th, 1977

Peter Massey was a month short of his 18th birthday in July 1977. Too young for the club life of New York City, he still lived it up with his cohort mates, former potential candidates for the position of Chosen One who were also being trained for leadership positions among the Conclaves.

On the night of July 13th, Peter and his cohort were at a party. I've heard more about this party than any I've ever attended myself. Peter had gone out along with Vasilij Orlov, the mystic of the group who came from a Russian noble expat family, Kenneth Ross, the class clown from Edinburgh, Tomas Pizarro, the Argentinian charmer or the group, and Clark Davis, the quiet Texan badass. They were all out trying to find somewhere to get a drink. Being 17, they couldn't get alcohol on their own, but Vasilij had some friends down in the Village who were having a party so they had set out to make the trip from Fifth Avenue to the lower west side. They were young and carefree. They felt excited and invincible

They were wrong. And it cost them their lives.

Every Chosen One is chosen by destiny to fulfill a prophecy, to save the world from an existential threat. Peter's prophecy was burned into my memory, a lesson in hubris.

> On the darkest night.
> In the city of smoke and grime
> The apple tarnished by man and money
> The scales will tip
> As life erupts from below
> And hope must descend, to rise again.

Normal, cryptic, understandable in its own esoteric way. But the conclave and the Chosen One had misinterpreted the first line.

Interpreting prophecy is a difficult art and the conclave had assumed that the darkest night referred to the winter solstice. Valid interpretation, but wrong. The five teenagers were wandering far from home, thinking the next potential darkest night was months away. But July 13th was the night of the New York City blackout.

They found the party around 8pm and by 9:30, things were going strong, the kids were drunk and happy when the power went out.

Clark had haltingly told my cohort of potentials about it as part of our education in the history of the Chosen One. At first, they didn't think much of it. They headed out into the streets and began to make their way home. But it quickly became clear that things were not that simple. As they moved through the city, people were reacting to the unexpected darkness with fits of intense violence.

Vasilij was the most spiritually sensitive of the group, the one that was most in touch with the magical landscape of the city. He noticed the weaves of magical force passing through the city and it was then they realized that the night had come. And more troublingly, it had come while they were far from their tools and mentors, unprepared for the dangers ahead.

The group debated what to do. I'll give Peter this, even faced with these obstacles, he still stepped up to his destiny. And the five kids headed into the darkness. And things began to go wrong.

Tomas was shot by police while the group tried to get supplies from a closed Rite Aid. They fled with only rudimentary supplies, entering the sewers below the city.

Kenneth was killed by a crocodile in the sewers. Not an alligator, a crocodile. The chaos in the streets was being caused by a cult of Sobek, trying to awaken human's reptile consciousness in order to return the world to savagery. They had brought crocodiles and were ready to fight.

Vasilij's mind slowly slipped away as they followed the paths of magic back to the source. Without their normal tools or the maps that would have helped them navigate, Vasilij had to try and follow the magical energies by feel, which left him wide open to their malign influence. It broke his mind before they arrived at the ritual site. They had to knock him out to prevent him attacking them. Last I heard, he was still in a Keeper run asylum in upstate New York and would try to eat anyone he was left alone with.

Having lost three of their companions along the way, Peter and Clark were hard pressed in their battle to stop the ritual. While they were able to stop the ritual, only Clark emerged, bearing the body of his best friend.

Peter was caught unprepared. He was not expecting that trouble could come at any time, as a result, he got lost and, in the end, it cost him his life. But I had much more, I had my tools, a sense of the enemies' plan and trained allies. Plus, I had 20 years' experience on him, hopefully all that would be enough.

Chapter 29

When Andrew and Boo made it up the ladder, I had a set of ship plans laid out on the deck. I signaled them close and spoke softly, "Simon pulled these from online. A ritual like what you described is going to need space, right?"

Boo nodded, "for protective circles and focusing symbols at the very least."

"Right. Well, open spaces are hard to come by on a ship like this. There's really only one type of space that would fit. The bottom of a cargo hold." I pointed to the plans. "This ship has 9. Five behind the center bridge and four forward from it."

"That seems easy. What's the catch?" Andrew knew me, knew how I thought.

"Well, it looks like the cargo holds are open to the sky, which makes sense if they are attempting something astronomical, but it means that we're going to have to look in from above." I pointed to the walkway over center of the ship. "We won't have surprise long."

Andrew nodded and checked his taser. "I'll cover our back as we go."

Boo unslung her simple wooden bow. "I can try to keep them at a distance."

"Don't kill anyone unless you have to." I looked seriously at Boo. "I'd like to get more information if we can. Plus, deaths are much harder to cover up than disappearances."

"Well, that's somewhere between flattering and morbid. I'm not exactly Kate Bishop with this thing." She waved off our lack of comprehension. "This pulls enough to pierce skin, but not break bone. It's discouraging, not deadly."

"Okay, Let's move out." I rolled up the plans and we moved along the raised edge of the cargo bay, towards the catwalk that led across the container bays, moving in a tight group. I walked ahead, peeking around corners with a handheld mirror. Behind me, Boo walked, arrow notched in her undrawn bow, book swinging in the satchel at her side. Andrew took up the rear, his hands spread to prevent backing into Boo.

We reached the center of the ship without seeing any motion and climbed the stairs quietly to the level of the catwalk. From further back, I heard some folks in heated conversation in Spanish. At least, I think it was Spanish. I could only hear one word in five and listening comprehension has never been my strong suit. I looked to Boo and Andrew and held a finger to my lips. The conversation was a ways away and seemed to be receding, so I gestured for them to follow as I moved towards it.

We came at them around a corner. I used my small mirror to get a peek, only two of them, and signaled to Andrew, pointing at him then to my right. He pointed to himself and then to his left in confirmation. I nodded, looked at Boo and the three of us moved around the corner. The two men saw us and moved into action. One of them lifted an air horn in one hand, but a well-placed arrow from Boo knocked it aside and drew a Spanish word that I recognized from kitchen accidents at the bar.

Andrew rushed the one on the left quickly, moving under Boo's arrow in a fighting crouch, the taser in his left hand, his right loosely clenched in a fist. The cultist dropped into a fighting stance of his own and swung a well telegraphed punch at Andrew's head. Andrew stepped into it, taking it glancingly off his raised shoulder and drove his fist into the man's solar plexus. The wind went out of him as he began to slump. Andrew jumped back and lit the taser before jabbing it into the man's side.

As he did this, I took a circular path towards the one Boo had shot. He pulled out a large folding knife with his off hand, fumbling it open while growling at me. I smiled back at him and spoke the name of fire, a burst of flame the size of a basketball bursting forward from my hands. As he stumbled back, he tripped, and Andrew deftly shifted his still lit taser from one prone figure to the other.

Things were still for a moment as we waited, tense. When nothing came, I smiled. "Looks like he brought a knife to a fire fight." Andrew looked at me like I was crazy and shook his head as he pulled zip ties and rope gags from his side and began to tie them up.

Boo giggled, "Normally I wouldn't find that so funny, but wow, does Adrenaline make me loopy."

I looked at Andrew, "Good move there." Mimicking his shoulder move and solar plexus punch.

"Big men often rely on reach. I've never been big, so I had to learn to fight close and to take a hit." Andrew finished tying up the men.

"We don't have time to take them back to the hoist. We'll have to move now." I pointed toward the center catwalk and Boo and Andrew nodded.

As we climbed the stairs to the catwalk, the wind gusted hard and pushed us against the rail. It was hard not to feel exposed up here. As we looked down, the open cargo bay yawned beneath us. Bay #9 was empty except for pools of stagnant water.

We moved past bays #8 and #7, also empty, and were on the edge of bay #6 when Andrew barked out his warning. "Shit. Guards." I ducked and turned to see three figures come up the catwalk stairway. One looked at us and raised high the air horn from his side. The blast was loud and carried around the ship. The other two pulled out small pistols and began firing at us, though we were out of accurate range and the sparks that flew were a few yards off.

"Move." I yelled, "there's some cover up ahead on the center bridge." We ran, occasional sparks flying around us as bullets flew by. We scrambled up the stairs and through the hatch into the central bridge area. But we had barely entered one door, which I briefly noted was marked with runes, before another group came in the opposite. Surrounded, my mind slipped once again, this time to Jakub Sobieski and the siege of Vienna.

Chapter 30

Jakub Sobieski's choosing came in an earlier period in Keeper history. Rather than an extensive network of standing conclaves based in cities, the associations were looser. So, when a group of seven learned men came to the court of Jan Sobieski in 1672, promising that his young son Jakub had a great destiny before him and that they would serve Jan as advisors while they trained young Jakub to the task, nobody knew quite what to expect.

But the prophecy was clear.

The crescent of the south

Will fall upon the eastmark

But winged knights beneath the eagle banner

Led by a royal prince

Will push back the tide.

Jan was skeptical. The King of Poland and Lithuania was young and hardy, unlikely to die soon. While Jan had drawn some support in the last monarchical selection, he was currently a pariah, considered an enemy of the state.

The Keepers assured him that they would help him with his troubles and were true to their word. Within two years, he had returned to prominence and aided by his military victories, now stood as prime candidate for King. In the choosing of May 1674, Jan became King and Jakub became the royal prince.

Over the next nine years, Jakub was trained by the Conclave in the Polish Court. For him, they focused on martial disciplines and battle leadership, anticipating his eventual test in battle. All the while, they kept a close watch on the Ottoman Empire, waiting for the prophesied moment.

It came in 1683 with the siege of Vienna, capital of Austria, the old Eastern Marches of the Holy Roman Empire. The Habsburgs had called for aid, but the negotiations stalled the departure of Polish forces until late summer. As they arrived in September, the situation was dire, but Jan swiftly took control of the armies present.

A few days later, Jan and Jakub were together in the Village of Gersthof at the outskirts of the city. The battle had been raging since before dawn, but they were confident that their allies had contained the Ottoman advances and maneuvered into the perfect position for a single strike. They held the high ground with 18,000 cavalry, including 3,000 winged hussars, the elite of the Polish forces.

While historians say Jan led the charge, the lore of the Keepers has Jakub the Chosen One charging out of the west, the setting sun behind him, at the head of 3000 elite knights, as his allies swiftly surrounded the Ottoman forces and drove back the tide. The battle that day was the pinnacle of Ottoman power in Europe, the tide was turned.

I considered my own situation. I was not so lucky. I had the meager force of a scrappy tobacconist and a nerdy witch against cultists that now surrounded us on both sides, surprise was lost.

Chapter 31

I didn't have long to think, though. As they moved into position and we tried to keep them from surrounding us entirely, one of them raised his gun. I braced for a shot but a voice from behind me yelled, "Idiota! Watch where you point that shit." As the man lowered his pistol, I realized that the close quarters could at least work in our favor, but six to three was terrible odds.

But they didn't seem ready to take advantage of them. Fighting in a coordinated group is difficult and as I looked back and forth, I could see that the cultists who had come from the front of the ship were dressed slightly differently than those from the back, betraying previous allegiances. The ones who came from the front covered their faces with some sort of voodoo face paint while the ones who had been pursuing from the rear had shaved heads with stylized central american designs tattooed on them.

Boo noticed the difference too. She called out to the trio with the shaved heads. "Hey, what brings el Sangre Derramada this far north?" She pronounced the Spanish well, rolling her r's skillfully. She looked at me, "Salvadoran Nihilists."

The one in the middle looked at her and spat "Fuck you, bitch!" before lunging at her. But that took his attention off Andrew, a big mistake. Andrew reacted swiftly and thrust his taser right into the cultist's groin. The man screamed in pain, his scalp tattoo flaring with energy as he struggled and crumpled to the ground.

And just like that, the fight began. In a fight this chaotic, it's easy to lose track of things. Everything shrinks to what is going on right in front of you. I do have a few clear moments, though.

I remember Boo at one point had one of the cultists in an arm lock of some sort, using his wrist and shoulder to maneuver him around like a piece of furniture she kept dodging behind, using him to keep another cultist just out of reach on the other side as the first cultist flailed helplessly with his other hand.

I remember Andrew getting grabbed from behind and pushing himself upwards into the cultists arms before coming down hard with both legs on the cultist's foot. The sound of the break was sickeningly loud, and the cultist lost his hold as he lost his balance.

At one point, I had pulled a fire hose off of the wall and was swinging it around, trying to keep the cultists out of reach with their knives. A thrown chair, I honestly didn't see who threw it, came from behind them and knocked one of them aside. I took the momentary distraction to whip out more hose and use the weight of the nozzle to wrap up the cultist who remained standing before kicking him hard in the diaphragm.

I began to turn towards the remaining cultists but was brought up short by a bellow from the cultist who Andrew had first felled with a taser blow. The bellow was tremendously loud and carried with it the echoes of the otherworldly. As I watched, the figure grew in height, superimposed on his features was a twisted skull which turned its rictus grin towards me and breathed out a burst of flame.

I backpedaled and swiftly brought the name of fire to mind, I spoke it firmly but with a subtle intonation, channeling the fire around myself and hurling it back towards the cultist. "Guys, we have a problem here!" The flames broke over the cultists outstretched arms, but he did not flinch.

Boo was entangled with one of the remaining cultists, shifting back and forth, trying to achieve a martial arts lock of some sort, but mostly moving around in circles. "It looks like...an avatar of Santa Muerte...I can banish it...but I need its name first." She said, as the two of them struggled.

Andrew heard that, caught my eye and delivered a hard shove to the cultist in front of him, backing him up against the wall. I moved in as Andrew shifted over, keeping the cultist engaged and backed up against the wall while Andrew began to stomp his feet and chant.

I only caught glimpses of the dance between the two of them, but it had a strange elegance. Andrew danced around, stomping his feet rhythmically as he called out syllables in a methodical fashion. The possessed cultist swung violently at Andrew and tried lashing out with fire, but Andrew, deeply in tune with the creature's movements, incorporated his dodges into his dance. As he came full circle around the creature, he cried out a series of syllables, a combination flavored with the glottal stops of Yucatec and the possessed cultist flinched at the utterance.

Boo shouted, "I'm up!" and broke away from the cultist she was fighting. I spoke the name of wind and blasted him back with a burst of wind. Boo moved forward, pulling a handful of salt out of her cargo pants pocket and drawing a small knife with her other hand. "I cast you out by salt and stone." She threw the salt at the creature in a spray. "I cast you out by blood and bone." She knelt and drew a quick cut from one of the fallen cultists, not deep but enough to draw blood. "Spirit from the world beyond/ hear your name and journey home." She spoke the name aloud, mimicking Andrew's delivery and the spirit screamed, separating itself from the cultist, who collapsed to the floor.

As he fell, there was a moment's pause, everyone briefly stunned before the battle came back into focus. It was down to two of them vs. three of us. I moved around the one Boo had been grappling, trying to get on the other side of him from Andrew, but he was swinging wildly with his short knife and yelled something in an unfamiliar language that sounded vaguely French.

At that, his companion who was facing off against Boo dove for the door to the back of the boat, dodging behind his friend who lunged to guard his escape. I saw the runes on the door as the cultist began to touch them in some order while murmuring. With grim realization, I yelled out "It's a trap!" and spoke the name of fire, hurling a blast of flame toward the door, but with a burst of energy, the fire spread against the wards now glowing all around the room. Andrew tased the final cultist and commanded him into unconsciousness, but we were trapped, like Chretien Fortier back in 1349.

Chapter 32

Thursday, January 1, 1349

Chretien Fortier saved the world and then died, a victim of his own hubris. An orphan of noble birth, Fortier was chosen while still a child and raised by a group of Keepers in Paris.

He was trained in all of the arts of the Keepers and had become a fine specimen of medieval manhood by the time his destiny came due. The details of his prophecy have been muddled over the years, but I do know a few things about his life, partially because he did something few Chosen Ones do, at least before their destiny is fulfilled, he had a son.

Chretien was 17 at the time, a man by the standards of the day and a ward of some of the most notable residents of Paris. He caught the eye of a young woman of noble birth and the two of them began a secret love affair. What can you say? Between courtly love and the threat of the Black Death, people were eager to make hay while the sun shone. The two of them married in secret, something much easier back then before social media, not that I was tempted.

Chretien lead his secret life for nearly a year and had fathered an infant son when destiny came calling. The plague was worsening, and Chretien had learned that its spread was being fueled by a group that had devoted themselves to an avatar spirit of Death, one of the earliest recorded Nihilist cults.

Venturing into the catacombs below Paris, he swiftly dealt with the cultists, dodging snares and traps, finally confronting the master of the ritual. The cultists spoke no language Fortier knew and when he killed the leader and the summoning circle began to collapse, he took the spirit of disease into himself, keeping it contained within his own body until he could get back to the Keepers and entrap it somewhere safe.

But he fucked up. He would never return home. Leaving the cult's lair, he stumbled into a warding trap that the cult had set off and flush with success, focused on keeping the spirit in, he blindly tripped it.

Fortier was trapped within a magical circle, unable to read the strange characters that made up the magics, later Keepers have theorized that they were Viking runes and that the Nihilists were a cult devoted to Hela, but we don't have a real record. Normally, he could have waited and hoped for rescue, but trapped within him was a spirit of plague and disease. Time was not on his side.

The agents of the Keepers sent after him found him three days later, dead of the plague within the circle. When they were finally able to unweave it, they found parchment on him, written in his own blood, telling the tale of what happened and revealing the existence of his wife and child.

Several things came of his death. With the spirit of plague contained, the plagues sweeping Europe lessened in intensity and died out. At least he fulfilled his destiny.

Second, the Keepers decided that it was forbidden for the Chosen one to wed. Too much danger in the dilution of focus and worry about the potential inheritance of those born of the Chosen One. Those who had fulfilled their prophecy were free to do as they will, but only if they survived of course.

And those who Chretien left behind? The Fortier family was embraced into the Keepers, and persists to this day, including such famous members as Scaevola Fortier, the traitor I chased now. It was Scaevola who told me the story of his ancestor and dispensed one of his million nuggets of wisdom, "Just because the enemy is dead, doesn't mean his tools are." Scaevola, who waited just beyond these wards.

Now, I was trapped like Chretien, contained by an unknown spirit. But I had something he didn't. Friends.

Chapter 33

We stood in the room in the silence that fell as the fires burned away. Boo looked over at me. "Thanks, Admiral."

I looked at her in confusion. "Admiral?"

She returned my look, incredulous. "Admiral Ackbar? It's a trap? Return of the Jedi?"

Andrew looked at me, "even I knew that one, Joe." He knelt over the twitching form of the cultist and began to zip tie his wrists.

"Sorry, I had a very restricted set of media I was allowed to watch. I haven't gotten around to it yet." I was flustered. "Still, we're trapped. There's a ward over the room and unless we can figure out the spirit powering the ward, we're trapped here."

Boo smiled, "One. We'll fix the Jedi thing once this is done. Two. Let's get to work figuring the spirit out. Did you see the glyph?"

I focused for a moment, trying to bring it to mind. As the image formed, I spoke. "Tree of life, surrounded by an image of the room. He was touching Chokhmah as he invoked the name. I couldn't hear it, but that's a start, right?"

"More than a start," Boo pulled out the book and began flipping through marked pages. "I have the wards and such labelled here. It'll just be a minute." She flipped to a page and let out a yip of excitement. Turning it to me, she pointed. "Like this?"

"Yes." As far as I could tell, this was identical to the glyph on the door. "Is the spirit's name there?"

Boo's smile widened. "Yup. Give me two minutes and I'll have this set." I nodded and helped Andrew move the bound prisoners to the side of the room, leaning them so they wouldn't have trouble breathing.

Andrew grunted as we dropped one and touched his arm. I noticed the blood staining his shirt. "Here." I reached for his arm and pulled back the sleeve, there was a long shallow cut on his forearm. I pulled out the first aid kit and took out an alcohol wipe, cleaning off the wound. "This doesn't look too deep; a butterfly bandage should do it." Andrew flinched slightly but let me continue my work. Soon, I had his arm wrapped in a light layer of gauze.

"Thanks." Andrew's response was terse but genuine. We exchanged nods as he patted me on the shoulder.

As we put the last cultist against the wall, Boo spoke up. "Okay, I think I have this done. If I've got this right, the ward is fueled by Raziel, chief of the erelim."

"Archangel of secrets." I spoke automatically, Boo nodded in agreement. "Alright, summon him up, let's get out of here."

Boo began to chant in Latin, reading from the book and half a minute later, an indistinct presence, humanoid but hazy appeared in the center of the room as Boo continued chanting. As Boo grew silent, the figure spoke, its words echoing against the wards.

"Those who would pass my ward must pay my price. Who is willing?"

"I am." The three of us spoke nearly in unison.

"Very well. My price is one secret. For that, you may pass my ward." The figure extended shadowy hands outwards, as if to embrace or accept and offered bundle.

We looked between ourselves. Andrew stepped forward. "When I was 18, I tried to kill myself." His face was tightly emotionless, and he didn't look at Boo or myself as he spoke. As he said the words, the world dropped away around us.

We stood invisibly on the wide-open prairie. As we watched, a much younger Andrew walked slowly towards a set of train tracks. His face had softer features, his cheeks were streaked with tears and one of his eyes was heavily bruised. Young Andrew approached and sat cross-legged on the tracks. Off in the distance, the whistle of a train blew loudly.

Andrew closed his eyes and began to weep openly. As the train drew closer and closer, the sky began to rumble, and rain began to fall. As the whistle blew loudly, the engine coming on fast and unstoppable, another sound joined it, a fierce cry from the sky. At this, Andrew threw open his eyes in surprise and saw before him a massive figure in the sky outlined by lightning. He spoke in surprise, "Thunderbird!" And the with the echo of the spirit's name, he was gone from the tracks, and we were back on the ship.

"Okay." Boo exhaled sharply, a bit shaken, "I knew my mother was going to run away, but I didn't tell anyone." This time, as the world dropped away, we found ourselves on the porch where I had met Boo earlier. Teenage Boo was sitting at the table, a ticket envelope in front of her, waiting. Her hair was cut short with a longer fringe in front, and she wore a loose L7 t-shirt.

A woman walked out the front door looking worried. Boo spoke up, "Looking for this, Mom?" Boo held up the ticket envelope.

Her mother's face fell as she saw her. "Boudicca, you don't understand."

"That you're going to leave us? I think I understand that pretty well." Boo's face was full of emotions competing for dominance, a twitch of anger, a slight downturn of sadness, a furrow of confusion.

"I didn't understand what it meant. I thought I would be able to just let go, to move on and return to the coven. But he hasn't faded in my mind. And I haven't faded in his. He was looking for me, I saw it in the mirror. Down in New Orleans. Where we met. Where you were conceived."

"Eew, I don't need to hear that part." Teenage disgust won out on Boo's face.

"Aren't you even a little curious about your father?" Boo's mother spoke softly.

"Mom, you'll be cast out of the coven if you do this. You'll be alone." Boo was calm as she said this, quiet. "Why don't you ask Agnes? Maybe she'd let you if you explained."

"She wouldn't. There are traditions and we follow them. No matter what sorrow they bring." Boo's mother looked downcast and then looked up to her daughter. "Are you going to tell her?"

Teenage Boo was silent for nearly a minute, thinking hard. "No." She finally said quietly, pushing the tickets across the table. "I don't understand what you're doing, but I won't stop you."

Boo's mother came over and picked up the tickets and embraced the seated Boo, kissing her on her forehead. "Little Boudicca, never forget that your mother loves you."

The world faded around them and the adult Boo sniffled and looked away, pulling a bandana out of her pocket and wiping her eyes.

It now fell to me. Neither Andrew nor Boo looked at me, both somewhat lost in their own pasts. I took a deep breath. "I think I could have saved Trevor, and if I had, I wouldn't be the Chosen One." I closed my eyes. I wasn't sure I could face this.

It was the feeling of the water on my face that brought me out of it. I opened my eyes to see the lake in turmoil and was brought back to that day. It was a normal training exercise, we had all been sent out on the Lake in crews of two in Scorpions. It was a race from Edgewater beach to the South Shore country club and back. The way down had been windy but calm, but returning back north the storm had rolled in. Trevor and I had passed Daniel and Gunter's torn sail on our way back, the two of them fighting and we had seen Bertie and Underwood's boat turn towards shore as we passed the downtown harbor, but Trevor was determined to go on and win.

We were North of Montrose Harbor when we capsized. A big wave blew in on a major gust and took us over. We tried to right the ship, but the current kept driving us towards the broken concrete off the lakeshore and we finally made a break for it, swimming as hard as we could. We hadn't been wearing our life jackets out of twelve-year-old bravado and the buffets of the waves kept pushing and pulling us back and forth. I reached the concrete first, climbing up the ladder as the storm crashed over me. I had just reached the top and turned around to look for Trevor when I heard him cry out and a loud thud. I looked over and saw him thrown hard into the concrete shore before being swept back out, then I lost sight of him.

I watched now as I looked around in the water. I saw myself frantically waver between diving into the water and running for help. There was nobody else around, but I could see the fear in my eyes as I looked back towards the crashing waves. And I saw myself turn and run towards the beach, frantically looking for help, as things faded.

We all stood around, looking at each other. I felt exposed and raw.

Raziel nodded and spoke. "Very well, you three may pass my ward." The figure glowed with energy for a moment and the three of us then the wards glowed with a faint luminescence to match.

Andrew moved first and opened the door. He looked back at us and nodded before passing through to onto the catwalk. Boo and I swiftly followed.

As we moved out, we heard the chanting. Just before us, at the base of one of the cargo bays, was laid out a ritual. Ornate diagrams made up the circle and four participants, all bearing ritual tools, stood at equal points around circle. It only took a moment to recognize one of them as Scaevola, reading from a ponderous tome. It reminded me viscerally of the day I was anointed as the Chosen One. I recalled the day from my memory, the first one that I anchored in the mantle of the Chosen One.

Chapter 34

It was my 13th birthday and I waited in an antechamber, outside the central ritual chamber in the Chicago Conclave's headquarters. I adjusted the robe I wore. It was newly tailored, but as scratchy a garment as I had ever worn. In my mind, I recited the words I had been practicing, the counter responses to the statements I knew were coming.

Over the last week, representatives had come from conclaves around the world. I had helped welcome delegations from London, Buenos Aires, Qingdao, Goa and Cape Town. I knew that several of my cohort were helping entertain other visiting dignitaries. Gunter was responsible for the Munich delegation, including his uncle the Count.

Notably absent was the delegation from Boston. After Trevor's death, a coolness had reigned between the two conclaves, though Anthony assured me it would pass.

At the ring of the bell, I stepped through the parted curtain into the ritual chamber. The attendees were arrayed around the edges of the room with the center taken up by the ritual circle. At the corners stood four hooded figures, and at the end of the aisle up which I walked was an altar. Behind it stood two other hooded figures. I hesitated briefly as I saw all this arrayed before me, but Anthony, his robe neatly pressed, stepped up behind me, placing his hand on my shoulder. "Come Joseph, your destiny awaits."

The two of us walked up the aisle towards the circle, his hand still on my shoulder. As we reached the edge of the circle, we stopped and one of the figures at the altar spoke. "Who speaks for this boy, unknown to our mysteries?" The hood stayed down, but I knew Casimir's voice.

Anthony spoke, "I speak for my sister's son, now a man and ready to open his eyes."

Casimir responded. "Very well, let him enter and pass the four tests."

I stepped into the circle and turned to my right. I was nervous, but not about the tests. These were ritual, I knew the answers better than I knew anything with how much they'd been drilled into us. But in front of everyone, I was not sure. It had been less than a year since Trevor died, the one we had all assumed to be the likely candidate. While his death proved he wasn't chosen by destiny, it had still been a shock and that hung over the proceedings.

I reached the northern point of the circle. The hooded figure raised his hand and I stopped as he asked, "Why do we fight?"

Without pause, I replied, "To end those who would tear down progress and to protect those who cannot protect themselves."

The figure pulled back his hood to reveal Clark, who smiled as he handed me a roman short sword and scabbard attached to a belt. "May your arm be true, and your blade cut through deception and danger alike." He aided me in securing the belt and I moved on.

I continued to the right, reaching the western point. Another hooded figure raised his hand. As I stopped, he said, "Why do we seek power?"

"As the steady hand holds the tiller, we keep the ship from the reefs." I intoned.

The figure pulled back his hood, revealing Simon and he handed me a heavy coin. "May you always control everything you need to prosper." I ceremonially placed the coin in a small bag and secured it to my sword belt.

At the South point of the circle, the figure asked, "Why do we study the mysteries?"

I replied, "From deeper understanding comes higher aspiration. We study that we may do more than others of lesser ambition."

This time, Prospero revealed himself as he presented me with a wand. "May your mind be always quick and may the world obey your words." I tucked the wand into my belt opposite the sword as I moved on.

I approached the eastern edge of the circle. There stood the fourth hooded figure. The twisted shoulder left little doubt as to his identity. Scaevola spoke, "How do we deal with those who betray us?"

My voice cracked slightly as I spoke. "With death, that their betrayals not lay us bare." I stood straight, unwavering before the stern Keeper.

Scaevola pulled back his hood and presented a filled cup. "May your eyes remain clear and unclouded." He favored me with a narrow but genuine smile as he passed me the cup. I drank the water within, and attached the cup to the clip on my belt.

Anthony stepped behind me and guided me towards the central altar, speaking as we proceeded. "This boy has passed the tests and is prepared to hear his destiny and to accept it as a man." He led me forward and I stood before the altar. I was aware of a hush in the room. This was the first time the prophecy, my prophecy, was to be shared.

Ephraim stepped forward on the altar, pulling back his hood. His voice echoed around the chamber.

"In the city built on fire and blood
Beside the great saltless water
An Elder Spirit Reversed
Will set loose the flood.
The waters will rise
And the city will fall."

The sounds died away as he finished as Casimir stepped forward. "Joseph Samuel Palevsky, I hereby invest you with the mantle of the Chosen One, selected by destiny to save the world."

The cheers echoed in my mind as I felt the power flow through me. I was no longer a scared boy, but a man who must now bear the weight of the world.

Chapter 35

I watched below us, as Scaevola directed his ritual. At the edges of the circle stood three of his cultists, chanting in unison as Scaevola directed the proceedings. In the center, Jennifer lay bound upon an altar.

Andrew, Boo and I watched as they moved about the circle. I leaned over to Boo as Andrew kept watch. "How much time do we have?"

Boo flipped quickly to a page late in the book, on which a diagram similar to the one laid out below was laid out. She skimmed the page, flipped a few pages further and her finger settled on a point in the ritual script. "Hmm. It looks like they just started the final segment, as in, just moments ago. I'd guess there's less than an hour, but this is a very weird ritual."

"Alright, I guess we're just in time." I snorted to myself. "So much for Scaevola's advice."

"What?" Boo's response was abrupt.

"Scaevola always told me you could never count on arriving in the nick of time, that the enemy would never wait for you...among other things." Recalling the advice given by the traitor below set me ill at ease.

Andrew looked back from the ritual, directly at me. "Joseph, you asked me to look for anything...hinky." He paused before the last word. "That ritual is not what it seems."

I looked at him and nodded. "Show me."

Andrew kneeled and pointed. "There are ways people move, flows of energy that define them. They are not right around Jennifer and Scaevola. "

"When you say not right, what do you mean, is it an illusion? A trap of some sort?" I watched the proceedings below, everything seemed in deadly earnest to me.

Andrew breathed in and placed his hand on my shoulder, looking me straight in the eyes "Listen as I tell, look as I show." I felt a tingling in my mind as he gestured and spoke.

Then I saw it, as if through Andrew's eyes. Jennifer was bound and acting scared, but it was just that, an act. There was no real fear in her, just a show. As I looked to Scaevola, I could see her acting mirrored. He was not a man ready to make a sacrifice. He stood defensive, waiting for something, nervous and determined.

I pulled back, blinking my eyes. "This is a lie. But why?"

Boo looked to both of us, "What's going on?"

I breathed deeply, "He's not going to kill her, and she knows it."

Boo flipped through the book and moved her lips silently, as if adding things together. "Maybe there's some other focal point? But no, the circle is built to channel a sacrifice. But there isn't tolerance built in for that level of energy. I don't know."

"Boo," I looked at her, "if they were to complete that ritual, could you contain it?"

Boo breathed in and out, looking at the book, "I think so."

"Think or know?" I asked, catching her eye.

"Think. Way too many variables for certainty, I'd go as high as 80%. And if I fail, I can probably make it so that the ritual won't summon the full force, it'll only kill everyone on the ship. If that's a comfort." Boo looked apologetic but firm.

"That'll have to do." I stood up. "You two stay here. I'm going to try something."

"What?" Boo and Andrew spoke in a unified hush.

"Well, there's something not right here. I'm going to see if I can stop it." I touched the tattoo on my chest, whispering up my guardian spirit. "I can take a few of them, and maybe get some answers first."

Andrew looked angry and Boo confused. I continued. "I'm not saying don't help if shit starts, but I have a feeling me going in alone might get me more answers."

Andrew relaxed a bit, but still looked concerned. "It's a long walk down, don't start trouble without alerting us."

We both looked to the scaffolding leading down into the cargo bay. "Okay, I'll use the word shenanigans if I am going to start something."

Boo snorted, "Yeah, that won't sound suspicious. Why not dastardly or nefarious? I'm sure those'll slip in easier."

I looked at her and smiled. "Tell you what, any of those will do just fine. Just be ready if everything goes south. The fate of Chicago may be at stake here."

I began my descent.

Chapter 36

As I descended the stairs built into the scaffolding, I watched the scene below me unfold. The chanting of the three cultists continued to drone as Scaevola made the ritual motions with an ornate knife I guessed was for the pretend sacrifice. Without Andrew's aid, the scene was less clear to me, but his movements still had a ring of falsehood to them.

Much of the area deep in the cargo bay was masked by shadows and years of practice sneaking out for fun had taught me something about being quiet, so I reached the bottom of the stairs without any hue and cry. Only a few feet away was a cultist, chanting aloud from an open folder, absorbed in his task.

I took a deep breath and pulled out my taser. I wondered for a moment if any Chosen One before me had gone in so unsure of what to do. None came to mind. I lunged forward, ready to improvise.

The cultist screamed as I jammed the taser into his kidney, crumpling to the ground in pain. The sudden shift in noise set everyone in motion. The cultists to either side dropped their folders and pulled out knives, moving toward me as I conjured forth a ball of flame, holding it in the air above my hand ready to throw.

"Stop!" the two of them were brought up short by Scaevola's shout. He strode forward towards the altar. "He is too late."

"Hold it!" I gestured with the flame and held up my other hand towards Scaevola. He paused, a few steps away from the altar and the bound figure of Jennifer. "Your man's not dead, just out for a bit."

"Did you come here alone? It's three against one, Joseph, what hope do you think you have?" Scaevola stood, not advancing, eyeing the flame in my hand.

"Hope? I'm not here for hope. I would like some answers, though." I tried to keep my expression diffident, though I was sure some fear showed through. "Why did you do it?"

"Why? You ask me why?" Scaevola gave a sharp bark of laughter. "One does not question the Deluge!"

"The Deluge?" I shook my head. "Are those your new friends?" I gestured to the two cultists with my hand not currently occupied supporting a ball of fire. "Don't seem like much to me."

"The Deluge was old when the Keepers were learning to write. Our ancient order will sweep away this unjust world and all that will be left is us. You cannot hope to stop us now." Scaevola's look was intense, but I thought about Boo's research on the book and its provenance. I needed to be sure, I decided on a plan, it was risky, but I didn't have a lot of options here.

"I'm too late?" I tried to look unsure. "Really more ancient?" I kicked myself inside for the phrasing, but Scaevola seemed to respond to it.

Scaevola drew himself up. "The ways of the Deluge predate Ancient Rome. Our arcane lore is timeless. These associates of mine may be new to our ways, but we have always been here and we will be all that is left and will rule the new world."

I let my doubt be plain on my face, then I released the ball of fire, letting it dissipate. "Well, if you can't beat 'em, join em. Where do I sign up?"

Scaevola looked unsure, "What do you mean?"

"I mean, where do I sign up? I know when I'm outnumbered. You always told me never attack against overwhelming odds. I'm all alone at this point, and the wisest of my teachers is here, so how do I join the Deluge?" I held back my fear as I watched Scaevola watch me, uncertain. "I'm in."

"You would simply let us sacrifice your true love?" He gestured towards Jennifer with his knife.

As if on cue, Jennifer spoke up, "Joe? Joe are you there?" I shut out her words and hoped I was right.

"Okay, let's not get carried away here. We went on two dates, one and a half, really. And it's simple. I prefer my life to hers. If my choice is between both of us dying or just her, I choose her." I stared at Scaevola's eyes, searching me, and tried not to hear Jennifer's whimpers of fear. "Besides, if you are on this side, then why can't I join you. We'd be more powerful together."

Scaevola and I watched each other for a long moment, neither of us moving. I saw his face waver and twist into an expression of contempt. He looked to the people to either side of me. I couldn't see their expressions, but their body language in my peripheral vision betrayed uncertainty. "No." he said as he reached into a hidden pocket in his robe, drawing forth a heavy pistol.

I scrambled backwards instinctively as I summoned up a wind buffer, but as Scaevola raised the pistol, it was aimed not at me but at the cultist to my right.

Scaevola murmured as he fired and the bullet caught the cultist in the chest, exploding outwards. The other cultist turned in alarm in time for Scaevola's second bullet to pierce his eye. The words died on my lips as Scaevola pointed the gun at me. "Joseph Samuel Palevsky. Can't you do anything right?" His voice seethed with anger.

"What?" I was at a loss for words, I hadn't expected this, I could only repeat my feeble question. "What?"

"You can't even fulfill your god damned destiny right. You had the advantage, the unarmed cultists, the free-flowing energy, you could have made short work of this. But you had to treat it like it was some sort of game. You are a disgrace."

I snapped back to the present a bit with that. "Hey. I don't know what you want me to do here." My speech started slow but found momentum.

"What I want you to do?" Scaevola barked out a harsh laugh. "Do your duty! Destroy the evil cult and win the girl! I want you to fulfill your destiny so we can all move on."

"You want me to kill you?" I was incredulous, though I tried to keep my voice calm.

"Kill me, end this threat, rescue the girl!" He gestured nonchalantly at the bound Jennifer. "The prophecy will be fulfilled, and this will all be over. You will get your happy ending."

I took this in as he said it and I watched him. He was offering some sort of deal...was this a suicide thing...was Jennifer really involved in this...what did this mean about the prophecy...had he turned against the Keepers just to throw it all away for my sake? A moment passed before I broke the silence. "No."

"No?" His response was contemptuous.

"I think you heard me." I began backing slowly towards the stairs.

"Stay where you are." Scaevola pointed the gun menacingly.

"I'm not going to do that." I spoke slowly as I continued to move. "Whatever is going on here, whatever it is you want me to do, I'm not going to do it. You're the one who told me, never do what the enemy wants you to do. Besides, I don't think whatever you're planning works if you kill me, so I'm leaving." I was at the base of the scaffold by now, still watching Scaevola.

"Get back here!" He waved the gun at me, trying to be threatening, but no shot came.

I began swiftly climbing the stairs as he hurled invectives. I was startled by a single gunshot as I climbed but couldn't see what was happening below. As I reached the top, Boo caught my arm. "The shot?" I asked.

Andrew spoke from the edge of the cargo bay. "Killed the henchman you disabled. We need to get out of here." We began to hustle back to the boat.

Chapter 37

As we climbed down the ladder to the boat, my mind raced. What had just happened? Was I doing the right thing? If I hadn't been sure going in, Scaevola's actions had me convinced that everything I knew was wrong.

On the hunch of a friend and the quick research of a woman I'd just met, I had just put the entire world in danger. But I had been right, right? Scaevola had wanted me to kill him. And Jennifer seemed to be in on it. To know she was in no real danger. Was this just a more elaborate trap? Some way of me fulfilling his plan? Maybe some way of turning the energy of the chosen one against me? My feet unexpectedly hit the floating dock, interrupting my train of thought.

I jumped into the boat. "Daniel, let's go."

Daniel looked at me, "Where's Jennifer?"

"She's not coming."

Daniel looked distressed, "Shit, man, I'm sorry. Were we too late?"

I looked to Andrew and Boo before answering, but their expressions gave me no guidance for how to answer. "Not really. But the world should be safe."

"Should be? What the fuck happened?" Daniel looked between all of us for an explanation.

"Just get us out of here!" I yelled and everyone jumped. "Sorry. Please, just get us back to shore." Daniel moved to the bridge and got the boat underway as Andrew untied us from the dock.

We rode in silence for a while for a while, all of us lost in our own thoughts. Boo finally broke the silence. "Joe, what happened back there? Why did he want you to kill him?"

"I... don't know. Maybe it would have powered the ritual or something? Some kind of suicidal endgame?" I shrugged, not looking up.

Boo shook her head. "No, I mean, not unless he was a sacred virgin of some sort. And I mean a vow sanctified by a greater power sacred virgin, not just never been laid."

"No. On both counts." I looked up at her. "I know from my Uncle Casimir that Scaevola used to have a regular girlfriend before he came to Chicago."

"So, no. He wouldn't have triggered the ritual." Boo opened the book. "What did he mean about the ancient ways? Do you think he knows the book is fake?"

"I'm sure of it. He didn't take things on faith. He doubled checked the math at restaurants. He wouldn't have been suckered by something like this. Hell, he might have written it himself" I rose and began to move about the deck. The boat was small, so I just paced in a tight line.

"Could he have?" Andrew's comment was quiet. He sat with his hands clasped and his elbows on his knees.

"I don't know. It feels like there's a lot I don't know right now." I stopped, looking out at the city as we drew closer.

Daniel called down from the bridge. "We're coming in, should I radio for backup?"

I looked up at him. "No, I'll make my way home on my own. I need some time to think."

"What about the prisoner?" Daniel leaned out and pointed to the cabin. "Shouldn't I arrange pickup?"

I cursed to myself. I'd forgotten about the first guard. I looked into the cabin and saw her there, still in a magically induced sleep. "No, I'll...just a sec." I turned to Andrew and Boo. "I need answers and I'm not sure where else to get them. Did either of you drive?"

Andrew shook his head, but Boo nodded. "I live in Hyde Park; you can't get by without a car. My grandmother's house has some secure rooms, too. They're mostly for magical detox, but we could hold her. But..."

I looked at her, "what?"

Boo sighed. "Right. You'll have to promise no torture. Period. I want to help, but there's a line I won't cross."

I looked startled. "Right, of course. I promise, I wouldn't..."

"Just being clear. "Boo looked away and began packing up her stuff. "I've heard stories about what happens to Keeper prisoners."

I paused, troubled, before I went up to the bridge. "Daniel, I'll handle the prisoner. You were on guard duty long enough."

"Alright." Daniel nodded as we pulled up to the dock. "I could use the fucking sleep."

"You get some. I'll talk to you soon." I looked at Daniel, steering the boat, a concerned look on his face. "It'll all be okay. Things just weren't what I expected out there."

End Act III

Chapter 38

Thursday, June 25th

One peculiar part of being the Chosen One is that I have protocols for waking up. Trained into me from a young age by Clark and Scaevola, I go through a short procedure whenever I regain consciousness.

It's a checklist of sorts, assessing any situation for peril and readiness. Do I know where I am? Am I wounded; can I move/speak? Has time passed? Do I have my tools? Over the years, I've learned to do these things subtly. Nothing spoils a morning after like leaping out of bed yelling 'Where the fuck is my wand?'

Today's inventory was more complicated. The first thing I realized is that I did not recognize the room I slept in, which put me on alert. I looked around, there weren't any obvious threats. I was lying on a couch under an afghan, still wearing undershirt and pants. My boots were beside the bed and my shirt and Kevlar hung over an easy chair nearby.

Scanning the room, I appeared to be in a quirkily decorated living room. Art dotted the mantelpieces and sat atop the baby grand piano. There was an elaborate wooden sculpture hanging from the ceiling that looked like some sort of fantastical airship. Searching, I found my bag of materiel beside the couch, with my taser and zip tie bundle next to it.

I got up, and as I did, I recalled the events of last night and sat back down. I had faced down Scaevola and called his bluff. Had it really been a bluff? Scaevola had all but admitted that things weren't what they seemed. But what did that mean?

As I sat there, I saw the note. Sitting on the chair next to my bed was a folded note card with my name on it. I picked it up and read. *Joe, you were asleep when I had to leave. I am doing some research, my grandmother would like to talk to you, she'll be on the back porch. -Boo. P.S. this is just to say don't touch the plums in the icebox, I'll fucking cut you.* I snickered. So, I was at Boo's house. That made sense. I remembered coming down here. I had better make myself presentable.

I put on shirt and boots and a quick search revealed a half bath under the stairs. I splashed water on my face and got my hair in order, gargling with a bit of salt water from my magic kit.

Leaving the powder room, I looked around. The back porch was not hard to find, right off of the kitchen, and there was an old woman, sitting in a rocking chair, reading a book. I stepped through the screen door and cleared my throat. "Hello ma'am. I understand this is your home."

The woman looked up as I spoke. She was in her late 70's at least, but her eyes were very clear, piercing even. "You understand correctly." She spoke calmly, her finger saving her place in her book.

"Thank you for your hospitality last night." I gave a long nod.

"You weren't in any shape to go anywhere, so it was for everyone's good. Can you make coffee?"

The question surprised me briefly, but I rallied. "I can, ma'am."

"The materials are in the kitchen. I take two fingers of milk in mine." She reopened her book and resumed reading.

A brief time later, I re-emerged with two cups of coffee. Boo's grandmother gestured at the second rocking chair on the porch. I set the coffee cups on the table between the chairs and then sat. "I hope this turned out well, I couldn't find a tablespoon, so I had to estimate, ma'am."

She blew on the coffee and took a sip. "It's fine and call me Agnes. We have some things to talk about, Joe." I sipped my coffee and continued to listen. "First, you are welcome here, everyone is, but you need to understand the rules of my house. By accepting my hospitality, you agree to cause no harm to anyone else under my protection."

"Of course, ma'am...Agnes." I corrected myself at her glance.

"Two, the young woman upstairs in my attic. She is also my guest while she is here. Do you understand?"

It took me a moment to realize who she was talking about. My prisoner. "Right. Is she secure up there? I need a chance to talk to her."

Agnes nodded, "I'm willing to have her here for a bit. Boo says she may be a danger to herself and others."

I jolted forward at the suggestion, remembering the spattering of blood as her fellow cultist had killed himself before me. "Oh my god, suicide, I didn't think. Is there anything..."

Agnes raised her hand to cut me off. "Don't worry. She's safe. Ivan wouldn't let her hurt herself."

"Ivan?" I wasn't sure anyone could easily stop someone as determined as the Deluge members proved to be.

"My Domovoi. He enforces the rules here. No harm means no harm."

I sat back down, relieved. A powerful house spirit could protect people from all manner of harm, even self-inflicted. "Thanks."

"Don't thank me. I'm not doing this for you. I'm doing this because it's the right thing." Agnes looked straight at me. "Which brings me to three. If you are lying or trying to take advantage of me or Boudicca, I will curse you as only an ancient witch crone can. Do you understand?"

I paused, listening and composing my response. "I understand. I take the responsibilities of guest and host very seriously and promise that I am not intentionally lying to you." I took a moment before continuing. "I say intentionally, because I am not sure what is going on here. I am trying to get to the heart of a matter that is proving to be very confusing, but I promise to tell the truth as I understand it in the moment."

"Oh, honey." Agnes reached over and patted my knee. "Keep grappling with it. Truth is an elusive goal, but as long as you're acting in good faith, I won't bring about your grisly end." The kindly smile of the old woman only partially softened her words. At that, she returned to her book with such decisiveness that I understood my audience with the lady of the house was complete.

Chapter 39

I made my way upstairs as Agnes directed me. It was time to meet my prisoner. The attic was reached through a narrow staircase that led up from the second-floor landing, winding upwards to a small wooden door. I knocked gently upon it, disturbing the silence of the attic.

When I heard nothing, I knocked again, louder. "I'm coming in. I'd just like to talk." I opened the door and immediately saw a chair speeding towards my head. As I began to duck, the chair stopped in mid-air and gently floated down to the floor, alighting softly on its legs.

I stared at the chair and as I looked, up, the woman across from me was staring at it too. When she saw me looking at her, her face became defiant. She had removed her hood and I saw her face, young and bold. She looked to be of South Asian descent, but I couldn't tell more than that. If she'd ordered a drink at Brando's, I would have carded her.

She stared at me for a moment and then gestured to the chair. "How did you do that?" Her words had a clipped quality to them, hints of an Indian accent tempered by time in the US.

"I didn't." I stepped in and closed the door behind me. We remained standing on opposite sides of the room. "That's the spirit of the house. He won't allow harm to be done." I looked around the room. There were small rooftop windows and a door leading to what must be a bathroom. There was a single bed and a desk without a chair, I guessed that was where she had gotten her weapon. There was a shelf with some well-worn paperbacks on it beside the bed, but the room was otherwise sparse.

"Is he what won't let me open the windows?" I shrugged at her question. "So, I am your prisoner again." She seemed slightly deflated as she said this, though her expression remained defiant.

"Well..." I paused, hearing her question. "Again?"

"I've been in Keeper custody before. I won't tell you anything. Your mind games won't win you any favors. And if you try anything..." She shivered slightly, tensing her muscles in anger to stop herself.

I moved into the room and took the chair over near a window. I set it down and sat, facing her. "You aren't a prisoner. Not really."

"Why can't I leave, then?" Her retort seethed with anger.

"It's for safety. So, you don't harm yourself or anybody else." I looked at her, trying to seem friendly, "I just want to talk, find out what's going on."

"When does the bad cop get here?" She looked at me with an angry sarcasm, gesturing towards the door.

"There is no bad cop, this isn't an interrogation. Let me start over. My name is Joe." I tried to keep frustration out of my voice.

"You think I don't know who you are!" She shouted.

I was taken aback by the vitriol. "I…" Before I could continue, she spat at me.

"Where are the others, what have you done with them?" She was shaking with anger, though it seemed to be warring with despair.

"You are the only one we took off of the ship."

"You killed them all?" She was wide-eyed and furious.

"Will you give me a chance to finish!" I spoke forcefully, but tried not to yell, to keep from seeming angry. "Please." I added as an afterthought, softening my tone.

She said nothing but sat firmly on the bed staring at me. She was short, though she carried herself much taller. I hadn't noticed how short until I saw her feet didn't reach the floor.

I collected my thoughts and continued. "Okay, we went, my three friends and I," I cut off her question, "to the ship to rescue the woman that you kidnapped, Jennifer. We used tasers and sleep magics to disable the guards we encountered. You were brought back because we knocked you out first and couldn't risk you waking up and alerting everyone." I paused.

"So, you just snuck in and put everyone to sleep?" She was terse.

"Well, no. We had to fight a few folks, but we didn't kill anyone. Scaevola did, though. When we tried to stop the ritual, he killed the other people involved. It all went weird. I don't quite understand why he did it." She looked at me, incredulous. "I swear. Honestly, I forgot we had you back on the boat. That's why you're here."

She looked at me, appraisingly. "And you want me to betray my comrades to you? You think these lies will convince me?"

"Yes? No? They aren't lies. I want to figure out what the fuck is really going on. I think you might know and that it's safer for everyone if you aren't out there helping them end the world." I stumbled over the words.

"Ending your world." She muttered to herself angrily.

I took a deep breath. "Look, we've gotten off on the wrong foot. Let's start over. Do you want some breakfast?" She glared at me. "I'm going to bring you some food. Do you have any dietary preferences?"

"No beef." She was reserved, not saying more.

"No beef." I repeated. "I'll be back in a bit, and we can try again, okay?" She said nothing as I shut the door behind me.

Chapter 40

I was downstairs assembling food on a tray when Boo came in. "Agnes already got ya doing chores?" She poured some coffee from the pot.

"No. Well, yes, I made that coffee, but this is for...our guest upstairs." I pointed upwards.

"Ah, paying a visit? You need me to join you as weird cop?" Boo looked over the tray.

I shook my head, "I'm not playing any sort of cop. I was up there earlier, and I didn't make much progress." I poured some milk into a pitcher on the tray. Boo's expression shifted a bit. "What?" I asked.

"Oh, you went up all alone?" She seemed reserved, but skeptical.

"Yeah, she tried to throw a chair at me." I watched her face, concerned. "It didn't hit me."

"That's not what I was wondering about. Look, Joe. I don't know you very well. Do you prefer things blunt or gentle?" Boo leaned against the counter; her arms crossed.

"Blunt, I guess." I was apprehensive, but I continued. "I'd rather have it clear."

"Okay, she was probably afraid you were going to rape her." Boo's tone was clear and calm.

"What?!" I dropped the milk and barely caught it.

"Okay, that might have been too blunt. But seriously Joe, you kidnapped her and she's in a strange house and you come in there all alone."

"I! I would never!" I sputtered.

"I know. Andrew wouldn't have vouched for you otherwise. But this isn't about you."

"But she thinks I'm a..." I was distraught.

Boo cut me off with a raised hand. "Slow your roll, Joe. Think about it from her perspective. She wakes up trapped in an unfamiliar bedroom and then a man shows up, all alone. You have all the power, and she has none. It's not you, it's the situation. Of course, it doesn't help that you're the public face of an organization she's trying to destroy, too, but."

I started to argue and then forced myself to take a deep breath. A few years back, Andrew had taught me some tricks for approaching tough issues without getting defensive. I took another breath, was this about me specifically? No. Not really. I took another breath. Was this something I actually knew from my own direct experience? No. I took another breath and let it out slowly. "You're right. I didn't think about it that way. I should have considered the situation more directly before jumping in."

"You aren't acculturated to. You don't have to take the statistics personally." Boo shrugged and her expression softened. "How about this? We deal with her in pairs for a while. So, it doesn't have the same overtones. Or maybe just me or Agnes for now, okay?"

"That makes sense. I feel like an ass. I didn't mean..."

Boo waved it away. "Take that feeling and turn it into determination to never do it again, okay?" She smiled at me. "Anyhoo, I've been trying to figure some things out research wise and could use your help."

The subject change was a relief. "Sure, what's up?"

Boo sipped her coffee. "You know a lot about previous Chosen Ones, right?"

"More than just about anyone." I nodded.

"Well, my records are a bit spotty and the libraries I have access to are missing a lot of information. I'm looking for a pattern, but there are too many missing pieces. Could you help me out?" Boo gave me a cheerful and hopeful look.

I thought about it. "The best thing would be the Keeper Archives, but I don't want to do that right now. Not until we know more. I have a few things in my own collection at home that could help, though."

Boo nodded, "Great, I'll tell you what. You go get those and I'll take this food upstairs." She gestured to the tray.

"Alright, I'll be back shortly." I began to leave before turning back. "Thanks for telling me directly how I fucked up. I really hadn't considered things from her perspective. I'd rather know, even if it's uncomfortable."

"Thanks for not getting all defensive. Lots of people really freak out at things like that." Boo winked as she picked up the tray and headed for the stairs.

Chapter 41

Thursday, June 25th

I could tell something was wrong when I entered the apartment building. Craig the doorman paused for a long moment before returning my greeting and as I passed through to the elevator, I saw him pick up his phone.

When I arrived on my floor, I could see the reason. Several men in jumpsuits were moving furniture out of my apartment. As I approached, Daniel emerged from my front door, putting his phone back in his pocket.

I looked at Daniel, throwing up my hands. "Dude. What the fuck?"

Daniel looked back at me, his expression a mix of shame and anger. "I should ask you the same thing. What the fuck did you do?"

"What do you mean?"

Daniel looked at me, "On the ship? The conclave is super fucking pissed at you. They say you ran away?" His expression was incredulous.

I looked back at Daniel. "Ran away? No. Not really. Things weren't what they looked like. I didn't want to...things were...Look. I didn't run away, but I chose not to fight Scaevola."

"Dude, why not? The bastard betrayed us and was going to kill everyone." Daniel threw up his hands. "You should have brought me. I'dve shot the fucker right between the eyes." Daniel made his hand in the shape of a gun. "Bam"

"The situation on the ground was not what it seemed. And you may have noticed. Everyone is still alive." I was guarded. Torn between explaining everything and holding back. I didn't know if I could trust Daniel at this point, especially with... "Daniel, what's going on here?" I gestured to the men moving a table out of my apartment.

"You're being kicked out. Prospero's orders." Daniel looked a little sheepish.

"But you can't." I sputtered.

"Joe, you don't have a lease. You don't have any rights here." Daniel wouldn't meet my eyes but was firm.

"What about...what about...squatter's rights?" I grappled with this in my mind. "I've lived here for years. You can't just throw me out on the street."

"You think you can find a judge in this town that would risk pissing off Casimir?" Daniel was sarcastic. "Be my guest."

My heart sank. There was no way I could beat them through the legal system. Casimir had his checkbook in every judicial election in Cook County for nearly three decades. Daniel was right. "I'm sorry Joey, but they've got all the cards."

I sighed. "Daniel. Can you do me a favor?"

He looked up, skeptical. "What?"

"Can you give me a few hours? I'll have everything out by the end of the day, just let me get a truck and some friends."

Daniel hesitated but softened. "Fine, but you need to be out by tonight or Prospero will literally murder me." He turned to go, waving down the movers who had a scrying table between them.

"Daniel." I called out as he moved away. "I didn't run away. Everything was all fucked up and I'm trying to figure out why."

Daniel shrugged, "If it's worth throwing your life away to do that, good fucking luck. But think about what you're doing, bro." He walked away. "Think about what you got to lose."

Eight hours, 37 phone calls, three pizzas and two cases of 312 worth of emergency moving help and one long discussion with a police officer as to why trucks weren't allowed on Lake Shore Drive and what counted as a 'historic parkway', I pulled the rental truck into Agnes' driveway.

Boo came out as I walked up to the porch. "When you said you had a few things that might be useful, you weren't kidding."

"I got evicted. Do you think your grandmother will let me crash here?" I handed Boo the box of research materials that I had set aside during my hasty packing.

Boo smiled, "She had Ivan make up a guest room this morning."

Chapter 42

"Aren't you supposed to be the Chosen One?"

I was chopping limes on the bar the next night, getting ready for happy hour (newly reinstated in Chicago, Casimir had talked the mayor's ear off about that one), when I heard her. Miriam was standing in the doorway to the back bar, glaring at me.

"Hello, Miriam." I spoke calmly, scooping the limes into the garnish case.

"Hello?" Miriam walked angrily up to the bar, facing me across it. She was apparently still dressed from work, wearing a dark skirt suit. "That's what you have to say? Why aren't you doing something?"

I looked at Miriam, what did she know? How involved was she? Was this part of some plot? "I have to work today, Miriam. Jennifer is safe, I'm doing everything I can to resolve the situation."

Miriam stared at me. "Safe? How can you be sure? Have you seen her?" Miriam was panicked.

"Miriam, do you have any idea what is going on?" I was torn inside. If Miriam was part of this, I was telling her what I suspected and potentially confirming that I was a threat to whatever was going on. If she wasn't, I was being unspeakably cruel. Jennifer was her friend; she was kidnapped as far as Miriam knew.

Miriam looked confused, "What do you mean? Jenny's being held prisoner by some crazy cult! She could be out there being tortured and killed while you tend bar?! Why aren't you doing something?!"

I looked at Miriam across the bar. I wished Andrew was here, but there was no subtle way to say, 'let's continue this conversation at the tobacco shop across the street with my friend who can magically sense sincerity.' I wanted to be honest, but I just couldn't trust her. "Miriam. There is a lot going on with this situation. I don't think a direct assault will work, but I have reason to believe that Jennifer is safe for the time being."

Miriam looked at me, plaintive. "How can you be sure? She is...well, they could use her for all sorts of things."

I reached across the bar and touched Miriam's hand. "Don't worry. I won't allow anything to happen to her. She has protections about her, and I have reasons to believe they need her alive and unharmed." I tried to keep my face sympathetic, but neutral. I couldn't know if she was taking what I said as comfort or as some sort of wordplay by implication and I couldn't know who she would tell about anything I said. "I have a plan, but the time isn't right. I want to resolve this safely for everyone."

Miriam looked at me and reached across the bar with both hands. I reacted instinctively, fearing danger at first, but then I realized she was trying to hug me. It was awkward with the bar between us, but I managed to hug her back. "Thank you, Joe. Please keep her safe."

As we released the hug, I looked at her. "I'll do everything I can." She left quickly, sniffling as she went.

By the time I left work, the streets of the loop were empty. Andrew had come by the bar as usual, though he had stayed later than he normally did, waiting for me to close out the till. We both had less sleep to look forward to, him because he had to open his shop again in 6 hours, me because I had research to get back to.

"Did you drive?" Andrew looked around, eyeing the empty streets.

"No. I still don't have a car and I'm not sure enough about funds to rent one." I lamented, "I'm on the redline to the 55, just like my misspent college days."

Andrew nodded and the two us headed north. As we passed the first blue line entrance with its ascending elevator, Andrew spoke up. "I can walk you to the red line stop."

"I'll just use the underground pass through, that way it's not out of your way."

Andrew shrugged and we went down the stairs into the Jackson Blue line station, past the stylized compass rose and through the turnstile. I silently thanked my luck that my monthly pass was still active, I wasn't sure I could afford another just yet.

Andrew wasn't particularly talkative, I could tell he was feeling tired, so we said little as we went down the stairs. I noted the LED monitor as we reached the platform. "It looks like 12 minutes to the next O'Hare." Andrew simply grunted as we moved down the platform towards the stairs marked for the red line. "I'll try and drop by the shop tomorrow. Boo has some research to do at the Spertus, I'll bring coffee."

Andrew smiled at the suggestion and gave me a quick hug. "Stay safe." He patted my shoulder as I started down the stairs.

I was halfway down the tunnel when I heard the noise. Above me, in their plastic bubbles, I saw the security cameras above me move, pointing at the walls. Looking down the tunnel, I saw the other sets move similarly.

I began to quicken my pace but stopped short when the two men stepped into the archway ahead of me from the red line platform. They were breathing heavily but had just pulled on their face masks beneath their hoodies.

I heard the two behind me before I saw them. As I turned, I saw I was surrounded, two on each side. I paused. They were definitely Deluge cultists, but I wasn't sure with the face masks if I'd faced them before. "Hello. I didn't realize we had the same commute, maybe we should try carpooling." I chuckled nervously as they began to advance. "But seriously, I won't bother you again, let's just take a step back and talk about this."

One of the pair coming from the blue line spoke. "You killed Vervain and think you can talk your way out of your threefold vengeance!" The speaker's voice identified her as female and the mention of threefold vengeance told me that the speaker was probably part of a witch coven, the brandished dagger subtly hinted it was probably one of the militant ones.

I turned towards her and her companion. "I don't want to sound callous, but I don't know who Vervain is. I didn't kill anybody when I attacked your ship."

The speaker snorted at that. "You murdered her when you stopped the ritual, how else could you have prevented our transcendence." She pulled out a cursing effigy doll as she spoke, I could feel her intense concentration as I watched, binding me to the fetish. Fortunately, I also saw Andrew peek his face around the corner behind her. We made brief eye contact as I saw him, and he ducked back behind the wall.

I moved towards the two witches, walking fast and closing ten feet as I talked. As I hoped, they stopped moving and one even took a step back, maintaining distance. They were too far away for me to reach, but only a few steps away from Andrew. "I can assure you; I didn't kill anyone. I was present when Vervain was shot, but I didn't even have a gun. Your leader Scaevola shot her."

They paused ever so slightly as I said this but scoffed. I heard the footsteps of the cultists behind me and continued my approach, trying to delay my inevitable flanking. "I mean, I'm sure you won't take my word for it, I could be up to all sorts of shenanigans." As I saw Andrew move, I spun, bellowing the name of fire downwards towards the cultists approaching from the red line.

Andrew rushed forward and grabbed the effigy and hurled it against the wall. The bond between witch and effigy channeled the force into her body, knocking her prone while the incomplete bond to me resulted in only a nudge.

The wave of fire coursing along the floor caught one of the approaching cultists in mid step and caused flame to lick up his legs. He screamed in fear as his clothes began to catch. His companion fared better, leaping over the wave and closing the gap. I beat my chest, activating my guardian spirit and blocked his truncheon with my arm, painful, but nothing broken.

A glance behind showed Andrew facing off with the still standing witch. She had a wicked knife and the two of them circled in the wide hallway. Andrew dodged a swipe from the dagger, watching the witch's fighting form closely for weaknesses.

I was brought up short by another blow from the truncheon. The mystic force imbued in it was enough to sting, but my fortifications held. It was enough to make me realize I had to do something to stop this. I wasn't sure how many blows I could take. My taser was deep in my satchel and he wasn't going to give me a chance to grab it.

I took a chance. I knew it was dangerous, I didn't know the amperage of the lights down here, but it was what I had to hand. I called the name of lightning, releasing the power coursing through the cables. Out of one of the lights jumped a massive bolt, shattering the bulbs in the middle of the hallway. The cultist was thrown backwards and landed hard and unmoving on the tiled floor.

I turned to see Andrew holding the witch in a sleeper hold. He had her well in hand her knife swings increasingly desperate as she struggled against him. Andrew looked down the hall at the man I had just attacked then back to me. He said two words. "Not breathing."

I looked back. The cultist who had been lit on fire had extinguished himself but was now leaning against the wall nursing the burns on his hands. His companion lay motionless on the ground. I cursed the overzealous electrical engineers as I ran forward and kneeled over the fallen man. I felt for his pulse and found it thready, his breathing stopped entirely. My first aid training rushed in, I needed to get his stabilized and get him breathing again.

I looked over at the other cultist and pointed forcefully. "Stay still, I'm trying to keep him alive." I fished in my bag and pulled out my taser. I needed to do this precisely or I could stop his heart entirely. I took a focusing breath and whispered the name of lightning carefully as I lit the taser. The shock jumped from the device through the heart, causing the cultists muscles to contract forcefully.

As he writhed, I moved in and carefully grabbed his head, tilting in backwards. I spoke the name of air, inflecting it carefully. I could rupture his lungs if I wasn't precise. The man sputtered as he took a ragged breath and then another. I heard steps behind me, and Andrew came rushing up, the witch's knife in his hand. "Come on."

The two of us emerged onto State Street, breathing heavily. I waved down a cab, looking around to make sure nobody else seemed to be a threat. As the cab pulled up, I got into the back and slid over to let in Andrew. "Head for the Eisenhower. Take Congress." I said to the Cabbie.

Andrew looked to me. "Good first aid back there."

"I haven't killed anyone so far; I'd rather not start now." I looked at the cabbie. "No problems, just a rowdy drunk at the bar," I turned to Andrew. "So, we can either drop you off at your place, or grab your things. What do you say?"

Chapter 43

I was finishing making breakfast when the knocking came at the front door. Andrew had taken his to go, reassured by the safety in numbers of the morning commute. Agnes was out on the back porch with her coffee and Boo was taking a shower upstairs. I was assembling a tray for the 'guest in the attic', as we'd begun calling her. I hoped today would bring progress, but as we hadn't even gotten her name, my hopes weren't high.

Agnes called from the back. "Joe, why don't you check on that."

I paused. After last night, I was wary, but it seemed really rude to answer someone else's door armed. I had to hope it wasn't someone dangerous. I opened the door, the name of the wind on my lips, but it died away as I saw Ellis Green standing there.

"Well look who we have here," he said, smiling a bemused smile.

"Ellis?" I looked around, he seemed to be alone. "What are you doing here?"

"No need to be all accusative." Ellis smiled and stepped past me into the foyer. "Agnes out on the back porch?"

I looked briefly dumbfounded before recovering my wits, "Yeah. I hadn't realized you knew her."

"I stayed with her when I first ran away from home." At this point, Ellis was halfway through the kitchen. "Agnes, you out there?"

Agnes' voice came through the screen door. "Is that Ellis? Come out here and let me look at you." And just like that, we were all standing on the porch as Agnes assessed Ellis' look (woefully underfed), fashion (delightfully retro) and life choices (happily still working with the teens, sadly still single).

After a few minutes of this, I tried to excuse myself. "I am going to finish breakfast up."

Agnes nodded an acknowledgement to my excuse, but Ellis spoke up. "Actually Agnes, I came here to see Joe too, so if you don't mind, we can catch up more after. I have some music recs for you." Agnes smiled and waved her dismissal, picking up her book.

As we walked into the kitchen, I rounded on Ellis. "How'd you know I was here?" I kept my voice low but menacing. "What's the deal?"

Ellis held his hands up, moving them in a protestation of innocence before gesturing to the living room. I let him lead the way, following him in at a close distance. He sat down in front of the piano, facing me. "I didn't. Honestly. I came here to see if Agnes had heard anything about where you were. She knows everyone in the South Side magic community in one way or another."

"That's great. I've saved you a step. Why are you looking for me in the first place?" I was guarded in my speech and stayed standing, arms crossed.

Ellis looked up at me, taking in my posture. "Easy, Joe. I'm not here to hurt you. My Pops called me, looking for you. My Pops, who only sent a get-well card when I got run over by a cop car, called me up and was all 'hey, you seen Joe lately?'" Ellis shrugged, "I mean, that's bizarro world, right? You're the good boy who might have information, I'm the wayward runaway. You can see why I got curious."

I looked at him skeptically, "So you've found me. You can go rat me out to your Pops."

Ellis snorted, "Things are backwards, but not that backwards. I'm here to help you out."

I looked at him, "What do you mean, help?"

Ellis smiled and put up two fingers. "I figure there are two possibilities that have you on the outs with the Uncles. One, you fucked up. The world is still standing, so that seems unlikely. Two, you realized what lying, manipulative fucks they are and got out."

I started to take umbrage, almost reflexively, but I stopped. The last week had stripped me of any certainty.

Ellis smiled wider. "See, that reaction right there tells me it's number two. Am I right?"

"So what if you are?" I frowned at his perceptiveness.

Ellis breathed out and his face turned serious. "Okay. How to put this. You are in a unique position. You may have access to information that can blow the lid off of a world-shattering pot of bullshit. I can help you know what to look for and help you get it out there when you find it."

I sat down on the couch. "Look, I don't even really know what's going on here. I'm not ready to agree to anything until I have a clue what 'it' is."

"That's fair, that's fair." Ellis nodded, leaning forward. "But just let me help you out for now. I swear to keep your secrets. I won't tell my Pops or your uncles where you are. I won't release anything unless you agree." He spoke the words solemnly, sanctifying the oath.

As I pondered, I heard footsteps on the stairs and a moment later, Boo emerged into the living room, her hair wet. "Ellis, what are you doing here?"

Ellis looked at Boo, smiling. "Just trying to get Joe here to let me help him smash the patriarchy."

"Sweet, when do we start?" Boo looked from Ellis to me.

"This is serious." I looked between the two of them.

"I know." Boo smiled, "We can smash the patriarchy afterwards. Have you taken care of the…?" Boo gestured upwards.

I looked at Boo and then at Ellis and then back at Boo. "Subtle much?"

Ellis looked between us, "What, you two getting it on?"

Boo and I both blurted out "no!'

Ellis chuckled, "Kidding, kidding. Look, I swore to keep your secrets, what would it hurt to tell me?"

Boo spoke up, "We've got a prisoner in the attic, part of the fake cult that kidnapped Joe's girlfriend."

"We went on two dates!" I exclaimed louder than I meant.

"Is everything alright in there?" Agnes called from the back porch. Boo and Ellis both looked to me.

"Yes, Ma'am. I'll keep it down." I looked at both of them and lowered my voice. "She's not my girlfriend."

"You have a better term?" Boo spread her hands in mock helplessness.

"How about the evil woman who is apparently in league with my traitor mentor? The one who was apparently in on her own kidnapping and fake sacrifice?" I seethed. "Does that work better?"

Boo looked a little bit abashed. 'Sorry. I didn't mean, I just." I waved away her apology, frustrated.

Ellis spoke up. "So, you've got a prisoner? Can I help? Let me help."

I looked at Boo and she shrugged. "Good luck," I said, "We haven't even been able to get a name out of her. We were just about to bring her breakfast once Boo got out of the shower."

Ellis smiled. "I got this. Give me five minutes, I'll show why you need me."

A minute later, the three of us were walking into the attic room. The prisoner sat on the bed, reading, but she set the book aside as we entered. She looked between the three of us, "Who's he?" Gesturing at Ellis with her forehead.

Ellis stepped forward, pulling out his wallet. He rifled through and pulled out a card. "My name is Ellis Green, and I am a certified affiliated observer by the Alexandrian Order. I'd like to offer my services as a neutral party"

The prisoner took the card and looked it over. She smiled. "Him, I will talk to. Alone." Ellis looked at us and I set the food tray on the desk, and we exited the room.

As we reached the second-floor landing, I turned to Boo. "Did you know about that?" Boo shook her head.

After a moment, she spoke. "I'm sorry about earlier. I joke when I'm nervous."

"It's okay. I just don't know what I'm doing right now. Plus, I got ambushed last night and nearly accidentally killed someone." my phone buzzed. "Hold on." I looked at the message. "Son of a bitch!"

"What?" Boo looked worried. "Did something?"

"No. But now I need to find 3000 dollars." Boo looked confused at me. "A few months back, I borrowed some money from one of my Uncles to help Andrew publish his chapbook."

"Two Spirits, One City?"

"Yeah, the loan is being called in."

"Andrew hasn't repaid you?" Boo looked quizzical.

"He's been doing it slowly; it wasn't a big thing. It was a no interest loan; the tobacco business isn't really booming. He pays me back regularly. 3000 is what's left." I sighed. "Now, I need to find quick money on top of everything else."

Boo looked at me sympathetically. She was about to say something when the door opened from upstairs. Ellis came down to the landing. "She'll talk if I can verify my neutrality by getting a message from her father."

"Really?" Boo was exited. "Can you do it?"

Ellis shrugged. "We'll find out." He began to descend the stairs. "Oh, and her name is Renuka."

Chapter 44

Saturday, June 27th

It had been a long day. A late morning visit from an antique buyer had disposed of my better pieces of furniture. I had saved my scrying table and best bookshelf. My collection of antique glassware had gone immediately on craigslist for much less than they were worth, though I took cold comfort in the fact that I could joke that I was low-balled on my hi-balls.

The rest of the day had been spent driving the U-Haul around to used bookstores around Chicagoland unloading my collections. I held onto my serious magical volumes, but I had heartbrokenly parted with nearly all the rest. My first American edition of Machiavelli's Prince had gone to Powell's along with a number of other antique volumes. My Lovecraft ended up in Ravenswood while my Burroughs found a home at Bookworks. Armadillo's pillow got my signed first printings of the Harry Potter books (ha ha Uncle Anthony), and the rest went to Half Price Books up in Skokie. I'd be lying if I said I didn't cry a little to lose some of them, but I needed the money.

I spent some time switching banks. I withdrew what I had left in my personal accounts at banks that I knew Simon had friends in and put it in fresh accounts elsewhere. Finally, I emptied what was left in the truck into Agnes' garage and returned the rented truck up on Fullerton.

It was early evening when I finally climbed the stairs to the red line. I had enough money to pay back the loan and enough to hopefully find a new place and get set up once everything blew over, if I had to. It felt weird, like my life had come to an end and would need rebuilding. Andrew's regular repayments would help, but I wouldn't have much extra after Brando's and Myopic.

I kept my eye out for trouble, hoping that the deviation from my routine would prevent any pursuit. As far as I could tell, the other people sharing the ride were normal folks. The Wrigley Field concession worker, half asleep from a double header. The Columbia College students, rambling about their upcoming art projects. The impeccably dressed old Black man, humming Motown to himself. All seemed normal for a southbound red line.

171

At the Chinatown stop, something shifted. I felt an odd vibration move outwards from the satchel on my lap. At first, I looked for my phone, but as I was doing so, I saw the last of my fellow passengers moving through the door in a quasi-stupor.

I leaped up as the chimes sounded, 'doors closing' sounded over the speakers but I was not fast enough, exhausted from the day. The train began to move. 'Sox/35th is next. Doors open on the left at Sox/35th.'

I contemplated my options. I was alone in the train car. I moved back a car. Also empty. I tried the emergency call button. No response. The driver must be in some sort of trance. I looked back a car, were they already on the train? Were they ahead of me or behind me? No choice. I reached out and called in a spirit of observation. This was sloppy and would be pretty costly, but I wasn't spoiled for options here. The spirit appeared instantly. The El was full of people watchers, the spirits were never far.

"See who walks in these cars and where and return to tell me. I offer one boon." The spirit was gone in a moment, rushing half visibly along towards the front of the train, passing through windows with the ease of conceptual intangibility. It returned in seconds, rushing through the car towards the back of the train.

In a moment, it returned to me. It projected an image of the train with its eight cars. At its head was the driver. Moving back from the front were two cultists, moving front from the back were two more. Not unpredictable. Scaevola loved flanking maneuvers as anyone who had played De Bellis Antiquitatis against him knew. Plus, they had tried this in the ship and the subway. I was trapped in the middle. I nodded and the spirit vanished.

Alright. What were my options? We were coming up on Sox/35th. I could try and make a break for it there, I could outrun them, but that wouldn't matter if they had guns or vans. I would be dead or kidnapped too quickly. I had to do something unexpected.

I brought up a mental image of the sox/35th stop. I pulled out my phone. This needed precision. Would there be a train on the other side? The transit app said two minutes for my southbound 95th and three for the northbound Howard. That was cutting it very close. But close was better than dead.

I crouched down beside the far door and summoned up the elements in my mind. I hadn't done this except under very controlled circumstances at the circus school up on Campbell and Homer back during training. I heard the door beside me begin to rattle as we slowed into the station.

This was it. As the doors opened, the cultists emerged from the rear of the train car, and I started sprinting. I didn't spare them a thought. I looked quickly to my right as I ran. There was enough clearance, but just barely. As I reached the edge of the platform at a dead run, I summoned up the named I needed. As I jumped, I first spoke the name of stone, inflected for the gestalt concrete of the platform. The floor beneath the metal plate at the edge of the platform rippled, hurtling me upwards and forwards before snapping back to rigidity. As I took to the air, I called the wind to my back as I had practiced years ago. As I felt the gust at my back, propelling me forward, I summoned up the most commanding voice I could and bellowed the name of fire.

The flames erupted beneath me, and I took a moment to assess my position. I soared smoothly over the Dan Ryan, cars and trucks moving beneath me. I hoped nobody crashed as a result but didn't have long to think as my arc of movement began to trend downwards. I concentrated and spoke the name of earth, calling the bare ground to catch me. The landing was hard, but I rolled through it and took off running almost immediately. A glance back showed the cultists looking back and forth at the ramps leading out of the station, both far out of their way, before the incoming train obscured them

Chapter 45

By the time I got back to the house I was exhausted. I had run all the way to the Green line then taken that to Garfield and caught the 55 bus, jumping off a few blocks early when I thought I saw a white van and running through back alleys to get back to Agnes' house.

I was winded when I finally opened the door into the foyer. Boo was in the living room when I stumbled in. "Goddess, you look like hell, Joe."

"I was attacked on the train. I had to flee." I was still breathing heavy, so my words stumbled out between breaths.

"Through the woods? You're covered in mud and grass stains."

"I guess that explains the dirty looks." I joked. Boo smiled but didn't laugh. "I need to figure out how they keep finding me." I said seriously after a moment.

"Right. We'll do that. But first, let's get you cleaned up. You aren't really fit to sit, as Agnes says." Boo walked over. "Take your shoes off to start, then try not to drip mud all over the carpet. I'll put the shoes back with the gardening stuff."

I was halfway up the stairs when Boo called out. "Oh yeah, hey Joe. I'm glad you're not dead!"

One shower and change of clothes later, into a comfortable old Smashing Pumpkins t-shirt and track pants, and I felt more like myself. Exhausted but no longer working on adrenaline and grit.

As I came downstairs, I found Boo sitting at the dining room table, my bag in front of her, still closed, but sitting on a drop cloth with a makeshift warding circle painted on it. Boo was wiping the mud off the bag with a rag. Beside it were my shoes, damp but clean.

Boo looked up. "Good. Go grab your clothes, let's see if they're tracking something on you." She held up a small dowsing rod, freshly cut.

I quickly trotted upstairs and came back down with my dirty clothes. "Sorry, these are really sweaty and gross. Do you really think there's something on me?"

"Well, you ward yourself, right? You'd know if there was someone pulling at your essence to find you." I nodded at her question. "Right, and anything that was attuned to you would be off limits. So, let's see if there's anything with a different resonance."

I shrugged, "Resonance has never been my strong suit."

Boo smiled, "I can help. It's much easier to detect for someone else. It's like smell. It's really hard to smell yourself." Boo reached out and took my hand, placing one branch of the dowsing rod in it. "Let's begin."

Boo guided the dowsing rod slowly from object to object, quietly humming to herself. First, we touched my clothes, piece by piece, the contents of my pockets and my shoes.

Boo then gestured at my bag. "We'll need to test everything in there, too. If there's anything confidential?"

"Confidential? Why would I have..." I puzzled at her.

"I'm used to working with people who have a lot of mystical secrets. I even made some inroads with the Hopi, and after what Voth did to them, that was no easy feat, let me tell you. I feel like I've done half my fieldwork blindfolded." Boo was standing very close to me and after her earlier comment about smell, I felt hyper aware of her presence, her face just a foot away as we held the dowsing rod together. Her eyes moved slightly, alternately focusing on each of mine.

After a brief, lost moment, I realized she was waiting for me to say something. "Right. No, no, there's nothing that's top secret." I dumped my bag on the tablecloth one handed as I broke eye contact.

The bag was full of random objects from the past few days. We ran through bank paperwork, truck rental receipts, Clif Bar wrappers and other detritus of days of running around before moving on to regular things. Keys, taser, wallet and phone came next before delving into my various magical tools. Rods, coins, flasks, blades, all came back highly attuned. Even the bag of makeshift tools from Pilar were attuned to me.

Boo looked troubled, "None of the random junk has any stray resonance, your tools are strongly attuned to you. Is there anything else?"

I lifted the bag and looked inside. Something glinted deep within, I reached down and tugged on it where it had caught on a tag. Looking at it, my stomach dropped. I set Jennifer's cross necklace on the table. Before the dowsing rod even touched it, it was straining away from it. "Well, we know how they're tracking me. That's Jennifer's, highly attuned to her."

Boo looked at me. "Oh, sorry. I mean, I..." She touched my shoulder with her other hand and trailed off as our eyes met. The tension of the moment was palpable, her touch electric. I shivered despite myself.

"It's okay." I let go of the dowsing rod, very aware of our closeness. A moment passed as we looked at each other before I stepped away. "Look, I'm sorry, this is just...very confusing right now. I'm not..."

"Not..." Boo looked confused. "Oh, I'm...I...no, I understand." Boo was waving her hands somewhat frantically at this point. "I wasn't, I guess, I mean. Dowsing for resonance can get intense, I should have..."

I raised my hands, showing my palms. "It's okay. I'm not upset, I just. And I don't mean to jump to conclusions or anything. I mean, I've read a lot about crisis situations and their effects on people. For obvious reasons. It's completely normal, it's like an instinctual thing, a way of propagating the species before dying." My voice kept getting faster as I spoke, and I took a deep breath.

Boo looked at me for a long moment, then broke out laughing.

I was startled for a moment, then began laughing with her. We got into a bit of a giggle loop, just unable to stop cracking up. It was a good ten minutes before we could both catch our breath enough to talk.

"Sorry, I shouldn't have said anything, I didn't want things to get weird." I said.

"Well, it's a little late for that. Propagating the species..." Boo laughed and shook her head as she said it and we both smiled. "Okay, how about this." She pulled open a drawer on the buffet that seemed to be full of cloth bags. She passed me a small one. "That should shield it. We get volatile stuff that needs warding around the house all the time." She said in explanation.

I tucked away the necklace and began repacking my satchel. "Thanks. Hopefully this means that I won't be randomly attacked anymore. At least no more than usual."

"Well, once you're finished there, I have some research results." Boo moved back to the living room as I finished packing the bag. I joined her a minute or two later after tossing out some garbage.

"Whatdya got?" I dropped onto the couch across from her.

"Okay." Boo slid forward, excited. "I've been looking at the history of the Chosen One and I've noticed three patterns, based on your works, cross referenced against a few, let's call them critical accounts, for balance."

"Okay." I felt a little energized. This sounded promising. "Lay it on me."

"Has anyone ever told you that you talk like a senior citizen?" Boo looked at me.

"Whatya mean? I'm hip, I'm groovy, now we're cooking with gas." I smiled. "I spend a lot of time around old men. Okay? Hazard of my line of work."

Boo shrugged her assent. "Okay. Thing one. Regularity. The Chosen One has been around a long time, right?"

I nodded, "In some form? Since Ancient Greece at least. Even our records are spotty, but you might have heard of Achilles?"

"Right. So, for a long time, even with spotty records. Chosen Ones were infrequent, there weren't necessarily crises that called for them, so one would arise only when needed. This changed about 500 years ago, give or take. Around then, there seems to always have been a Chosen One, crisis after crisis, every 15-20 years, almost like clockwork."

"It's a more dangerous world. Things are happening more quickly." I looked at Boo, skeptical. "Besides, I haven't faced my crisis yet and I'm nearly 40."

"We'll come back to that. Alright, fine, more is happening, but I think it's deeper than that. Let's look at thing two. Location. Based on history, it looks like the Chosen One is located in the city where the Conclave is most powerful." Boo looked to me for acknowledgement.

"Sort of. The Conclave of the city with the Chosen One is considered Ascendant. Others defer to them." I explained.

"Correct. But it looks like that isn't always actually cause and effect. It looks like sometimes; the Conclave of an area is either already in power or trending that way or is somewhere the Keepers have been looking to establish." Boo again looked at me.

"That could just be a result of the nature of prophecy. They simply knew where they would be needed." I sighed.

"Okay, but let's look at thing three. Reason. The Chosen One protects the world from ruin, right?" I nodded at her question. "Well, some of the prophecies are a little biased."

I looked skeptical. "What do you mean?"

"Well...Sobieski in 1683 Vienna or Murphy in 1899 Peking. They weren't really saving the world. They were saving Western interests. The world wouldn't have ended with an Islamic Austria or an independent China."

"But what about 1959 or 1804?" I protested. "Both of those times ash would have blanketed the world."

"I'm not saying that everything is bad. Nobody wants Yellowstone to explode, but these things together point to something more going on. I think this is part of what's happening now." Boo looked serious, her usual smile absent. "I don't think the Chosen One is real."

"The Chosen One isn't real?" I made a play show of patting my chest and arms.

"Okay, not real is the wrong way to put this. I think that there is something deeply suspicious about the choosing of the Chosen One. It's too regular and the benefits for the Conclaves are way too convenient."

"Are you saying that they just choose a Chosen One when they need one?" I had trouble keeping the skepticism out of my voice.

"I think they do. I'm not sure how, if they just engineer a crisis for the Chosen One to face or what, but it would explain what you said about Scaevola. Maybe it's just time for it to happen?"

"I don't know. There have been a lot of Chosen Ones who have nearly failed, who have died or been gravely wounded. It would be really cold blooded to just sacrifice them like that. Even Scaevola..." I thought about Peter, about Trevor, about all the others who had come before me.

Boo put her hand on mine. "Maybe it's not that. But there's just too much here to not question it."

I thought about it. "You're not wrong. These questions are very interesting, but I don't really know what good they do us. It's not like there's anyone I can ask about things, not since after it...all...happened." I trailed off as I remembered something.

"What?" Boo looked worried.

I pulled out my phone and texted Simon. After a minute of back and forth, I had laid out the circumstances under which I was willing to meet, where, when, and with whom. Boo was still looking at me as I finished. "I have a second conversation to have."

Chapter 46

Sunday, June 28th

The next day, I stood in front of the Art Institute at 11am, as I had proposed in my text. I had a money order in my pocket for the full three thousand and was ready to flee through the crowd if anything untoward happened. I hadn't received anything since last night, but I wasn't sure if that meant yes, no, or something in between.

Just after 11, a limousine pulled up in front of the museum, just North of one of the lions. This was the deciding moment. If Simon stepped out, or one of his assistants, then I would simply hand over the check and go. Nothing could be gained by engagement, and I couldn't really tell if it was a trap.

The driver got out of the limo and moved to the back passenger door. As he opened it and reached down his hand, I saw what I had hoped for. Ephraim stood up from the car awkwardly, leaning on the driver's arm.

I moved towards the car, looking around, making sure nobody suspicious was following. "I can take it from here." I said, offering Ephraim my arm.

"Ah, Zar-Ptak. Yes, that will do Pulaski. I will call when I need you." He took my arm and gestured to the driver.

We walked towards the museum steps, and I spoke. "Sir, would you like to see some of the museum today as we talk?"

"That would be very nice. We have much to discuss and art may make it nicer." We took the stairs up and passed easily through the members line as I showed my membership card, a Christmas gift from Simon, I thought ruefully.

We passed through the Women's Board Staircase into the long hall of South Asian Art, long and wood floored, faintly smelling of ancient clay and granite. "Ephraim. You said we would have a conversation 'after'. Is this that conversation?"

Ephraim nodded, "It is, Zar-Ptak. But let's not jump to serious matters immediately. How are you doing? Where are you staying? Are you getting enough to eat?"

I kept my voice cool, "I am staying with a friend, sir. It's a temporary arrangement, but I am sure I'll find somewhere more permanent. I hadn't realized my prior accommodations were so temporary."

"Hmph. That was Prospero's Idea. Casimir said we needed to convince you to return, and Prospero thought the threat of being cut off would be enough. The man whispers in Casimir's ear like a worm and eyes my chair like a hungry buzzard." Ephraim snorted. "He still thinks you're a boy who fears missing his supper."

"That's a common misconception." I let a little frustration creep out. "Anyway, I've got a warm place to sleep and a hook to hang my hat."

"Warmth. Once some time ago I had a vision about warmth." Ephraim stopped before a statue of Lion Headed Vishnu. "It was not long after Peter. I wanted to try and understand the monsters who had done such a thing."

"I forget sometimes that you were Keeper of the Flames for so long, sir." I paused alongside him. "You were there for Peter's choosing and for his...."

"Yes, and I was part of the Conclave that misinterpreted the prophecy. Casimir, too." He paused, dour. "But I was talking about warmth. As I descended the qlippothic tree, I saw the part of us that is still the cold little reptile, hungry for warmth and willing to do anything to get it. I was not in a good mind at that point. I saw all love as hollow, as reptile lust for warmth. I was in a dark place and felt very alone."

"Why are you telling me this, sir?" Ephraim had begun walking again and I followed him.

"People who think like that are dangerous. The little reptile does not know when to stop sucking the warmth from the world. I want to make sure you know that. There is more to love than just desire for warmth. There is more to family than just who pays to feed and clothe you. Consider this a thing not to forget." Ephraim stopped and looked at me as we reached the end of the hall.

I looked at him standing there. "Yes, sir."

"Good. Now let's go downstairs and get some tea. You have many questions and I want to give you your answers. Though you won't like them." We continued through the Greek and Roman section and paused only briefly before Chagall's windows. "I'll look at these after we talk." Ephraim waved his hand and we continued to the elevator. "If there's time..." he muttered.

At the member lounge I scanned my card again and helped Ephraim to a seat. I returned after a moment with two cups of green tea, setting them on the low table between us. As I sat, I looked directly at Ephraim. "Sir, is Scaevola really a traitor?"

"Ah, so we're starting, are we? Okay, just a moment." Ephraim sat forward and breathed in the warmth of his tea before taking a sip. "I'll answer, but what do you think, Zar-Ptak?"

"I think he wasn't really going to sacrifice Jennifer and that he wasn't willing to kill me. I also think the cult is a fake. Or at least isn't what it seems."

Ephraim nodded. "All correct so far. What else do you think? Let's get things out so I don't miss anything that matters."

I sighed. "I think Jennifer is in on it. I think...that I disrupted what was supposed to happen."

Ephraim smiled wanly, "That is also correct, Zar-Ptak."

I looked at him, somewhat apprehensively. "I think, well, Boo thinks."

"Boo?" Ephraim raised his prodigious eyebrows.

"Oh, Boudicca Esthersdottir. She's a friend."

"Ah, that's Agnes' granddaughter, right? Is that where you're staying?" Ephraim asked casually. When I didn't respond, he waved his hand. "Don't worry, I won't tell anyone. If you see Agnes, give her my regards."

I processed this for a moment, then moved on. "Right. Well, Boo thinks that the whole Chosen One thing might be...well...fake."

Ephraim smiled, tiredly. "Now we get to your real question. Ask and I will answer truly."

"Is it? Has this all been a lie? All these decades, all these centuries?" My anger crept into my voice as I talked, causing several other people in the room to look at us. I smiled with tight lips at the onlookers and continued in a quieter voice as they looked away, still harsh. "I don't want to believe it, but she has some pretty compelling circumstantial evidence, enough to make me question all of it. You have been more honest with me than anyone. Tell me the truth. Am I really the Chosen One?"

"I've been wondering for a long time what I would say when you asked me about this. Yes, Joe, you are the Chosen One, but you aren't asking the right question."

I thought for a moment, frustrated with my enigmatic old master, not least because I could tell he was right. "What is the Chosen One?"

Ephraim waggled his head from side to side. "That's closer, still not quite right, but of course it's hard to find the question that encompasses your entire existence. The Chosen One is a young man from a Keeper family chosen to fight a great threat and protect the world. Try again, go deeper."

I thought hard for a moment before asking again. "Who chooses the Chosen One?" I looked skeptical.

Ephraim nodded. "There is a process. The Keeper of the Laws and the Keeper of the Flames make the selection. The Keeper of the Flames identifies an upcoming threat and with the Keeper of the laws chooses one of the candidates most likely to end that threat. We invest in that candidate the hopes and dreams of the Keepers and their allies through the mantle of the Chosen One. And they go and fight the threat with those powers. They serve as a symbol of the power of the Conclave, reassuring our allies that we can handle whatever they fear and striking fear into the hearts of our enemies." Ephraim took a long drink of his tea, "At least, that's how it usually works."

"What do you mean, usually?" I looked questioningly. "Do you mean me?"

"I chose poorly." Ephraim looked sad. "You have to understand, I had just seen poor young Peter die because of my misinterpretation, losing most of his cohort, the best and brightest of a generation. I couldn't bear to send another child against something so terrible, and Casimir wanted something likely to happen soon, to overcome the shame. I chose a threat that while dangerous, wouldn't be likely to outright kill someone."

"What do you mean? What was I supposed to be dealing with?"

"You remember the great flood of 1992?" Ephraim smiled, ruefully.

"Not really. I was sick that week, my appendix burst, and I had to spend the week in the hospital." I thought back, "That was my threat?"

"Yes. We thought it would provide a good challenge but be unlikely to kill you. The spirit of the Chicago River had grown twisted after the engineers reversed it, so many years ago. It had broken through its bonds and would have brought down the city if it hadn't been stopped. It would have toppled the foundations of buildings and crashed the world economy as the heart of Chicago collapsed. The waters will rise and the city will fall."

"But. I didn't stop it. What happened?" My mind raced, "Why didn't it destroy the city? Was the prophecy false?"

Ephraim sighed. "You were too sick to go fight it. We did everything we could, hoping we'd have a day or so to get you in fighting shape, we even tried to prevent anyone else from getting to the area, but someone, I never knew who discovered what was happening. They healed the spirit of its malaise, and someone brought in mundane authorities to deal with the aftermath. By the time you were healthy enough, it was done and behind us. There was nothing left to do."

I did some mental calculations. "So, I was supposed to be done 23 years ago? What has been going on since then?" I was livid but I kept my voice low.

"Casimir made the decision not to say anything. How would it have looked if we had said, 'oops, sorry, I guess we didn't really need a Chosen One this time.' It would have undermined confidence in the Keepers. And the next time there was a major crisis we needed the Chosen One's power to resolve, we wouldn't have it. So, we waited." Ephraim looked downcast. "Kept watch for another disaster, one that we could have you resolve."

I considered what he said. "When did you decide to fake a crisis?"

Ephraim gave a grim chuckle, "Five years ago. We were coming up on 20 years and Casimir was worried nothing else would happen. Casimir talked to Scaevola, because he knew we couldn't act behind his back and get away with it. Scaevola volunteered for the rest." Ephraim shrugged, "He volunteered to die to save the Conclave."

"So, this was Scaevola?" I looked at Ephraim. "All of it?"

Ephraim shook his head. "Casimir orchestrated things. Simon was brought in to fund the project. I... wrote the book." Ephraim looked dubious.

I smiled, "Not well enough, Boo recognized it as fake."

"Did she now? Good for her." Ephraim actually smiled, though wanly, "What gave it away?"

"I'm not sure precisely. Something with the cover and word frequencies." I shrugged, "Where did the cult come from? You can't just buy one."

"Scaevola assembled it. I don't know how. I tried to keep out of it as much as I could, tried to find a legitimate danger we could send you against rather than this." Ephraim shrugged. "I've been searching the flames, but they only showed me today, over and over."

I blinked for a moment, then shook my head. "What about Jennifer?" I looked seriously at Ephraim.

"Scaevola thought she would be good motivation and help sell the story afterwards. Love vs. betrayal. You could marry her afterwards; it could be an event." Ephraim looked at his tea.

I looked down at my hands. At the cuts and bruises that several days of violence and danger had left on them. Casimir, Scaevola, Simon, even Ephraim, they had all used me. Tried to play with my heart and my loyalties. They had hurt and killed people. They had wasted twenty years of my life. I felt the rage build in me.

I tried to keep it in, tried to remain calm, but it all came bursting out. "You...You took my life from me. I mean, I've been doing everything you said for 25 years, 25 years! And I was okay with it. I was okay with the sacrifices, okay with the lack of future."

"I was okay with it all because it meant something. I was waiting because I was going to be a hero, someone who would do some good in the world. And now you're telling me that it was all bullshit! A political power play! I... How could you do this to me? To me!" I reached into my pocket, pulling out the check. "Here's Simon's money." I threw it down on the table. "You were right about one thing. This will be the last time we talk." I turned and walked swiftly from the room before the room attendants could throw me out.

As I left, I caught a final glimpse of Ephraim through the window. He held his face in his hands, weeping silently. I hardened my heart and kept going. I didn't know if it was the right thing to do. I don't know if I could have gone back in and fixed things with him, but I just couldn't do it and then the moment had passed, and I was heading out of the museum.

Chapter 47

I didn't have time to go back to Agnes', so I was still fuming that afternoon at Myopic when I showed up for work. As I came in and headed for the counter, Kim waved me over. "Hey Joe. David wants to talk to you. He said to send you in when you got here." She seemed apprehensive, but I couldn't tell if it was worry about my mood or something else.

"Thanks, Kim." I waved back and turned towards the office. David was waiting inside with a similarly apprehensive look.

"Hello, Joe. Have a seat." He gestured to one of the chairs as he sat in the other. I sat down, quietly worrying. "Joe, I've heard from someone that you were selling off a large number of rare books at a number of different places around the city yesterday. Is that true?"

"Yes. I wasn't aware that would be a problem. They were all from my private collection." I tried to remain hopeful, but I could see where this was going.

"I heard from the same source that some of these were potential Myopic purchases that may have been diverted into your personal collection. As a book buyer, you would be in a good position to do such a thing." David spoke with a pained expression.

"I would be, but I haven't been doing that. I promise." David began to reply, but I cut him off. "Look, Sir, I am in the middle of some family conflict right now. I'm sure you're under pressure from the owner to get rid of me, just as I'm sure this is connected to this family thing. Can you give me a few weeks? Take me off the schedule, but don't let me go just yet. I'll see if I can resolve things."

David thought for a moment. "I can only give you a week. I will be meeting with the owner then and he'll want to know the situation."

I stood up. "Thanks, I promise you, sir, I haven't been stealing from the store."

If I had been in a bad mood coming into Myopic, I was in an even worse mood coming back to Agnes' house. The only positive thing I could say is that nobody tried to kill me on my way home, which is a depressingly low bar to set.

When I walked in the front door, I heard laughter coming from the living room. Ellis and Boo were sitting on the couch and talking. They looked at me as I came in, smiling.

"Joe. Ellis was just telling me about the time you tried to teach him to ride a bike down by the lake." Boo still had laughter in her eyes.

I thought back. We were down at the Lake Shore Path near the curve. We had been picnicking at North Avenue beach and Ellis, who was seven at the time, wanted to try my new bike. I had let him, but as I was watching, he lost control and started heading towards the steep drop off at the lake's edge. I ran to try and grab him, but he swerved at the last second, falling on the concrete and I ended up tripping over him, turning my rescue into a headlong flight into the lake.

I smiled wanly. "I'm sure he undervalues the heroism behind my actions." I pulled up my pant leg, "I still have a scar."

Boo and Ellis looked at me, concerned. Boo spoke up, "You okay? How did things go?"

"Well, I paid back my loan, but I lost my job. Apparently, some anonymous tipster told the owner that I had been selling stolen books at used bookstores across town."

"Check and mate." Ellis shook his head.

"That really sucks." Boo made a pained face. "How did the conversation go?"

I sat down in the armchair. "Well, apparently, my destiny was due 23 years ago, but I was busy dealing with sepsis, so I missed it." Boo and Ellis looked confused, so I launched into it, telling them all Ephraim had said.

"I fucking knew it. I fucking KNEW it." Ellis said excitedly when I was done, "Please tell me you had a tape recorder or something."

I shook my head. "No, no tape, nothing on record. All I have are memories of betrayal and two and a half-wasted decades."

Boo spoke up. "You think he was telling the truth?"

"Yeah, Ephraim has always been...well, I guess not always been straight with me, but he wasn't lying about this. Well, at least we know why the book was false and the ritual did nothing." I sank into my chair.

Ellis looked over, "Well, I have some good news. I got word from Renuka's family." He gestured upstairs.

"Right, I didn't have a chance to ask about this before. Tell me how all that works. Take my mind off of my imploding life." I leaned back into my seat, rested my hands on my head.

"You mean getting word?" Ellis looked questioningly.

"The whole Alexandrian observer thing. I thought they were just scribes."

Boo looked surprised. "You don't know about the Alexandrians?"

Ellis looked over, "No. It makes sense. I forget what Keeper education is like. Okay, so, you're right. The Alexandrians are scribes, well, recorders. They take vows of neutrality to capture confidential information, a kind of dark archive against another catastrophic loss of information."

"Okay, that much I knew." I felt a little better, I wasn't totally in the dark.

"Well, the last century, they've developed into an informal go-between. In exchange for right to record, they serve as neutral messengers, impartial observers, essentially an official third party. It's nice when you want to make sure that if you get killed someone will record the information." Ellis shrugged.

"So, you're a neutral observer? You?"

Ellis and Boo both laughed at my question, sensing my skepticism. Ellis spoke. "No, like my man Howard Zinn said, you can't be neutral on a moving train. I'm just a certified affiliate. I deposit things with them and am empowered to negotiate third party services. That's what I did with Renuka. She wanted verification, I got it."

"Why have I not heard of this?" I leaned forward.

"Same reason the Major League owners opposed salary arbitration. When you're the one in power, you don't want neutrality, you want bias. Keepers use in house counsel."

I let out a long and dejected sigh. Ellis made sense. With what I'd learned lately, it seemed obvious. "Alright, how are we doing this? Is there a formal process?"

"Well, my part is that I'll go up and talk to her. After that, it's up to you." Ellis shrugged.

"Okay, well, I'd like to hear how she came to be involved in the fake cult and if she can help us take them down."

"I've got some ideas with that, actually." Boo spoke up, adjusting her glasses. "If this is a fake cult, then maybe we can send her back with this information. Convince others in the cult."

"That's a lot of risk. What can we offer her to make it worth it?"

"We can offer her something that might help her feel safe and trust us a little more."

"Well, that's a start. What do you propose?"

"Money for a ticket to wherever she wants to go home or to start a new life or whatever." Boo looked over at me.

My stomach clenched. I thought about the money I'd just paid, the job I'd just lost. "Okay, I just...I need to figure out how I can afford that."

Boo waved her hands. "Joe. Stop. You aren't the only one involved in this. I know some people who work on things like this. Help get runaways to safety or people out of abusive cults. I appreciate the willingness, but you don't have to take everything on yourself."

I breathed a sigh of relief. "Well, let's hope that's enough for her. Ellis, bring her down. Wait. Let me grab some food so I'm not hangry, then bring her down."

Chapter 48

Renuka moved hesitantly coming into the living room. She looked around, taking in the weird art and antique furniture, but also obviously looking out for danger. I had vacated the armchair and brought in a kitchen chair for myself. "Please, have a seat." I gestured to the armchair.

Ellis came in behind Renuka and sat beside Boo on the couch. Boo sat with the book of the Deluge in her lap. "It's okay. We'd like to ask you a few questions and offer some help. The help doesn't depend on your answers, but we would greatly appreciate anything you could tell us."

Renuka seemed apprehensive but sat. She looked over to me, "Ellis here says you aren't currently with the Keepers, but you definitely aren't part of the Deluge, even if you do have the book. Who are you with?"

The question took me a moment. "I guess I'm currently unaffiliated. I know that isn't much of an answer, but I hope that it will make sense if you hear me out."

Renuka nodded, "Okay. What are we doing here?"

Boo and I looked at each other. We really hadn't put much planning into this. I decided to just plunge in. "I have a few questions about the Deluge. How long have you been a part of it and how did you come to be a member?"

Renuka looked at Boo with the book in her lap. "Two years, and it's a long story." I gestured for her to continue, and she shrugged. "I guess the short version is I was blackmailed. I was working on some liberated histories with my research cell."

Ellis spoke up, "You were with the Subaltern revisionist clique out of L.A., right?"

Renuka turned her head a bit to the side. "I disagree with the loaded term revisionist, but yes, I was with the Subaltern. We had liberated some documents from the Keeper compound outside San Jacinto and were working on decryption."

"It was me, Deanna and my boyfriend Seunghee. We were squatting in a friend's guesthouse in the valley, running decryptions in shifts, living on Trader Joe's trail mix and coffee. That's when we got caught. The Keepers had the police haul in Seunghee on a traffic stop and grabbed Deanna and I back at the guest house based on the tags of a borrowed car. Shattering windows, flashbang grenade, and the next thing I knew I was waking up in a locked room. The next few days were interrogation and torture. Keeper agents telling me how my friends were turning on me, trying to get me to confess. I thought I'd breathed my last free breath."

I hung on her words. When she paused, I couldn't help myself. "How did you escape?"

"The Deluge rescued me. Scaevola himself."

I looked at her with disbelief. "Scaevola Fortier rescued you from a Keeper prison?"

"Yes. One morning I was in my cell and instead of my normal guard, he came in and told me to come with him. He rescued Deanna too, though he said it was too late for Seunghee." Renuka closed her eyes, pausing for a moment. "Once we'd gotten out, he told me about the Deluge and that he would help me avenge my lost love. Deanna and I spent the next year in his compound, learning the traditions and rituals of the Deluge. He wouldn't tell us what the final goals were, just showed up with new recruits he'd rescued every so often. Deanna and I were overseen by a pretty militant witch named Vervain while we were there, but we weren't allowed any contact with the outside world. There were a few folks from other parts of the world, a few Haitians, David from South Africa, I didn't really know everyone. About three months ago, Scaevola came and this time he brought in a group of central Americans, real heavies. He told us the time had come for the end came and showed us the ritual book." She gestured to Boo, "That one you have in your lap."

Boo touched the book but didn't interrupt.

"I think he'd waited til late because he wasn't sure how we'd react to the plan. The idea of bringing down a meteor and flooding the city didn't sit well with some of us, but the more violent were pretty loud in their approval. Of the rest of us, some were very committed, some of us were just terrified what would happen if we were retaken. Scaevola made sure we knew the things the Keepers did to their enemies."

I snorted. "The things that he did. Scaevola has been the primary interrogator for years. But hey, he probably wasn't lying, at least about what would happen. Sorry. Continue."

"I don't know what else there is. We brought the ship in and sabotaged it enough to fool the coast guard but not enough to require us to move it. Deanna was in the ritual prep team, I got assigned to front guard. I think he deliberately split us up to prevent us talking. Anyway, we were waiting out there a few days, starting to get antsy. He had a group of some of the more committed violent types, Eliot, Vervain, some of the Living Tonton Macoute, go along to kidnap a girl, but then we just waited around. He kept saying, we'll begin when the time is right. Then the night you grabbed me, he brought us all together and sent us out on our different duties. Deanna said that they had been double checking the ritual setup when Scaevola got a phone call. I was still on guard duty, while she was part of the ritual team, so we didn't get to talk more."

I spoke softly. "I have some bad news. Scaevola killed Deanna."

Renuka looked blank. "I'm not surprised. Was she trying to escape?"

"No. He killed those who were helping with the ritual when I refused to stop it."

Renuka's expression shifted to confusion. "What? You...what? Why?"

I looked over to Boo. She picked up the book and set it on the table. "The ritual was a fake. The whole cult was." She opened the book, full of her index cards and colored tags. "I had done some preliminary research before we went to the ship. There were some mathematical deficiencies in the ritual design, at least, there was nothing that was designed to channel the energy from a virgin sacrifice to summon a meteor, though it was designed to look that way. Can I ask a question?"

Renuka looked at me, then when I said nothing, she spoke. "Are you asking me?" Boo nodded. "Fine, ask."

"Did you <u>all</u> have a tattoo marked on you?" Boo laid an image on the table, a photocopy of one of the photos from the file I'd shared with her earlier. Boo seemed eager, but restrained, like someone trying not to spook an animal.

Renuka nodded and touched her chest over her heart. "Before we left on the boat, there was a ritual. We were all marked together. I think it translates to 'Continuity of Action, Commonality of Mission, Ancient Traditions of the Deluge', my French isn't great. Scaevola was marked first, then marked three others, who marked three others, and so on."

Boo nodded. She pointed to an image on the page that matched the image of the tattoo from Eliot, the man who had killed himself to avoid Keeper capture. "Well, I think I know what the ritual was supposed to do." Boo paused.

"Okay," I waved my hand, encouraging her to continue.

"I think it was a sacrifice ritual, just not how it was supposed to seem. I think it would have killed the entire cult of the Deluge when Joe killed Scaevola. The tattoos tied life forces together, those energies would have been channeled through them and...." Boo made a gurgling noise and stuck out her tongue.

"Man, that's some cold shit." Ellis spoke from the side. "Even for a man like Scaevola."

"Wait, couldn't he just have killed himself then?" I was sure my confusion was evident on my face.

"Wouldn't have worked. Suicide takes a lot of the will; the body really doesn't like harming itself. I doubt he could have done that and channeled the energy of the spell." Boo took out some tracing paper from her notebook and laid it on the ritual. She traced some lines from the pattern and showed them around. "It makes sense now. There was a fake ritual sketched over a real one."

"That seems a lot of trouble to go through." I shook my head. "And all because he thought I'd kill him without noticing what he was doing?"

Boo shrugged. Renuka had been silent as we discussed this, but she finally spoke up quietly. "So, I've answered your questions and apparently, I've been spending the last two years enslaved to a double agent who planned on murdering me. You said you could help me?"

I jumped in. "Boo, do you think we could find funds to help more than one person?"

Boo paused before speaking. "Probably. What are you thinking?"

"Renuka, is there anyone else in the Deluge that thought like you did? Wasn't really interested in the violence and was there against their will?"

Renuka thought for a moment. "Yes, I'd say about a third of them. But if Deanna's dead, that's one less. The rest of Vervain's coven was mostly there for Vervain and there were some other former prisoners who mostly kept to themselves. The rest are mostly killers, though."

"If we can get you a moment to talk to some of them, do you think you could convince them to turn on the bastard who enslaved you and plotted your deaths?"

Renuka thought for a moment. "Why? What are you thinking?"

I smiled, "I think we can take down the Deluge."

Chapter 49

"You should have told me." Andrew counted the cash from the day's business onto the counter.

"I understand your perspective, but I think you're wrong." I leaned on the wall looking out the window. The plan relied on a lot of moving parts, I had tried to plan contingencies, but things would be best if the Deluge continued to act predictably. If they attacked us here, I wasn't sure what I'd do.

"Joe, it was my loan in the first place. Without me, you wouldn't have borrowed the money in the first place." Andrew wrapped up a bundle of bills and tucked them into a deposit bag.

"That is true. But we agreed when the loan was made what the terms were. You've been on time with payments, and I don't want to change that. Just because someone pulled the rug out from under me doesn't mean I need to do the same."

"I appreciate your thinking of me, but I would still have appreciated being part of the decision-making process." Andrew came out from behind the counter and shut off the lights in the store. He moved towards the door and nodded his chin at the window signs advertising lottery tickets.

I reached up and switched off the signs and joined him by the door. "You're right. I'm sorry. I made assumptions and tried to make this into some sort of grand gesture. I should have talked to you, even if I intended to do what I did."

"Apology accepted." Andrew closed and locked the door to the store. "You've changed, Joe. A week ago, you would have argued that with me, at least, it would have taken me longer to get you to admit you were wrong."

I gave a little snort as we set off to the south towards the bank. "A week ago, I was a lot more certain I knew what was right." Andrew shrugged.

"Do you remember Holly? Back in 2010?" I said wistfully as we walked. "I really thought she could have been the one. We could have settled down and had some kids."

Andrew nodded, "She loved you. At least before all the secrets. Secrets change people."

"Yeah, how was I supposed to explain to her, I am investigating a pre-Islamic death cult that seems to have set up in Garfield Park and may be trying to release an ancient water spirit." I grumbled, "So I just had to 'tend to a family emergency' every few days. I felt like the college freshman with five dead grandmothers."

Andrew patted my shoulder quietly and knowingly. "I'm sorry, Joe. Have you heard anything from her recently?"

"No. She stopped talking to me when she got that coding job in San Francisco, and I couldn't go with her to help her find an apartment." I shrugged and fell silent for the rest of the walk.

At the bank, Andrew dropped off his deposit, withdrew the loan repayment, which I put right into my new bank account. I didn't have much margin for extravagance right now.

We parted ways at the corner. "See you tomorrow, I'm gonna try to catch the next Metra back to Hyde Park, but I gotta run." Andrew headed North as I jogged east.

My route took me quickly towards Michigan and I headed north towards the Van Buren station. It was one of my favorite underappreciated spots in Chicago, a replica of a historical Paris Metro station with an Art Nouveau entrance.

Down the stairs, I slowed up. I felt the necklace in my pocket grow warm. Well, this part was working. Leave it to Scaevola to try the same strategy a third time. Hopefully, everyone was in position.

I emerged up the ramp just as the scheduled southbound train pulled away. Everyone who had been legitimately waiting for a train would be gone. Still, three figures sat on the wooden benches, rising as I moved in. Two were familiar, women from the subway tunnel fight. I heard some others behind me quicken their step. I stepped forward and spoke in my most commanding voice, looking between the two groups. "Hold!" The word was loud and clear enough that it stopped them briefly.

Recognizing that surprise wasn't an option, they moved more warily. As they moved to surround me, one of the witches spoke, the one who had held the effigy doll in the subway fight. "Hello, Chosen One. Come with us quietly or it will go hard on you."

I stifled a laugh. "Do you really expect that to work?"

"You are all alone. There are enough of us to take you down even with the power of the Chosen One." The witch watched me; the others seemed to be taking their cues from her.

"You might want to double check that math, sister." Ellis' voice came from the doors of the train platform. He and Boo came in from the outer doors, on the other side of witches. At the same time, Andrew emerged up the passage behind the ones who had followed me.

The standoff was tense for a moment, everyone sizing up tactical edges. The lead witch broke the silence. "We still have you outnumbered; you can't hope to win in a fight."

I held up my hands. "I don't want a fight if I can help it. I'd like a chance to talk."

"What do you think you have to say that's worth listening to?" One of the other witches spat. "And what's to stop us just attacking you?"

I smiled. "Boudicca, why don't you show them our trump card."

"Now who's being dramatic, Joe?" Boo reached into the pouch at her side and drew out an ornate drop spindle with a golden needle at the top. "Anyway, any funny business and I prick my finger. We all know what happens next."

The lead witch looked to Boo. "We have no quarrel with the coven of Agnes Lilithsdottir."

Boo smiled, "Then let's talk this out and I won't have to play sleeping beauty."

Ellis picked up the thread, pulling out his cell. "My phone is programmed to call 911 if I don't tell it not to every five minutes. I have a feeling you don't want that kind of attention. Am I right?"

"Besides," I said, "It's not me that's going to be doing the talking." I raised my voice. "C'mon in, Renuka." As Renuka emerged, the whole mood of the room shifted.

Renuka smiled weakly, "Hey everyone."

The other witch stepped forward, I recognized her from the subway fight, and she looked at me warily. "Renuka, are you okay?"

"I'm fine. I haven't been mistreated." Renuka nodded quietly. "Scaevola has been lying to us. We've been played."

The lead witch looked at me, "You can't think we'll believe this. You have her spirit bound, or some sort of threat hanging over her, a Jinn or something similar, if she tells us the truth she dies."

I kept my tone neutral, non-threatening. "You are free to examine her and talk to her until you are satisfied. We'll wait, nobody will start anything as long as you don't try to hurt her."

The witch gestured to Renuka forcefully, pointing to one of the benches off to the side, Renuka looked to me and nodded her approval before joining the witch, who began to take materials out of a bag beside her.

The rest of us stood in tense silence for a while, waiting as she began her tests.

The other witch looked over at Boo, "You're Boudicca Esthersdottir, right? I recognize you from your author's photo."

Boo looked surprised, "Oh, cool, I mean, I feel like I went way too intense in that pose. I never know what to do with my eyes. But cool."

"I loved your book, though I think you were a little too hard on the Crowley-influenced covens."

Boo shrugged, "Yeah, it's a restriction of the methodology. I try not to actually do value judgements myself but restrict the work to people with firsthand experience. The only people I could find that weren't inside the covens were really bitter ex-members. Though I think it says something about an organization if everyone who leaves it does so with a bad taste in their mouth."

The witch smiled, "If I'd known you'd be here, I'd have brought my copy for you to sign."

"Oh! That's so sweet!" Boo gave a shy smile.

"Enough, stop mooning, Rosemary." The witch walked back over with Renuka beside her. She turned to her companions. "She is who she says she is, she's not under any normal mind control and as far as I can tell isn't under mundane threat either." She turned back towards Renuka, who had come to stand by Boo. "You said we are being played? What do you mean?"

Renuka took a deep breath. "Well, working with Boudicca and Ellis here, I have learned that the Deluge is an elaborate fake. Scaevola has been working for the Keepers the entire time, gathering us together to try and fake a crisis and get us all killed."

One of the other Deluge members stepped forward, a middle-aged man who I supposed to be Slavic from his accent, "and we just take your word for it? I am not as gullible as a little girl."

Both the witches looked harshly at the man, and he shied away slightly. The head witch turned back to Renuka, "Sexism aside, Dmitri has a point. Do you have some sort of proof of this?"

Boo stepped forward and pulled the book out of her bag along with a folder. "You recognize this?" The head witch nodded, "I have a list of inconsistencies and hidden rituals embedded within the text. For instance, let me show you this one." She opened the book on the floor and pulled a transparency and a photo of the tattoo from Eliot's autopsy out of the folder. "This was the ritual to summon the meteor down, which, seriously, just as an aside, here, that was a really stupid final plan." The head witch glared impatiently at Boo, "Anyhoo, most of the ritual design is false. Boo laid the transparency over the ritual, revealing a pyramid structure. "This was the real ritual design. I assume you are all marked with these tattoos? They would have served to channel necrotic energies from the death of Scaevola into each of you."

The Deluge members drew closer to look at the ritual, Rosemary spoke first, "If I'm reading this correctly, this would only have worked if Scaevola himself was killed, right?"

Boo smiled, "Yes. The whole thing was set to trigger upon Scaevola's death. All the energy being raised by the people in the circle was being used to fuel this."

Renuka spoke up, "Think about it, what's more likely. That Scaevola Fortier, the scourge of the Keepers, would be a double agent, or that he would be laying a trap. He took advantage of all of us."

Boo stepped back from the book and folder. "Those are yours to keep and analyze. Check it for yourself. I promise it checks out."

The head witch took a deep breath. "We need a moment to talk about this." She gestured for us to step back. "Renuka. Get over here." She continued as Renuka began to step back with us before joining the Deluge members.

We retreated back to the edge of the room, keeping an eye on them. I turned to Andrew as they continued to talk, "Think they believe us?"

Andrew smiled, "They believed us immediately. They were just waiting to see if we were trying to get them to do something. Now they are debating whether to leave or to go after Scaevola themselves."

Ellis snorted, "Helped that Boo Radley here had a fangirl."

Boo smiled, "I have a very specific audience for my work."

"I'd love to read it, once things blow over." I looked over to her.

"Well, I only have about a dozen copies at Agnes' so it might be tricky to put my hands on one."

We waited for a few minutes as they continued to debate among themselves. Finally, Renuka came over to us. "It's done. We're going to bring this to the rest of the group and at least some of us are going to try to get away from all this." She looked at Boo. "Thank you."

"Hey, Agnes is the one who does the whole Underground Railroad thing, I just told her you'd be a good candidate." Boo and Renuka hugged, she nodded to the rest of us, and the members of the Deluge walked away down the hall back towards the exit.

Boo drove as we pulled away down the McCormick Place bus road. I still had the code to the gates, which had given a good vantage point to sneak into the station. "Thanks, Guys." Boo cleared her throat. I thought for a second. "Sorry, thanks, folks." Boo nodded.

"I just feel bad for lying to them like that." Ellis chuckled.

I looked back at him. "What do you mean? You said you could program your phone to call the cops."

Ellis looked over his glasses at me. "I can. Doesn't mean I did. I don't turn anybody over to CPD unless I want them tied up in Homan Square with electrodes connected to their junk. And I wouldn't do that to my worst enemy."

"What would have happened if they called the bluff?" Boo sounded nervous. "That's a potent curse. We would have all been out for hours."

"Not me." Ellis said, smiling. "My phone was rigged to trigger my watch to shock me awake if I didn't tell it not to. I would have carried us all out to the car and gotten us out safe. I had a plan. Just not one what would have involved betraying anyone to Keeper prison."

I was about to get into it when my own phone rang. I looked at it. Daniel's number. More aggravation. I thought about sending it to voicemail, but I didn't want them to think I was afraid. "Hello Daniel, what's the fresh hell today?" I kept my tone acerbic; it wasn't hard.

"Hey Joe." Daniel's voice was subdued, and he paused before continuing.

"What. Do you need me to wash your car, or you'll ruin my credit rating? Is Prospero complaining about missed homework?"

"Joe. It's Ephraim." Daniel was speaking quietly.

"What does he want? I thought I made it clear to him how I felt." I was upset. I had trouble getting Ephraim's tears out of my mind.

"He's dead, Joe." I was stunned as Daniel continued. "The funeral is this Saturday at Graceland. Casimir is offering a truce."

I mumbled something affirmative into the phone before hanging up. Ephraim was dead. And right after talking to me, confessing what they'd done. Had they killed him? Had I driven away a friend? My only ally among the Keepers?

Andrew was the first to notice. "What happened, Joe." He reached up and touched my shoulder.

I sat quietly for a moment. "My uncle Ephraim is dead. I think they killed him for talking to me."

Chapter 50

That night, the four of us were sitting around Agnes' living room. Ellis and Andrew were playing cribbage. Boo was reading a few books and taking notes, her materials spread out on the piano. I was laid out on the couch. Ephraim's death was hitting me harder than I thought it would. I hadn't said much of anything since we returned from the ambush.

I had accepted a cup of cocoa from Agnes before she went to bed, I had declined offers to talk from Boo and from Andrew, I had murmured assent when Ellis had called Ephraim 'one wacky old man, really did his own thing, I always respected that.' But otherwise, I had laid silent on the couch. I hadn't even responded when Agnes brought word from Renuka that she and half a dozen other former Deluge members were headed out of the city while a bunch of the rest were headed back to confront Scaevola. I noticed the others occasionally looking at me, trying not to seem worried.

I stood up suddenly, "I need some air. I'll be back, I just need some air."

Andrew looked at me and nodded. "Do you need any company?"

I shook my head and walked out the front door into the night. I couldn't stand being cooped up anymore. Everything from the past week was eating at me and I just...I had to walk. When I got into that headspace the only thing that could get me out was my feet.

My life was...gone. I had lost my home, lost my possessions, lost my family. Family? Were they really my family? They had betrayed me, put me in danger and strung me along. Were they all in on it? No, I had no family. My parents had abandoned me to this life when I wasn't even a teenager. My uncles, ha, only Anthony and Casimir were really my uncles and one of them was the architect of this whole thing. No. I didn't have family.

So why did it hurt so much to lose Ephraim? He had been my teacher, my mentor and then later on my friend. He was the only one who ever treated me like a colleague rather than an intern. He had helped me open the doors of perception for the first time. We had met esoteric spirits and climbed the Tree of Life. And now he was gone.

He had been part of the lie. He had put me in the position of Chosen One and he had been in on the plot. But he had come clean. And maybe even tried to warn me? That last tarot spread. Now I wouldn't even get the chance to ask him. They had killed him because he had told me the truth.

I stopped and looked around me. I had made it all the way out to Promontory Point, the city glowed to the North over the lake, from here it looked so small. From here it was easy to believe that a malevolent force could reach out and snuff out a million lives in an instant. I had lived my life thinking I needed to stop that from happening, thinking I was waiting for my moment, only that was a lie used to save face by my supposed family. My supposed leaders. Now they were cleaning up their mess and didn't care who anymore had to die. If they ever did.

No. I couldn't let them do that. I couldn't let them get away with this. I started walking again. I needed to do something. Their motivations didn't matter. I did what I did because it meant something, because I wanted to help people, because I was in a position to do something. But I couldn't do this alone.

I strode through the front door forcefully, startling everyone. "I'm hungry. Let's go eat some food. Where's open right now down here?"

Boo and Ellis looked at each other. "Clarke's."

"There's a Clarke's down here now? Where was that when I was in college. Let's go. I need to talk to you. All of you." I grabbed my satchel and moved back towards the door.

Ten minutes later, we were in Clarke's. It was empty enough that we had claimed a circular table in the corner. We ordered when the waitress came over and then settled into silence.

Boo spoke first in a nervous joking tone, "Well, I'm gonna have to do a lot of rewrites. This whole revelation really puts a new spin on a lot of the inter-tradition political dynamics. I mean, it completely recontextualizes the Treaty of Madrid if the Keepers were playing dirty pool the whole time."

"That's a drag." Ellis nodded his head to the side sympathetically.

"That's research. You have to be ready to learn something and let it move you, otherwise you're just James George Frazer." She looked around the table, and only Andrew reacted. "I need more anthropologist friends."

"We need to do something." I said forcefully.

"About Frazer?" Boo quirked an eyebrow. "It's a little late."

"No. We should do something about what's going on."

Ellis smiled. "What did you have in mind?" He leaned forward on the table, folding his hands together.

I sighed. "I don't have a plan. I don't know what action looks like against something like this. I was trained to fight people who thought differently than me. I was taught arts of direct conflict, ways to attack people physically. This isn't something I know how to fight." I paused, thinking about how to continue. "But I was also trained to search out trouble and end it. To find people who sought to harm others and to stop them. And I see no reason to stop doing that. If anything, I feel like this just shows how much that is needed."

I looked around the table. Ellis was smiling eagerly, Boo had a look of curiosity on her face and Andrew looked solemn, though he was nodding his head. I continued. "I know I can't do this alone and I'd like all of your help, but I'd like to know why you're interested. I've taken motivations for granted for too long."

Ellis jumped in. "That's easy for me. I've been chasing this truth my whole life. Ever since I learned about Keeper involvement in the Atlanta compromise, I've been sure there was something like this and I've wanted to prove it to the world. As far as I see it, I'm not helping you with this, you're helping me."

"Fair enough." I nodded. "I'm sorry it took me so long to realize you needed help."

"Nah, I know you. You always run to help; you just fall in the lake sometimes." Ellis gave quick twitch of his eyebrows "We're on the right track now."

After a moment, Boo spoke up. "I guess for me it's about curiosity. I've been studying intergroup dynamics of the magical community for years and lacking this crucial piece of the puzzle. This changes everything and makes so many things make sense. I need to know more. Besides, I like wearing my patriarchy smashing boots and this is a chance to lace 'em up."

"I'm not sure I can handle another earth-shattering revelation on this scale, but if one pops up, I'm glad you'll be around to contextualize it for me." I smiled at Boo.

"Boo smash." Boo mock stomped her feet under the table. "Plus, you still need to see Return of the Jedi."

Ellis looked at Boo, "He hasn't seen?" He turned to me. "Tell me you've seen Empire at least."

"Sorry, No. You know how Casimir felt about movies made after Psycho." I shrugged and looked over at Andrew.

Andrew sat in thought for a moment. "I'm not sure what I have to offer in all this. I'm not a scholar or a truth seeker. I'm not looking to make my mark upon the world. I am here because you are my friend. When I came to Chicago, I didn't have much of anybody and I had resigned myself to it." He paused.

We were all silent for a moment. Andrew thought and then continued. "You changed that, Joe. You have been a good friend. And that didn't change when you learned I was trans. It's hard as a namer, someone who can see the internal truth behind every reaction, but it meant a lot to me that you took it as a challenge to learn and be better, not an excuse to grow distant or stop taking me seriously. I wish you weren't an exception, but you are. You know my taste in ginger beer, you are a good crossword buddy and an even better wingman, you are my best friend. That means a lot to me, and I am not one to abandon friends."

I smiled through some tears. "Well, you've always treated me as just Joe, not as some grand fulfillment of a prophecy. That's meant a lot to me over the years, someone I could just do the crossword with where it wasn't a test of my worthiness." I leaned over and gave Andrew a hug.

The waitress showed up as we broke the hug and looked around. After the plates were handed out and the coffees refreshed, I reached into my bag and pulled out a notebook. "Alright. Let's come up with a plan."

End Act IV

Chapter 51

Monday, June 29th

I felt dramatically overdressed standing in the Red Line train. My somber black suit contrasted dramatically with the chattering college students and summering tourists sharing the ride north. My mood was just as discordant. As they bustled with excitement, I was deep within my own despair.

I had lost my mentors, all of my mentors. The men that I had trusted with my life and future. They had cultivated me as a lie, raising me to fight and die to maintain their stranglehold on the world. I had been fed a steady diet of half-truths, sent on meaningless tasks and taught methods of oppression. Used as a symbol for a regime of cultural hegemony without my consent.

They had sent a woman to seduce me and serve as bait, a fake prisoner of a fake cult to fulfill a fake prophecy. They had set me up to kill a man and with him, an entire group of people, at least some of whom were there against their will. They had planned a quiet ignorant retirement for me married to a co-conspirator. And expected me to be thankful. And then they would have started again with a new Chosen One. A new lamb sent to the slaughter.

Ephraim had told me. At least, he had come clean when asked. Hell, maybe he had even been trying to hint with that tarot spread. Had there been hints before that I missed? And less than a day after telling me the truth, he was dead. Had he been killed? Did that even matter at this point?

The train nearly emptied at Fullerton and Belmont, and I had a few minutes breathing time before I had to get off. I had to prepare myself. This was a space of truce. I trusted that enough to come here, or at least to come prepared. I had bound an air spirit into my suit, enough for one mighty leap over Graceland's walls if I needed to run. A week ago, I wouldn't have thought that necessary preparation for a funeral. A week ago, my entire life wasn't built on lies.

I would go, I would say as few words as possible, and then I would give my eulogy. I would take the opportunity to see how people reacted. Who thought what about what was going on. And I would have a chance to test Ellis' psychometric camera.

Ellis had placed it himself, connected to a tie pin specifically designed for the purpose. Less a typical camera, the device was one of Ellis' own design, an active psychometric recorder, taking passive recordings that could be reconstructed later for easy reproduction. Ellis had developed it for monitoring police interactions on the South Side, catching things police wouldn't do before a known camera. Hopefully, we'd get some results that could be examined later by Andrew, looking for subtle clues in behavior that told us who was part of this and who wasn't.

"This is Sheridan." The familiar voice brought me out of my reverie. "Doors open on the right at Sheridan." I disembarked and headed out to the street. The entrance to Graceland was only a few blocks away. It had always been on the train line, built after the great fire along the model of the London Necropolis, far enough from the center to avoid overcrowding, easy to reach by train. While the city had grown around it, it was still open green space, one of Chicago's great cemeteries. As I passed through the gates, I saw the funeral tent in the near distance.

The gathering at the graveside was small. A couple dozen people, all in black suits, wearing long black sashes of mourning. They were milling about together in hushed, informal conversation. I pulled my own sash from my satchel and draped it over my shoulders as I approached. Voices grew quiet as I drew closer, my appearance was noticed in waves.

As I entered the tent area, I looked at the layout. The Conclave themselves were in the front of the tent, around the table, with associate members and allied groups. I saw Casimir speaking softly to Simon, his eyes boring into me from across the tent. I stood near the edge in the back, held back by the emotional force of that glare. None of the conclave made any move to approach me and I remained as far away as I could without leaving the tent.

I felt someone standing beside me and glanced over to see Daniel, looking somber in his suit. "Hey Joey." The tension in his voice told of nervousness and withheld emotion. "Glad you could make it."

"Well, I wouldn't miss it. Ephraim was a friend." I kept my own voice quiet.

"A lot of us thought we were friends, Joey." Daniel kept his eyes looking towards the front of the tent. "If it was me up there, would you still be standing here?"

I looked over at him. "Yes, Daniel. I would be." He didn't look back at me, but I could sense an easing in tension. "We've been through way too much together."

Daniel snorted and pulled a flask from his pocket. He took a sip and offered it to me. "They are really fucking pissed at you, Joe. Casimir has been talking about 'irresponsibility and shirking of duty and ungratefulness' more or less non-stop." Daniel glanced around and spoke more quietly. "They have Simon trying to find a way to nullify Ephraim's will, you know."

I took a sip of the flask before handing it back. "Okay?" I was uncertain. "What does that have to do with me?"

This time Daniel did look over. "He left you everything. He drew it up, certified and sanctified the night before he died. Casimir says you won't see any of it unless you stop running around and playing at rebellion." He took another sip and put the flask away.

I was surprised. Ephraim and I had parted on such bad terms. "What do you mean, playing at rebellion?"

"Casimir says you're drawing things out, sure the prophecy will keep you from failing. He doesn't say why, but he keeps hinting that you must have chickened out. Clark is champing at the bit to go after Scaevola himself, but Casimir won't let him." Daniel looked at me. "Joe, why didn't you just finish this bullshit out on the ship?"

"I couldn't."

"Happens to a lot of guys."

I shook my head and gave Daniel a dirty look. "I saw that my actions wouldn't have actually resolved the prophecy. I needed more information. So, I withdrew."

"Why don't you tell them that?" Daniel was hushed, but insistent. "Shit, Joe, this could be over right now."

"They already know, but they won't accept the truth." I nodded forward as the ceremony began. The Chicago Conclave of Keepers sat around the front table with three empty chairs. Ephraim's, Scaevola's and mine. Around the tent Keepers from nearby conclaves, family members and associates all sat and stood. I contemplated sitting down, but I knew that it would take enough willpower for me to make myself speak, I decided not to add standing up to that.

Casimir rose, "Ephraim Baumann served as Keeper of the Flames for over fifty years, vigilantly watching the sacred fires for signs of danger, keeping us safe through many tumultuous times. He served as mentor to two of the Chosen, Peter Massey and Joseph Palevsky. We are lessened without his insights, but he has gone to a better place and rests now beside his maker. I would like to invite those who knew him best to say a few words in his memory."

Many spoke of Ephraim, eulogizing his wisdom, his peculiar sense of humor, his love of good cigars. They spoke of his life. I watched, waiting. As things began to subside, I saw Casimir begin to rise, to close out the ritual and I knew the moment had come.

"I would like to say a few words." All eyes in the tent turned to me as I strode forwards to the front of the tent. Casimir stared, but he couldn't simply tell me no in front of the visiting Keepers, I figured none of them knew the nitty gritty of what was going on, fuck, I was banking on it. Casimir sat back in his chair, brooding.

I strode forwards, taking a position off to the side. I needed to be able to see everyone. "Prophecies are often referred to as Revelations, something that Ephraim taught me a lot about. Prophets reveal things, they lay aside the lies we tell ourselves about the future, show us what is to come and force us to ask ourselves what we are going to do about it. Ephraim took that responsibility seriously. He wanted us all to be asking the right questions about what is to come. In the process, I think he revealed more than he imagined. I think he revealed to each of us a bit of who we really are." I paused and pulled out a piece of paper. "I would like to share a passage from Scripture.

For we know in part, and we prophesy in part.

But when that which is perfect is come, then that which is in part shall be done away.

When I was a child, I spake as a child, I understood as a child, I thought as a child: but when I became a man, I put away childish things.

For now we see through a glass, darkly, but then face to face: now I know in part, but then shall I know even as also I am known."

"Thank you." I left the front of the stage, no longer able to hold back my tears, walked down the aisle and out of the tent as the assembled Keepers watched me.

Chapter 52

Tuesday, June 30th

I returned to Agnes' house that evening after work. I had been nervous leaving the bar alone, constantly watching the shadows for movement, but all of the others had important tasks and I still needed to earn a paycheck. Besides, Scaevola didn't have a cult to come after me anymore.

Everything was busy in Agnes' living room. Andrew and Ellis were on the sofa, watching something on Ellis' laptop that appeared to be connected to his psychometric apparatus, my tie pin sitting in the center. Agnes was at her antique desk in the corner, reading glasses on, paperwork in front of her, humming as she shifted numbers in a ledger.

I got nods from each of them as I entered before they returned to their tasks. I saw Boo through the door to the dining room, seated at the table in conversation with two people. She waved me over as I entered, and I came into the room. "Joe, I'd like to introduce you to some people. This is Tina and this is Lobo." Boo stood up and gestured to her visitors. "Tina, Lobo, this is Joe."

They each stood up as I entered and took my hand as I offered it. Tina was a darker skinned Latina, short and strongly built. As she stood, I could tell she was pregnant, though not too far along. Her handshake was strong, and she looked me straight in the eye. "Agustina Lopez. Tina to my friends."

"Joseph Palevsky, and I hope to be one of those." I turned to Lobo. He was also Latino, though taller and with lighter skin. He looked older than Tina, a bit of gray in his temples. "She said you were Lobo?"

"Miguel Villalobos. Got stuck with Lobo as a teen, it's more or less permanent now." His hands were calloused and his handshake firm.

Boo smiled at the introductions. "So, we talked about potentially getting some protection, these are some folks I thought might be able to help. Tina and Lobo are part of the local Ocelomeh, dedicated to Tezcatlipoca, they do community protection down in Little Village." Boo sat and the rest of us joined her around the table.

"Tescat..." I struggled a bit with the pronunciation. "That's Nahuatl, right?"

Tina looked at me straight. "Tezcatlipoca, the smoking mirror. Patron of the Jaguar Warriors who fought Cortez. We are the inheritors of their mantle." I nodded in understanding, noticing that both of them had some piece of clothing with jaguar pattern highlights. Tina a stretchy top, Lobo a handkerchief in his back pocket.

"So, has Boo let you know what we're hoping for?" I looked back and forth between them.

"She mentioned it, but we haven't talked any specifics." Lobo smiled. "We got a bit caught up in catching up."

"No problem. So, I am going to be doing some investigation and potentially confronting Keeper forces in the city. I don't anticipate any violence, I won't be instigating any, but having some people to back me up would make them think twice about starting trouble. I am only thinking of a few specific situations, but it would be very helpful if you could provide backup."

Lobo and Tina exchanged a look. Tina turned back to me. "This can be arranged, but there is a price. Tezcatlipoca demands a sacrifice for our service."

I was taken aback but I tried to take the request in stride. "Okay, um.... I'm just gonna say I am not comfortable with human sacrifice, but, but I do have a reliable source for sanctified animals. I could get a lamb or a goat fairly easily, would that do?"

Lobo, Boo and Tina exchanged looks, and then laughed out loud. Lobo spoke first, "We were thinking more of you coming down to the community center and volunteering. We have a book sale coming up and the abuelas can always use help using the computers. Though my cousin Nitzi got a really good jerk goat recipe from this Jamaican girl he used to date, so if you really want to throw a cookout, we could figure something out."

I nodded, a bit peeved, but grateful I wouldn't have to spring for a whole sanctified goat. "I'd be happy to help with the book sale and with the abuelas. If things go on for a while, then we'll talk cookout."

"Then you have our help." Tina didn't smile, but her expression did soften some. She stood and Lobo stood with her. "La Fantasma knows how to contact us." I nodded, shook hands with both of them. They hugged Boo and departed.

After they'd gone, I turned to Boo. "La Fantasma?"

"Long story."

"Like, a ghost? A ghost that might say Boo?"

"Okay, not a long story. Can't I just have a cool mysterious nickname?"

"Hey, I won't tell. So, I hope I didn't offend them by mentioning human sacrifice or offering up animals. I don't know a lot about Mesoamerican practices, just what my teachers said, and now that I think about it, I don't think I can trust much of that."

Boo smiled and patted my shoulder. "Don't worry, I think you're fine on the first count, it's not like the Aztecs didn't sacrifice people, just offer to take care of Senora Juarez when you help out at the community center, she's the toughest one."

"Mean?" I felt weird asking how intimidating an old Hispanic woman was.

"No, but she has 20 something grandchildren back in Cuautla and will want to see pictures of all of them. You may have to send some pointed emails to her daughters-in-law who don't post enough." Boo smiled. "Tezcatlipoca smiles on those who face adversity willingly."

"Tina's not planning on joining us in the field in her...condition?" I gestured to indicate her pregnancy.

Boo raised her eyebrow. "Oh? No. Ocelomeh groups are always led by a midwife and a warrior. The Jaguar god protects women in childbirth as well, you know. They just make decisions together." She smiled as we joined the others in the living room. "It's too bad for you. Tina's the real badass of the two."

Chapter 53

I was finishing making dinner when Ellis came into the kitchen. I had been working hard to pitch in around the house since I'd been staying there and while I wasn't a fantastic cook, I'd picked up a few tricks working in bars over the years. Tonight was a caramelized onion couscous with garbanzos and falafel. It fit various dietary restrictions and still felt good and substantial for those used to eating meat.

"Joe, we've got some results." Ellis looked at the food and grabbed a piece of falafel, crunching into it.

"Hey, hands off the grub until it's served." I smiled and picked up the plates, heading into the dining room. "Dinner's ready."

Once everyone was sitting down and the meal begun, Ellis spoke up. "So, like I said, we've got some results." He pulled open his laptop and started playing the video. I looked over to Agnes, expecting her to object, but she kept eating.

"Okay." I said, "What'ya got?"

Ellis started the video. He'd isolated the facial expressions of the Keepers at the table in separate windows. The faces of Prospero, Clark, Anthony, Casimir and Simon all looked back. "We broke things down by time and Andrew watched how they reacted to the different parts of your speech." He clicked through, "Here's the main point, where you talked about the aspects of prophecy and truth. We get some really interesting reactions here. Andrew?"

Andrew leaned forward, pointing as he went. "Casimir knows, but he doesn't feel any more guilt about it. He used to, but not now. He's committed. Simon knows. He's not entirely sure, but he is in favor of whatever keeps him comfortable and is following Casimir's lead on that. Prospero knows, but only recently, he's still getting used to the idea. That said, he's not losing sleep. Based on what you said Ephraim said, I think he wants to replace him and sees his chance."

"Of course he does." I said with a resigned sigh. "More power, more prestige."

Andrew nodded. "The other two don't know. Anthony was pretty broken up over everything, but Clark was suspicious of what you were saying. I think he might have mistaken your meaning."

"Tell him the other thing with Clark." Ellis nudged Andrew. I looked between them.

Andrew rewound the video. The quality changed slightly. "This is the part where Casimir mentions Peter. Clark is still deeply hurt by the loss of his friend."

"They were close." I shrugged. "He never wanted to talk about it." I leaned my head on my hands. That's our in, isn't it. I feel like such an..." I paused and restrained my language, looking at Agnes.

"An asshole?" She said, smiling.

"Yeah, an asshole." I continued, I guess I didn't need to watch my language quite so much.

"You're looking at this the wrong way, Joe." Ellis leaned forward. "You ain't the one who sent his friend in unprepared. You ain't the one who leveraged his friend's sacrifice for prestige."

I shook my head. "Neither is he. I would be dragging it out."

"Clark is as much a victim of this as anyone. He deserves to know, painful or not." Ellis was vehement. "I know it's going to hurt, but it'll hurt however he learns. Shit, at this point it's a mercy. The man has been lied to about the death of his best friend for nearly 40 years!"

I was about to reply when Ellis' phone rang. "Sorry." He looked at it. "I need to take this." He stepped into the living room. The rest of us went back to eating.

Boo joined the conversation, "I know you don't like to hurt people. But think about it this way. How's Clark going to feel if he learns from someone else? You know more than anyone what he's going to go through."

Ellis came back in. "Joe, I need you to finish eating. That was my contact with the Alexandrians. They are willing to meet, but in five minutes."

"Okay. Right. Where? I could probably enchant this carpet to fly if..." I grabbed a falafel ball and tossed it whole into my mouth.

"Upstairs, Joe. This'll be virtual." Ellis chuckled at my surprise, "C'mon, man, It's 2015."

Chapter 54

Ellis had set up his laptop upstairs with webcam and microphone. The room seemed strangely empty without Renuka. As I approached, Ellis was fiddling with the program. "I have the security set up. Are you ready?" I nodded and sat in one of the chairs.

Ellis clicked a button on the screen, and it came to life. On the screen were three figures split between multiple frames. They were all wearing identical featureless masks with hoods. The center one spoke, indicated by a light before them that illuminated. "We have come to hear the petition from Joseph Palevsky, supported by Ellis Green. I have gathered a committee of three as required to hear a petition for a single party consent recording. Please identify yourselves and affirm your intentions." The light went out as they concluded their speech.

Ellis sat forward. "My name is Ellis Jaleel Green; I am a certified affiliate of the Alexandrians. I bring forth this petition as affiliate and affirm my intentions for the revelation of truth." He nodded to me.

I leaned forward. "My name is Joseph Samuel Palevsky. I also bring this petition and affirm my intention for the revelation of truth." I spoke the phrase as Ellis had taught me.

"We acknowledge your affirmed intentions and accept your right to petition. Please present your case." The central figure said.

Ellis sat forward. "We have collected evidence that the Conclave of Keepers has arranged an extensive cover up related to their internal office of the Chosen One. We want help distributing a recording of a confession, but we need permission for a single party consent recording." He sat back.

The Alexandrian on the right spoke. "You are aware that under normal circumstances we only allow two party consent when it comes to distribution. We have specific requirements to fulfill in order to break that policy."

Ellis leaned forward again. "We understand those requirements. I have submitted supporting material to establish that the content is both intentionally concealed and materially harmful. As I understand, we need within the recording to establish the intentional deception and give those involved in the cover up a chance to willingly reveal the truth. Am I correct?"

"You are." The Alexandrian on the left said.

"We accept these requirements and consent to have this material stored and disseminated by the Alexandrian Order." Ellis nodded at me.

"I also consent to these requirements and to storage and dissemination." I spoke exactly as Ellis had told me.

"We therefore accept your oaths. You have 28 days before this covenant expires. Ellis, you have the transfer protocols, correct."

"Correct."

"Then our business is concluded." The video stopped suddenly.

"Whew. I thought the Keepers had a monopoly on mysterious and creepy." I sat back.

"Yeah, different reasons though. They go for anonymous and interchangeable not sinister and dominant." Ellis closed his computer. "That's one more thing down. Now to get something to leak."

I looked at Ellis. "Hey, I wanted to talk about something."

Ellis was slipping his computer back into his bag. "What's up, Joe?"

"About the train station. You changed the plan without consulting me." I tried to keep calm, but this had been digging at me. "That whole stunt with the phone could have put us all in real danger."

Ellis sat back in his chair. "Well, no offense, Joe, but the plan sucked. You know how close Clark is to the police. We would have ended up in a Keeper prison and everything would have gone to shit."

"What the fuck is so bad about Keeper prisons?" I blew up. "Everyone seems so willing to die rather than go to them. They imprison terrible people who want to destroy the world! People who have been convicted of terrible things!"

Ellis looked at me, slightly baffled. "You really don't know what they're like, do you? Have you ever been to one?"

"I've been to the holding cells below the lodge, they aren't that bad. It's no feather bed, but it's no hell."

Ellis smirked, "That's jail, there's a world of difference between jail and prison. Look, Joe. It's not your fault you don't know. Your uncles sure weren't in a rush to show you their dirty laundry. Tell you what, I know some folks who can tell you more. Give me a day, then if you still want to fight about this, we'll row over to Weehawken."

Chapter 55

Thursday, July 2nd

Ellis' apartment was easy enough to find. He'd sent me the address and asked me to stop by, but he hadn't told me why. Still, it wasn't too inconvenient a walk from Agnes', a trip across the UofC campus and past the law school into Woodlawn. Back when I was a student, I don't think I would have braved the journey south of the Midway, but I didn't think I had anything to fear in the middle of the day and the trip down had only brought me into contact with people enjoying the sunny weather on their porches.

I reached the apartment and knocked on Ellis' door. I heard some locks being undone from out on the landing, but when the door opened Ellis stepped out rather than inviting me in. "Hey Joe, thanks for coming." He pulled his door mostly shut and gave me an overhand shake. "Alright, so I wanted to talk to you before I brought you inside. The people inside are a bit nervous and I want to make sure you know how things are going to go down."

"Sure." I shrugged, "I'm not exactly sure why I'm here, but I figured you know what we're up against, so you wouldn't call me down for nothing."

Ellis smiled, "This shit's vital. Okay, so I work with a support group, documenting abuses of power by the Conclave and their cronies. These are some of the folks I've interviewed. They are here to tell you their stories, but they only agreed based on a few specific rules. One, no interrupting. They are telling their stories, and it's hard enough to talk about. Two, you can ask questions afterwards, but they don't have to answer. If they say no, then that's it, no follow-ups, no rephrasing the same question. And don't ask anything that seems like it might be used to identify them to the Conclave. They are already a little skeptical of your presence here."

"Didn't you vouch for me?" This wasn't feeling very comforting.

"Joe, there isn't enough mystical cred in all Chicago to convince these people the Chosen One isn't a potential danger. These were the three who I could get here. You don't want to know how many said no." Ellis gave a short laugh. "So, you up?"

I gave a brief thought before nodding, "Sure. Let's do this. Ellis led me in and through his apartment. I was surprised at the size. The front part of the apartment had two rooms facing the street, one that seemed to be set up as an electronics and metals workshop and the other with a computer and a mountain of peripherals. "You some sort of hacker?" I looked at Ellis.

"Video editing and encrypted communication. I make videos, I send them out. It's not all glamorous, I mostly do weddings, bar mitzvahs and graduations. Citizen journalist for the magical world doesn't pay the bills." Ellis smiled at me as he beckoned back down the hall.

At the end of the hall there was a dining room across from a kitchen, and around the table, there were three people seated. Ellis entered first, "Hey everyone, this is Joe. Like I told you, Joe is a member of the Conclave of Keepers, but has been questioning the things he's been told, so I wanted to give you all a chance to tell him your stories, help get some of that wool off his eyes."

I nodded as he spoke. "Yup. Hello everyone, I want to thank you in advance for this. I can only imagine what you've been through." I looked at Ellis and the table and he gestured me to a seat with my back to the window, furthest from the door. It wouldn't be my first choice, but I figured my own comfort was the lowest priority here.

There was a moment of silence as I sat, Ellis smiled and closed the door, before looking around the table. The first to speak was the fairly conservatively dressed African American woman next to me. "I'll start. My name is Martha. I used to have a very good relationship with the Keepers. I was brought up in the Atlantan community and studied down at the Tuskegee Institute, working in the mystical crafts. I was near the top of my class and specialized in protective jewelry. After I left school, I was employed by the Conclave in Washington D.C., working at the main North American offices of the Praetorians, crafting sword pins."

"I had been working for several years and had gotten good at the work. I could easily craft in the defensive enchantments, but I was curious about whether I could improve on the design. I borrowed some library books through a friend of mine, a Kappa Tau Omega, and came up with a way of creating an ablative shield against flame using the name of fire carved into a small lead plate at the back. It would only protect against one attack before melting but could easily be incorporated into existing designs."

"I went to share my invention with my supervisor, sure that I'd be rewarded or at least praised for my initiative. Instead, I found myself in front of the high council of the Praetorians.

"Apparently, the magic I had learned for my crafting was forbidden, only available to trusted members of the Conclave. I was told that I was lucky I was not being imprisoned for what I did, but they would have to pronounce anathema on me, there would be a Jinn bound to my spirit to prevent me from using magic and, oh yeah, I was fired." She paused for a while at the end, shaking a bit with contained anger. "Of course, my friend got away with just a slap on the wrist."

"Do you know what it is to live under anathema?" She asked, I shook my head. "It's like losing your hands. Only, you still have your hands, you just know that you aren't allowed to touch anything, or your hands will fall off. I spent years training in magical jewelcraft, now I can't practice that. I have had to move cities, I've had to try and start over, all because they couldn't trust me not to burn down Keeper facilities because I'm naturally subversive or something."

Everyone around the table was quiet for a moment as Martha finished. Ellis looked around and turned to me. "Joe, do you have any questions?"

I sat for a moment in thought. I knew certain magics were kept secret, though I hadn't really thought through the repercussions. I cleared my throat. "Who was it pronounced the Anathema on you? I know only a few people know that ritual."

"The Keeper of Laws in ascendance, Casimir Palevsky." Martha smiled ruefully, "Honestly, that's part of why I came to Chicago, I had some sort of naive idea that I could find a way to meet him and convince him to lift it. Yeah, I'm not that naive anymore."

"Thank you for sharing that with me, Martha." I spoke softly and bowed my head slightly. Martha shrugged a bit and leaned back in her chair.

Next to Martha was a blonde woman, dramatic undercut and punk trappings, the stylized sun pendant around her neck identified her as a witch in one of the Slavic traditions, though I couldn't quite place it. She had been leaning back during Martha's story but leaned forward once it was clear Martha was finished. "Hello, my name is Ruslana Susanivna, I was trained by the Crimean Sun coven in Kyiv, but came to Chicago 10 years ago. I had kept in some touch with the Crimean Sun during the first few years, but when our leader Stepania died, I drifted away. I didn't know the new leader and my sister had told me she was very angry. I am not violent, I am, what is the word, pacifist. I lived quietly, practiced alone."

"You know about the war in Ukraine last year?" She looked at me as she asked.

"I read some about it, I don't know everything, though." I said after pausing to make sure it wasn't rhetorical.

"There was a lot of...unrest in Kyiv, people marching, spirit of revolution in the hearts of people. I was watching news, worried about my family." Ruslana sighed, "Then my sister Oksana came to my home. She had not called, but she was family, I took her in. She had run from the Crimean Sun, the new leader Ana had been making war on Keepers, Oksana had run to avoid getting killed. I did not know what she did, but she is my sister, I let her stay with me."

"It was two days when men came. They took us both, killed my cat. They had tracked my sister. We were tortured." Ruslana put her hands on the table and removed her gloves, revealing hands scarred all along the fingers. "I did not have anything to tell them, I had been gone from Ukraine 10 years, my sister had only just come to me. They kept me in prison for six months, brought in truth-seers, made me swear oaths. Then one day, they put me in a van and dropped me off on a street corner. They told me I was going to be watched, and that I should stay quiet, and nothing would happen. I have not seen my sister since then. Ellis has been trying to help me track her down." Ellis nodded solemnly as Ruslana gestured to him.

Ellis looked to me, "Do you have any questions for Ruslana, Joe?"

I sat for a moment. "I do, but I am worried they might seem like a search for identifiable information. May I explain my reasoning and ask?"

Ellis looked over to Ruslana, "It's up to you. You are free to say no. You are also free to say yes and not answer."

Ruslana nodded with a set expression. "Go ahead."

"I want to know when and where this happened. I'm not doubting what you are saying, but if this happened here in Chicago, I think...thought, I guess, I would have heard about it."

Ruslana nodded, "I was taken from Chicago, It was in February. I do not know where they held me"

I sighed. "Thank you. This isn't something I knew of. I'm sorry about what you went through."

As I finished, the last person at the table stood up. A tall and slender East Asian man, he had been wearing a long-sleeved shirt, which he removed. Beneath, he was wearing a small undershirt and he was covered in tattoos from where a t-shirt collar would be to where the cuffs of his shirt had been. He set the shirt on the table in front of him, but he remained standing as he spoke in unaccented English. "Call me Saigo. I don't have a lot to my story, I grew up in San Francisco as part of one of the Shadow Yakuza families, I was initiated into the darker elements of the family business when I was 13, before I knew better. I was arrested when I was 15 with some illegal imports, but instead of being sent to Juvie, I found myself in a Keeper prison without trial and without the possibility of release. I was pretty much fucked."

"I was in there for three years, long enough to regret getting into trouble...Long story short, I escaped. I'm not gonna tell you how, but it was that or kill myself. I've been on the run since. I don't really know what I'm going to do long term. I don't want to go back to my family, I don't want to get into that sort of shit anymore, but I don't really have anywhere to go. I'm 20 years old and the rest of my life I going to be on the run because of stupid teenage bullshit. Fuck the Keepers, Fuck my family, Fuck the whole goddamn system." Saigo picked up his shirt from the table and walked out the door, glaring at me.

I sat quietly and looked at Ellis. He nodded at me and spoke up. "I want to thank you both for sharing your stories. I will see you at the next meeting I hope, and Saigo too." He added as an afterthought. There were some strained pleasantries as Martha and Ruslana gathered up their things and departed, I remained at the table while Ellis showed them out through the kitchen.

"I had no idea." I said as Ellis returned.

Ellis looked at me, "That's why I showed you."

"Why didn't you tell me about this, why didn't you come to me? I thought we were...well, we were friends once, right?" I had trouble keeping my anger down. "Seriously, I could have done something, I could have stopped this and instead, you just held this back and left me helpless."

Ellis paused, an enigmatic expression on his face. "You gonna tell me you would just have gone, 'sure Ellis, I believe you, the runaway outcast, about the shit that's being done by the folks that raised me.' Because you just gotta look around you to see that's not how this shit goes down. I can tell you for sure that I go to any of your uncles with this shit, I get locked up myself, so no, I didn't take the immense risk to trust someone I haven't really seen for the past decade." Ellis shook his head, then continued a little quieter. "Look Joe, I know you didn't do this shit. And I know you didn't know. But you're an adult. You need to start asking questions, looking into the shit around you. Because when you don't ask, that's as good as saying you don't care. People notice when you don't stand up, when you don't look around."

I sat there, a little speechless under the weight of Ellis' rebuke. I felt anger and indignance start to rise up and I stopped myself. I took a deep breath. "You're right...I'm sorry."

Ellis sat down next to me. "Shit, Joe. I ain't slamming you. Just saying, wake up and smell the oppression. I wish we could have been in this together the whole time, but this ain't over yet. We're in this shit together 'til the end, right?" He offered me his hand and pulled me into a quick one shoulder hug. "Let's start fixing."

I nodded. "Okay, what's next?"

Chapter 56

Saturday, July 4th

We had to wait a few days before finding an opening for a confrontation. Members of the Ocelomeh kept their ears open and Boo had some of her contacts looking around. Trying to find a situation to intervene in, a chance to find Clark in action and engineer a confrontation.

I spent the time keeping busy. In between my shifts at the bar, I split my time between filming some interviews with Ellis and working at the community center. Boo hadn't exaggerated Señora Juarez' number of grandchildren, but the Señora decided fairly quickly that I was a nice young man and that I needed feeding up and introducing around. Agnes' fridge was full of tamales and tres leches cake, nobody was complaining.

Ellis' interviews were hard. He had me talking about things I'd done as Chosen One, going over some timelines, looking at photos of people I'd helped arrest. Boo had supplied some legwork on tracking down results. There were some hard truths to confront there, some questions where the truth hurt a lot. But I wasn't backing off this.

Saturday ended up being the roughest. I lay on a hammock in Agnes' garden, staring at the trees above me, trying to clear my head. It was too early to start drinking, but I didn't have any other ideas.

It was hard not to think about all the things I would be doing if my life hadn't fallen apart. In other circumstances, I'd be down on Daniel's boat, drinking fancy beer or whatever ridiculous literary cocktail I'd invented for the occasion and flirting with the women on the other boats. Maybe I'd be out at a picnic with the other folks from the bookstore, grilling brats and reading bad sex scenes from self-published novels out loud for laughs. I doubted Daniel was partying right now and employees let go for suspected theft weren't usually invited to the cookout.

No, I was alone on the hammock in the backyard. Agnes had gone to Michigan City for the weekend to get away from the inevitable warzone atmosphere of neighborhood fireworks brought over from Indiana. Boo was out running down some leads places where I'd either be in the way or get stabbed somewhere uncomfortable. Her words.

Ellis was documenting police harassment on the South Side with his film team. Andrew was...where was Andrew? Well, he wasn't here.

I had made a pitcher of margaritas earlier, something to do with my hands while I waited, making a fancy lime syrup from scratch, mixing them up in just the right proportions, but it was way too early to start drinking alone.

I looked at my phone. 2pm. I looked at the pile of books I'd brought out one by one, none of them enough to distract me for more than a few pages. I needed to get out of here, out of this funk. I needed a distraction. I pulled up Andrew's number and hoped I wasn't interrupting something.

Andrew answered pretty quickly. "Joe, what's going on? Everything alright?" His tone was matter of fact, but there was definitely concern in his voice.

"Andrew, hey. Everything's fine. I hope I'm not interrupting anything, I..." I paused; a bit lost for words.

"Joe?"

"I don't know. I don't really have anything to do right now. I mean, I'm not, I guess that doesn't really sound like much of a problem, but..."

"You stopped moving long enough to look around." Andrew was succinct.

"Yeah, I guess, yeah. I don't really know what to do with myself and all the things that seem appealing seem a bit...I don't know."

"I hear you. Give me ten minutes, I'll give you a call back. Put on some real pants." Andrew hung up before I could ask how he knew I was still in pajama pants.

A few minutes later my phone buzzed. "Yeah?"

"Are you sober?" Andrew was speaking loudly over the noise of traffic.

"Yeah, I made some margaritas, but haven't...."

"Great, stay that way, closed toed shoes, meet out front of Agnes' in about 20."

"Cool." I threw on some boots and grabbed my bag. About 20 minutes later, I was on Agnes' porch when a battered gray pickup pulled up with Andrew in the passenger seat. He waved me over and slid to the middle of the bench seat. I got into the truck and buckled myself in.

"Joe, this is my friend Sharlene. She's gonna teach you a new skill today." Andrew gestured to the woman driving, an Asian woman with short hair wearing a sleeveless vest and heavy boots.

"Ah, nice to meet you Sharlene." I extended my hand across Andrew.

"You too, Joe." Sharlene's grip was firm, and her hands were lightly calloused but smooth.

"No offense, Andrew, but I don't know if I have the bandwidth for personal development right now. I'm a bit all over the place."

"Trust me, Joe." Andrew smiled as he continued to watch the road ahead.

"The trick is to get the rotation just right, so it hits just as the blade comes around." Sharlene hurled the axe two handed over her head with a grunt. It twirled through the air and sunk with a satisfying thunk into the log target. Sharlene's backyard in Pilsen was set up with a row of targets and a plywood backing against the concrete wall. She walked over to the wall and pulled the axe out of the log. "The weight of the axe head does the work for you." She handed me the hatchet. "Give it a shot."

I squared up, trying to emulate what she had showed me. I tried a few gentle dry swings then hurled the hatchet with both hands. It struck the wall next to the target and bounced to the ground. "I can see why you said closed toed shoes." I smiled ruefully at Andrew who nodded back.

"Give it another try." Sharlene grabbed the hatchet from the ground. Square your shoulders and hips and stand just half a step further back." She set me up behind a 2 X 4 that served as a distance marker.

I threw again and the axe hit squarely, though not hard enough to stick in the wood. "You're getting it. Don't move your feet, I'll grab it." She picked up the axe and brought it back to me.

A few throws later and I was hitting the target well about half the time. Andrew was taking a few shots at the target next to mine, doing a bit better than I was.

"You're getting it. You two okay out here on your own for a bit?" Sharlene looked to Andrew who nodded.

We took a few turns, throwing the axes and drinking some of the homemade kombucha Sharlene's girlfriend had brought out. I felt a bit of soreness in my shoulders, but the hurt didn't bother me much. "This is a weird choice, Andrew. Not saying it isn't fun, but axe throwing?"

"My writing group did a thing out here a few weeks back. A bunch of Queer poets of color throwing axes at logs, Sharlene broke out a few labryses? Labri? What's the plural of labrys?"

"I'm going to decline to answer that." I waggled my eyebrows at the pun and Andrew stared back blankly. "You know, because it's a declension?"

"Oh, I understood what you said, I'm just not going to dignify that as a joke." Andrew kept his face blank, then smiled.

"I'm not saying it's not a cool image, but why are we here? If there's some sort of counter prophecy that I'll need to kill someone with an axe, I don't think I can handle it."

"We're here because you're angry, Joe, and you can take that out on some logs or on yourself." Andrew was still smiling, but his eyes were serious.

"I mean, sure, I guess, I'm a bit angry, but I'm not...I'm not gonna do anything stupid. It's fine. It won't stop me from getting this done, from figuring all this out." I laughed a bit.

Andrew looked at me hard, looking up and down in silence, his smile a bit thinner.

"Fine, I am upset, everything is hard. I can deal with it."

Andrew looked at me and sighed. "Joe, you are furious. You are so furious you can't even admit it. You haven't let yourself feel this because there's always one more thing to do, one more lead to chase, one more problem to solve. But right now, there isn't. So let it out a bit. These logs don't care."

I looked over at the target, walked over and pulled out the axe. "Alright, you're right. I am angry. I just learned that the Keepers have been running secret prisons and abusing people." I threw the axe. Thunk.

Andrew nodded, "And."

I fetched the axe, "And I learned that all the time I thought I was serving a greater good and helping the world I was really just keeping them in fucking power." Thunk.

"And?"

"And... And they lied to me and tried to set me up in some sort of goddamn secret arranged marriage to a goddamn...I can't even think of a word to call her. All the ones that come to mind are just really not things I want to say anymore."

Andrew smiled a bit and looked pensive. "Let's give her a name, something to break her power over you. There's a long tradition of that. Something simple, easy to remember, but with layers. Spinning Jenny. Spinning because she tells lies, spins tales. A Jenny is a name for a female donkey, and she's definitely shown she's an ass."

"She hates being called Jenny. It's too ordinary. And she'd hate being named after a piece of industrial equipment. Right. They tried to set me up with fucking Spinning Jenny." I threw the axe again. Thunk. "I think...I think that might be what pisses me off the most. I mean, I care about the big shit. I think it's a big fucking deal what they're doing, and I need...need to get through this and get this done but they tried to set me up with fucking romance and love!"

Andrew was silent, nodding in solidarity.

"They know how I feel about this, I have wanted a relationship with a future for years. I am 38 fucking years old, Andrew, I want to have a real fucking relationship where I can plan. I want to settle into something that can last and isn't built on lies. I just want a goddamn life and they send this...Spinning Jenny to try and trick me into a fake one, to get me out of the way and as a side note to prop up a fucking corrupt and murdering power structure. They are bastards. Cold hearted evil bastards and I have been such a fucking idiot." I dropped the axe to the ground and sat hard beside it.

Andrew watched and came over to sit down beside me.

"How could I not look deeper? Why did I fall for all this? If you hadn't been there on the ship with me, I would have gone through with all this, murdered a bunch of people and fallen for the lie of the century. And they used some hackneyed meet cute at a bar to do it. Of all the fucking gin joints, for Christ's sake, can you get more cliche?" I fell silent for a moment, my breathing tinged with hints of mania.

Andrew put his hand on my shoulder. "It's fucking infuriating."

"It fucking is." I got up and picked up the axe from the ground. "And I can't let it get to me. I can't let it affect me. Because this is all so much bigger than my own hurt feelings. People are dying out there, but I'm upset because my uncles lied to me? Boo fucking hoo. I just have to keep it together and finish this." Thunk.

Andrew fetched the axe from the target for me. "You won't do that by keeping this in, though. That's not the way to do it. You are right to feel angry and you are right to feel hurt. Not only are you right, but you have the right to feel those things and feel grief for what you've lost."

"I'm 38 years old and my entire life has been built on trying to live someone else's lie. I don't know where to fucking begin."

Andrew nodded to me solemnly. "I will help you figure that out. For now, let's just get this out in the world. I know what it's like to hold in anger til it turns on you. I will not let you do that to yourself. You need friends, real friends here to support you and let you be angry. You have me. And you have Ellis too, I know you're worried about it, but he wants to help you through this. And you have Boo." Andrew caught some change in my expression and smiled. "I'm not telling secrets, just saying, she's a good friend if you let her be one."

Andrew walked over with the axe, but I pulled him into a tight hug. "Thank you."

"Of course." He handed me the axe in his hand as we let go. "Let's throw some axes, then let's go watch people blow things up to celebrate people signing a piece of paper."

Chapter 57

Sunday, July 5th

Sunday morning, I woke to a knock on the guest room door. I mumbled a brief phrase, not really words yet, requesting a moment and pulled on some pants. I opened the door to find Boo standing there, nearly bouncing, two cups of coffee in her hands. "I've found him. I've figured it out and I found him. Who shall say I am not the happy genius of my household?"

I looked at her, letting my brain take a moment to process. "It's too early for William Carlos Williams." I took one of the cups of coffee.

"It's never too early for modernist poetry!"

I smiled and drank from my coffee, "Found who?"

"The guy that did your job, the one who saved the city while you had appendicitis." Boo looked excitedly at me.

I turned quickly from the door and hunted for a t-shirt. Boo followed me in and sat on the chair in the corner as I pulled on the shirt, my fogginess lifting. "Start from the beginning."

"Okay, so when you said that the whole thing was related to the Chicago flood, I remembered I'd heard something in some of my fieldwork years ago. Do you know about the Shepherds of Machines?" I shook my head and Boo continued. "They're a group of practitioners who tend to the functioning of mundane urban spirits, the spirits of things that sustain life. They're pretty low profile, don't get involved in politics, well, human politics. They have strong feelings about how machines deal with each other. Neither here nor there. Well, I was doing some interviews for my research a few years ago and I remembered that one of my consultants mentioned that he dealt with spirits like the trains, the heating vents and the <u>great</u> <u>twisted</u> <u>river</u>."

By now I had woken up a bit. "So, wait, you spoke to the guy who fulfilled the prophecy?"

"And I think I've found him again. I pulled out my notes and put the word out that I was looking for him and I heard from a friend that he had been seen down near that old rusty bridge south of Roosevelt." Boo said excitedly.

"The St. Charles air line or the B&O CT?" I sipped my coffee. Boo gave me a surprised look. I sighed. "I can list the bridges all the way down to the city limits from memory. I spent 25 years learning the waterways of the city. The waters will rise and the city will fall. I had river and lake minutiae drilled into my head."

Boo nodded slowly, "Have you considered giving riverboat tours?"

I paused. "Didn't really fit my schedule. I could only do jobs where I could get away quickly. Can't just say 'world needs me' and dive off the boat into the river mid tour."

"I mean, it would make the tour memorable. Anyhoo, we need to get moving if we are going to find him. Dress for muddy." Boo left quickly, grabbing at my half-empty mug. I quickly drained it and handed it off.

Less than an hour later, we were slogging through the empty wetlands near the river. This part of the city had avoided development so far through a combination of being inaccessible to most roads while being close to freight and passenger railroad lines. The area was a combination of native plants trying to find a foothold and windblown trash with the occasional illicit dump site or feral animal, while still being close enough to see the Sears Tower.

Boo and I spent several hours searching around the area before finally stumbling upon what we were looking for. In the shadow of the bridge, just out of view of Ping Tom park, lay a fallen scrap of corrugated metal. At first glance, it seemed to be trash, but a small wisp of smoke rose from it.

"Okay Joe, I want to prepare you here." Boo stopped in front of me, holding up her hand. "The Shepherds are a little odd. They're people who have devoted themselves to tending the needs of the city. Not the people, but the city itself. They're kind of a combination between urban survivalists, wandering monks and well, object fetishists. So, they kind of redefine weird. Just be nice and accept their hospitality. Don't argue."

I looked at Boo. "No problem. I've had to deal with different practitioners for years, I'll play nice. Do you have the camera?" She nodded and we approached the makeshift shelter.

Boo called out as we approached. "Hello? We're looking for a Shepherd. Are we in the right place?"

From under the metal emerged a figure. An older Black man with a matted black and white beard and hair and a light patina of dirt on him. He wore a Chicago Cubs 2003 National League Champions t shirt and a pair of green camo BDUs. He stood barefoot looking at us curiously. "Who is asking?"

I stepped forward. "Hello, my name is Joe. I'd like to talk to you about the river. Would that be possible?"

The man smiled, "Well, I always have some time to talk about the river." He looked over his shoulder. "Come in."

A few moments later, we were seated on milk crates around a camp stove in the middle of his shelter as the man prepared tea in salvaged cups. As he handed me the cup, I spoke. "Thank you. Do you mind if we record this? We're working on documenting some events in Chicago and would like a record."

The man looked at me and at Boo with the camera in her hand and reached out for it, not insistently, but clearly. As Boo handed him the camera, he looked it over, checking the hinges and buttons. He held it close to his ear and closed his eyes. "The battery is ailing. You need to get some rest." He passed the camera back to Boo. "Yes, I will speak with this camera, it seems most curious."

It ended up taking well over an hour. The first obstacle was getting him to understand what we wanted to talk about specifically, which finally ended up being 'the day he befriended the great twisted river." The second was getting him to put things in coherent order. He seemed to always want to talk about how whatever part of the city he was describing impacted phone service or sewage treatment or elevated rail maintenance. I had to gently steer him back to the events of the day multiple times.

In the end, his story boiled down to this. In the early morning of April 13th, 1992, Reg, which was what he asked we called him, short for his chosen name of Flow Regulator, came across trouble beneath the Loop while wandering the old Narrow Gauge Railroad Tunnels. Following a trickle of water through the tunnels, he realized there was a leak coming from the river. However, he was initially delayed by several men who were guarding access to the tunnel. He couldn't describe their faces, but he did describe the official swords of Keeper guards. He apparently knew a hidden path around them and found his way to the site of the growing leak. Plunging into the water, he communed with the spirit of the river and then, and I'm unclear on how, I'm sure his actions would make sense to another Shepherd of Machines, but not to me, he purified the river of the madness that had driven it to try and bring down the city.

He emerged from the experience strongly bonded to the spirit of the river. He contacted a friend who worked for the city to tip them off about the existing leak. While the mundane flood still spread, he had been able to prevent the river from washing away the deep foundations of some of the taller buildings, averting what would have been a serious catastrophe. Since that day, he has served as the protector of the river spirit, helping channel its anger.

Boo and I were returning to the car afterwards. I had been silent for most of the walk, but something had been bugging me. "I can't stop thinking about me at 14 trying to deal with this. Down in the wet and the dark, hoping that whatever air spirit I had bound to me kept me in breathable air and that my flames were enough to unweave the malevolent spirit. And I don't know if I could have done it."

Boo looked at me, serious. "I'm sure you would have done something clever and won the day."

"But, better than Reg? I would have killed the spirit, but he healed it. I probably would have sacrificed my life, but Reg made a new friend. I had no business being responsible for that." I paused for a moment. "That's what it comes down to. I can't imagine a problem that is better trusted to a lone teenager than to an expert."

Boo looked thoughtful. "Maybe a Snapchat based crisis? A vengeful ghost who will only be mollified by the proper use of on fleek? A plague of people who just can't even?" She looked seriously at me, and we were able to hold that seriousness for about five seconds before breaking into laughter.

As we recovered, I smiled at her. "I wanted to thank you, Boo. You've helped so much in so many ways and I just want you do know I couldn't have done any of this without your help."

She nodded, a look of mock confidence on her face. "I know. Without me, you'd be dead in a ditch being eaten by raven-coyote hybrids." She dropped the look. "Honestly, I just ask myself what Agnes would do and try to do that."

"Well, thanks." I extended my hand for a handshake, but Boo looked at it skeptically and extended her arms for a hug, looking inquisitive.

My phone rang as we finished the hug. As I answered, Lobo's voice spoke in my ear. "Joe, how soon can you be at Maxwell St? I think we have what you're looking for."

Chapter 58

With Maxwell Street Market in full swing, the closest Boo could get me was the south end of the market on Roosevelt. I jumped out, pack in hand, still muddy, but as presentable as 10 minutes in a passenger seat with a handful of wet wipes could make me.

I had arranged to meet Lobo at the red metal frames that marked the South end of the market and as Boo left before traffic could insist, I saw him approaching. "Hey, Joe. That was quick."

"I wasn't far. What's the situation?" I paused. "Sorry, hi Lobo, thank you for calling, I didn't mean to leap into action."

"No problem. This is big stuff; I don't blame you for being all business." He nodded north and started walking.

"Still, no need for rudeness, always time to say hello." I followed him.

"So, two of my guys were up here, doing some shopping when they came across something. You know a curandera named Pilar?" He was moving slowly, occasionally trading nods with merchants.

"Yeah, is she okay? I buy supplies from her sometimes, helped her out with a tricky exorcism a few years back." I followed looking around for trouble.

"She's okay. I've got guys keeping an eye on the situation, they said there were some guys dressed like Keeper guards harassing her. They had the sword pins and everything. Accusing her of being involved with a cult."

"Shit. I bet Scaevola fed back the info that she was who I bought supplies from. Clark is probably jumping to conclusions. Was Clark there himself?" I began to move ahead of Lobo, making my way to Pilar's usual spot.

"No, at least my guys didn't think so. They didn't have a photo." When I looked back, Lobo slowed. "They weren't actually here on work; they were just shopping. But they know opportunity."

"Well, double thanks. You have a well-trained...staff? I don't know what to call them."

"Well, staff is definitely wrong, but yeah, I try to bring in the smart ones. Idiots lose sight of bigger goals. Tezcatlipoca hates idiots." Lobo smiled as we approached Pilar's stall.

I saw immediately what was going on. The two men were in what passed for casual clothing among the Praetorian guard, magically reinforced summer weight suits without ties. I recognized them instantly, Austin and Francisco, part of the investigative unit. They were standing on either side of Pilar, keeping her exits blocked while asking questions. Pilar was obviously uncomfortable but seemed to be complying. Lobo waved and two young men came over. They were dressed casually, both wearing t-shirts with screen printed Jaguars. Lobo spoke Spanish to them, too quick and low for me to catch much. They spoke hurriedly back, pointing and gesturing.

Lobo turned to me. "They've just been hanging around, asking her questions about you. How you met, what she sold you, if she knew where you were. Then they started talking lower and my guys couldn't hear."

"Alright. I need someone to film and some backup. Who wants the camera?"

One of the young men raised his hand. "Can I just use my phone?"

"Yeah, sure, that'll work." I put the camera back in my bag. "Right, so, no violence, unless they start it. Don't rise to any provocation, okay?" Lobo gave a nod of approval. "Ready?" I signaled the camera bearer and we all started forward. "Hey, fellas, are you lost?"

They turned towards me and took their attention off of Pilar. She relaxed a bit but was still nervous. I continued. "You guys just shopping? I know there's some good deals here, but that's no reason to crowd the shopkeeper."

Austin stepped forward as Francisco stayed back, touching his sword pin and speaking lowly. Probably summoning backup. Austin spoke up. "We're just investigating, Mr. Palevsky. Seems our normal chief investigator got a case of the jitters; we've heard he's taking a vacation."

"Well, I'm here now. Figured I'd investigate why you need to harass an innocent woman." I moved slowly, not letting the two of them stay completely still.

"We're just doing our jobs." Austin said, "You know, the things that are our responsibility? You may have heard of people doing that." Francisco was moving up now, he whispered in Austin's ear. Austin continued. "Would you have a moment to talk? I'm sure you have information that could help our investigations. After all, you were seen in contact with our main suspect. Right near here in fact, wasn't it?"

I thought for a moment. Was I a suspect? I was sure at least some of them knew where I was, why didn't they just try and take me there? "Are you going to try and bring me in now?"

"No. Just keeping you here long enough for the boss to finish the ambush." He nodded and I turned. Approaching from across the lot was Clark, the glamour masking his features melting away.

Clark strode right up to me, pushing Lobo aside. "Joe. Where the fuck is my niece?"

There was a tense moment as I watched Clark. Had I misjudged his rage? Would he just attack me outright in public? I didn't have much choice at this point, so I pushed on, waving back Lobo and his men. "Hello, Clark. Your niece was safe the last time I saw her, in the hands of someone who had no intention to harm her." I spoke slowly and with a neutral tone. "You and I have both been lied to."

Clark continued to stare at me as the forces around us slowly positioned themselves. Austin and Francisco made their way behind Clark while Lobo and his boys moved behind me. At least Pilar was behind me now. I didn't want hostages to come into this.

"Explain yourself." Clark used minimal effort; his eyes hard on me.

"Scaevola didn't really betray the conclave. He and Casimir set this all up, including the fake kidnapping, because they screwed up the original prophecy." I had to keep myself from rushing.

"What original prophecy?" Clark looked over at the camera. "Why are you filming?"

"Put down the phone." I gestured to the Jaguar Warrior, and he lowered it. "We were trying to document what was going on in pursuit of this false traitor. As for the original prophecy, my original prophecy. I was supposed to deal with the Chicago Flood back when I was 14, but I had appendicitis. The problem was dealt with, but not by the Chosen One."

Clark looked at me skeptically, "And you know this how?"

"Ephraim told me. When we spoke at the Art Institute. And I just spoke with the man who actually resolved the problem. Do you remember being told to send guards down there before the flood hit?"

Clark looked thoughtful, though he didn't take his eyes off of me. "Casimir said there was a spiritual disturbance, but nothing came of it."

"That was supposed to be my crucible. The day I fought my great evil and completed my prophecy. And we missed it. So, Casimir and Scaevola made up this new evil. Scaevola would pretend to betray the Keepers and I would stop him, fulfilling 'the prophecy' in the process." I marked the words with finger quotes.

"The kidnapping was fake, Jennifer was in on it, part of the whole plan. But I figured out that it wasn't what it seemed, that the ritual wasn't real. So, I confronted Scaevola. Then he killed his lieutenants in his fake cult and tried to get me to kill him. But I'm not a murderer. So, I withdrew, tried to get some answers."

Clark looked at me. "That's a very interesting theory. But it doesn't address my question. Where is my niece?"

I swallowed. "I don't know. I lost track of her and Scaevola when I broke up the fake cult." I hurriedly added. "But I can find them, I can show you she's safe. I have what I need. Give me til tomorrow."

Clark looked at me hard and I thought for a moment it was going to come to violence. "If anything happens to her, I will kill you."

"Tomorrow, sir. I promise." Clark turned and walked away into the market, trailing Austin and Francisco.

I walked over to Pilar. "Are you okay? They didn't hurt you, did they?"

Pilar was seated behind her table, fanning herself. She looked at me, questioningly. "What is going on, Joe? Are you in some sort of trouble?"

I paused, thinking about it, and Lobo came up beside me. "Joe, we should get out of here. I don't trust them not to try and fuck us over here. I'll be back at the van."

Pilar looked at Lobo as he left and then turned her disapproving gaze on me. "So, you are hanging out with that sort of people now and fighting with your Uncles?" She shook her head. "Joe, you need to stop looking for trouble or it will find you."

I sighed and gave her a rueful smile. "Trouble finds me, Pilar. I'm the Chosen One. But I promise, everything will be clear soon. You have my phone number, call me directly if anyone else gives you any trouble." As I left, she was looking at me with suspicion, I'd be lying if I said it didn't hurt.

Chapter 59

"Well, this doesn't make any sense." Boo stared at the map. "Is she the outdoorsy type?"

"What do you mean?" I pulled the map over, looking at the lines Boo had drawn.

"Well, the bearings triangulate to part of the cook county forest preserve. Maybe they're camping out?" Boo tried to put some optimism in her voice.

Ellis snorted from the driver's seat of the van. "The only way you'd get Scaevola out in the woods is if someone said the trees were plotting against him."

"Ellis is right. Scaevola's unlikely to sleep rough. Are you sure you tracked this right?"

"Are you sure you have the right bearings?"

I pulled out Jen's necklace and the compass. I pulsed a bit of will into it, whispering her name through the pendant. It tugged upwards and held rigidly away. I compared it to the compass. What did I give you before?"

Boo checked the map. "280"

"Alright, well it's 275 now. I think they're on the move." I put down the necklace and compass, tucking them into the warded bag. "Goddamnit."

"They're probably moving safehouses or something. Scaevola probably has some sort of three days rule for how long you can stay in one place." Ellis opined.

"48 hours, actually." I sighed. "Okay, we just have to wait. We should have done this last night."

"Sorry, man. I had a Know-Your-Rights training to run, and I don't know if you've ever had to cancel on a whole bunch of church ladies, but it ain't pretty." Ellis shook his head. "You sure we can't just follow the necklace?"

"Too risky. Hopefully she'll dismiss the occasional tingles from momentary readings, but a sustained follow is sure to get her attention. We know she knows how to scry." I sat back. "Okay, we just need to wait. If they are stopping in Chicagoland somewhere, they should be stationary in two hours at most. Anyone feel like Polish food?"

We ate borscht, pierogies and bratwurst at my favorite restaurant in Belmont Cragin and waited. Andrew swung up to join us after closing the shop for the evening and the four of us set out again. Triangulation works much better on a stationary target, and it was only an hour before we found ourselves standing across from the Chicago Marriott Midway."

"That makes sense. Scaevola knows I don't spend a lot of time out at the edges of the city. They were probably up by O'Hare before, and we caught them on the expressway. Now to find them inside."

"Alright, that's you and me, Joe." Ellis smiled. "Same method, different sites. Boo, Andrew, y'all okay with waiting in the bar?"

Ellis and I made our way over to the corner of the building. "Here." He passed me a cigarette as he lay out a mat with a grid and a set of short metal rods. "Light up. That's why we're out here if anyone asks." I hesitated before lighting it. "Don't worry, it's herbal, I know you quit."

"How do you know I quit?"

"Please, after the week you've had any non-quit smoker would look like a Beyonce show." He finished laying out his grid and rods.

"You sure you can do this?" I looked at the complicated contraption.

"Don't ask me that." Ellis kept his mind on the set. "You just smoke your fake cigarette and keep watch. "I did as he said, nodding to a security truck that passed, flashing the cigarette and shrugging. That seemed to satisfy and a moment later, Ellis nudged me. "You're up, Joe. Hurry."

I turned and saw the rods had assembled into a scale framework model of the hotel. Ellis was touching the building with one hand and the mat with the other. The task was obviously taking concentration. I knelt beside the model and held the necklace, whispering the name through it. It pointed up at an angle. I measured it quickly with the protractor and Ellis let it drop. "I've got a reading. They're in the front half of the hotel at 65 degrees from the northwest corner." I tucked the necklace away in its bag as Ellis began to back. "That's a really impressive setup by the way."

"Thanks, it's my own design. Been working on a few things."

We cleaned up quickly and made our way inside. Boo and Andrew had snagged a corner table and we came to join them. I made a quick run to the bar to make sure we didn't seem neglected and brought back a round.

Ellis had already set up his mat again and was preparing to activate it. I looked around and watched as he touched the wall and the mat. This time, I watched the building spring into existence piecing itself together. I reached down and repeated my reading. This time, the angle pointed differently. I marked the X in my head. "They're in a top floor suite either one from the end or at the end. I'm not sure how the rooms are laid out."

Andrew chimed in. "I can check the fire escape map in the stairwell."

"Good idea. Alright, now we need to rent a room and call Clark." I said.

"And hope they use standardized furniture." Ellis added.

Chapter 60

Monday, July 6th

Andrew and I stood in front of the hotel, waiting. I had sent Clark a message and gotten back a simply <Okay.> I looked over at Andrew, "Are you sure the message was genuine? That we aren't waiting on a trap."

Andrew looked back. "If he wanted to lure you into a trap, he would have said more. But I'm out here with you in case I'm wrong." He smiled.

"Well, that's reassuring." I said, half-sarcastically. We waited more. "Andrew, I'm not sure how this is all going to end. I don't know if people who have been willing to commit fraud on me my entire life will give up. I'm just saying, if I don't make it through, I'll miss our daily crosswords."

Andrew stood silently. "Don't think like that. I don't want to have to find a new wingman."

I smiled at Andrew as we saw Clark's truck pull into the parking lot. He wasn't alone in the cab, but I didn't see any vehicles following.

Clark parked his truck and walked over to us, followed by Austin and Francisco. "I'll give you this, Joe. If this is an ambush, it's an unusual place for one."

"I promise you it isn't one, sir. If you'll come with me, we're set up in room 237."

Clark followed me along with Austin, leaving Francisco downstairs to watch the truck. I wish I could say that inspired confidence, but I knew Keeper guard procedure. Clark was still anticipating trouble.

In the hotel room, Ellis had set up one of the bedside tables with a number of pieces of equipment and was in the process of replacing the light bulb in the table lamp. He looked up as we came in and then resumed his work. Boo moved around the room, waving a miniature broom and incanting to herself.

Clark looked around the room. "You said you had evidence?"

"We traced Jennifer here. She is currently in one of the suites at the top of the hotel. Ellis is setting up a scrying device right now."

Clark looked over at Ellis curiously. "Wait, you're George Green's son? How the hell did you get involved in this?"

"That's a long story. I'll tell you later. You want an explanation of the how of what I'm doing here?" Ellis gestured at the table as Clark nodded. "Remote psychometry is tricky but can work with very similar objects. I've attuned the lamp here to its closest duplicate in the suite upstairs. That should give us a picture of what's happening. The tech I'm installing now will project that in the room here."

"How do I know this isn't just faked?" Clark's expression remained hard to read as he looked over the lamp.

"It would be much harder to fake this than to do it for real, y'know, like the moon landing. What you should be asking is if we're working with Scaevola." Boo chimed in. I looked at her, incredulous. "What? It's the more relevant question. But the level of convolution required is way outside Occam's Razor territory." She looked to Ellis, "We're pretty much clean of psychic interference here." She set down her broom.

"Alright." Ellis said, eagerly. "Let's get this going." Ellis signaled Andrew who turned off the overhead lights. The room was dimly lit, but not 'dark.' Ellis completed the turn of the light bulb contraption and suddenly the room was illuminated by shadowy forms and full of faint sounds. We all moved around to be out of the way of the new additions and get a clear view.

The center of the room was dominated by a group of chairs and a sofa around a table. On one of the chairs sat Scaevola, one hand bandaged, facing a chess set on the table. Across from him lay a figure on the couch. It took me a moment to recognize him, but Clark got there immediately. "Morse? Austin, where is Morse supposed to be right now?"

Austin thought for a moment. "On loan with Cumberland and Laramie to the Keeper of Coins. They're supposed to be guarding the vaults to make sure the cult doesn't try to get any of the armaments. Keeper Simon asked for the extra guard help a few days ago."

Clark looked over at me. "Where is Jennifer?"

I looked at Ellis, who shrugged. "The range on this is limited. She might be in one of the adjacent rooms." As we spoke, the soundscape shifted. There had been a white noise that I had attributed to static that suddenly stopped. The figures in the image shifted, Morse stood up and walked towards the side of the room, picking up a pad of paper. Scaevola turned the chess board around, assuming the other role.

"Is he playing by himself?" Boo asked.

"He always does." I answered, "Thinks it helps him put himself in the minds of his enemies. I can't tell you how many 'Scaevola's playing with himself again' jokes Daniel made over the years."

Morse knocked on what was apparently a door and then called through it. "Hey, what do you want for dinner?"

Muffled, but still audible through the scrying came Jennifer's voice. "Chicken Caesar Salad. Dressing on the side."

I looked over to Clark, but his expression was skeptical. "This doesn't prove anything. She could be a prisoner that they don't want to starve."

I grumbled. "Come on. What are the chances that Scaevola would be talking about his plans the exact second we looked in. This at least proves that Simon is on it, and that Jennifer is safe. You have to admit that."

Clark wagged his head in uncertainty. "It does show that things are weird, but what are we going to do, watch all night?"

Ellis shook his head. "This thing overheats after 20 minutes at best."

Boo chimed in, "Ooh, we could go in pretending to be room service. Ask about their plans." She looked at the blank stares that met her. "Okay, fine, you're right, that would be ridiculous."

"I need to go in," said Clark. "I'll ask what's going on, pretend I tracked Morse here. They can explain it to me. If Jennifer's a hostage, I'll get her out. If not..."

We all considered this possibility. "I don't have anything better." I said. "We'll watch and back you up if there's trouble."

Boo piped up. "Just try to casually work in the word shenanigans."

Clark looked at her, deadly serious, and then strode out of the room.

Chapter 61

Ellis was sitting on one of the beds fiddling with the sword pin as we waited. Austin eyed him suspiciously, nervous about the pin despite Ellis' reassurances. Clark had left the room a minute ago wearing his own guard pin and Ellis was racing against the elevator to reattune his equipment for the scrying.

"Done." Ellis placed the pin on the mat and flattened it out. As we gathered round, an image of Clark rose from the mat, surrounded by a ghostly miniature elevator. As we watched, the doors opened, and the image extended to include the hall as Clark exited.

Clark looked from side to side and turned to his right, the sliver of hallway moving with him. He strode with purpose, and we soon saw his destination. Before one of the doors stood a guard who had come to nervous attention as Clark approached.

"Cumberland." Clark approached the guard casually, as if he was supposed to be there.

Cumberland remained tense. "Sir, what are you doing here?"

Clark eyed the guard, then leaned in. "Are you asking your commander what he is doing, Praetorian?"

"No, sir." Cumberland resumed rigid attention. "I was unaware of your visit, sir. Sorry sir."

"Knock on the door, Cumberland. I want to see what you're guarding." Cumberland hesitated, but knocked on the door in a staccato pattern, seven times.

The door opened and there was a brief moment as things resolved before Clark was pushing into the room, past the astonished Morse. We saw the room resolve, a smaller version of what we'd seen before. Scaevola was standing quickly as Clark entered and bellowed "What is going on here?"

Scaevola held up his hands. "Clark. What are you doing here?"

"I should ask you the same thing, traitor!" Clark reached into his jacket for his gun, and I tensed. Violence wouldn't help, not right now.

"Please, wait. It's not what it seems. Just give me a moment to explain. I am unarmed." Scaevola seemed worried, taken about by the sudden intrusion.

"If you've harmed my niece, I will kill you." Clark kept his hand on his weapon, not drawing it, moving to the side, checking the room for other people. Scaevola waved for the guards to go outside. They paused, looked to Clark who nodded and closed the front door behind them.

As the front door closed, the door to the other room opened and Jennifer stood framed there. She had her hair up in a towel and was wearing what appeared to be silk pajamas. "Uncle Clark? What are you doing here?"

"See. She's safe." Scaevola kept his hands visible, gesturing at Jennifer. "Can we take a moment and talk?"

Clark removed his hand from his gun but stayed rigid. "Are you okay, Jenny?"

"I'm fine, Uncle Clark. Safe and sound." Jennifer walked over to the table and sat on the couch. She patted the seat beside her. "Come have a seat and let's talk about it."

Clark walked over and sat beside her. "You aren't being held against your will?"

"No. I'm here helping Scaevola and the Conclave. I want to be here." She spoke quietly, gently, as if calming a wild animal.

Scaevola sat in one of the chairs. "Let me explain. The Chosen One's destiny was in peril. He missed taking care of his true destiny, so we arranged for another opportunity, a chance for him to be the hero we need and for the Conclave to move on. Casimir asked me to help, and I did. I volunteered to lay down my life for the greater good and in the process save the Keepers. But Joe chose to ignore this chance and walk away. Now we're just trying to get things back on track."

"What is Jennifer doing here? Were you going to lay down her life, too?" Clark glared at Scaevola.

Scaevola shook his head. "No, she was always to be kept safe. Her involvement was to help inspire Joe. Love spurs on the hero."

"I wanted to do this, Uncle Clark. Our story would be romantic and inspiring. The Chosen One going into danger to save his lady love. It would be a story that would help restore faith in the Conclave. Help people believe." Jennifer's smile turned my stomach. I had to turn away for a moment.

When I looked again, Scaevola was speaking. "How did you find us?"

"I decided to check on the detail assigned to Simon. Since I couldn't find them where they were supposed to be, I followed their insignias." Clark tapped the pin, which caused the whole scene to shake.

"Damn." Scaevola grumbled. "We should get rid of those. If you can track them…"

"I'll take the insignias with me. It wouldn't do for anyone to see official Praetorian guards here." Clark stood. "It might blow your cover."

Scaevola spoke as he stood up too. "Go talk to Casimir. He can explain everything more fully."

Clark hesitated, then nodded. "I will. And you keep her safe." He pointed to Jennifer and started for the door.

She ran up and gave him a hug as he left. "It'll all be okay, Uncle Clark. You'll see."

Ellis released the energy of the scrying and the image faded. In the absence of the light, the room felt dim and dour. I got up and turned on the overhead light. Nobody said anything for a few long minutes, then a knock came on the door. Austin beat us all to it and Clark walked in, his expression haggard.

For a long moment, nobody said anything. Clark broke the silence. "Tell me one thing. Is it all a lie? Did Peter die for nothing?"

I thought for a moment. "No. He died fighting for what was right. But you shouldn't have had to do it on your own. They could have helped him. They could have saved his life."

Clark nodded and sniffed. "Just tell me what you need."

Chapter 62

I rode up to work the next morning with Andrew. He had crashed at Agnes' and so we sat together on the 6 bus as it headed north on Lake Shore.

"Joe. I do want to apologize." Andrew broke the sleepy morning silence. "I'm sorry I didn't see Spinning Jenny for what she was."

"It's okay, Andrew. We were both fooled. You only had a few minutes with her in the first place." I shrugged, "Someone willing to buy into a lie that big must be pretty good at deception. Besides, you had her number when it really mattered."

"I'll try and do better in the future." Andrew smiled. "The next crazy plot that tries to throw a femme fatale at you, I'll be all over it." We both chuckled. Andrew continued. "So, how are things with you and Boo?"

"What?" I looked over at him. "What do you mean?" Andrew just looked at me significantly. "There's nothing. We had a weird moment a few days ago, heat of the moment thing. Danger does that to people."

Andrew nodded. "Boo is a nice girl. You hurt her and I would, well, let's just say we'd have words."

"What? I wouldn't, I... wait. You're just giving me shit, aren't you."? Andrew broke out smiling and I softly punched him on the upper arm. "You and your goddamn laconic western wit." I shook my head, smiling.

"Seriously, though. When all this is done, she wouldn't say no to a date. Just keeping an eye out for you." Andrew rubbed his arm where I'd punched it.

I spent the rest of the morning in the shop with Andrew, waiting for lunchtime. We worked through a few puzzles, joked about our love lives, talked about the local news. It was like old times, two friends, hanging out.

I looked up at the clock around 11. "Alright, it's time."

Andrew nodded, "Are you sure this is how you want to do this?"

"Anthony is the easiest to get alone. He's blood kin so he won't respond with violence and he's the only one not in on things. Besides, I know where he eats lunch."

Anthony was at his normal table at Bistro Zinc, just a short walk from the library. He ate here nearly every day, his time to himself, his time to read. Today, he was reading the Man Who Was Thursday. I recognized the worn paperback from twenty feet away. He read this whenever he was stressed or worried. I couldn't blame him with the month we were having.

When I sat down in the chair opposite, he looked up. I saw his face go from confused to surprised to panicked in a few seconds. He looked around, but before he could yell, I had placed my hands on the table. "Don't worry Uncle Anthony. I'm not here to hurt you or anything. I just want to talk."

His panic subsided some, but he still looked worried. "What are you doing here, Joe? Are you going to take me hostage?"

"What? No. I'm not going to take you hostage. I'm also not here to recite Anarchist Poetry." I gestured at the book.

Anthony looked down. "Well, that's good, I don't know if I could handle Anarchist poetry." He smiled, wanly.

"I'm here to talk about coming in and discussing terms of my return." I waved away the approaching waiter. I wouldn't be here long.

"Shouldn't you discuss those with Casimir or Clark? You know I don't handle security and that sort of thing." Anthony fidgeted nervously stirring his tea.

"Honestly? I don't trust them as much as I trust you. You are my mother's brother. You sponsored my membership in the Keepers. I trust that you will listen and bring back my conditions." I calmly spoke, my hands clasped before me.

"Okay." Anthony closed his eyes and breathed through his nose. "Tell me your conditions. I'll bring them to the conclave." He opened his eyes, looking nervous but determined.

"Alright. First, I want safe passage to the meeting and safe passage from the meeting. Okay?" Anthony nodded. "Second, I want written amnesty for my associates. Andrew Two-Spirits, Boudicca Esthersdottir and Ellis Green, Okay?"

"Ellis? I didn't know you and he were in touch." Anthony seemed puzzled.

"Misery acquaints a man with strange bedfellows." I quipped.

"Tempest, Act Two, Scene Two if I remember correctly." Anthony smiled. "I'll bring those demands."

"I have one more. I will only meet with the entire Chicago Conclave of Keepers, including Scaevola."

Anthony looked shocked. "Scaevola? The traitor?"

"Bring those demands. The written amnesty can be delivered to Ellis by his father. Once the others are arranged, I want you to call me. Nobody but you. Do you understand?"

Anthony nodded, "Joe, I don't know why you have turned, either away from or against us, I guess. But I promised your mother I would keep you safe. I know things can be hard, we've all had to make sacrifices for the good of the Conclave. Choices we've had to make. Sometimes personal happiness is not as important as the greater good."

I wasn't sure what Anthony was talking about. A moment of regret washed over me as I sat there. Was I closing the door on my family? I didn't know if I'd see him again after everything came out, but I couldn't back out now. "Help me with this now and you can consider that promise fulfilled." I got up from the table. "Let's talk after this is over and you can tell me about it."

Chapter 63

Tuesday, July 7th

When Ellis sent a text, <MEETING W/ POPS> I knew it was coming together. Anthony's call of confirmation came an hour later, and the meeting was set. 9am tomorrow, Keeper HQ, the normal monthly meeting time for the council. The time and place of my greatest test. You'd think that growing up under the shadow of a prophecy of doom would make this kind of thing easier, but all I really had to comfort me was a lifetime of thinking about what I'd do the night before, if I had the chance.

When I was a teenager, I would probably have driven town to Hammond with Daniel to visit a strip club. Though most of my twenties, I would have had an epic night of drinking and dancing and the ultimate one-night stand. Facing down my end at 38, all I wanted was a good dinner with friends, especially those I could talk to about what was happening. So, I booked a table for four at Cafe BaBaReeba! and pulled out a gift certificate, last year's Christmas present from Casimir. Tonight's final dinner would be on the man I was going to confront tomorrow.

We ate copious amounts of tapas, drank several pitchers of Sangria, with ginger ale for Andrew, and spoke of anything except what loomed before us. We laughed, we told stories, in short it was just what I wanted. As the last of the plates were being cleared, I stood up and raised my glass.

"I want to raise a toast to friends. To old friends, new friends and friends rediscovered. Without your help, all of your help, I would be living an oppressive lie right now, none the wiser. I want to thank you for being here with me throughout all of this. For helping me when I was right, for telling me when I was wrong, for helping me see the truth." I lifted my glass high. "To friends."

The others raised their glasses along with me, drinking their sangria and ginger ale. As I sat down, Boo looked at me. "Joe, I have a question that's been bouncing around in my head for the past few days. You asked all of us why we were doing this. Why are you?"

Ellis and Andrew looked from Boo to me, obviously interested in the answer as well. I wondered if they'd talked about it among themselves.

"There's a lot of reasons. I'd be lying if I said there wasn't a little vengeance. They did waste 25 years of my life. There's a little bit of trying to prevent them from doing this to someone else, maybe a bit of glory hunting, being the man who revealed the truth, but what it really comes down to is choice. I'm doing it because I have the choice. When there's danger, you make the choice to try and save people, even if you don't always know how. Do any of you watch disaster movies?" I looked around. "I love disaster movies, they're a total guilty pleasure of mine. There's a specific type of scene you get in disaster movies that just gets me every time, where people who don't have any special skills or abilities help those they can, even if it means running into danger. In Armageddon, there's this bit right at the beginning where this cabbie played by the guy from Hangin with Mr. Cooper is helping get a tourist couple to safety, just pushing them ahead of him as the world crashes around them. He doesn't know them. They haven't even paid their fare yet, but when he has the choice to help them or abandon them, he puts himself at risk to try and help. I honestly get a little choked up, just thinking about it." I sniffled a bit. "That's what it's about for me, why I do what I do. I need to make this choice. I need to do something about this because I can. If I don't, then I couldn't live with myself. I could get all Spiderman here, and yes, Boo, I know who Spiderman is, and talk about power and responsibility, but it's not about responsibility. It's about the choices in front of you. Every choice has the opportunity to try to make the world better, and if you don't do that when you can, then things get worse. Right now, I have no idea what will come next. I'm honestly a little terrified, but I know I'm the only person right now with the ability to make this choice. So yeah, I'm not backing down, I hope that's enough."

The others were silent for a moment. "Well, somehow you just made me hate Armageddon a little less." Ellis smiled.

"Hey, I'm not taking responsibility for all of it. But that scene stuck with me." I shrugged.

"Well, I got shit to do." Ellis stood up. "I'll bring you the recorder tomorrow morning."

I stood up with him. "You sure it won't be detected?"

"It's a two-part system, like the lamp trick from the hotel, only intentional. There's nothing in the tie pin to actually detect this time. Plus, it's recorded on the other end so even if they kill you mid-meeting, we'll still have a recording."

"You always know how to reassure me, Ellis."

"Hey, if it means anything, I hope they don't kill you." Ellis grabbed my hand overhand and pulled me into a quick hug, smiling. As we broke the hug, he waved to the others and headed out.

"Well, if we're heading out, I'm going to divest myself of some liquid assets." Boo headed back towards the bathroom, leaving Andrew and I alone at the table.

"I wish there were a way I could be in there with you tomorrow, Joe." Andrew drained his ginger ale.

"Well, I'm counting on you all to be there on my way out. I don't relish the idea of just slowly walking away all alone."

"We'll be there." Andrew and I sat in silence until Boo returned. We caught the red line south to Jackson and said goodnight to Andrew as he went over to the Blue line. At the top of the stairs, Andrew gave me a quick hug and passed me a flask, as I sniffed it, the familiar scent of Andrew's concoction wafted out. "For tomorrow morning. You wouldn't want to face this hungover, would you?"

Boo and I caught the 6 down to Hyde Park, riding in tired and tipsy silence until we reached Hyde Park Blvd. As we walked the last few blocks to Agnes', Boo spoke up, "I'm really glad I met you. I almost didn't agree when Andrew asked me to help. I was sure it was some sort of sting operation at first, like, you were trying to use me to get to Agnes or something. Instead, I have firsthand knowledge of the biggest shift in magical culture since, well, I don't know when."

"You're welcome?" I said, a bit awkwardly, "I'm glad to have helped."

"I mean, you're not bad yourself, nice enough guy, but you don't really compare to new knowledge, even if I have to start my entire dissertation from scratch." Boo gave me a kidding look.

I smiled and stopped walking, turning to Boo. "So, I wanted to say something that's been bugging me."

"Sure," Boo smiled. "I promise I won't make fun of you for crying at Armageddon, if that's your worry."

"It wasn't until just now." I smiled back. "No, I wanted to say, about the other day."

"Oh, the N.A.T." Boo noticed my confusion. "Nose avoidance turning, prelude to a kiss. Don't worry, I'll show you Coupling after I show you Star Wars. At least, the parts that hold up."

"Okay, well, I know I shut things down fast back there and such, I just wanted to say, I like you, and I'd like to maybe explore that, but not with doom hanging over my head. Does that make sense?"

"I understand what you're saying. But I have a question. Is it what you want or is it you making a decision for me because you think it's best?" Boo's expression was frustratingly enigmatic.

We walked another block. "My last date included the unspoken assumption that she would be a literal trophy wife. I think I have some of my own shit to work out first."

"I concur," said Boo, "I just wanted you to be sure as well." She smiled as we walked up the path to Agnes'.

"Also, I might die tomorrow and oddly enough, I'd rather not get involved in something right before that. I don't think 16-year-old Joe will ever forgive me, but hopefully I'll have a chance to live with that."

Chapter 64

Wednesday, July 8th

I stood outside the room; near the door I had entered so many times as the Chosen One. Not dressed in the traditional robes, but in a simple blue suit, though admittedly with some armored enchantments. I checked the tie pin Ellis had given me. He was outside, in the back of Boo's car, his equipment spread out to capture and record everything. I was thankful for his craftsmanship and subtlety. They had searched me as I entered, examined my standing enchantments with slightly excessive interest but hadn't paid anything more than passing attention to my accessories. They were afraid of violence. Which made me afraid of violence.

At the ringing of the bell, I stepped through the door. The room had been reorganized, the chairs reassembled so there was one before me and seven others arrayed around the other side of the table, one draped in black cloth. Four of Clark's Praetorians stood around the edges of the room, rigidly watching the entrances. I noted that Austin and Francisco were among them, but neither of the guards that had been on Scaevola's detail. That was a good sign, I hoped.

The Keepers had not donned their robes of office either, the only nod to official authority came from Casimir, wearing the stole of the Keeper of Laws. We all sat in silence, Scaevola and Clark taking seats at opposite ends of the row of chairs, with others finding spots in between.

For a moment, nobody quite knew how to start things. Years of practice and tradition had set us in certain habits and if we were doing things differently today, we were working without a script. Finally, Casimir rose. "We are all present here to discuss the resolution of the current crisis. As you requested, Joseph, we have assembled, I trust you received the written amnesty for your...associates?"

"I did, sir. Thank you for agreeing to meet. I believe the time has come for things to come to an end." I kept my voice respectful, no need to blow things up before they got started.

Casimir resumed his seat and sat back, crossing his hands over his stomach. "Joseph. How do we move forward here? So much has happened, I'm sure you've been through a lot in the past few weeks. It's been a trying time for many of us."

"I have, sir. It's been a rough time. I've lost someone close to me, found myself unexpectedly homeless, been attacked multiple times and nearly had to kill someone. It's enough to shake someone up." I pushed thoughts about the loss of Ephraim out of my mind.

Casimir looked over to Simon. Simon stood and spoke. "Yes, my turn. At the behest of the Keeper of Laws, I have put together an offer of settlement. As a gesture of good faith, we have officially dropped all probate challenges to the will of Ephraim Baumann. The paperwork is filed with the county this morning." He slid a paper across the table to me, looked at Casimir and sat.

"That is just part of our offer, Joseph." Casimir continued, "Joseph. We would appoint you Keeper of the Flames. We know you were troubled by the way we have done things in the past, this way, you could have a leading hand. You could help us choose the next Chosen One. Choose the challenge to prove his strength. Help us change from within, after all, we don't want to throw out the baby with the bathwater." Casimir smiled widely, spreading his hands. "The world needs leadership; you could help provide that. Help us correct our course. What do you say, Joseph? Will you help us?"

I thought about this. I hadn't been expecting this offer and I looked to the Keepers across from me as I considered. Clark's face was stern and unreadable, which made me nervous. I hoped this wasn't testing his resolve or worse, him testing mine. Anthony beside him seemed eager. I could tell that he wanted me to take the offer, wanted a peaceful resolution to all of this. As I looked to Prospero, I could see from his grin where the idea had come from. Prospero had been my teacher for years, he knew what would motivate me, if anything would.

I looked to the other three. Casimir was unreadable, Simon was taking his cues directly from Casimir, nervous. Then my eyes fell on the brooding Scaevola. He did not like this idea.

"What about Keeper Fortier? He's a known enemy of the Conclave at this point? How will we resolve that?" I looked at Scaevola as I said it.

Casimir leaned back and spread his hands. "Easy, we tell people he was possessed by an evil spirit that drove him to assemble the cult. You were able to drive that spirit out of him, resolving the threat in a peaceful manner. A good example for future Chosen Ones."

I sat in silence, considering their offer. Could I reform things from within? Could I make a difference? I decided to let the temptation in for a moment. Let myself consider this. If I didn't, I knew I'd always wonder. My life could be simple again, I could return to a life of assured privilege. I could try and fix things. Maybe when Casimir died, I could move to the head of the Conclave.

But no. There were too many people among the Keepers who knew, who would push back with everything they had to stop the change. The only option was to push forward, to take them down from the outside. I drew up my resolve and crossed the Rubicon.

"I have a few questions before I can accept your generous offer. May I ask them?"

Casimir's smile faded slightly, but he still held his hands out, placing them on the table. "Go ahead, Joseph."

"How long have the Conclave of Keepers been choosing the crisis the Chosen One will face? Has it always been fake?" I kept a concerned look on my face, trying hard to mask my anger.

"It isn't fake, not as you mean it. We have always seen what the greatest challenges that will face the magical community are and we have always chosen one of those challenges to be the responsibility of the Chosen One. Then we give them the support they need to succeed."

"As you did with Peter?" I asked softly.

"What happened with Peter was an unfortunate mistake. We can do better. With your help, of course." Casimir spoke firmly but put some regret in his voice. "But what we do now is not fundamentally different from what we have always done. We have always protected the world from danger."

"Why not involve other people? If there are dangers, why not enlist help? Warn people. We could solve things together. Build a world of cooperation." A bit more real emotion crept into my voice this time. I couldn't hold it all back.

"You have no idea what it's like out there. There are people who would join anything we consider a threat just because we oppose it. Nihilists would tear down the world we built If we gave them the chance." Casimir's smile was gone at this point, replaced with a deep scowl. "The world needs people of strength and learning to lead it Joseph, how can we trust our enemies to not take the chance to put a knife in our back."

I waved my hand, giving up this line of argument. There was no convincing him and I was afraid of getting him too angry. "I have another question. Who knows about this? This isn't common knowledge among all Conclaves, is it?"

"No. Traditionally, only the Keeper of the Laws for each Conclave knows, along with the Keeper of the Flames. Plus, everyone in this room, now, of course."

I nodded. "I think that we should tell people. Come clean, move on, make allies. There has to be a better way than hiding behind the sacrifice of good men. I would only be able to join the Conclave on the condition that we tell people the truth. I implore you."

"You implore us?" Casimir scoffed, his voice rising. "What do you think would happen if we just told people about this? Do you think they'd throw a party, and all would be forgiven? That we'd be rewarded for our honesty?"

"What do you think will happen when they learn from somewhere else?" My own voice rose to match. "Please, tell people the truth."

Casimir glared at me. "No." His hands were clenched into fists at this point.

"Fine. Then I will. I am not going to become your pet prophet and be part of your lies. I am going to tell the world what I know." I stood up.

"What makes you think we'd allow you to do that?" Casimir's smile was cruel.

"I was offered safe passage." I began.

"Jebać to! To Hell with your safe passage!" Casimir cut me off as he slammed his fists on the table. "Praetorians!" He pointed at me.

"Belay that!" Clark rose from his seat.

Casimir stared at Clark. "What are you doing?"

Clark looked back. "I am honoring Joe's safe passage, and so are my men."

"You know I outrank you!" Casimir stood up. "You will do what you're told, or you will pay the price."

"You should have thought of that before you killed my best friend." Clark and Casimir locked eyes, a burning stare between them. I held still. The guards beside me were well armed and I didn't want to risk them taking matters into their own hands.

Casimir broke the silence. "Keeper Fortier, I hereby relieve Keeper Davis of his duties. Confiscate his badge of office and his sword."

Clark spoke up forcefully. "I call for a vote of no confidence in the Keeper of Laws."

Casimir sneered. "You think you can get out of your treason with parliamentary maneuvering? You're alone here Clark. I may remind you that the Chosen One is not a voting member of the Conclave. You need a second for a vote of no confidence and you have no friends here."

Anthony stood up, shaking. "I second." It came out meekly at first, then he repeated himself more forcefully. "I second the motion of no confidence."

Casimir grabbed out at Anthony with one beefy hand, Anthony scrambled away, nearly tripping over his chair, coming to stand behind Clark. Scaevola moved up as Clark's hand went to the short sword concealed beneath his jacket. The guards moved forward, Simon and Prospero both broke for the back of the room and in the chaos I moved for the door. As I slipped outside, the Most Esteemed Conclave of Keepers of Chicago were locked in a standoff, neither side making a move.

As I left, I moved quickly, not running, not wanting to bring attention to myself. I heard a cacophony of raised voices erupt in the room behind me as I approached the outer door. Once in the hallway, I broke into a jog, moving down the hall and out towards the daylight.

As I approached the door, I saw another figure standing there that brought me up short. "Jennifer." I said tersely. I wasn't sure I had time for this, but I couldn't risk her raising an alarm at this point.

"Joe." Jennifer's enigmatic smile was muted. "Are things okay? I thought you'd be in there longer."

"Things are fine. All the lies are out in the open." I looked at her coldly. "Why did *you* do it? Why get involved in this whole plan?"

Jennifer looked at me, "It's the game, Joe. What else could I do? When your life is a rigged game, you can play to win, or you can give up. When your only prospects are arranged marriages with powerful men, you try to make the best one you can. We would be legends, Joe. The Chosen One and his true love who he saved from the traitor. People would be talking about our love story for a hundred years. It's not too late..." She began to move towards me.

"I'm gonna stop you right there." I held up my hand. "It's way too late. It was too late the moment we met under false pretenses. It was too late the moment you became part of this. Goodbye Jennifer, I hope we never see each other again." I moved towards the door and paused. "You should call Miriam, she's worried about you." I left before she could respond, stepping out into the sun.

Boo pulled the car up to the side entrance as I emerged, and I quickly got into the passenger seat. We began to drive as I loosened my tie, passing the tie pin back to Ellis.

"You were brilliant in there," Boo smiled. "Ellis played the audio for us as he was recording."

"You got it all?" I looked back to Ellis.

"Every word, every image." He reached up his hand. "Well, up until the end." He winked as Andrew gave him a high five.

"Thanks for that." I smiled. I leaned back as Boo drove. We pulled onto Lake Shore, and I saw the city skyline over the green of Lincoln Park. "I wasn't sure I was going to get out of there alive."

Boo laughed a nervous laugh. "Yeeeah, I don't think any of us were sure of that. But hey, you're still breathing, right?"

Andrew smiled, "Well Joe, you're free, what do you want to do next?"

I thought for a moment. It had been a long time since that question had any meaning for me. I could leave Chicago. I could leave the country. I could get married and have kids. I could spend a day doing nothing with my phone turned off. It was a different world for me. I looked around the car at my friends. "I have no fucking idea. Really? I'm just glad it's over."

Boo glanced over at me. "Over? Let's just call this a good start."
And we drove south towards home.

End Act V

Fin

Made in the USA
Monee, IL
18 September 2021